Endorsements for Remembered Lives

Fascinating reading! Scenes described so well, at times I felt like I was in the story; going to a footy game or riding a horse across the dusty African plains! As a Liverpool fan, a lot of the story is very close to my heart. Well written words pulled me into the story, causing tears to be shed. The linking of history, and non-fiction with fictional characters is so very well done, making the whole story very believable.

Sioux Gijzen, South African Liverpool Supporters Club.

Hebrews 24 ... "and let's consider how to encourage one another in love and good deeds, not abandoning our own meeting together, as is the habit of some people, but encouraging one another; and all the more as you see the day drawing near."

Remembered Lives — What a perfect title for this kaleidoscope of well-researched history and life; then and now. Remembrance unites people of all faiths, cultures, and backgrounds. Remembrance honours those who serve to defend our democratic freedoms and way of life. It does not glorify war; it is a sign of hope for a peaceful future.

From the ashes of the tragedy of the Battle of Spion Kop,

part of the rich tapestry of our history, Anna Jensen pays tribute to the people that were touched by the bloody events of 1899-1902. She seamlessly and cleverly weaves this together with the story of the families and survivors of the horrific football incident of 1989 in the UK, and how Spion Kop plays a role in their lives thirty-five years later.

Raymond & Lynette Heron, Directors of Spion Kop,
Woodlands Farm, South Africa

REMEMBERED LIVES

where the past and present collide

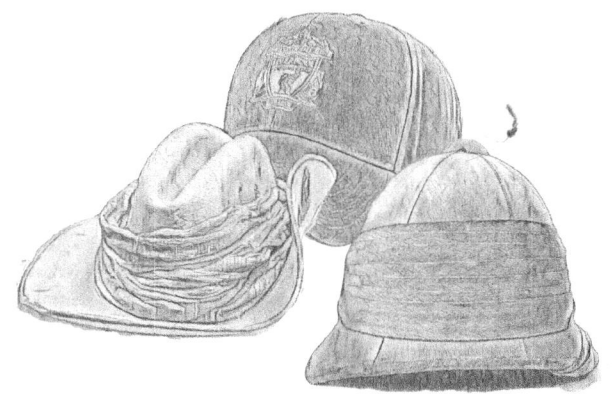

Anna
JENSEN

Contents

Dedication

To all who remember.

Acknowledgements

A book of this scale and ambition needs a lot of assistance. I had the best, from so many different people, in so many different ways.

To Craig, Caragh and Leal – for being the sounding board for ideas, unravelling plots and timelines. And helping me with my football knowledge (or lack thereof!)

To Dominic, Julie and Marc Bigara – for accompanying Craig and I on my first research trip to Spionkop and entering into the spirit of the moment with me.

To Raymond and Lynette Heron – for your hospitality and welcome at Spionkop Lodge on more than one occasion, and for allowing me to pick your brains for the stories behind the story.

To Sioux Gijzon and the rest of the South African Liverpool fans – thank you for allowing me to join you at the unveiling of the Andrew Devine memorial chair at Spionkop Lodge. It truly was an honour and privilege to be included. And thanks to Sioux for the input and feedback she gave which helped ensure Remembered Lives would be as accurate an account of the horrors of the Hillsborough Disaster and its aftermath as I could make it.

To Alison Theron, Gwethlyn Meyer and Jeannette Harbottle – the best, eagle-eyed beta readers I could wish for. Thank you for checking my facts and helping me find better ways to say things.

To Allyson Koekhoven – for your excellent, helpful and timeous editing. You polish my sentences and fix up my grammar. Really!

To Sheena Carnie – those sticky notes were above and beyond! Thank you!

To my ARC readers – thank you for your feedback and your kind words as I shared this precious story with you.

To you, the reader – thank you for buying this book, and taking the time to read it. I hope your heart is stirred to remember these and others who live ordinary lives under the loving gaze of an extraordinary God. And may you know the same, for yourself – you are seen, you are known, you are loved.

To Jesus – thank you for it all.

Are not two sparrows sold for a penny? And not one of them will fall to the ground apart from your Father. But even the hairs of your head are all numbered. Fear not, therefore; you are of more value than many sparrows.

Matthew 10:29-31 ESV

Map 1: South Africa, 1900

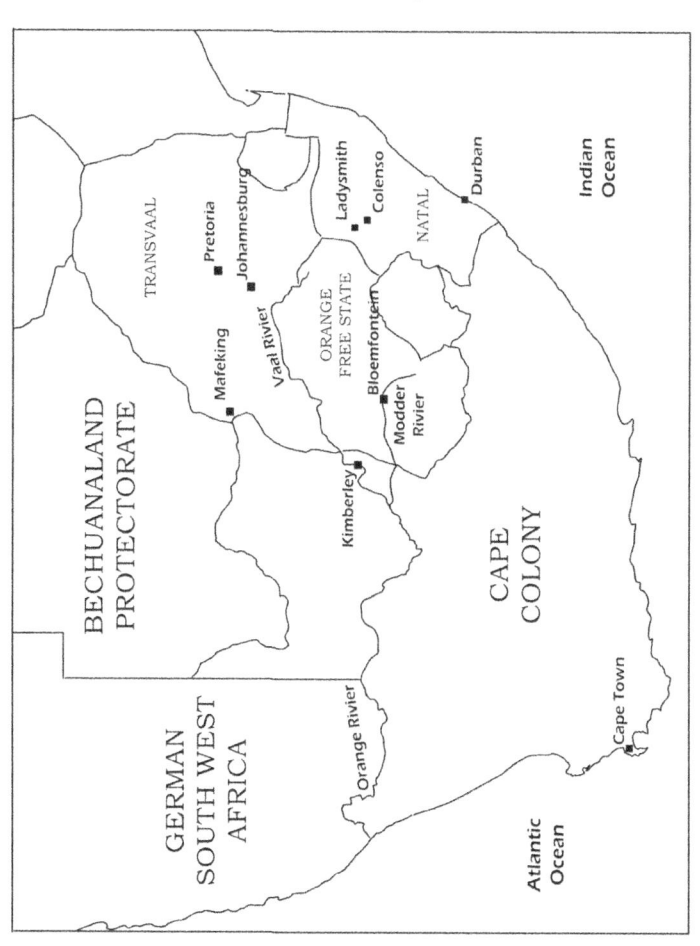

Map 2: Battle of Spionkop

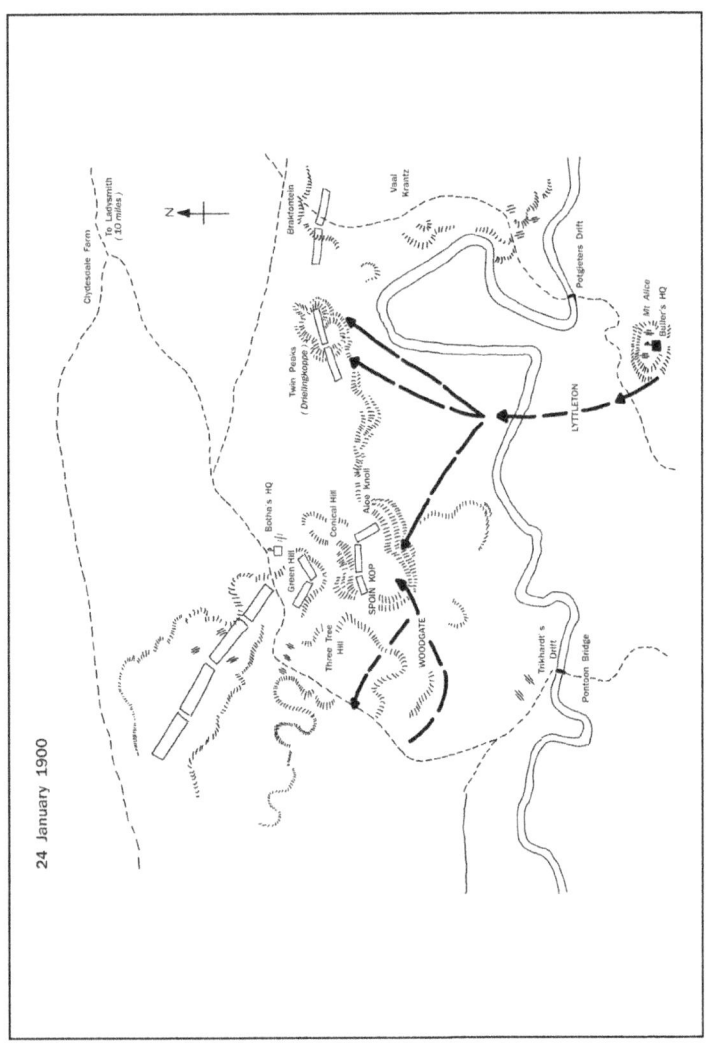

Prologue

Liverpool, England
Saturday 15 April 1989

"Come on, Tina. The game's about to start. What are you doing?"

A splosh of water and a sigh. Mam appeared in the doorway between the sitting room and kitchen wiping soapy hands on the front of her flowered apron. The smell of fried eggs, chips, and lemon-scented washing up liquid wafted into the room with her. Her permed, bottle-blonde hair clung in tight curls to her forehead, victim of her after-dinner exertions. Brown eyes flicked from one person to the next. Jimmy avoided her gaze, his attention returning to the blurred images moving on the television screen.

"What do you think I'm doing, Derek? Clearing up from dinner, that's what. There's dishes to see to and the leftovers..."

"Ah, we can do it after the match, love. It's the FA Cup semi-final. Win this and we make it to the final. Football's most prestigious competition. The dishes can wait." Dad hitched along the sofa, elbowing Jimmy in the ribs. "Budge up, son. Make some space for your Mam."

Jimmy, wedged up against Nana's red-and-white dressed marshmallow bulk, edged forward and slipped to the floor. "I'll sit here. More room for everyone." Jimmy grinned up at Mam. "Dad's right, Mam. We'll do that after."

"Well, that would be grand. If I hadn't already finished it." Mam untied the apron from her waist. "Anyone for a cup of tea before I get myself settled?"

Dad raised his can of beer. "Not for me, thanks, love. I'm all sorted for the duration." He patted the six-pack at his elbow.

Behind Jimmy's head, the clack of needles indicated Nana had picked up her knitting again. "No, dear, I'm so full from lunch. Lovely eggs. Although the chips were a tad on the cold side, I thought."

Jimmy bit his lip. Mam would love that one.

Grandad leant forward in the armchair, cigarette smoke drifting out of the open window at his elbow. A breeze stirred the net curtains, swirled the smoke in Jimmy's direction. He coughed.

"Stop your bothering, Tina. We're alright, all of us. Sit down and hush up. I want to listen to the pre-match build up." The cigarette waved. "Turn the volume up, lad. Can't hear with the sound of traffic outside." A bus lumbered past, yards from the window, highlighting the old man's point with a belch of diesel fumes.

Jimmy scooted forward. The commentary team's voices boomed into the room.

"Maybe not that loud, Jimmy." Mam touched his shoulder as she passed behind him, taking her place between Nana and Dad. The sofa exhaled a breath in protest. "Oo, it's good to take the weight off my feet. You alright there, Mum? How's Kirsty's cardi coming along?"

A vision of sister Kirsty enrobed in the bulky hand-knitted, mustard coloured cardigan floated across Jimmy's imagination. He shook his head at the idea. Last time she came home from Uni, black was her colour of choice. For everything. Jeans, boots, shirt, jacket, hair. Make-up. Mind you, her tastes changed as often as the Merseyside weather, so who knew? Maybe it would appeal to the arty crowd she belonged to.

"Ssh. If you need to chat, there's always the kitchen…" Dad slurped at his beer.

The volume sorted, Jimmy lounged back against the arm of the sofa. Long legs, poured into the tightest drain-pipe jeans he could find, sprawled across the swathe of beige shag-pile carpet. Sweat prickled around his forehead where the red and white Liverpool hat hugged his hairline. Jimmy scratched at the wool. Full supporter's kit was essential for every match, no matter whether watched from an overheated sitting room or a windy, ice-blasted winter stand at Anfield. His scarf hung at his neck, limp and uncomfortable, tasselled ends obscuring the logo on his last-season's shirt.

A few schoolmates had tickets for the semi-final. They'd left on a coach early that morning. Jimmy, pedalling up and down deserted streets, shoving newspapers through letterboxes with a page-ripping ferocity, muttered under his breath at the unfairness of it all. By the time he finished earning his pocket money, the exuberant fans would be halfway to Sheffield. His friend Desmond amongst them.

"I wish you could come along in the car with us." Des was kind enough to commiserate with Jimmy, rather than rub his nose in it. "But Dad's taking a couple of clients. Treat them right, and they'll keep giving him business. So he says."

Jimmy shrugged at the memory. The pundits wrapped up their banter as referee Ray Lewis spread his arms wide in preparation for the start of the game. Liverpool against Nottingham Forest in an almost identical rerun of last year's semi-final. Jimmy held his breath, his heart beating faster with anticipation as Lewis lifted the whistle to his lips. Three o'clock on the dot.

Would the Hillsborough Stadium be as good to the Liverpool team today?

The teams surged forward as the game got underway; Liverpool in red on the left, Nottingham Forest, in unfamiliar white, on the right. Shadows chased the players as the afternoon sun shone down on the pitch. Chants and songs rose around the ground. The whistle blew a second time. Liverpool given the first free kick of the match, penalising the Forest captain, Stuart Pearce.

"That's it, boys, that's the way to get started." Dad thumped his fist into the settee.

"Watch it, you'll spill beer everywhere if you're not careful." Mam shuffled in the seat behind Jimmy. Nana's needles paused mid-stitch.

Jimmy clenched his fists as the ball swung wide, missing the Liverpool forwards and curving instead into the reach of the Forest defenders. They pushed the ball away from their danger area and back down the pitch. Liverpool responded to the challenge. Alan Hansen retrieved the ball, to the cheers of Liverpool fans.

"Good player, that." A grunt from Grandad.

Forest regained possession as the game drifted to the other end. The referee awarded a corner, taken by Tommy Gaynor.

"Seems the crowd are getting a bit out of hand there." Mam watched the crowd as much, if not more, than she did the players and the ball. "They're all walking…Oh, well, never mind, they're not showing it now."

Jimmy shifted his position on the floor. Forest took another corner. Movement at the top of the screen distracted Jimmy from the action.

"See?" Mam leant forward, pointing at the TV with one hand, while tugging on Dad's arm with the other. "People are walking around behind the posts. Isn't that the police there, too?"

"Hooligans. They're probably being escorted out of the grounds." Dad gulped his beer. "As they should be. A disgrace to the game. Don't you go getting mixed up with that crowd, our Jimmy."

"No, Dad." As if. Desmond wouldn't say boo to a goose, despite his superior height and strength over any of their mates. Jake might be a likely hooligan, always buzzing around on his BMX, chatting up the girls and fist-fighting with anyone who looked at him wrong. But he didn't like football.

Play shifted to the Forest half, the defenders scrambling to prevent a Liverpool goal. A free kick sent the ball flying out of danger. Jimmy thumped the floor, frustrated at the loss of possession.

More people surged onto the field behind the goals. The camera swung to the opposite end of the pitch before Jimmy could focus on the crowd.

"There's definitely something wrong, Derek. Look next time they show the goal." Mam's voice sounded urgent. But she could be dramatic.

"Can't be anything much. The commentators would mention it." A click and fizz as Dad opened his second can of beer.

Jimmy's concentration kept wandering, his attention distracted as more figures moved from behind the goals and around the edges of the pitch. Some were running in one direction, while uniformed police officers strode in the other. The game continued, the cameras panning away from whatever the disturbance was. A missed goal-kick by Forest. The ball kicked away, waiting to be collected by a Liverpool player. The stands at the Liverpool end in shot once more. More spectators spilling onto the field.

Jimmy's heart skipped a beat as the camera zoomed away from the game, focussed on the crowd. Fans were scaling the metal safety fence, tumbling to the grass below while behind them, others pressed forward. Policemen reached up as they tried to stop the invasion. The commentators wondered about the activity, mentioned a gate being opened to allow the fans easier access. Play carried on. Seated spectators continued to sing and cheer. The police strolled on unhurried patrol. Beardsley kicked for goal, his attempt foiled by the crossbar rather than the Forest goalie.

"Oof, that was close. Better aim next time, old son." Grandad lit another cigarette, shook its glowing tip at the TV.

Jimmy gritted his teeth. So close. Come on, Liverpool.

What? A policeman ran into the centre of the field, his dark clothes and flat hat in stark contrast to the shorts and shirts of the players. He waved over at the referee. The camera panned outwards as the commentators discussed developments. People poured over the fence, collapsing to the ground or wandering onto the pitch, dazed or raising their hands in anger. The police dashed in and out of the confusion.

"Oh." A sharp intake of breath behind him as Mam watched the scene unfolding. "Derek, they're getting squashed. There's too many of them."

As if hearing her, the commentators confirmed some members of the capacity crowd of 54 100 spectators seemed squeezed into the two central stands.

"They're taking the players off, Dad. See?" A shiver of anxiety tickled the back of Jimmy's neck, dampened the palms balled in his lap. Like waiting for an exam to start.

What were they witnessing?

"Well, I've never seen..." The sofa wheezed as Dad shifted his position. Jimmy smelled beer as it sloshed to the carpet beside him. Mam didn't comment. "Would you look at that?"

Fans reached down from the terrace above the open stand, hauling those below out of the mass of writhing bodies. Police converged from around the ground, outnumbered by spectators heaving over the fence and onto the grass. It was chaos.

The clack of Nana's needles stopped. Grandad's cigarette dangled from his lips, ash dropping to his chest. The clock on the mantelpiece ticked away the seconds, a metronome marking the slowest passage of time with a dragging, melancholy beat. In contrast to Jimmy's heart, which raced as though he'd run the one hundred metres around the school track. He transferred his right hand from his lap to his mouth, chewing on his thumbnail as images of disaster paraded across the television screen.

"I'm going to call Ethel…" Before Mam could huff herself up from the sofa, the telephone in the hallway burst into sudden, urgent life. "She beat me to it. I'm sure that'll be her. Winston and Desmond are — are at the game, aren't they?"

Moving as though in slow motion, every muscle tense and unresponsive, Jimmy turned his head to stare at Mam. Desmond. Yes, Desmond is at the game, with his dad. With Winston. The words strangled his throat, dried on his lips before they could be free. Free to pollute the air with fear.

The phone stopped.

A van coughed past the window, unaware of any drama beyond its own efforts to reach the top of Mitchell Hill.

The phone started up again. Determined to be answered.

Mam sprang from the edge of the seat, nails digging into the flesh of Jimmy's shoulder as she pushed upright. She stood for a second, swaying from the momentum of her sudden rise. Regaining her balance, she took the two or three steps to the mantelpiece and reached up her right hand, her fingers fluttering over the rough wooden carving of a cross hanging in pride of place on the chimney. Her lips moved in silent prayer.

The phone continued.

Mam let her arm fall to her side and hurried from the room. Jimmy lunged towards to the TV, turned the volume down on the commentators' bewildered conjectures.

"Ethel? Ethel, I can't hear you…yes, we were watching…don't understand…I'll come. Right away. Hang tight, Ethel."

"You should take her, Derek. We'll hold the fort here." Grandad's voice penetrated the fog of Jimmy's thoughts.

Dad was already on his feet, his beer abandoned on the coffee table in the centre of the room.

"I'm coming too, Dad. Don't think you can stop me, either." Jimmy scrabbled up from the floor. "He's my friend."

Dad laid a hand on Jimmy's arm, its weight leaden with understanding. "I wouldn't dream of stopping you. We'll drop your mam at Ethel's, check she's okay. Then we'll head for the ground. Find out the story from there."

Mam rustled in from the hallway, zipping her blue waterproof jacket with one hand, while gripping an umbrella in the other. Her knuckles shone white against the umbrella's garish pink and orange stripes.

"I'm going with Ethel down to the church. Father Malory is phoning around, said he'd hold a vigil until we know more of what's going on. Mum, Dad, will you be alright staying here while I'm gone?"

"Of course, dear, I'll rustle up some sandwiches. You can call back and fetch them later, if you need them. And I'll keep the kettle at the ready. We're in for a long night." Nana laid her knitting on the arm of the sofa. "Kirsty's cardigan will wait."

"Wait up, Tina, I'll give you a lift to Ethel's. I'm going to the ground, see if they've got any more news than the TV broadcasters. Though I don't think they know what's going on, any more than we do." Dad pulled the Club scarf tighter around his neck. The keys to the Ford Cortina jangled in his other hand. "Son? Are you ready?"

Dad and Mam exchanged glances. Mam raised an eyebrow.

Jimmy's jaws locked, his nostrils flaring, daring her to say no.

"Hurry up, then. And make sure you keep your eye on him, Derek."

The news broadcaster relayed the latest that evening, the backdrop of the afternoon's match playing on a loop behind her. Jimmy's stomach flipped and flopped at the sombre tones. His throat burned from too much talking. From holding back the raging torrent of emotion bubbling and lurching inside. Still nothing from Winston or Desmond. Or from any of his other friends. The officials at the ground had been wide-eyed and inarticulate, unable to even comprehend the day's events, let alone marshal any sort of response.

They'd bumped into Dad's friend, Steve, while parking the Cortina in a side street after searching for an available space for what felt like hours.

"Steve. Hold on." Dad darted across the road. A car hooted, the driver winding down the window to remonstrate. Dad shook his red and white scarf at him; the man ducked his head, waved a hand in apology, drove on at walking pace.

Jimmy jogged over to Dad and Steve.

"Derek. Were you watching? Course you were. Stupid question." The men shook hands, gripped one another's shoulders. "You heard from anyone yet?"

Dad shook his head, loped up the road toward the stadium. "That's why we came down here. See if there's any more information." He paused mid-stride, turning towards his friend. His skin was pale and glistening, reminding Jimmy of the time he'd been off school with the flu. "What happened, Steve? What on earth happened?"

No one could tell them. Candles flickered in shivering hands. Songs drifted over the gathering crowd. Everyone waited.

Pools of orange streetlight cast a dingy glow over damp pavements as Jimmy trailed behind Dad back to the car. Mum needed fetching from church; Nana and Grandad would be wanting their tea. Steve stayed at the ground, determined to remain rooted to the tarmac until he received more than angry speculation or vague reassurance.

"I'll ring you, mate, once I'm home." He'd turned up the collar of his coat, water dripping to the pavement at his feet.

"Yeah, right you are, Steve. Sorry, need to get back to the old folks."

Steve shrugged his dismissal, leaving Dad and Jimmy to weave their way through the gathering crowd still marching towards Anfield.

The image of the news reader faded as the footage from Hillsborough engulfed the TV screen. Fans milled around on the turf, distressed and dishevelled. A person in jeans and pale jumper lay prone on the grass. A stationary ambulance hugged the railings, inadequate provision for so many hurt. Men in pairs scuttled backwards and forwards, holding stretchers improvised from advertising hoardings. The broadcaster's voice continued in clipped, emotionless tones, belying the disaster she described.

"Dozens of football fans injured and, it is feared, some killed..."

Jimmy

Liverpool, England
Tuesday 15 April 2014

The turnstile clicked, metal on metal, as Jimmy leant his hip on the bar. The attendant returned his ticket stub. Urged Jimmy forward out of the way of the next person in line. Hurried to take the next ticket.

Like any other football match day. Only this wasn't a match. And it wasn't any other day.

Today, flowers adorned Anfield Road's pavement, tributes in red and white. Knotted scarves and flags hung from the metal railings of the Shankly Gates; the red of Liverpool entwined with the blue and white of city rivals Everton, the yellow and black of Hull City, with Aston Villa's maroon and pale blue. The crowd, far from shoving and pushing, raucous and excited for a spectacle of sport and entertainment, spoke in muted tones, eyes averted. Or, in more cases than Jimmy cared to count, leaking grief from under damp lashes.

He shuffled to one side, waiting for the familiar figure of his friend, head and shoulders above others in the queue, to reach the ticket official. A woman elbowed past, hurrying to keep up with the long strides of her companion. He sneezed, intense perfume tickling his nostrils.

"Gosh, luv, I didn't see you there." Breathless. Apologetic. A hand rested on Jimmy's forearm, nails painted white, tiny numbers in red on each one. 96. "If I don't hurry, I'll lose him in this crowd," she pointed at the bobbing figure. "Kev wouldn't even notice I'm not there, until he sat down. Big day for him. Lost his cousin."

"Sorry." There was nothing else to say.

The woman raced off, hand waving above her head. "Coo-ee! Kev. Wait for me."

Jimmy watched her part the crowd, a modern Moses fording the Red Sea. He shoved his hands in the pocket of his jeans, shoulders lifted and tense from the encounter. This wasn't a fun afternoon out in gentle spring sunshine, was it? It was about them. The Ninety-six. And their families. And friends.

"There are you. Look, I got programmes." His friend's bulk shielded the sun for a second, accentuating the chill tickling up Jimmy's spine.

"How'd I miss you? I watched that gate like a hawk."

"Different gate, mate, different gate." Expensive dentistry slashed a grin across the bottom of Des' dark features. "You alright? You look a bit peaky, if you don't mind me saying."

"Peaky? Don't be daft. It's you, creeping up and casting shadows over me." He shoved Des to one side, his fingers connecting with a solid, bulging bicep. "And what do you mean, you've got programmes? Did you get the hot dogs as well?"

A rumble of laughter, rising from the belly of a beast, was the only response.

"Let's find our seats, shall we? It'll be starting soon, won't it? Although they've let us through a bit early, I suppose. On account of all the people." Jimmy nodded at the queue of supporters and the throng pausing at the memorial just beyond the entrance. Heads dipped in respect as individuals laid wreaths beneath boards of gold-embossed names. One or two photos in silver or black frames nestled amongst the floral tributes, smiling faces stuck with frizzy 1980s hairstyles and wearing twenty-something-year-old fashions.

Des flicked his wrist, peering at the face of a gunmetal grey Tag Heuer watch. Titanium. Jimmy had looked it up on the internet, a whistle escaping between envious teeth at the price.

"We've got time yet. But we might as well amble in. Soak up the atmosphere." He blinked, shielding dark pools of unfathomable pain from view. But Jimmy saw. As he always did. Des straightened to his full height, opening his eyes wide, smiling. Pretending. For both of them.

Together, they joined the press of fans making their way to the stands. Progress was slow. Couples walked hand in hand. Friends — arms linked across shoulders, around waists — staggered in haphazard confusion as feet and legs tripped over one another. Strangers embraced, entwined in the commonality of collective grief.

Jimmy's hands returned to his pockets, refuge from the tumult of emotion surging through his body. Relief, like a helium balloon — free and untethered — that a paper-round and lack of funds had denied him a trip to Sheffield; the thud and fog of guilt, the sick weight in his stomach — how traitorous was he, that relief was his first sensation? A twist of pity for Des and the two wives who couldn't endure the cries of sweat-soaked nightmares despite decades of talk and counselling and medication. Another lurch of delight at thoughts of Sarah, at home with Kim and Tom, urging him to be there for his mate.

And beneath every thought, a pulsing anger, a bass drum of rage, that it happened at all.

No, Jimmy would never forget — twenty-five years since an FA Cup semi-final shattered the heart of a city.

Jimmy inhaled a swirl of perfume, cigarette smoke, more perfume, nervous sweat, as he squeezed and 'sorried' his way to their seats in the middle of the row. Missing was the tang of sloshed beer, the pungency of fried onions and steaming hot dogs. Missing too were the chants and the shouts, the whistles, and the laughter of a match-day crowd. Hands gripped his shoulders, patted his forearm as he passed; gestures of solidarity on a day without words. Des trailed behind him, stopping to greet each individual, grey-crowned head leaning in to catch their stories, their sorrow. A hand held between two elegant, manicured palms; an eye-lock of special recognition.

Des pulled out a white cotton handkerchief as he settled next to Jimmy. He wiped his eyes, blew into the fabric.

Jimmy kept his attention on the pitch in front of him, giving Des a moment to regain his composure. His leg jiggled in protest at the rollercoaster of emotions, memories resurfacing like the flickering images of an old film. Images he'd rather keep buried beneath the light-hearted banter and camaraderie of a lifelong friendship. He leant forward, resting his elbows on his thighs. Weighing down the fidgets, his head hanging low between stooped shoulders.

Shoulders on which a heavy arm rested. Jimmy wrinkled his nose at the garlic breath from lunchtime schwarmas as Des bent down towards him. Jimmy shrugged the arm away.

"You could do with a stick of gum there, mate. Everyone will know what you ate before coming out." He fanned a hand under his nose. The intensity of the occasion wafted away. For now.

"And whose idea was it to go to Ali's Kebabs before coming here, I ask you?" Des rummaged in his pockets, retrieving a packet of mints. He patted a couple into his palm, tossed one over to Jimmy. "I think you'll find your need is greater than mine, old friend."

They sucked in silence. Jimmy's eyes watered at the menthol fumes breezing through his nasal passages.

"Did you send one in?" Des scowled at the pitch, a patchwork of scarves forming the number 96 laid out in the centre.

"No. We come down and tie ours to the railings outside every year. You?"

Des bit into his mint with a crack and a grimace. "No. I thought it was for others to show their respects. For what we went through. I was there, they weren't. I don't need to post a scarf so I'll remember." He squared his shoulders, his glance at Jimmy causing a shiver to chase up his spine.

No, I wasn't there. And I'll never know what it was like. You don't have to remind me. He swallowed the words with the last of his mint. There was no point speaking them out loud, it would only lead to the same fight it always did. A fight from opposite corners, neither side able to cross to the other.

"But our Kenny did good. Must be thousands who responded to him." Des nudged Jimmy in the ribs, animosity and misunderstanding hidden from view again. "Mind you, who says no to Kenny Dalglish, right?"

Before Jimmy could respond, those seated around him stood, clapping and whistling. Jimmy forgot the scarves and Kenny Dalglish and the moments of friction between himself and Des. Supporters dressed not in Liverpool football kit, but in the sombre outfits of mourning filed into seats in the front row of the Kop. Jimmy recognised Margaret Aspinall from the TV, often interviewed as the Chairperson

for the Hillsborough Family Support Group. Groups of men and
women followed her. There was no one else Jimmy knew, but he assumed
they were club officials of some sort or other. Next came the full
Liverpool team; Luis Suarez for once not the centre of attention.

Behind the football superstars came a constant stream of
ordinary-looking fans, some clutching bouquets of red and white roses.
One held a photograph aloft; 'He's my brother' emblazoned on his shirt
in letters large enough for Jimmy to read from where he stood several
rows behind. Two more people carried a red and blue banner, declaring
Liverpool and Everton as 'two teams, one massive family' — rivalries
abandoned in the name of remembrance.

The clapping continued long after the survivors' families reached their
seats.

The choir sang the opening notes of Abide With Me, the hymn
gagging in Jimmy's throat, strangled into a croak by the band of emotion
tightening its grip, restricting his breathing. The paper order of service
rustled in Des' shaking hands, but his deep baritone flowed with no
discernible strain, despite another sniffle or two in his handkerchief
between verses.

On any other day, the hymn would conclude with a referee's whistle
and a ball thudded to one end of the pitch amid cries and shouts of
encouragement from fans high on FA Cup Final fervour.

Not today. Today, Jimmy held his breath as a hush descended over
the now-seated crowd. The Reverend Kelvin Bolton took his place
at the podium, a bank of seats draped with yet more multi-coloured
scarves before him. The microphone amplified his soft northern vowels,
dispersing his message of tribute around the stadium and, Jimmy
supposed, to the world beyond.

The vicar drew his remarks to a close. A murmur rippled through the
crowd at an unseen signal to stand. Feet shuffled, people coughed. Jimmy
rammed the back of his knees against the plastic seat, certain he would
need its support for what came next. Reverend David Smith and Father
Maloney joined their colleague.

A brief pause. The crowd sucked a collective breath. And the
Reverend Bolton began to recite the ninety-six names of those who died
on 15 April 1989 at a football stadium in Sheffield.

"John Alfred Anderson, aged 62; Colin Mark Ashcrof, aged 19; James Gary Aspinall, aged 18; Kester Roger Marcus Ball, aged 16..."

The names swam in a blur of black on the white page Jimmy gripped. He squeezed his eyelids shut, then blinked them open wide, determined to concentrate. His lips moved in silent solidarity with the three men's unwavering voices, gulping for air when the choir interjected the one repeated prayer; "In life, in death, Oh Lord, with me abide."

Des leant against him, his bulk shaking in spasms of anguish as the list continued. Jimmy fumbled for his hand, squeezing his friend's fingers until his own grew numb, locked in the grip of impossible comfort. Behind, a woman's cries crescendoed, faltered, faded, settled into a moan like the night-time howl of a sea wind rippling up the Mersey and into the city. The hairs on Jimmy's neck tingled. Further along the row from him, a man gave up any pretence at composure, collapsing back into his seat, head buried in a Liverpool scarf held to his face by nicotine-stained fingers.

Brothers, sisters, friends; teenagers, students, the middle-aged and the retired. Every name representing a broken family, a damaged community. Jimmy clenched his jaw against the bubble of rage threatening to explode from where it rippled like molten lava under the surface. Justice was one thing, healing quite another. And peace? Something else entirely. He needed a distraction, something other than the litany of victims reverberating through the sound system and bouncing around the stadium. He focussed on the O-shaped sculpture at the side of the podium, watched as light after light flicked on at the reading of each name; individuals represented by a pinprick of gleaming white. Jimmy released his jaw muscles, fiddled instead with his wedding ring, twisting it around between thumb and forefinger.

"The light shines in the darkness, and the darkness has not overcome it." The Irish lilt of Father O'Brien's voice floated into Jimmy's mind. Something he'd spoken of at a sermon a few weeks ago. Just the verse for the day, a nice-sounding platitude for a congregation seeking solace in troubled times. But now, surrounded by mourners and survivors, a ring of light shone ever brighter onto the sunlit pitch of Anfield. And a smouldering flame flickered in the darkness of Jimmy's soul.

"...Martin Kenneth Wild, aged 29; Kevin Daniel Williams, aged 15; Graham John Wright, aged 17."

The microphone hummed into silence. The men leading the memorial stepped back. The singers paused. Outside, the ubiquitous buzz and hum of traffic ceased; inside, twenty-five thousand people stood motionless, breath held. It was 3:06 p.m. Away in the distance, the first church bell tolled. Then the next. Then another.

Jimmy chewed the inside of his mouth, eyes closed, arms limp at his side. He was 15, on the floor of the sitting room, watching the referee blow the whistle, watching a game get underway. Then falter. Mam's fingers tracing the wooden outline of a cross hanging on the wall. The phone ringing.

The blood pounded in his ears. Dizziness swirled. Breath rushed from his lungs, an injured animal groan. Jimmy bowed his head, liquid pain escaping beneath squeezed eyelids, nose running, shoulders crumpling. The continuing silence pressed down on him, a weight anchoring him to the concrete stand beneath his feet. A quarter of a century condensed into a single, intentional minute.

Jimmy

Liverpool, England
Tuesday 15 April 2014

"You'll ne-e-e-ver walk alone."

Twenty-five thousand voices drowned out Gary Marsden's husky singing. Arms lifted, scarves waved, feet stomped.

Jimmy licked the salty tang of free-flowing tears from his lips. He wouldn't wipe them away. After the intensity of the minute's silence, more tributes from the Everton manager — football rivalries laid aside — and the local MP — finally admitting people other than the victims needed to shoulder blame for the events of twenty-five years ago — this was the soaring freedom of release. The familiar words rasped from Jimmy's hoarse throat, a battle cry to remembrance and camaraderie, the eternal flame given wings and flying alongside the ninety-six red balloons still bobbing skywards. It was victory torn from the teeth of tragedy, it was invincible courage, certain success, a winner's anthem.

It was the Kop at its triumphant, glorious best.

Des tossed the car keys over to Jimmy. "You drive."

Jimmy stretched out an arm in reflex response, fumbling to catch the bunch as it glinted in the low sunshine of evening. "Are you sure? This is your new one, isn't it?" He cradled the miniature Porsche Boxter in the palm of his hand, its elegant curves exactly matching the vehicle it belonged to. "You trust an old plumber with this thing? I'm usually cruising the streets in a panel van."

"It's just a car, Jimmy. You know how to drive. So, drive it." Irritation masked a weariness Jimmy knew consumed Des in the darker moments of forced remembrance. He wouldn't have missed today's memorial, but it would cost him over the next few weeks; it was the same every year. An itch he needed to scratch, but which reopened the wound each time he did so.

Jimmy hid the grin lurking at the corner of his mouth as they approached the jet-black Porsche waiting beneath the announcement *D. Graham, Senior Partner*. His trainers squeaked on the polished concrete. The key in his hand, he clicked the unlock button. Orange indicator lights flashed on and off. Des waved him forward, a grin of his own brightening the otherwise haggard features of puffy eyelids, glistening pink rims, a vein pulsing in his temple.

"What you do think of my baby, then?" He pulled open the driver's door, swung away to give Jimmy a clear view inside. "Kid leather, that. Soft like butter."

"Give over. Who sits on butter?" Jimmy bent forward, inhaling the new car smell not yet polluted by cigarette smoke or sweat. Dark walnut dashboard and shining chrome completed the luxurious effect. He whistled. "She's a beauty, mate. You sure you trust me to drive you home?"

He squinted back over his shoulder. Des shaded his eyes with one hand, the other gripping the open door of the car with white-knuckled ferocity.

Straightening up, Jimmy laid a hand on Des' arm. "Come on, let's get you back." He pulled Des toward him, steering him round to the passenger side, opened the door. He pushed on Des' head, as he'd seen the police do on TV — folding him into the seat, ensuring he didn't bump against the frame. Des responded like a tired child, slumping against the headrest, eyes closed, jaw slack. Jimmy yanked at the seatbelt, reaching across to fasten it. Des blinked at the sudden click, but remained motionless.

Jimmy slammed the door, trotted to the driver's side, slid in behind the wheel. He inhaled, abandoning concern for his passenger in the novelty of the moment. The moulded seat hugged his back and shoulders. Dials and displays reminded him of the cockpit of a plane he'd climbed into at an airshow a few years ago. The engine started with a roar, a vibration deep in his belly. He gave a few touches on the accelerator; the growl intensified to a full-throated roar.

Jimmy swallowed a whoop of delight.

He eased out of the parking and up onto the road. The streets were quieter, evening shadows lengthening across the pavement. A discarded paper lifted in a gust of wind; Jimmy recognised an order of service from the afternoon's memorial. He tutted, reassured by the crackle of his own copy folded in the back pocket of his jeans. He saved it for Sarah and the kids, making sure they understood his absence on a Tuesday afternoon for more than work or a game of footy.

Des grunted, twisting his head to turn away from Jimmy. Although only inches separated them, Jimmy knew they were as distant as two separate planets. Glassy eyes saw not a deserted street; ears heard not the delicious undertones of an engine straining for release. Did they see instead fear and panic and desperation? Did Des hear the screams, the shouts for help, the confused rush of the police? Or had his father, had Winston, pulled his son into his chest so all he saw was the red of a Liverpool shirt, all he heard was a beating heart?

"We should visit South Africa." Des rolled his head around to face Jimmy. He risked a quick glance. Eyes shone with the brightness of a new idea, a grand scheme. "Next year. For the anniversary. We'll go to South Africa."

Jimmy bit back a sigh. It was always the same. Something shiny and expensive to preoccupy the grieving mind. To avoid a too painful reality. "Why South Africa, Des?" What will you find there? he wanted to say. But didn't. He needed to get Des to his fancy waterfront apartment, drop him off, and catch the bus back home.

"Well, it's the Kop, isn't it?" He sat up in the seat, rubbing his hands together. Warming to his plan. "That's how it got its name, you know? From a battle in South Africa. I read up on it."

Of course you did. Jimmy flicked on the indicator, inched around the corner into the queue of cars retreating from the stadium. Too preoccupied to answer.

"There's a group out there who hold their own memorial. Of…of…" Des coughed. "At the battlesite. At the first Kop."

Jimmy swerved as a lad dashed into the road in front of him. "Watch it!" He honked the horn.

"Calm down, old son!" Des poked him in the ribs. "We'll be forty plus one next year. It can be a birthday extravaganza."

Jimmy imagined telling Sarah the money they'd saved for a weekend in Paris was being commandeered for a visit to goodness knows where with Des. Without her. He flinched.

Des waved a hand in his direction. "Bring Sarah. My treat."

Jimmy

Liverpool, England
Wednesday 8 April, 2015

"Are we all checked in, then?" Sarah leant on Jimmy's shoulder, a tendril of chestnut hair tickling his cheek.

Jimmy tapped away at the keyboard, tongue wedged into the corner of his mouth. Hitting 'enter' with a flourish, he reached an arm around Sarah's waist. "Yep! We're on our way to South Africa."

The printer clacked into life under the window of their home office. Jimmy scooted over in his wheelie chair to collect the tickets and boarding passes as they emerged. He waved the documents under Sarah's nose.

"I don't think we've had a holiday on our own since Kim and Tom were born, have we?"

"Well, this isn't exactly alone, is it? There's a dozen or more of the Supporters' Club coming. And Desmond." Sarah swatted the A4 sheets away from her. "Mustn't forget Desmond."

Jimmy paused in tucking the documents away into a plastic folder. The label on its front shouted 'South Africa' in red felt-tipped pen letters.

"What's that supposed to mean, 'mustn't forget Desmond'? It was his idea."

Sarah perched on the edge of the desk, folding her arms across her chest. Jimmy's jaw spasmed as she placed the physical barrier between them, a familiar symbol of a deeper gulf. A gulf named Desmond.

"I know it was Desmond's idea." Sarah avoided eye contact. "And I know he's having a hard time. But it's been twenty-five — well, twenty-six — years, Jimmy. Over a quarter of a century. He has to let it go sometime."

She paused, tugged on hair escaping from the haphazard bun twisted into place with a pencil from Jimmy's desk.

How does it stay there? Distracted by the mysterious physics of female hair techniques, Jimmy almost missed her next comment.

"And you do too, Jimmy. Let it go. You weren't there, and he was. Nothing you say or do will change that." She pushed up from the desk, the pencil releasing its grip in her twist of hair, clattering to the desk's surface. Dark curls, highlighted with streaks of sunshine blonde, tumbled around her face, curtaining her expression. "Let *him* go, Jimmy."

It was Jimmy's turn to hide his heart with crossed arms.

"Desmond's been my friend since primary school, Sarah. You know that." The truth in Sarah's remark seeped through his defences. He couldn't keep blaming himself — for what, exactly? He pressed his left thumb into the strip of gold encircling his wedding finger. "There's no one else. No one who gets it, anyway."

Sarah swept her hair back. "I know, I know. I just think — " she picked up the pencil from the desk, "— maybe on the trip you could talk to him. *We* could talk to him. Help him get closure. Or something."

"Perhaps." Jimmy couldn't hide the doubt from his voice. He shoved thoughts of any such conversation with Des to one side. Saving them for another day. Or not. He tapped the green folder in front of him. "We're going on a trip of a lifetime. And it's thanks to Des, so we can hardly begrudge his presence. C'mon, don't let him spoil the holiday he's paid for."

Sarah's smile ironed out the worry creases from her forehead, replaced them with the crinkled eyes and single dimple Jimmy had loved since they were sixteen. "Yes, you're right. And your mam is kind to have Kim and Tom for the whole time we're away." The dimple disappeared, like the sun hiding behind a summer's cloud. The worry frown returned. "Do you think she'll cope with all their activities and everything? They seem to get busier the older they are. Felicity from church said it gets easier as they finish junior school, but I'm not convinced. I've written out a list but..."

Jimmy whizzed the chair over to her and pulled her onto his lap. The holiday folder crinkled under her weight. The musky scent of her perfume — Noa, the new fragrance the lady at Boots persuaded him to buy as a Christmas gift — clung to her clothes. "Are you determined to make sure you don't enjoy this, Sar?" He picked up her hand, entwining his calloused fingers with her delicate ones. "Everything will be fantastic, just you wait and see. The kids will have a blast with Mam. It'll be all sweets and late nights and…" He let Sarah's hand drop, held his up to his face in mock self-defence as her eyes narrowed. "Joking! I'm only joking. She'll be strict with them, but fair. And she'll love the company, someone to start the day with, cook tea for at the end."

"I suppose so. Thank you — for trying to reassure me." Sarah wrapped her arms around Jimmy's neck, gave him a quick kiss. "Now, all those suitcases in the hall won't pack themselves, will they?"

She wriggled off his lap, pausing in the doorway. The dimple was back. "Did someone say holiday in the sun?"

Sarah twisted the tissue in her fingers. Shreds of damp white paper balled and fell to the footwell of the van.

"Oh, what are we doing, Jimmy? How can we leave our children for a fortnight? It's so selfish of us." She sniffed. "Maybe we could phone the travel agent. Check if it's possible to make a last-minute booking. We only fly late tonight. We could contact the school, that sort of thing. And I'm sure your mam prefers the peace and quiet than those two tearing up her house for two weeks."

Jimmy started the engine. He grunted, his attention on the rearview mirror as he indicated to pull out into the road. The lurch of his heart when hugging Kim and Tom goodbye, the walk down the garden path, the waved farewells from the street to the trio huddled on the porch of Mam's bungalow; that took him by surprise. He'd struggled for words. Speeches of warning and love and thanks — warnings to behave well; confirmation that he loved the kids always, no matter how far apart; and thanks to Mam for affording them the luxury of a foreign trip in the middle of the term — rehearsed in his mind for days, choked in a strangled throat, died on dry lips. All he could do was squeeze tight. So tight, Kim complained she couldn't breathe.

He pulled away from the kerb. A white Vauxhall Opel, caught in his blind spot, hooted a warning. The van stalled as Jimmy slammed on the brakes. He knew what Kim meant about not being able to breathe. Only anxiety, not a too-tight hug, squeezed the air from his lungs. He squared his shoulders, forced a deep breath.

"They'll be alright. They've probably forgotten about us already." He reached a hand over to clasp Sarah's.

"Yes, I suppose so. Like the first day of nursery all over again."

"And you remember how that turned out? Mrs Fraser phoned you at ten, telling you not to come early as Tom was having too much fun." Jimmy wobbled his head from side to side, the tension in his shoulders easing at the memory. Sarah beside herself, he trying to calm her down while all knotted up inside himself. The laugh they'd had after Mrs Fraser's call. "The same with Kim. We'll phone Mam from the airport. Check everyone's still in one piece."

Sarah wiped the wet tissue over her face.

"I must look a sight." She pulled down the sun visor, checked her reflection in its small mirror. "Ugh. I do."

"You look perfect, darling." Jimmy winked. She wagged a tongue at him. Dimple on display. "There's just time to get home, fetch the bags before the taxi arrives."

"And get tidied up. Although that may take longer than we've got." Sarah flipped the mirror away. "By the way, what did your mam give you before we left? She looked quite agitated. Intense."

Keeping his eyes on the road, Jimmy felt in his jacket pocket. His fingers traced the contours and bumps of the object Mam had pressed into his hands while Sarah settled the kids in their bedroom for the fortnight.

"This." He pulled out a carved wooden cross.

"Why on earth did she give you that? She's not usually into good luck charms and whatnot." Sarah took the ornament from Jimmy. "It is beautiful though, isn't it? It must be quite old. Your mam's had this on her sitting room wall for as long as I've known you."

"Turn it over. There's writing on the back, see?" Jimmy halted at a set of red traffic lights. "She says her grandfather brought it home from South Africa after the war."

Sarah squinted at the carved letters. "What does it say? It's not English, is it?" She nudged Jimmy in the ribs. "It's green. You can go. And what war? The First World War, you mean?"

Jimmy eased out of the junction. He sucked on his teeth, trying to remember the story of Grampy Percy. "No, before that. Mam said he was in South Africa when he was young. Before he got married or anything. Would you look at that? Red again." He waited a second time for green lights. "She was sure he brought the carving back with him. As a memento or something. But she said it always seemed important to him. Like it was more than a trinket, you know."

A lad in a grey hoodie ran to cross to the other pavement as the lights changed.

"Anytime, son, anytime." Jimmy shook his head. "Anyway, Mam wants me to take it with us. See if we can discover anything about it."

"Well, that's nice. But I don't know how she expects us to do that. Our itinerary looks pretty full." Sarah rested the carving in her lap.

"I thought that. But we're doing that history tour bit, after the match in Durban. Maybe someone there will tell us. I told Mam I'd try, but not to hold her breath." He indicated left, turning into their street. A silver BMW people carrier sat in their driveway. A tall, dark figure leant against the driver's side door.

"Desmond. He's early." Sarah rummaged in her handbag, pulling out a clean tissue and a lipstick. "Just as well I'm prepared for every eventuality."

"I'll make him carry our bags." Jimmy grinned. "All around South Africa."

Percy

Southampton Docks, England
Saturday 14 October 1899

Percy hitched the twin canvas straps of his haversack higher, the bag's weight pressing between his shoulder blades. The new haircut — haircut, more like a sheep shearing — itched under his cloth-covered field helmet, the chinstrap digging into the flesh beneath his jaw. He gave a tentative waggle of the head, certain this particular piece of protective gear was more of a hindrance than a help on the battlefield. He wanted to scratch his forehead, wipe the sweat away before it dripped into his eyes, but insufficient space between him and his neighbour prevented him. On either side, khaki-clad shoulder rubbed khaki-clad shoulder. In front, red necks and bristled hair; cigarette breath tickled from behind. Feet shuffled in black leather boots, mud from the recent rains tarnishing their polish.

The hum of nervous conversation bubbled around Percy, accents of north and south, of manor and miner, mingling into one indefinable voice. The oompah of a brass band harrumphed triumphant patriotism from the other side of the quay. Ladies in frothy dresses of pink and yellow and green held the arms of men in dull suits and shiny top hats. The less well-heeled sat atop stationary railway carriages or draped themselves over iron balustrades, desperate for a view of the day's proceedings. Overhead, seagulls swooped and circled, squabbling over any unattended rations, any discarded scraps. Rigging clacked and rattled as triangles of red, white, and blue cloth strung between sailing masts snapped and flipped in the wind gusting in across the harbour.

Percy inhaled the pungent tang of salt and seaweed. Images of afternoons spent poking around on the banks of the River Mersey flashed across his mind; of fishing for tiddlers or digging for buried treasure; of days filled with the innocent and simple pleasures of a childhood abandoned for a greater adventure.

And of evenings walking hand in hand along the edge of the water with Flo, dreaming future plans and prospects.

"I'll be back in no time. You'll see." Was he reassuring her, or himself? "Those Boers are spoiling for a fight. And we'll give them one. It'll be over by Christmas. Then I'll speak to your Pa, man to man."

Florence had giggled through her tears, a music-box tinkle Percy stored away in the recesses of his heart, to be retrieved in the din of whatever battle he found himself engaged in. Stowed in the pocket of his tunic, a more tangible reminder; the portrait photograph, letter and curl of auburn hair, Flo pressed into his hands on the platform of a crowded station of couples bidding the farewells of war.

Since then, there'd been weeks of marching up and down parade grounds until his feet blistered and head ached; hours cleaning and loading and firing rifles at targets, fingers calloused and stained with oil and the smell of cordite. He'd rushed at a scarecrow enemy, stabbing and slashing with his bayonet, screaming with all the breath in his burning lungs.

Sweat pooled in the hollow of Percy's back beneath the cotton drill of his uniform. Here he stood, a trained and proud private in the British Army, ready to defend the Queen and her Empire from an insolent President and his fellow upstarts. Chin lifted, chest expanded, and shoulders back, Percy consigned Flo to the hidden depths of his soul.

"Onwards to South Africa." To marching with a brotherhood of Britain's finest into a victorious destiny in a distant, dusty land. He bit back a triumphant cheer.

"It's exciting, isn't it?" The soldier on his right nudged Percy in the ribs. "Didn't think so many people would see us off, did you?"

Straining to hear his companion above the whistles and cheers, the brass band and the background chatter, Percy leaned closer. His helmet wobbled, threatening to tumble to the ground.

"I'll never get used to this stupid thing on top of my head. How are we supposed to fight with something balancing on our heads like this?"

He repositioned the helmet, tugging on the neck strap, hoping to tighten the fit.

"Better than getting your head knocked off by one of Mr Kroojer's bullets. Though by the time we get there, he might have given up and be waving a white 'kerchief instead." The man's red face crumpled into a frown. Wisps of damp, dark hair stuck to his brow. "Wish they'd let us on board. She's a pretty-looking vessel, isn't she?"

Percy bobbed up on tiptoe, too short to see over the forest of bulbous helmets. He glimpsed wagons drawn up at two gangplanks, stevedores offloading boxes and tin trunks of supplies for the voyage. One man wheeled a bicycle up the entryway; another scurried behind with an armful of what appeared to be swords encased in leather scabbards. Dangling from the ropes of a winch halfway down the deck, a huge crate swung in precarious motion. Two men leaned over the ship's railing, transmitting their alarmed instructions even from this distance with wild arm gestures. Twin funnels painted in pillar-box red and black belched steam into the misty air. Masts protruded at bow and stern, their nakedness awaiting the unfurling of sails. Rows of portholes ringed the vessel's sides, unblinking eyes observing onshore events.

Responding to the cramp in his calves, Percy dropped his heels to the paving.

"She is. Pretty, I mean. Not sure how we'll all fit on board, mind you." He glanced around at the assembled regiments and brigades, careful to limit any movement which could dislodge his headgear. His pulse quickened with the panic of those small in stature when in the presence of bulkier fellows.

"You stick with me, old son, and you'll be alright." Percy's new friend held out a hand in greeting. "Arthur Houltram. Lancashire Fusiliers. But you know that, of course."

"Percival Barnes. Percy to my mates." Percy shook the hand, calloused fingers wrapping around his far smaller fist. "Also Lancashire Fusiliers." He grinned, his pulse slowing to a normal rhythm.

"Private Percy. PP. Right you are. Although, if you don't mind me saying, that's not much of a Salford accent you've got there...?"

"No, I'm from Liverpool. Missed the call-up to the local regiment — stuck at work in Manchester with a boss who didn't see the point of involving myself in a war at the bottom of the world." Percy winked. "So, I left. And here I am."

Percy lost Arthur's response in a sudden loud roar of excitement, rippling from the front of the assembly, then crashing over him like a wave at high tide.

"General Buller has arrived." Arthur shouted into Percy's ear. "We're on our way."

Percy

Aboard the RMS Dunottar Castle
October 1899

Percy lurched against the guardrail of the third deck, swallowing bilious saliva as his insides danced the jig of the landlubber's stomach. Spray dashed up the side of the ship, dousing him in its salty drizzle. Gripping the rail with one white-knuckled hand, he wiped at his wet face with the other.

"You alright there, PP?" Arthur's nickname had travelled throughout the ship. Percy couldn't remember the last time anyone used his real name.

"Fine." One word through gritted teeth, the only reply he could manage.

"Only you're looking a touch green about the gills there." Percy's inquisitive friend flung a heavy arm across his heaving shoulders. Unsteady legs buckled at the additional weight. "First time at sea, is it?"

Percy nodded. His liquid stomach roiled. Squeezing his eyes shut against the rise and dip of the decking beneath his feet, he breathed through flared nostrils.

His companion continued chatting, a mix of sympathy and sadistic enjoyment in his voice. "You'll get your sea legs soon enough. This is my fourth voyage. Constitution like iron by now." A chuckle. A pat on the shoulder. "Wasn't always like that. First time I travelled out to India, I lost half my weight overboard. Couldn't even keep a cup of water down, let alone the slop they dished up for us."

The morning's porridge threatened to return for a second tasting. Percy groaned.

"Here, try a cigarette. It'll help."

"Don't smoke." Summoning up the courage to re-open his eyes, Percy squinted at his companion. "Miller, isn't it? Thanks for the offer. I'm sure I'll be right as rain in no time."

The ship's bow plunged into the trough of a wave. Percy staggered against the railing.

"Keep your eyes looking into the distance, PP. You need something steady to focus on." Miller pointed at the horizon with a smouldering cigarette. "Private George Miller at your service. I'm a couple of cabins down from you."

Whether it was the cigarette smoke he breathed in or his determination to keep his attention on the motionless line between sea and sky, Percy's insides stopped threatening to spill all over the deck. Or maybe the wind had died down. He risked a longer examination of George.

The man gripped the railing with a freckled hand. A reddish-blonde moustache crept across his upper lip, narrow and insignificant, the cigarette dangling from thin lips. Matching lashes shaded eyes the colour of a cloudless sky. Tanned skin stretched across bony cheekbones. His age was indeterminate. Campaigns on foreign soils would do that to a man, Percy guessed.

Would he return to Flo, an old man at twenty?

Beyond George, four or five other men leant against the railings in various degrees of travel discomfort. Sprawled across the deck, others read books or played cards. Some snoozed. One fellow, sheltering in the shade cast by the upper decks, sat with a sketchpad in his lap.

"You're like one of them reporters up top, Mickey. Forever drawing and doodling. Give us a look." One soldier — a troublemaker by the name of Jimmy Crosby; he'd already been in two fist fights with his cabin mates — sauntered over, bare feet and ankles protruding from rolled-up trousers. A dirty white vest revealed sunburnt, peeling shoulders. The fog shrouding their departure the previous Saturday no longer clouded the ship in its shelter. Crosby whisked the sketch pad from Mickey's lap, retreating a few paces. Mickey dived forward. The soldier whistled. "Well, what have we here, boys? There's me thinking Mickey here is drawing us all, recording the journey for posterity. When, in fact, he's composing portraits of his sweetheart from back home."

Mickey, cheeks stained crimson, snatched the sketchpad back. Clutching it to his chest, he gathered his pencils and hurried through the doorway leading to the cabins. Crosby waved goodbye, playing to the audience of bored onlookers.

Percy turned to the horizon, his cheeks hot with sympathy.

"I'm not sure I like the idea of reporters following us on campaign."

"Mm?" Percy, preoccupied with a sudden rush of thoughts about his own sweetheart, had no idea what George was talking about.

"That lot. Buller's entourage." George indicated the upper deck with a jerk of the head. Laughter and music carried towards them on the wind. "Although, from what I've heard, he's not keen on them being here either. He avoided them like the plague in Khartoum."

"Oh. The Press, you mean? I don't know. Isn't it good people back home hear the news, know what's happening?"

"When we're winning, maybe." George rubbed at a scar running from his ear to his jawline. Blinded by nausea, Percy hadn't noticed it earlier. "Not so good when we're not."

George leant on the railings, flicking the stub of his cigarette into the surging waters below. He followed its progress with his eyes, shoulders hunched, head lowered.

Percy remained silent. What could he say? He knew nothing of war. Only drills and exercises and lectures. He always devoured reports from battlefronts in India or North Africa, poring for hours over the detailed drawings and descriptions of the action. Every soldier was a hero, every general an infallible colossus destined to topple the enemy. Scraping together whatever money he could each week, Percy hurried to purchase the latest newspapers. His particular favourite was the Illustrated London News, closely followed by the Morning Post. Imagine if the great Melton Prior were on board the Dunottar Castle, steaming south on the same vessel currently reducing Percy's insides to a den of slithering snakes? Or Lord Randolph's son, only a few years older than himself, but already composing despatches filled with dashing exploits and marvellous victories. What was his name? Winston. Winston Churchill.

The Manchester Guardian and its premier reporter, Atkins, didn't suit Percy's tastes, so he didn't waste any precious shillings on its purchase. It was too small-minded in his opinion, too opposed to Queen Victoria and her desire to share her realm with the rest of the world.

"As if the words and illustrations aren't enough, they've brought moving pictures with them this time." George straightened up, feeling in his pockets for another cigarette. "There's a Biograph stowed away on the second deck. Hulking great thing, totally unsuitable to bring to battle."

"Is that what that is? I wondered." Percy recalled the crate being winched aboard. "I'd like to see that."

Percy's breath came in quick spurts, his heart pounding. Sweat dripped from his chin as he flung himself forward. The first to reach the tape. The winner.

He raised shaking arms in celebratory salute to the cheers and whistles breaking through his silent focus of the race.

"He might be small, but our PP's quick." Arthur grabbed a wrist and waved it at the crowd. "We'll send him in first, boys. Brother Boer won't see him coming."

Raucous laughter. Percy pressed his free hand into his side, squeezing away the stitch in his belly. Someone handed him a canister of water.

"Thanks." He took two deep gulps.

The Games were an impromptu almost-order relayed from the Upper Decks to both ease the crushing boredom of the final few days of the voyage, and to maintain some level of fitness amongst the men before they reached shore. Quarrels broke out between the men, intensifying the closer they drew to the Cape, breaking out into physical altercations if no one intervened. Crosby featured in most of the arguments. He began by poking fun, joking, and teasing. When his wit and humour went unappreciated, less friendly banter followed. The objects of his attentions skulked away, hiding out in their cabins until his focus switched to another unfortunate soul.

Percy, while keeping out of Crosby and his mates' way, found himself in the company of the teased and the outcast.

"You're like a loyal dog, PP. Standing in readiness to defend against the beatings of a bully." Arthur had grinned. Although Percy registered concern in the unsmiling eyes. "Just mind you don't get kicked about for your efforts."

The jangled nerves and tense ennui permeated the ship with its fever. One evening, when the wind was silent and voices carried across the moonlit waters, Percy overheard the ship's captain and the chaplain disagreeing over who should lead the Sunday services for the duration of the voyage.

"What if we've missed it all? What if it's over?" The question rose from everyone's lips, in every conversation.

The brief stop in the port at Madeira to load coal and offload passengers added to the gloom. News of Boers routed and in retreat raised cheers of triumph in public; worries about missed victory parades and party invitations in private conversation.

"What if we don't make it to the Front?"

Percy, lying motionless in his narrow bunk in the cabin he shared with Arthur and four other men, stared into the darkness of each night with his pulse quickened and his tongue dry. What if he didn't get to fight, didn't get to live everything he'd sacrificed for?

What if he did?

George, puffing away at a cigarette, assured him it would all work out. He'd seen enough action to know what he was talking about. So he said. But Percy saw the absent look each time his fingers strayed to the scar puckering his cheek. And he heard the indistinct mutterings and groans from his cabin during the night while everyone else slept.

Moments of excitement punctuated the journey before The Games; a whale chased by a shoal of small fish the most amusing of these. Percy, by that stage accustomed to the ocean roll and able to tolerate the tasteless meals dished out at regular intervals during the day, lay snoozing in the sunshine on the deck. Cigarette smoke and the smell of engine oil and unwashed bodies hung in the still, breezeless air. Quiet conversations hummed around him. The slap of cards accompanied by shouts of 'cheat'. The ubiquitous escort of seagulls screeching overhead.

"There. Look, there it is again."

Percy jerked awake at the sudden shout from behind him. He rolled over, propping himself up on his elbow, blinking. The card players threw their hands down, Queens and Tens skittering along the wooden boards of the deck as the men hurried to their feet.

"PP, you've got to see this." Arthur dragged Percy to his feet. "A whale, old chap. A great bloomin' whale."

Yards away from the ship's stern, a dark shape emerged from the ocean's glasslike surface, squirting a fountain of spray as high as the railing against which everyone leant.

"Thar she blows!" A voice bellowed from the upper deck. Percy twisted around. Squinting into the sun, he recognised the unmistakable tall build and broad-shouldered silhouette of General Sir Redvers Buller. It was the only time Percy had seen him since the raucous reception of his arrival in Southampton.

He turned back to watch the whale as it flipped its enormous tail fin out of the water, holding it poised in mid-air for two or three seconds. Then, with a mighty boom which shook the railing and rattled the rigging, the mammal slapped its tail on the water. Percy ducked, expecting the accompanying spray to pour all over him.

After the whale, dull routine returned to ship life. Until the ship's doctor embarked on a series of lectures outlining the benefits of inoculation against enteric fever. Accompanied by an extensive programme of said inoculation for all the ship's passengers.

Delirious with fever, muscles twitching and stomach griping, Percy crawled out of his bed to the deck, where the air was fresh. For the next twenty-four hours, curled into a groaning, retching ball, he almost wished for the earlier symptoms of seasickness in preference to his current situation.

Fine way to bring down the might of the British Empire and her army. Perhaps the doctors could distribute the vaccine to the Boers on disembarkation in South Africa; should conflict be ongoing, they could win the war without a single bullet fired.

Percy

Aboard the RMS Dunottar Castle
Sunday 29 October 1899

The trumpet played the last notes of 'Lord, abide with me.'

Percy, head bowed, patted the tobacco tin in his breast pocket; his love held close to his heart. It was Flo's favourite hymn.

His collection of treasures was one item richer; Mickey had pencilled a likeness of Flo, using the formal photograph as his model. Percy liked the new image better. Somehow, without ever meeting her, Mickey captured the essence of who she was. Percy could almost hear her laughter tinkling from the page each time he looked at it.

The two men had spoken at great length to each other about their respective sweethearts after Mickey's bruising encounter with Jimmy Crosby. His own cheeks burning at the memory, and hungry now that the ocean swell bothered him less, Percy had sought him out at supper on the evening of the altercation. Seated as alone as was possible on a ship of a thousand passengers, it was easy for Percy to squeeze in next to the humiliated man.

"I'd like to see your drawing sometime." Percy poked at a pile of watery carrots. "I'll be glad of some decent food when we get off this ship."

"You want to join in the fun, do you?" His chin lifted in challenge. Twin spots of pink shame blushed Mickey's cheeks. "Well, let me tell you, my girl's not for..."

Percy waved his fork. "Keep your hair on. I don't want to tease." He laid his cutlery down. Tugging at the flap of his pocket, he pulled out the old tin George had donated for his precious papers. An earthy tobacco smell overlaid the flowery scent of perfume. "Here's my girl. Flo. I wanted something less formal, but it was all she could arrange at short notice."

He held the photograph at an angle, catching the light from a window behind them.

"Don't let Crosby see you with that. You'll never hear the end of it." Mickey took the picture. "She's pretty. Fine cheekbones. Smile like Ethel's."

"Ethel? Your girl?" Percy retrieved the photo, stowed it back in its place in the tin.

Mickey delved into his pocket. He glanced around. Pushing their plates to one side, he spread a sheet of paper out on the table. Smoothing out the creases, he pointed at the parted lips of a curly-haired, wide-eyed girl. "See? They smile the same. They could be sisters."

The Chaplain's closing benediction recalled Percy to the present. "May the Lord bless you and keep you, may He make His face to shine upon you. Go in peace to love and serve the Lord."

Percy traced a cross in the air at the words of dismissal. Go in peace? Not quite what that particular congregation had in mind.

The men shuffled out of the saloon. Percy yawned. Another day of endless monotony stretched ahead now the highlight of chapel was over.

Shouts echoing from the deck outside startled Percy awake from a fitful afternoon nap. He elbowed his way past those blocking the doorway, eager to discover the source of the commotion, excited at the prospect of seeing another whale. Or perhaps even a distant purple outline of land on the horizon.

It was a ship. Telescopes clicked open. Men jostled with one another, pushing and shoving towards the front of the crowd lining the railings. Cameras flashed. Men lugged the Biograph into position on the deck above. General Buller emerged from his private quarters, binoculars in hand. His civilian shirt billowed in the breeze.

Phosphorescent water churned at the bow of the small steamer as she changed course to inch closer to the Dunottar Castle. Percy, his hand to his forehead as a shade against the sun, made out the name *Australasian* along her side. As she approached, sailors scurried around the deck. They hefted a large blackboard over the railings; letters emblazoned in white broadcast the latest news. Percy, lacking any magnification device, tapped impatient fingers while he waited for others to enlighten him.

A groan rippled around the assembled soldiers. General Buller lowered his field glasses. Without uttering a word, he returned to his cabin.

"What does it say?" The communication too far away to read with the naked eye.

"Nothing good, PP, nothing good." Arthur passed his binoculars to Percy, his mouth pinched into a tight line.

BOERS DEFEATED – THREE BATTLES – PENN SYMONS KILLED.

"But that means we're winning." Percy returned the glasses. "I suppose Penn-Symons is an important General or something. I dare say his loss will be felt by someone somewhere. But to win three battles that's...Oh."

"Yes. 'Oh', Private Percival. Oh, indeed." Crosby shoved away from the rails, a scowl pulling his eyebrows into a bushy line. "We've missed the game, wasting away on this floating hotel."

Percy

Cape Town, South Africa
Monday 30 October, 1899

R ain dripped from Percy's helmet. Water ran into his eyes, obscuring his vision. Further down the ranks, someone sneezed. His first glimpse of South Africa and Percy was as wet and miserable as on a winter's day in England. He shivered.

Bedraggled Union Jack flags hung in limp, silent welcome as the Dunottar Castle eased her way into Cape Town harbour. Two tugs nudged and corralled her towards an awaiting berth. Lights along the wharf blinked in the gloom of late evening. Three black cars drove in slow convoy down the jetty, headlight beams breaking into shards of reflected light as they splashed through puddles.

Behind him, the twin funnels belched dirty grey smoke as the engines manoeuvred the troop ship to her moorings. After the pristine, unpolluted air of the open ocean, Percy's lungs wheezed and protested at the oppressive, smoke-tinged atmosphere of the harbour bowl. A moment he'd anticipated with growing eagerness after three weeks at sea threatened to suffocate him in its anti-climactic gloom.

The cars halted a few yards from the ship. A gangplank rattled into place against the ship's side amidst shouted instructions muffled by the rain. Drivers emerged from the front of each car, military uniform indicating official visitors occupied their back seats. One of Buller's aides appeared at the top of the walkway. He stood to stiff attention as the vehicles disgorged their passengers, who scurried up the gangplank, heads bowed low and collars upturned against the damp. One man hugged an attaché case to his chest.

"Telling Buller to turn around and go back home, probably."

"Should have known we'd get here too late."

"Do you think they'll at least let us ashore first? I didn't join the army to become a sailor..."

Laughter rippled through the assembly.

While the military men conferred, others, laden with cameras and duffle bags, scuttled down the gangplank. The reporters, rushing to send their despatches to London. Rats and sinking ships sprang to mind. They dispersed in groups of two and three, indistinct shadows in the murky night.

Percy wiped a raindrop from the end of his nose.

"Looks like they've delivered the good news. See, they're leaving already."

The officials scuttled back to the awaiting cars. The attaché case wasn't with them.

"Might as well go return to your bunks, boys. That's all the fun for tonight."

Percy welcomed the first fingers of sunrise with relief. All night, his stomach bobbing and dipping in unison with the unaccustomed motion of the moored ship, he lay listening to the muttered grumbles and restless movement of men denied the opportunity of war. His bunk was too narrow, his cabin mates too noisy, his blanket too thin. Three weeks of dreaming and planning; of practicing imaginary manoeuvres; of shooting at real targets; culminated in this moment, in these few hours before disembarkation.

"You'll do us proud, son." Father's voice echoing through his thoughts.

"Come home safely, child. We'll be praying." Mother's damp handkerchief against his cheek.

"Write every day. Even if you can't send the letters so often." Flo's stern instructions.

He'd rolled over, his forehead against the cold metal of the cabin wall, biting his lip against the groan stirring in his soul.

The morning reveille sounded loud and insistent, penetrating the corridors and cabins of the lower deck with its urgent call to action. Percy, Arthur and the others danced around each other in a complicated choreography of bag packing, uniform straightening, and bedmaking. Percy tugged on the white leather straps of his dress uniform. His kit gleamed from hours of polishing and checking and polishing some more. Without waiting for his cabin mates, Percy hefted his knapsack and bedroll and joined the stream of soldiers flowing onto the deck.

The rain had cleared. Cape Town glinted in the laundered shine of a new spring day. Rigging clacked, flags waved. Cormorants and shags huddled on nearby rocks, vying with the seagulls for the best of any scraps dropped by the gathering crowd. A flat-topped mountain brooded over the harbour, homes and gardens cascading down its lower slopes. A cloud or two puffed over the ridge, dispersing in the sea wind.

"The Southampton of Africa." Percy, delighting in the warmth and the carnival atmosphere, started at Arthur's voice so close to his ear. "And we've not even fired a shot."

"And probably never will." Gordon Jackson, another of Percy's cabin mates, ran a hand over his glistening forehead. "Phew, it's hot when it's not raining."

"Hot? This isn't hot. It's early still, too." George sauntered towards them, a grin crinkling the skin around his eyes. "You should try India in the middle of summer right after a monsoon rain."

"No, thanks. This is fine for now." Jackson wiped his palms on his trousers. "Old Buller, he must be overheating in that get-up."

Emerging from his private cabin, General Sir Redvers Buller, dressed in all his regimental finery, surveyed his troops. Silver buttons and braids accented the dark navy of his tunic, the row of medal ribbons a checkerboard of battle-won colour. His moustache, twirled and waxed, dominated his square features.

A thousand hands raised in silent salute as their leader stepped towards the gangplank. On the quayside below, a pair of magnificent bay horses leading a liveried open landau waited for their distinguished passenger. A band struck up the opening bars of the National Anthem.

Cheers rose from the gathered crowd onshore. Percy lifted his chin, his heart fluttering and skipping as though the medals were his own and the applause for him. He was in Africa. And he was here to defend Queen and Country.

After the pomp and ceremony of General Buller's departure, the decks of the Dunottar Castle became a frenzy of organised activity. Boots thumped and clumped on the boards as men formed into companies ready to march to their next — undisclosed — destination. Percy whistled while preparing to disembark, certain of a motionless bed to sleep in at last, wherever that bed may be. Haversacks and shoulders bumped, helmets toppled and rolled underfoot. Orderlies arranged supplies and stores in neat piles on the decks. Percy, taking a moment to catch his breath, leant against the railing and watched as dark-skinned labourers prodded and poked pairs of oxen yoked to baggage wagons on the wharf.

"Come on, Private. Stop dawdling and fall in." An officer shouted over at Percy.

He hurried to the back of the line. A flutter of nerves harmonised with the march of boots descending the gangplank. Unable to see beyond the khaki shoulder of the man in front, Percy noticed a creature swimming and curving through the water alongside the gangplank. Its sleek body shone almost black as it emerged, whiskers dripping with diamond drops, curiosity obvious in the round, enquiring eyes. Although never having been near one in real life, Percy recognised the seal from a picture he'd seen in a book. Fascinated, he paused as it dived underwater again. The soldier behind him bumped into him.

"Watch it. Don't stop like that." A hand shoved into the small of Percy's back. "I'll remember not to be near you in any field advance against Brother Boer. Might get my head shot off."

The tips of his ears burning, Percy picked up speed, his legs shaky with embarrassment and the novel sensation of unmoving ground beneath his feet. A group of young ladies waved and smiled from under delicate parasols as the marching soldiers swung left, away from the Dunottar Castle and towards their barracks. Percy fixed his eyes forward, ignoring the whistles and boisterous comments from his fellows as they delighted in female attention for the first time in weeks.

The crowds of well-wishers and sight-seers thinned as the men left the harbour; their banter and light-hearted chatter diminishing with every step. The reality of the purpose of their visit wrapped around Percy like a thick blanket, dulling his senses and silencing his speech. He guessed others were confronting a similar realisation. Every step along the winding road inland was one step deeper into an unknown land of hostility and danger.

Wilhelm

Carolina, Transvaal Republic, South Africa
Tuesday 26 September 1899

"But is war really the answer, Dominee?" Pa tugged on his beard, his meal untouched in front of him. "Surely there's a different way."

Dominee Fourie removed his black hat, placing it beside him. Resting his hand on its stiff crown, he closed his eyes. A sigh ruffled his moustache.

"Marthinus, what more can I tell you? The Rand is a powder keg worse than any mine explosive. The match has already been lit. There's only one way to extinguish the fire…"

Wilhelm slurped his stew, the sting of hot vegetables burning his lips and tongue. Coughing, he reached for a cup of water. Pa's eyes flicked in his direction, brows drawn together in a familiar frown of disapproval.

"You'll have some food, Dominee? There's bread as well." Ma ladled steaming liquid into a fourth bowl.

Dominee Fourie raised his palms, shaking his head in refusal. Ma placed a dish in front of him, regardless.

"Very well. Thank you, Elise. I welcome your hospitality." The Dominee picked up his spoon, twisting it around his fingers. He didn't eat.

"You were saying, Dominee? Johannesburg is in uproar. You're right, I have heard that. But is there not a solution other than fighting?"

"An agreement of peace with the British is surely an accord with the devil himself. Besides, we already have an agreement. To live within the borders of our Republic, with President Kruger as our leader, enjoying no outside interference from any foreign power in any matters of policy. Including, and especially, the franchise." Dominee Fourie paused, his empty spoon suspended in mid-air. "Provision exists for the Uitlanders, these outsiders, to have the vote after fourteen years of living and working in a law-abiding manner here. It is only gold that stirs them to request anything different."

It was Pa's turn to sigh. He moved away from the table, sun-darkened fists clenching and unclenching as he paced in front of the window. A patch of sunlight caught the top of his head, highlighting streaks of grey in the dark brown curls.

Wilhelm scooped a piece of carrot from his stew. He blew on it through pursed lips, fragrant steam swirling in puffs of miniature clouds. He didn't dare have another coughing fit for fear Pa would send him from the room. And then he'd never know the outcome of the present discussion. He took a tentative bite.

"See all that out there, Marthinus?" The dominee twisted in his chair, the meal abandoned before it was tasted. "All that land? It belongs to you. Given to you by God Himself, a place for you and your family to prosper. A place for you to be free. Do you think the British and Uitlanders will stop at Parliament in Pretoria? Do you think they only want the vote? Marthinus, you know they want more. They want our country."

Pa stopped pacing. He leant against the window frame, gazing out at his farm beyond. Muscles bunched across his broad shoulders, visible through the thin white cotton of his shirt. A click of the tongue from Ma.

"What do you want me to do?" Pa kept his back to the kitchen, his voice low and quiet.

"Oom Paul is mobilising everyone who can ride a horse and carry a gun. They're gathering in Pretoria as we speak."

Pa turned round, eyes rimmed red and glistening. "And President Steyn. The Orange Free State. Are they with us?"

The Dominee bowed his head, avoiding Pa's glare of challenge. A rumble of thunder in the distant hills accented the tension. Wilhelm held his breath, spoon midway between his bowl and mouth. Gravy dripped on his shirt.

"Well?" Pa crossed his arms, sure sign he was trying to control a rising temper. "President Steyn and the Free State burghers. Are they with us?"

Dominee Fourie lifted his head. He stood, unfolding long, slender limbs from his chair. Pale fingers rested on Pa's shoulder.

"We are praying, Marthinus. President Kruger is a persuasive man, with a mandate from the Lord. It is only a matter of time." He dropped his hand to his side, bent, and scooped his hat from the table with the other. "Elise, my apologies for not eating. It is no reflection on you. Rather, on my troubled soul. Marthinus, I will leave you to think. And to pray. May the Lord guide you. And may He not delay in that guidance."

Thunder rumbled closer. Lightning flashed through the darkening sky, a searchlight casting the trees and shrubs of the veld into stark relief. The farm dog barked her alarm. The door to the bedrooms at the back of the house flew open with such violence the framed print on the wall shook. Isobel rushed in, hands over her ears. She hurtled into Ma's lap.

"Isy, were you asleep? You're not afraid of a spring storm, child." Ma rubbed her back with a slow, circular motion.

Isobel snuggled closer, removing her hands from her ears. Her thumb wandered into her mouth.

"There's more than a spring storm in the air." Pa returned to his seat. The chair creaked under his weight as he sat down. "Wilhelm, clear these dishes away for your Ma."

Wilhelm stacked the soup bowls, placing Dominee Fourie's untouched lunch with the others. Isobel sucked on her thumb, her eyelids drooping shut.

"What do you think, Marthinus?" Ma shifted Isobel's head. "Is the Dominee right?"

Wilhelm returned to his place, eager to hear Pa's response. His friends on neighbouring farms spoke of nothing other than the prospect of war. They rode around on their ponies, brandishing heavy sticks in place of guns, hats low over foreheads. Old man Mulder and son Piet, two years Wilhelm's senior at 23, had saddled up earlier that week, bound for Pretoria and Oom Paul's army.

Pa placed his palms on the table, fingers splayed out. He seemed to study his nails. "Even if he is, Elise, what can I do? We have a farm to run. Responsibilities…"

"But what about our responsibility to the volk, Pa?" Words blurted from Wilhelm's boiling heart before he could stop them. Now they were free, he couldn't catch them back. "Surely, if we stand together, we can beat the British and their plans. God gave us this land. He will give us strength to keep it."

Fearing an outburst of anger and dismissal to the bedroom, Wilhelm clamped his mouth shut, grinding his teeth with the effort of self-control.

Pa clenched his left hand into a fist, but remained silent. His nostrils flared.

Another flash of lightning. The first plop of fat raindrops pinged on the metal roof. Wilhelm inhaled the sweet scent of cool rain on hot dust.

"Wilhelm's right, Marthinus. Isn't he? If war is going to happen, we have to join the fight." Ma stretched her arm around Isobel's slight frame, her hand groping for Pa's. "You'll have to, Marthinus."

Pa bent his head, his shoulders hunched. He reached for Ma's hand. "We should pray. These are again ominous times for us, when the enemy threatens our homeland and our ways. We settled far from their influence, and yet they have followed us and again wish to take what is ours for themselves."

Wilhelm jiggled in his chair. What's the good of prayer if not accompanied by action? He'd read the Bible stories of battles fought by Joshua, by David, by Gideon — battles against those wanting to deprive the Israelites of the Promised Land. He knew the history of Dingaan, of the Battle of Bloodrivier, how only a few repulsed an army of thousands. God is on the side of his chosen people; victory is assured.

Pa rose to his feet. He always stood to pray. Ma nudged Isobel awake, swooshing the cat from his place on the rocking chair beside the stove and settling Isobel in the vacated seat. Winding her fingers through the child's hair, Ma closed her eyes. Wilhelm considered remaining seated, an outward sign of his inward lack of conviction. Knowing Pa rewarded such open rebellion with a hiding, Wilhelm settled on rising from his place in slow motion.

"Our God in heaven. You have protected us, kept us according to your promises in the past. We trust you will do the same now." Pa's Sunday voice filled the kitchen. "We pray for wisdom for our leaders, for Presidents Kruger and Steyn. We pray for a resolution to this present crisis. And we pray for courage and success for all those who respond to the call to arms."

"Amen." Wilhelm muttered the word under this breath. Rain battered down on the roof, poured in a sheet of water past the open window. He stepped from the table, avoiding eye contact with Pa. He would go outside, check on the dog and the horses. Allow the storm to wash away his disappointment.

"Where are you going, son?" Pa stood between him and the door, his bulk blocking escape.

"Outside. Make sure the animals are sheltered from the storm."

"The animals can wait. We have to plan, make arrangements."

"Plan for what?" A butterfly flitted inside Wilhelm's stomach. Were they...?

"A trek to Natal. We won't waste time going to Pretoria, only to travel back south." Pa stepped forward. He gripped Wilhelm's shoulders. Dark eyes bored into Wilhelm's soul. He resisted the urge to blink, to shuffle. "We'll journey to God alone knows where."

Wilhelm

Carolina, Transvaal Republic, South Africa
Sunday 1 October 1899

Dominee Fourie thumped a fist on the leather-bound Bible on the lectern. A dull thud echoed through the stone chapel.

"Men, you ride with our prayers ringing in your ears. You march, knowing your wives, your children are safe in the care of the Lord Almighty. You fight for independence, you fight for freedom. And you will return victorious."

The congregation rose to their feet, cheering and clapping. Pa draped an arm around Wilhelm's shoulder, held Ma's hand tight with the other. Isobel clung to him, her legs wrapped around his waist, and her arms around his neck.

Wilhelm whistled the whooping call he used when out hunting with the dogs. From the row in front, Katryn turned and smiled. Her blonde hair hung in two thick plaits between her shoulders, tied at the end with bows of white ribbon. More ribbons flounced around the neckline of her blouse and at her wrists.

Wilhelm pulled himself taller, winking at his girl. Blue eyes widened, then winked in reply. Well, he presumed she was his girl. She would be, when he came back. Of that, he was certain. Her lips parted as her smile twitched into a giggle. She turned to face Dominee Fourie once more.

"And now, brave men of Carolina, we wish you Godspeed. Let us pray."

The shouts died in the air as men shuffled and bowed their heads. Skirts rustled and a woman near the front released a low moan. The Dominee cleared his throat, wiped a shaking hand across his beard.

This was it. This was the commissioning before war. Wilhelm closed his eyes. He breathed in perfume and dust and men's nervous sweat. His fingers traced the knots and whorls on the wooden bench in front of him. A coucal chattered its call from the tree outside, heralding rain. He slit open one eye, risking another glance at Katryn. Her belt at her waist accentuated her figure. As though aware he watched her, her hand smoothed her skirt, and a dusky blush coloured her neck.

Wilhelm squeezed his eyelids closed, concentrating on the blessing.

"...and may the Lord bless you and keep you..." Yes, Katryn was his girl.

"May His face shine upon you..." He would return and make her his wife.

"...Amen!"

"Amen."

Reality settling in. Less triumphant, more reverent.

More sober.

The ponies nibbled at the grass, saddles strapped to their backs, bed rolls wedged in place. A cooking pot and water canteen clanked together as their heads dipped, tails flicked. Farm workers stood in a silent semi-circle at the edge of the field. Pa strode towards them, spoke one or two earnest words of thanks to each. The men bowed; the women cried.

Ma fussed over Wilhelm's jacket, straightening the collar, and tugging on the sleeves. Tears glistened in her eyes, but didn't quite spill over.

"Now, make sure you stay with your Pa, Wilhelm. You've not explored that far south before."

"Don't worry, Ma, I'll be fine." Wilhelm fidgeted under her ministrations. "We'll all travel together, so even if I lose Pa, I'll follow the others."

"Leave the boy alone, Elise." Pa gripped Ma's wrists, turning her away from Wilhelm. He planted a kiss on her forehead. "He can take care of himself. We've taught him well."

Decisions made and the journey almost underway, Pa seemed to have shrugged off his doubts and concerns. Father and son spent the previous day preparing the homestead as best they could. They mended fences; chopped and stored wood; secured fodder for the animals, enough for the next couple of months. They'd be home by Christmas; everyone said so. Ma packed parcels of coffee, strips of dried beef and fruit, and salted apricot sweets. Isobel brushed the ponies and polished the saddles.

"And I will travel with them, to care for both of them, madam." Petrus, their senior farmhand, stepped forward, his bare-footed tread silent in the long grass. Dark leathery skin folded in wrinkles around his eyes and mouth, giving him an aged, old man, appearance. But his shoulders were broad, his hands strong and his stubborn determination evident in the tilt of his head.

"No, Petrus. You must remain here, with Elise and Isobel. Your place is on the farm." Pa faced his herdsman. "I need you here."

"It is all arranged, sir." Petrus licked his lips. Disobeying orders wasn't his natural approach. "David here will take charge in my absence. I have explained all that needs to be done. I am coming with you."

Wilhelm waited. How would Pa react?

Pa looked from Petrus to David and back again. He glanced at Ma. She shrugged, gave a tiny nod.

"Petrus, I would be delighted and honoured to have you with us. We have a two-day journey ahead, much of which will be slow and arduous. Your expertise with the ponies is invaluable, as is your assistance with our belongings."

"Not to mention cooking. Petrus is a better cook than either of you can ever hope to be." Ma smiled at Petrus. "Thank you. I will sleep easier at night, knowing you are with them. And thank you, David, for stepping in to help me and Isobel keep everything going here. I'm sure we'll make a good team."

David bowed low. The other workers clapped and stamped their feet.

"We must be on our way, Wilhelm." Pa pulled Ma into his arms. "We shall pray for you all here at home."

"And we shall pray for you, Marthinus. Every day." Ma's voice was muffled. Whether with tears or the rough fabric of Pa's jacket, Wilhelm wasn't sure. "Shan't we, Isobel?"

Ma stepped out of Pa's embrace. He knelt to the ground as Isobel hurled into his open arms. She huddled into his neck, her shoulders shaking.

"Come, child. Be strong now. Your ma needs you to look after the farm with her. You remember how to milk the cows, don't you?" Isobel sniffed and nodded. "That is your special task. Be sure to get every drop, won't you?"

Isobel wiped her eyes with the back of her hand. Splodges of dirt stained her cheeks. Her face grew serious. "Yes, I will do that, Pa."

Pa stood, ruffling her hair, then turned towards his pony. He gathered the reins, pulling his hat low over his ears.

Ma gripped Wilhelm's upper arms with white-knuckled fingers. She reached up to kiss his cheek. He chewed his lower lip against the weakness of tears. Unable to speak beyond the lump in his throat, he nodded. She dropped her hands to her sides, and he stepped towards Flooi, his coffee-coloured pony.

"Wait! I have something for you to take." Isobel rushed to his side, an object cradled to her chest. "So you don't forget me."

Tears leaked from the edges of Wilhelm's eyes. "I won't forget you, Isobel. Not ever." His voice cracked liked a teenager's. "What have you got there?"

Isobel held out her gift. It was the carved ornament from their bedroom, from where it hung between their beds. "I used your knife and put my name on it. Look."

Wilhelm turned the object over, tilting it so the sun could catch the letters scratched onto the wooden surface.

Ek is lief vir jou Ouboet. Isobel Olivier xx

"And I love you too, little sister." Wilhelm hugged Isobel in his arms until the muscles ached.

Wilhelm

Transvaal Republic, South Africa
Sunday 1 October 1899

Wilhelm lay on his back, arms behind his head. A crescent moon slashed the star-speckled velvet sky. Shifting his position, Wilhelm found the bright dots of the southern pointers. With his eyes, he traced a diagonal line from them to the next glinting star — the tip of the Southern Cross. He recalled childhood nights on the farm, with Pa bobbed down beside him, pointing at the vast expanse of night above their heads.

"If you remember the stars, son, you'll never get lost."

"How, Pa? There are too many to know. Too many to count." He flopped down on the rough grass of the field beyond the homestead. "I'm hungry. Can't we go inside?"

Pa had pulled him upright, drawing their faces together until their ears touched. Whiskers of beard prickled Wilhelm's cheek.

Tilting his chin, Pa raised a finger. "Follow the line of my hand." Wilhelm tracked along the outstretched arm. A twinkling diamond dangled from the finger's tip. "See that star? That's the first pointer. Now…" the arm angled upwards. Wilhelm's intense gaze followed "…you can identify the second one. And a bit further…" Pa nudged his head to the right, pushing Wilhelm's into position "…you'll find the top of the cross."

"Yes, I can see all three. But — "

"We're not finished yet. Imagine a line drawn to that single bright star at the bottom. Got it?" Wilhelm nodded. "Keep that line in mind. Next, draw another line from between the pointer stars, extending it in the same direction."

Wilhelm squinted in concentration, his tongue wedged in the corner of his mouth. "Uh-huh."

"You see where your two lines meet?" Another nod. "Drop your eyes to the ground, right where that old thorn tree is. That's south."

Years of practice later, Wilhelm didn't need to imagine all the lines and intersections, the calculations so second nature he didn't even notice he was making them; he knew the hillock off to his left was south — their direction of travel, towards Natal.

Wilhelm pushed himself to his elbows. The campfire glowed orange in the centre of the laager, the circle of horses and wagons denoting their resting place for the night. Their destination was little more than a day's trek from Carolina, but once Dominee Fourie pronounced his blessing and the wives and children shed tears of farewell, no one wished to delay their departure until the next day. Wilhelm had trotted behind Pa, Petrus jogging along beside, waving and smiling at the friends and neighbours lining the street to the outskirts of town. Ma, flanked by Tannie Anneke, her sister, and Isobel, rose on tiptoes as Wilhelm passed. She blew him a kiss, pointing him out to Isobel.

Isobel darted forward, Ma too slow to grab her shoulder and prevent her.

"Goodbye, *ouboet*. I'll keep your bed warm for when you get back." She pirouetted in front of Flooi, the white ribbon she held billowing and flicking as she danced and skipped. Flooi reared her head away, snorting in alarm.

"Mind, Isobel! You're spooking Flooi. She'll trample you." Wilhelm hauled on the reins, keeping them short and tight to restrain the pony's wild movement.

Brown arms reached around Isobel's waist, lifting her out of danger. She squealed.

Ma rushed over. "Thank you, Petrus. Thank goodness you were right there." Petrus placed Isobel on the ground. Ma grabbed her hand. "What were you thinking, child? You might have been hurt."

"I want to say goodbye. Properly." Isobel's lip quivered. Tears gathered in her eyes.

Wilhelm, once more in full control of Flooi, leant down. He pulled one of Isobel's plaits. "You've given me a goodbye to remember for always, *sussie*." He tickled her nose with the wispy ends of hair. Isobel giggled. "And I don't think Flooi will forget it, either."

Dropping the plait and straightening up in the saddle, Wilhelm shook the reins. "Come on, Flooi, we're getting left behind. Goodbye Ma, Isobel. Goodbye Tannie Anneke. We'll see you at Christmas."

Before sunset, the leaders of the group established camp at a farm dam, circled with trees. In the damp surroundings, bright spring grass grew in abundant clumps, providing free fodder for the animals. Weaver birds chattered in noisy evening conversation in the bank of reeds above the water, half-finished nests bobbing in the breeze. Overhead, swallows dipped and swooped in the fading light as they caught invisible insects.

Violent sparks spat upwards as someone threw a new log into the blaze. Men sat or stood around the fire, silhouetted figures in slouch hats and boots. Several kept rifles slung over their shoulders, on the lookout for hyenas or leopards on a nocturnal prowl. A black cast-iron pot hung over the fire, steam escaping from the lid each time Petrus or one of the other farmhands accompanying their masters, lifted it to stir the contents.

Wilhelm's stomach growled. He'd nibbled on the dry meat and fruit during the afternoon's trek, but that could only sustain him for so long. He wanted a proper meal. Would Ma and Isobel have eaten already, gone to sleep early in the empty bedrooms? He thought he'd overhead Ma telling Isobel she could sleep in her bed, on Pa's side. But perhaps that was his hopeful imagination, not a real conversation.

Flooi cropped at the grass beside him. Fearing he might start nibbling on it himself if the stew wasn't ready soon, Wilhelm rolled to his knees and bounced to his feet. Flooi, alarmed by the sudden movement, shied away.

"Sorry, Flooi. I didn't mean to scare you." Wilhelm grabbed a handful of oats from a bag, a peace offering for his disquieted mare. "Here, aren't these better than boring old grass?"

Flooi advanced, ears twitching, nostrils flared. Wilhelm waited. The pony stretched her neck, snuffling at the oats. Wilhelm reached up his other hand and stroked her nose.

"There now. I can't have a spooked horse before we've even got started. You know the drill, Flooi. It's just like any other hunt. We'll stick together, you and me. Nothing to worry about." Wilhelm leant his cheek against her, breathing in her warm smell.

A sudden clanging of metal on metal — a spoon or cup banged against a plate — announced dinner.

"My turn to eat, Flooi. And I'm famished." He slapped the pony's rump. "See you later."

With quick strides, he crossed the laager, identifying Pa and Petrus on the other side. Pa held a steaming bowl with his fingertips; Petrus carried two others, teeth showing in his smiling face.

Wilhelm returned the grin, saliva pooling under his tongue at the smell of herbs, spices, and slow-cooked beef.

In the morning, they would ride out, refreshed and ready for the hunt. As Wilhelm plucked a bone from his bowl, scalding his fingers in the thick broth, he could almost believe this was just another spring expedition with Pa, the stars their only roof and the wild tract of open country their boundary. Almost.

Wilhelm

Transvaal Republic, South Africa
Monday 2 October 1899

The sun shone in a cloudless blue sky. At first glad to banish the chill of a night sleeping in the open, Wilhelm now lifted his hat, hoping for a breeze to cool him. When there wasn't one, he ruffled his fingers through his hair, fanned his face with the hat. Thirsty, he patted around for the water bottle hanging from the straps of his saddle. He gave it a tentative shake, but there was no answering splashing sound. Empty.

Wilhelm hoped the dark bump on the horizon was their destination; Volksrust. The journey south from Carolina was flat and dull, with few stops or breaks. All thoughts of fun hunting expeditions, tracking buck or warthog with Pa and his friends, of lazing beside evening fires together, discussing the shoot, vanished from Wilhelm's mind as the men pushed onwards. They'd rested for a few hours' sleep, breaking camp while the moon still reigned in the night sky.

Urgent, hushed conversations passed between the community leaders, Pa amongst them, as they urged the group to keep up the pace. More groups joined them, with slaps on the back and greetings of delight, or nods of acknowledgement and whispered words. Wagons and ponies, cattle and sheep, clogged the dusty highway towards the border between the Transvaal and Natal. Twice, Wilhelm trotted along alone, pushed aside by larger horses ridden by heavier men. Gripping his saddle between tired, shaking thighs, he'd raised himself up enough to see over the other riders and spot Pa's battered brown hat, porcupine quills tucked behind the ear, a useful identifier, not only for him but all the Carolina men. Although not their official leader — that distinction was for Commandant H.F. Prinsloo — Pa drew people to him as the heather and aloes of the veld attracted bees.

"Petrus, do you have more water?" Petrus perched on the tail of a wagon, legs dangling.

"No. We ran out last time you asked."

"We'll have to wait until we reach camp, then." Wilhelm sucked on his lip, cracked from hour after hour of exposure to sun and wind. He tasted dust and salt. And blood. "Won't be long now. I hope."

But water was the furthest thing from his mind as they approached Volksrust. They'd been following the railway line for the last several miles. Wilhelm's excitement grew as trains, decorated with flags of the Republic, puffed past at regular intervals. Men hung out from open doors, whistling and waving at the riders on their horses.

"Let's have a race. See if we can't outrun the train!" The man next to Wilhelm rode a magnificent jet-black mare. Tossing her mane in response to her rider's furious flick of the reins, she burst forward as though the shout was a direct challenge to her.

Wilhelm prodded Flooi in the withers. "What do you think, Flooi? Shall we try?" Flooi lowered her head and nibbled on a clump of grass beside the track. "No, I thought not."

Petrus, watching from his position in the wagon, threw his hands up in the air, his body twitching with laughter. "A wise and experienced pony. No point wasting energy until you have to. She will need to run on other days."

He hopped off the cart, strolling over to join Wilhelm, who'd slipped from the saddle and stood, stretching the stiffness from his hips and thighs.

Out of the corner of his eye, Wilhelm caught sight of a man stepping from behind a glade of low trees, his dark skin camouflaged in the lengthening afternoon shadows. Wilhelm squinted to watch as the man took two or three steps towards them. He brandished a long stick — or was it a spear? — in one hand. Muscles flexed in his arms as he raised the stick above his head, pointing it straight at Petrus. The man hurled, not the stick, but a tirade of words Wilhelm didn't understand.

Petrus straightened up from where he'd been fussing over Flooi. Legs apart and arms crossed, he lifted his chin as though daring more than talk.

The stranger lowered the stick, spitting on the ground at his feet. He spun around, stalking into the shadows without uttering another word.

Petrus wiped a shaking hand over his face.

"What was that for?" Wilhelm peered at Petrus. His expression was impossible to read.

"Nothing. Nothing about you, anyway." Petrus pressed his lips together.

"No, Petrus, that wasn't nothing. Tell me. What's going on?"

Petrus stared straight ahead. "This is a white man's war, Wilhelm. It is not for people like me to get involved in." He clucked his tongue and shrugged. His usual expression of regret, he could have been talking about a wayward sheep or goat back at the farm. "Or so many think. I am not one of them."

"No one will ask you to fight, will they? You won't need to. You're just coming to help with Flooi, and supplies and so on. The fight's between us and the British." Wilhelm chewed the inside of his cheek for a second. "Isn't it?"

"You might think so. But there are no bystanders in war, no spectators." Petrus shrugged. "My people will serve your people wherever you lead us. And those like me in Natal? They will serve the British. And all will lose."

Wilhelm was about to reply, rebuke Petrus for his negativity, explain it wouldn't be like that. Not this time. But a great shout rose from the front of the procession, preventing further discussion. A ripple of conversation, confusion, and excitement passed down the ranks.

"What is it? Has something happened? Petrus, run on ahead and find out what the commotion is about." Petrus hesitated. "Flooi and me, we'll be alright. We'll keep up with everyone else. You can come back and find us. Here, give me the reins."

Doubt puckering Petrus' brow, he tossed the reins to Wilhelm. "Now, Flooi, you stay calm and guide young Wilhelm to wherever we're going."

Flooi flicked her head in reply. Wilhelm grabbed the reins and hoisted himself back into the saddle. With a gentle squeeze of his thighs, he encouraged Flooi into a trot. Ahead, Petrus darted between wagons and horses and riders standing in their stirrups.

Unsure of what the commotion was about, Wilhelm urged Flooi forward through the throng. His mouth was dry again and the encounter with the hostile stranger had unnerved him. Casting quick, darting glances to right and left, he realised he'd lost contact with the rest of the men from Carolina.

"I hope Petrus finds Pa." He gripped the edge of the saddle with tight fingers. "And then finds us, Flooi."

"No need to worry, son. Everyone's headed to the same place. You'll find your people." The man on the black mare. Flecks of sweat foamed on the horse's neck and rump. He held out his hand in greeting. "Hendrik Venter. Standerton."

Wilhelm released his grip on the saddle, shook hands. Hendrik's skin was smooth, free from the callouses and scratches of a farmer. Neat hair the colour of corn brushed into a side parting and slicked down with a mysterious, shiny product. A trimmed moustache, and high-collared shirt. "I'm a clerk in the bank. Not as used to these outdoor treks as you burghers, but I'm here."

"Wilhelm Olivier. From Carolina. Farmer's son. Used to being in the saddle for days at a time." He grinned, the tension easing from his shoulders.

"But not so familiar with trains and this number of people all in one place, I would guess?" Hendrik released Wilhelm's hand. "Think of the next few days as a great celebration, like Dingaan's Day, only bigger. They'll break us up into smaller groups once we head for Natal, I'm certain of it. Only the British are stupid enough to travel around this kind of terrain in regimental columns."

"You know the British, then?" Curiosity beat shyness.

"I've studied." Hendrik waved an arm back in the vague direction of Pretoria. "Read up on British campaigns in Sudan. Or India. They have no idea what they're letting themselves in for. We'll chase them back into the sea at Durban before they've finished disembarking."

Wilhelm, squashed between Hendrik on one side and a slow-moving wagon bumping along next to him on the other, wondered if he would ever move at faster than walking pace.

"Oh, did you win?" He remembered Hendrik charging off in pursuit of the train.

"What? Win? Oh — " Hendrik's moustache twitched "— the train. No, of course not. It was fun though. Hunter here enjoyed herself. I might sit behind a desk all day, but we enjoy a wild ride now and then, don't we, girl?"

Before Wilhelm could reply, Petrus appeared at his elbow. "Oh, there you are, Petrus. Did you find Pa?"

Petrus nodded. Hendrik raised a hand but didn't speak.

"Yes, he's a little further ahead. There's a camp set up at a railway siding a few miles on. You're to meet him there."

"Very well, lead the way. And Hendrik here will join us. Won't you?"

Hendrik shrugged, his moustache a straight line above thin lips. Wilhelm wondered at the disapproving expression, but, with the road becoming more congested as groups of riders, horses, ponies and wagons joined the procession along the railway line, he needed to concentrate on guiding Flooi. Wagon drivers shouted and gesticulated. Individual riders hauled on reins to halt their animals. Those on foot flitted and weaved through the chaos.

After half an hour, the siding was in view. Tin-roofed sheds and one or two ramshackle buildings hugged the edge of the railway line. A train belched black smoke from its chimney as men disgorged from its carriages. Piles of crates and boxes littered the platform. A team of men struggled to offload a contraption strapped to a wheeled cart. Shock rippled through Wilhelm as he recognised a field gun from Pretoria from pictures in the newspaper.

Suddenly, this was war.

Petrus elbowed deeper into the crowd, Flooi's reins looped over his forearm as he led the way in search of Pa and the other Carolina men. Wilhelm half-rose in his saddle, scanning the hats for three porcupine quills. There!

"Petrus! To your left. Near the end of the train."

Petrus swerved around a donkey pulling a loaded cart. Flooi, sure-footed despite the sudden change in direction, flared her nostrils.

Wilhelm leant forward, pressing his mouth as close to her ears as he could reach. "It's alright, Flooi. Nearly there. Then we'll get you settled somewhere quiet, with fresh water and hay."

The pushing and shoving intensified as they neared the train. Wilhelm slid from his saddle, taking the reins from Petrus. The crowd in front of him parted and there was Pa, beckoning them forward.

"Son! It's good to see you." Wilhelm breathed the musky aroma of the two-day journey as Pa embraced him. "Our arrival coincides with good news from the Free State. President Steyn has finally understood that war against the British is inevitable. His troops will start to assemble and move forward this very day."

"Good news indeed." Hendrik, remaining seated on Hunter's back, stretched down to shake Pa's hand. "Hendrik Venter, sir. Pleased to meet you — and on such an auspicious day."

"Marthinus Olivier. Pleased to meet you, Hendrik." Pa patted Wilhelm on the shoulder. "It seems you have been taking care of my son here. I thank you."

"He is a fine man, well able to care for himself I believe." Wilhelm kicked at a stone, heat rushing across cheeks at the compliment. "I have enjoyed his company. But I must find my own people. Wilhelm, we shall meet again soon. Perhaps in Durban!"

With a jaunty wave, he whirled Hunter around. Admiring glances followed their progress through the crowd.

"So then, my fine man. Our camp is this way, alongside those acacias there." Pa pointed, squeezing Wilhelm's shoulder as he steered him in the right direction.

Wilhelm

Volksrust, South Africa
Tuesday 10 October 1899

Wilhelm slid from his pony, patting her neck as he looped the reins over a convenient thorn tree branch. The animal nuzzled at his pocket.

"And what might you be looking for, Flooi?" Wilhelm pushed the velvet nose aside, digging in his trousers for the treat his mare sought.

Flooi chewed on the carrot top, ears and tail flicking at flies. Wilhelm gave her a farewell pat, then strode across uneven ground towards his commando's laager. Smoke curled upwards from the main campfire where half a dozen men squatted, tin coffee mugs steaming in their hands. Today was President Kruger's birthday. The assembled burghers planned on throwing a party in his honour, although Oom Paul himself was still in Pretoria.

A paradoxical combination of boredom and anticipation had prevented Wilhelm from sleeping beyond the breaking notes of the dawn chorus. Careful not to disturb his slumbering tent companions — older Carolina men who seemed able to wait for something to happen with a patience Wilhelm wasn't sure he'd ever possess — he wriggled through the tent flap into the damp morning air. Stretching, his spine clicking at the release of night-time cramp, Wilhem filled his lungs. He pushed his feet into the leather boots cleaned by Petrus each evening. Without bothering to tie the laces, Wilhelm clumped over to the campfire, kicking at the ashes. Dusty clouds billowed upwards, catching in his throat, and giving him a coughing fit. He spat the acrid taste from his mouth.

Wilhelm grabbed a cup from a makeshift table and drew water from a nearby bucket. He swallowed the icy water in two breathless gulps, liquid dribbling between his lips and into his fledgling beard, consequence of three weeks of camp life. He replaced the cup and went in search of Flooi; a ride to clear his head before starting the day's work was appealing.

The swish of Flooi's tail, the thudding of her hooves in the soft soil as Wilhelm galloped away from the camp, revived him. He whooped with delight as the wind of movement brushed his hair, made his eyes water. The fingers of early sunrise tickled the landscape, dappling the early spring growth with pink and orange. A plover rose from her nest in the grass, flapping and chirping her alarm and indignation at their approach.

Wilhelm reached the top of a small incline, his favourite vantage point from where to survey the plain. He wheeled Flooi around, releasing the reins to allow her to nibble at the long grass at her feet. Below them, the Boer camp spread for miles. Out of a haphazard gathering of men from across the Republic, a loose organisation of military units had emerged, each with their designated leader.

Circled tents and wagons, the camps of each separate commando, spread outwards from a single white marquee — General Joubert's headquarters. Dark dots scurried between the shadows as his immediate staff hurried for their morning briefing. Wilhelm had heard rumours the General's wife accompanied him here, but he had yet to see her for himself. Curls of smoke wound upwards from the veld as the native helpers, like Petrus, prepared breakfast. A distant whistle sounded as the first of the day's trains from Pretoria steamed into view.

Wilhelm's stomach rumbled. "Time to go, Flooi." He retrieved the reins with a flick, digging his heels into the pony's flanks. She responded, tossing her head and breaking into a breathtaking gallop down the hill.

A pot of steaming porridge greeted Wilhelm's return to camp. Coffee fumes escaped from another pot on the edge of the smouldering fire.

"There you are." Pa strode over, slurping from a mug as he walked. "You need to hurry. A train has just come in. It needs to be offloaded before the birthday parade starts."

Wilhelm dragged his feet, rolling his shoulders and stretching stiff arms above his head. He'd hefted box after box labelled AMMUNISIE from the morning train onto wagons waiting to transport the cargo to the central stores of the encamped army. Oxen strained under their harnesses, snorting, and dipping their heads at the crack of a leather whip on their rumps. Wilhelm thought enough guns and bullets had lumbered across the African plain to keep the commandos supplied for months. Certainly, sufficient to break the advance of any British troops who dared venture into Boer territory.

As would today's arrival of fighting men, their slouched hats pulled low and new Mauser rifles slung over their shoulders. There'd been much hand-shaking and cheery greetings as the train emptied of her passengers. Groups huddled together, Wilhelm catching snatches of news from the capital as he struggled beneath his loads. Something about President Kruger at last issuing an ultimatum to the British. A final effort to avoid war or the first definite steps towards it?

Wilhelm picked up his pace, eager to discover if Pa or the Commandant possessed more information. But by the time he returned to the laager, only Petrus and a few other natives rested under the trees.

"Petrus, where's Pa?" He accepted the cup of coffee from Petrus, burning his tongue on the bitter liquid as he took a hasty gulp.

"He told me to tell you to join him at the parade for the President's birthday. Over there, look." Petrus pointed to a low hill beyond the camp. "You'd better hurry. I've saddled Flooi ready for you."

"Thanks, Petrus. And thanks for the coffee."

Urging Flooi into a canter, Wilhelm rode along the outskirts of the camp, passing the laagers of the other commandos, many of which he'd visited over the previous couple of weeks. Lack of any indication of an imminent war had him seeking activity and friendship, first to Hendrik Venter's camp. Together, they'd ridden out to hunt for rabbits or small buck, exercising their horses while practising their shooting. Hunter always beat Flooi over long, straight stretches; Wilhelm was delighted to discover her more sure-footed across streams or on boulder-strewn paths.

In the evenings, they'd toured the tents and campfires, listening to the songs and stories of the older men, playing cards or, in Hendrik's case, smoking with the younger.

On the lookout for Pa's porcupine-quilled hat, Wilhelm passed row after row of riders waiting their turn for the military procession. Horses and ponies chomped on bits and scuffed at the ground, heads bobbing up and down as they stretched for morsels of grass. There was Hendrik's Standerton commando; beyond them, one of the Pretoria groups, larger and more vocal. On a little further, and Wilhelm found Pa and the others from Carolina.

"Wilhelm! You made it just in time. Let's ride." Pa let out a whoop of delight, his horse leaping forward. Holding the reins in his left hand, he lifted his hat in the other and brandished it as he cantered past a man sitting on a motionless horse. Commandant-General Joubert, ready to take the salute on behalf of President Kruger, flanked by his aides and officers. And a lone woman — his wife.

Heart pounding and legs shaking from the exertion of holding on while standing in his stirrups, Wilhelm urged Flooi up the incline. He released a screech of joy, a child on his first gallop again. Wind cooled his cheeks, billowed his shirt sleeves. His eyes watered. He bowed over his hat as he passed an impassive Joubert.

His breath coming in spurts, Wilhelm raced down the other side of the hill. Reaching Pa, he hauled on Flooi's reins and drew her to a panting halt. He grinned.

As the last commando filed past in pre-battle triumph, Wilhelm's heart rate settled back to normal. A hush fell over the crowd as the General prepared to deliver a speech to his army. Too far to hear more than the odd snatched word blown in their direction by the gathering afternoon wind, Wilhelm slumped in his saddle and allowed his thoughts to drift.

A sudden shout startled him awake from a doze the drowsy afternoon sun had lulled him into. His eyes flew open, his head snapping up. The shouting gathered force, roaring towards him like a rush of water down a flooding gulley.

"It's war! It's war!" The words repeated over and over.

Wilhelm turned to Pa. Tears glistened in the corner of Pa's eyes.

"What is it, Pa? What's happened?" His heart skipped and fluttered.

A vein pulsed in Pa's temple, his jaw a tight line of tension. "The British have received President Kruger's ultimatum. An ultimatum they are unlikely to accept." He pinned Wilhelm with piercing blue eyes, rims red as though with the flush of a head cold. His voice cracked. Clearing his throat, he started again. "We are at war, son. Tomorrow, we march into Natal."

Jimmy

Durban, South Africa
Thursday 9 April 2015

The 'fasten seat belt' sign flashed orange. Passengers fumbled to obey. Jimmy pulled on the end of his seatbelt until the blue webbing strap cut into his stomach.

"You don't have to do it that tight, you know." Sarah prodded the overhang of flesh, giggling. "Bit nervous of the landing, are we, darling?"

Jimmy grunted, eyes fixed on the screen extended down from the luggage compartment above everyone's heads.

Des leant over him, craning to see out of the window. Jimmy inhaled musky aftershave and coffee. He wrinkled his nose, his own scent the distinctive odour associated with fourteen hours pressed into a flying tube of metal. He regretted not taking time to address his personal hygiene in Johannesburg where they'd changed flights from British Airways to some funny local airline; it's green and white livery glowing on the rain-drenched runway.

He cringed at the memory of the landing in Joburg — as the locals all called the city with knowing nods and conspiratorial smiles — a bumpy, lurching affair as they descended through boiling storm clouds. Babies cried, and a woman at the back of the plane, paper 'sick' bag rustling as she pulled it from the seat pocket, groaned.

Jimmy had retrieved the carton of orange juice saved from breakfast, piercing the foil opening with the blunt point of its plastic straw. After three or four attempts, his reward was a fountain of lukewarm sticky liquid squirting all over his red Liverpool shirt. By the time he'd clambered out of the aircraft on stiff, uncooperative legs and shuffled through the terminal to Immigration, the stain was dark and crusty.

"Would you look at that queue? We'll be here for hours." Jimmy gripped the handrail as the escalator descended from the Arrivals level into a vast hall packed with weary passengers from at least two international flights. Individuals hurried forward, heads down, elbows out, determined to be first to the front. Family groups waited to one side, kids whining while parents sorted passports and pieces of paper. African staff in official uniforms herded passengers into their respective lanes — one for South African passport holders; the other, for foreign visitors. Neither crowd seemed smaller than the other.

"I hope we don't miss our connecting flight."

"Stop worrying, man." Des massaged Jimmy's shoulders from the stair behind. "We're on holiday. If we can't board our plane, we'll book on another. Get some coffee or lunch. Or whatever meal we're supposed to be eating by now."

"But won't it be expensive to change our tickets?" Sarah twisted around, looking beyond Jimmy at Des. A frown worried her features.

"That's for me to know and you not to find out." Jimmy could hear the wink in Des' voice. *Here we go again. We won't forget who paid for this trip in a hurry.*

Bumped and shoved off the escalator and into the snaking 'foreign nationals' queue, Jimmy let the matter drop. Des was right — they were on holiday, the first proper one for him and Sarah since they got married. Since forever, if he was honest. He took his place in the line, manoeuvring his wheelie carry-on bag into a space in front of them. Wrapping his arm around her waist, he pulled her close.

"Happy holidays, luv. You deserve it." He kissed her cheek.

"Aw, look at the lovebirds."

Jimmy had spun around, puckering his lips in Des' face. "You jealous, mate? You want one too?"

Des swatted him away with a roar of laughter. Everyone turned at the sudden sound bursting over the muted mutterings and grumbles. Smiles broke out on tired faces, tense expressions relaxing.

The queue shuffled forward until, at last, the official directing individuals to specific windows indicated for Jimmy and Sarah to step over the red line. The woman behind the glass panel smiled a candyfloss-pink welcome as she propped their passports against her computer keyboard. She pecked at the letters, her head listing to the right as she read the screen. Sucking in a breath, she tapped some more. Jimmy waited. Was there something wrong with their papers?

She flicked backwards and forwards through the pages, her eyes darting between the book and their faces. Jimmy willed himself not to fidget or glance away, aware of his heart beating with the urgency of needing to be somewhere else.

"Welcome to South Africa, Mr and Mrs Brightmore." The official shoved the passports back to them. "Enjoy your stay. Next!"

Des stood waiting by the empty carousel. He waved them over. "Grab a trolley from over there. We'll make a run for it!"

"No bags? But we've been ages getting through passport control." Jimmy veered off to the left and unhooked a trolley for the non-existent suitcases. After a wrestle with the handle, he jerked one free and negotiated his way around groups of travellers, all seeking their luggage in vain. The wheel squeaked. He swerved alongside Des and Sarah. "Oops, sorry, bit difficult to drive, these things. Are you sure this is the right place? What about those bags over there?"

"That's the flight from Switzerland." Sarah plopped down onto the edge of the trolley. She rested her chin in her hands, her eyelids drooping. "Wake me when it's time to move again."

The carousel clanked into life. A shiny black suitcase pushed through the dangling rubber flaps. Not theirs. But it was a good sign.

Half an hour later, they were racing from international arrivals to domestic departures. Jimmy careened along the smooth tiled floors, his trolley-wheel squeaking like a mouse in the last throes of life. Sarah strode on ahead, brandishing tickets and passports. Des brought up the rear, calm and casual, strolling without hurry.

Once checked-in for the flight to Durban, Des disappeared, his leather holdall in hand. "See you in a minute. Want to freshen up."

He returned moments later, clean-shaven and wearing a fresh shirt. Even his teeth gleamed. Jimmy wiped his tongue around his furry mouth, folded his arms over the juice stain. He groaned, aware his personal grooming couldn't compare with his friend's.

"Sorry, luv, I didn't think to bring a change of anything in my hand luggage. I thought we'd do all that at the hotel." Jimmy whispered in Sarah's ear as they hurried down the ramp, trying to talk without breathing foul fumes over her. She smelt of fresh flowers — all those squirts of perfume from the testers in Duty Free.

She patted his chest. "You scrub up just fine, don't you worry."

A metallic voice floated over the small plane's speakers, recalling Jimmy — with a degree of gratitude — to the present.

"Please remain seated with your seatbelts fastened and your cellphones switched off until the aircraft has come to a complete stop and the seatbelt signs have been switched off. If you need any assistance disembarking, sorry for you, help yourself. Only kidding folks, we'll ask one of the greasy engineers to come and assist you."

Laughter rumbled around the cabin. The lad in front held up his mobile phone, the camera set to video record. What was going on?

"Please be sure to take all of your belongings. If you're going to leave anything behind, it will be shared by the cabin crew, so please make sure it's something we'd like to have."

Des barked a laugh. Sarah giggled. This was the strangest landing announcement Jimmy had ever heard.

"We'd like to thank you for flying with us today. And the next time you get the insane urge to go blasting through the skies in a pressurised metal tube, we hope you'll think of Kulula. Welcome to Durban!"

Jimmy

Durban, South Africa
Friday 10 April 2015

Curtains swished. A click and a squeak of a sliding door on well-oiled rails. Sunshine atomised the room, accompanied by a roar of ocean bouncing off the walls.

Jimmy squeezed his eyes shut against the glare, burrowing deeper into the pillow.

"Wakey, wakey, sleepyhead." Sarah's singsong greeting elicited a groan. "It's a magnificent morning. And we're right on the beach. Look."

Jimmy prised open one eye. Sarah leant against the door frame, half inside and half on the balustraded balcony stretching the width of the glass-panelled doorway. Two wicker chairs and a black wrought-iron table occupied most of the small space. Sarah's flowery dressing grown fluttered in the breeze. Beyond, a bright blue sky and an occasional wispy cloud.

Propping himself up on an elbow, Jimmy rubbed his palm over his face. Before he could speak, Sarah squealed and stepped out onto the balcony.

"Jimmy! Jimmy, there are dolphins." Her excitement pierced the deep rumble of the ocean.

This he had to see. He flung off the duvet, swung his legs to the tiled floor, reaching Sarah's side in a few steps.

"Where?" He rested his elbows on the balustrade, scrutinising the frothing waves beyond the hotel gardens and the public walkway. "Are you having me on? I can't see anything."

"No, wait. They'll come back up." Sarah shielded her eyes from the sun with a raised hand. "They were near those rocks, to the left. Going towards that lighthouse. Oh, there they are."

Jimmy squinted into the sunlight. A woman and child clambered over glistening rocks. A few metres from where they played, a dark shape curved out of the water. Then another. And another. Dolphins. Ten, twenty, perhaps fifty of them, dipping in and out of the rolling waves.

"They're surfing, Jimmy."

Sleek bodies tumbled down the front of an oncoming wave, their twisting shapes clear in the toothpaste-blue water.

They watched until the dolphins swam out of view. Below, dog-walkers and joggers resumed their promenade along the path.

"It's so lovely, we should go for a walk before breakfast." Sarah pushed away from the railing. "Although, do you think it's safe? You hear such terrible stories. I overheard a couple talking in the airport yesterday. Something about a robbery in a restaurant somewhere. It sounded awful. They said the police didn't turn up, but a private security firm arrived, and then there was some sort of gunfight."

"I'm sure they were exaggerating. It doesn't exactly seem like the Wild West out there, does it?" Jimmy waved at the beach. "Still, we should probably hide our passports somewhere, in case the cleaners come while we're out."

"Oh, I saw a safe in one of the cupboards. One where you set your own keypad number. I wondered why it was there, to be honest. Can't say I've ever seen one in a hotel room before."

"That's because we don't normally stay in these sort of hotels, Sar." Jimmy exhaled a huff. "Only the best for Desmond. Of course."

"Ah, don't be like that, Jimmy. We wouldn't be here if it wasn't for Des. And maybe, while we're not distracted by everything at home, it'll be easier to talk to him about, well, stuff." Sarah scanned Jimmy's face. He avoided her scrutiny, returned his attention to the ocean as though seeking the return of the dolphins. "You will speak to him, won't you? You promised..."

"I'll try. When the time's right. And there he is now." Jimmy lifted a hand in greeting as Des appeared beside the pool below. "Good grief, what is the man wearing?"

Sarah peered at the garden below. She giggled. "I think that's what they call Designer Beach. Hey, Desmond. Morning!"

Des glanced around before looking upwards. He whisked his white Panama hat from his head, bowing in mock formality. "Good morning, Sarah. Jimmy. Trust you had a good sleep?" He straightened up, twirling his hat in his right hand while smoothing the creases from the orange and pink flowery shirt he wore with his left. His toes wiggled in open sandals. "You're missing the best of the day. Hurry on down. We can have a quick paddle in the sea."

A uniformed member of staff appeared, a collection of glasses balanced on a tray. He advanced to Des.

"I've even organised refreshments for us." The waiter placed the drinks on a small round table, exchanged a word or two with Des, then retreated to the bowels of the hotel. Des stretched himself out on a pool lounger, his legs crossed at the ankles. "I'll wait for you here. But don't be long. We don't have all day."

Jimmy and Sarah hastened inside, bumping against each other as they hurried in through the sliding doors. Jimmy hauled their suitcase onto the bed, its contents spilling in a haphazard pile across the ruffled bedding as he rummaged for something to wear. Sarah, plucking a green dress from the top of the growing jumble sale of belongings, disappeared into the bathroom where the splutter of the shower soon mingled with the sound of her humming.

Jimmy riffled through the clothes, finding patterned Bermuda shorts and a plain yellow T-shirt that would do for a stroll and lazy breakfast on the pool-deck. He would change into jeans before leaving for anywhere else; no way was he showing his legs in public other than at the seaside.

He stuffed the discarded clothing back into the suitcase. They could tidy up later, unpack and make use of the bank of cupboards against the far wall before they moved to their next destination. Thinking of unpacking reminded him of the passports. He must stow them in the safe before he forgot. They were still in the rucksack he used for cabin luggage.

Retrieving the bag, he delved inside, feeling through the contents for the plastic wallet he kept all the travel documents in. His fingers connected with a hard, rough object. The ornament Mam gave him. He pulled it out, holding it up in the sunlight. Behind him, the bathroom door clicked open, and a waft of perfumed steam trailed Sarah into the bedroom.

"Do I look alright?" She twirled the dress backwards and forwards, mimicking the swirl and tumble of the waves beyond the window. "You brought it then? I thought we agreed we're not likely to discover anything."

Jimmy propped the cross up on his bedside cabinet. He shrugged. "Yeah. But I felt bad. Mam was pretty insistent about it, like it really mattered to her. You know? And besides, it's not such a huge chunk of wood that it won't fit into my bag. There's no harm in packing it." He grabbed up the shorts from the bed, moving towards the bathroom. "I doubt we'll be able to solve any mystery about it, but you never know, we might meet someone who knows something. Anyway, let me get dressed and we'll go and find Des and his drinks."

He paused at the door, grinning. "And you're very pretty in that green dress, Mrs Brightmore. Can I interest you in a date?"

He winked, then ducked into the bathroom before the towel Sarah threw in his direction could land on his head.

Jimmy

Durban, South Africa
Saturday 11 April 2015

The coach nudged through crowds of pedestrians towards a gate manned by yellow-vested marshalls. The driver leant out of the window, gesticulating. A marshall nodded and waved while another hurried to open the gate. The outer precinct of the glistening white stadium teemed with fans hurrying for the match. A decorative arch soared from the ground to span the width of the structure.

Des bounced up from his seat in front of Jimmy and Sarah. "Isn't this fantastic? Can't you feel the vibe already? And we're not off the bus yet! Did you know you can climb to the top? I heard there's a bungee swing. Brilliant."

"Mm, it's certainly...different." Jimmy swallowed a rising flicker of panic, hoping it wouldn't crash over him like the ocean waves battering the beach and rocks outside their hotel. He wiped a sweating palm on his jeans. "We'll be lucky not to get lost inside."

"Liverpool. Liverpool, Liverpool..." The chant, started by Des, gathered momentum as the coachload of fans rose from their seats. The driver shouted something about remaining seated until they'd parked, but he wasted his breath; no one other than Jimmy seemed to notice he spoke. Even Sarah was on her feet, waving her Liverpool scarf as much as the confines of the coach allowed.

Within moments of the swish of the doors opening, Des grabbed his jacket and raced to the front. He was first down the steps and onto the concrete pavement. Jimmy marvelled at the easy greetings he bestowed on the various officials gathered to receive them.

"He's born for this, isn't he?" Sarah pointed outside. Des had his arms draped around a steward, the latest mobile phone glinting in the sunlight as he took photos.

Jimmy grunted, concentrating on stowing their belongings into the safety of his rucksack. "I wish you'd left your necklace at home. It's too easy for someone to grab it."

"And my pockets might get picked at any of the matches at Anfield. You're not worried then." Sarah nudged Jimmy into the aisle. "We'll just stick with Des. Everything will be fine."

"Alright there, Jimbo?" Nick, a fellow fan who lived down the street from Jimmy, waved him forward. "After you, mate. I figure they won't be starting without us. You ever seen such an amazing crowd?"

Jimmy hadn't. He'd been attending football matches all his life, enjoyed raucous singing and boisterous exchanges. He'd sat in train carriages, whistling and jeering at supporters of the opposing team as they'd pulled out of railway stations around the country. He'd laughed at drunken friends weaving their way home, staggered under the weight of revellers worse for wear. But this was different.

As he clambered down from the steps, a wall of sound slammed into him. Loudspeakers thumped to a deep bass rhythm. Spectators streamed in groups of three, four, five towards the tunnels leading inside the stadium. Several carried long plastic trumpets, their single-note toot piercing all other noises. Vuvuzelas, so someone told Jimmy at the hotel; South Africa's reply to English football chants.

Hawkers draped in flags — the red and white of Liverpool and the black with skull and crossbones of the Pirates, the local team — called out for customers. A queue snaked around the edges of the main concourse as patrons waited in line to buy their first drinks of the afternoon. The smell of cooking oil wafted over from another stall selling chips in paper cones. Plastic bottles of sauce ranged along the counter.

Jimmy felt for Sarah's hand, gave it a reassuring squeeze. Or was he reassuring himself, keeping her close? He hitched the backpack up on his shoulder and shuffled through the disembarking fans to where Des stood, head thrown back in laughter.

"Jimmy. Over here. Meet my new friend, Goodnews. He'll take us to the hospitality suite I've booked."

Jimmy shook the offered hand. Goodnews held out a coloured armband. "Welcome to Durban. I hope you enjoy your stay. You'll need this. For security." He wrapped the orange strip around Jimmy's wrist, ripping the cover paper from the sticky end.

"Thanks, er, Goodnews." Jimmy wriggled his wrist. The band caught against his watchstrap, a garish slash of identity against the dull leather.

"Nice for some, getting to live the high life." Billy, a twenty-something-year-old electrician with acne and mousy brown hair, sneered his envy as he approached them. "Some of us have to sit in the stands like everyone else."

Jimmy's face flushed with sudden warmth. "Sorry, not my doing." He glanced over at Des, loud in expansive conversation with the dozen others being treated to the 'high life', as Billy put it. "You'll probably have more fun, anyway. There's your escort now."

A woman in a bulky luminous vest, black blouse and skirt strode over. A radio hung from her belt. She smiled, false eyelashes flicking in greeting. "Good afternoon. Welcome to Moses Mabhida Stadium. I'll be showing you all to your seats. Is everyone ready?"

Billy waggled his fingers in reply. The self-appointed spokesman for the group, his lanky frame towered over the woman. "Yes, we're all here." He turned his back on Jimmy.

The steward nodded, gestured for them to follow her. Like Moses parting the Red Sea, the crowd moved to one side as fifteen men and women dressed in their finest Liverpool livery hurried behind her. As they passed, people reached out, patting their shoulders, or shaking hands. Others held up mobile phones and cameras; most waited with apparent indifference for the visitors to pass.

"Jimmy, we're going." Sarah looped a hand through his arm. Her eyes danced with excitement, reminding Jimmy of Kim at her recent birthday party. She'd twirled and giggled in a new frock, lapping up the attention and the festivities. So like her mum.

He smiled, swallowing a stab of homesick guilt at thoughts of the kids, and Mam having to look after them while he and Sarah had a party of their own. "Lead on, then. I wonder what Des organised this time?"

Goodnews walked backwards for a few paces, checking his guests remained together as he led them across the concourse. His shoes squeaked on the polished concrete surface as he spun around and continued walking.

"I know what you mean about getting lost." Sarah trotted at Jimmy's side, her handbag bouncing against his hip. "Can you still see Goodnews?"

"Yes, there he is. Over by those lifts."

A security guard inspected their wristbands, then stepped aside for them all to enter the lift. He reached in, pressed a button, and retreated to his post as the doors slid closed. Blue numbers on the control panel indicated their upward progress.

They stopped at Level 3 with a lurch. Doors opened, then they alighted into an empty reception area. Floor to ceiling windows — sunshine slanting in through the tinted glass — muted the thud of music pulsing from the stadium. A troupe of four dancers in pale tracksuit trousers and patterned tops hopped and jumped on a makeshift stage built at the edge of the gathering spectators. Flickering screens at either end of the pitch displayed television pundits sitting on sofas in a studio.

Goodnews leant against a set of double doors, tapping his foot in time with the drumbeat. "Follow me, everyone. Your hostess is waiting for you. Third door on the right."

Jimmy

Durban, South Africa
Saturday 11 April 2015

"Hi, I'm Melissa. Welcome to Moses Mabhida Stadium." A dark-haired woman in her early twenties, sporting tattoos and a nose piercing, held open the door to the hospitality suite. "Please help yourself to drinks. Snacks are on the counter over there. The caterers will serve the main course during half-time."

Self-service drinks? Snacks? And a main course? This wasn't the overpriced Coke and crisps Jimmy grabbed at Anfield on match days.

Des flung open the fridge door, surveying the contents. "What'll it be, Sarah? A gin and tonic to get the party started?"

Sarah, leaning against the bar, giggled. "I wouldn't have had you down as barman, Des. But seeing as you're there, I'll have a fruit juice, if there is one."

Des grimaced. "We travel halfway around the world, and you prefer fruit juice?" He rummaged in the fridge, moving packs of beer and bottles of wine aside. "But what the lady wants, the lady gets. Here you go..."

He placed the drink on the counter. Condensation beaded on its metal surface. He flicked up the tab, reached for a glass, and poured the syrupy liquid over the ice he'd tossed in. Sarah raised the glass, frozen cubes knocking against its edge with a satisfying clink.

Jimmy's mouth watered at the sound. "That looks good. Same again, mate."

"What, juice for Jimmy? Am I hearing right? Here, have one of these local beers — a Castle lager."

"It's fine, thanks. Lent…" Jimmy clenched his jaw at Des's snort of derision. He wasn't about to admit he liked the change from the usual round after round of beer — or worse, whiskey — Des subjected him to most times they met up.

"So long as you keep praying for us while you're getting cosy with the Man Upstairs, then drink as much of that stuff as you want." Des whizzed a second can along the bar. No glass this time. "Nick, what'll it be…?"

Jimmy wandered over to the snacks. Bowls of chewy cured beef strips — biltong, they'd said at the hotel — sat in unappetising fatness in the middle of the spread. Giving them a miss, Jimmy grabbed a plate and selected a crumbed chicken drumstick, a couple of calamari rings and a stodgy ball resembling a miniature onion bhajee. Other platters contained triangle sandwiches of egg mayonnaise or slices of cheese and ham. But the corners of the bread curled in protest at the cold blasting down from an air-conditioning vent in the ceiling.

"Do you want anything?" Sarah hovered at his elbow, peering at the dishes.

"No, I'll wait until the proper meal. Save my appetite." She took a sip of her drink. "Shall we go and sit outside? We have a wonderful view of the whole field from up here."

They wandered off. The door closed on another shout of "What will it be, Kevin?" from Des.

Jimmy was unprepared for the intensity of noise, which greeted them as they shuffled to their seat. Vuvuzelas buzzed from every corner of the stadium, like an angry swarm of bees fighting for release. The sound system bellowed out dance tunes with an unmistakable African beat. A singer poured her soul into a microphone, her voice rising and swelling with the melody. The three dancers gyrated on stage, leaping up and down, arms akimbo. Men and women danced and clapped and shouted and sang in the stands beyond the private suites. It was a carnival of chaos.

Jimmy grinned as he settled into a plastic seat, balancing his can and plate on his lap with care. He dropped his shoulders from where they'd hugged his ears since leaving Heathrow, blew out a breath in a guffaw of sheer delight.

"Isn't this fantastic?" He leant over to Sarah, his mouth close to her ear. Strands of hair tickled his lips. "Football. It brings the world together, doesn't it?"

He kissed the ear. Sarah squirmed away. "That tickles." She giggled. "So, you're glad we came then? I was getting worried..."

"What? Can't hear you over the din." Jimmy turned as the others emerged from inside, sloshing drinks and loaded plates accompanying them. "Des, here, sit by us."

Des nudged his way down the row, stepping on Jimmy's toes. He slurped at a bottle of beer. "Cheers. Even if it is only with orange juice."

They clinked their drinks, metal against glass, old friends celebrating years of familiarity.

"There're lots of spare seats, look." Sarah elbowed Jimmy in the ribs. "I thought the match was sold out?"

"It is. Or so I heard." Jimmy scanned the empty terraces. He chuckled. "Perhaps no one sits down here. Everyone's over there, by the entrance."

Beside him, Des sucked in a whistling breath. "That could be trouble. All those people, jostling to see the action. I don't like..."

Jimmy lost the rest of his comment in a sudden roar from the crowd. Players strode out of the tunnel onto the pitch. The black and white clad Pirates led the way, each player gripping the hand of a child dressed in the same, albeit smaller, kit.

"Sweet. They look so serious, don't they?" Sarah waved at the children.

"You do know they can't see you, don't you?" Nick leant forward between Jimmy and Sarah.

"I know. But I can see me. And waving seems the right thing to do." She waved again.

Jimmy shook his head. "Daft woman. What can I do, Nick? I bet your Glenda doesn't do things like that."

"No — she leaps up from her chair and yells a greeting."

"Don't give Sarah any ideas..."

Another almighty cheer. The Liverpool team, a touring side of youngsters picked especially for this afternoon's friendly, jogged into the stadium.

Jimmy leapt to his feet, knocking over his half-finished drink. He linked arms with Sarah as she sprang from her seat. "Liverpool. Liverpool." He sang himself hoarse in minutes.

A sea of red and white surged and soared as the other Liverpool fans in the main stand hoisted scarves and flags in a display designed to impress — and intimidate — the locals.

The teams waited in the centre of the field. Were they singing national anthems today? Des shrugged, seeming as nonplussed as Jimmy.

A silence descended on the packed stands. The thumping bass of the music stilled, replaced with the skipping beat of Jimmy's heart.

A man stood alongside the players. He wore a dress suit and sunglasses. Not the referee. He lifted a microphone to his lips. *"When you walk through a storm. Hold your head up high. And don't be afraid of the dark..."*

The TV show previously broadcast on the giant screens switched images. On one, the singer appeared, his mouth shaping the words of the Liverpool anthem. On the other screen, the Club crest and the Eternal Flame. And a list of names scrolling in slow motion.

The 96.

Jimmy bowed his head, unable to watch any more. Sarah sniffed. On his other side, Des' arm trembled where it touched his. Like a patient with fever chills.

Jimmy

Durban, South Africa
Saturday 11 April 2015

Jimmy slumped on the bed, head in hands. A gentle breeze from the balcony rustled the curtains. A muted rumble of the ocean hitting the beach, the only other sound.

"It's going to follow me for the rest of my life." His posture sagged. "I'll never escape, no matter how hard I try."

A half-moon lit the room. Sarah had flicked on the light-switch after opening the door. Wincing against the cheery brightness, Jimmy thumped it off with his fist.

A salty tang wafted up from the shore, giving his mouth a metallic taste. Fingers ran through sticky hair. He closed his eyes, images slapping into his mind like photographs thrown in haphazard confusion onto a dirty tabletop. The never-ending scroll of names on the big screens; the wail of reassuring voices, declaring no one would ever walk alone; a singer in a black suit hustling from the stage as the referee raised his arm and blew a whistle to start a game Jimmy could no longer bear to watch.

Des crashing past him, spilling drinks and overturning plates, his features contorted with anger. Or pain.

Sarah, perched on the edge of her seat, attention fixed on the moving figures chasing a ball around a green field. Lips tight. Shoulders tense.

The hostess urging her guests to eat; his dazed dishing up of some sort of curry with rice. Pushing food around with a fork. Abandoning the pretence.

Three goals. A winning team. A silent coach journey to their accommodation.

The mattress sighed as Sarah flopped next to him, their shoulders touching. Her bracelets jangled together as she reached out for his hand, tugging it from his face. Jimmy resisted, pressing his fingers into his forehead with greater force. Another jangle and her arm moved away, a gap opening between their bodies.

A sudden burst of light illuminated the wall behind them. Jimmy's watch ticked the seconds away. One. Two. The next flash. The lighthouse, a few metres from the hotel, intruding on his misery, chasing shadows. He shifted positions, creating more space between himself and Sarah. She rose, mirroring his rejection as she moved outside. A chair scraped as she settled into it.

A door banged in the corridor outside. Voices, loud and jarring, hurried past on their way to the stairs at the end of the hallway. Not anyone he recognised.

Des, first off the coach, surrounded by a protective bubble of hostility, headed straight for his room. Jimmy overheard him asking a passing waiter to send up a glass — a bottle? — of whiskey. The rest of the party drifted off, some out to the promenade, others to the bar.

"He'll be alright by tomorrow, don't worry." Nick stood in the foyer, hands on hips, watching as the lift doors slid closed on Des' pinched countenance. "Pity that happened, but it was to be expected. First time the team has played here and the locals wanting to pay their respects and all that. And it's the anniversary in a couple of days. He should have prepared himself better for the possibility."

Jimmy shoved his fists into his jeans pockets, torn between pragmatic agreement with Nick and defensive loyalty for his friend.

Sarah saved him from saying anything, pulling the rucksack from his shoulders and claiming a headache. She pushed the lift button, watched the numbers descend from Des' floor down to Ground.

She stepped through the open doors, her arm wedged against the frame to prevent their sudden closure. "You coming? Or you heading for the bar as well?" Her eyes darted from Jimmy to the waiting lift, and back again.

"Sorry, Nick, I'd better go." Jimmy raised a hand in farewell. "I'm not much company myself, anyway. See you in the morning."

They'd not spoken as they ascended to their level, nor as they entered their room. What was there to say?

Another searching, probing beam from the lighthouse. Jimmy sighed, his breath catching as he dragged himself to his feet.

"Sorry." He leant against the door frame; all strength consumed in taking the few steps from the bed. "I'm just sick of it. Always being on my guard, waiting in case someone says something, mentions it when I'm not expecting it. I'm exhausted."

"Yes. It is tiring."

Sarah's simple words, her gentle voice, incensed Jimmy. Her gaze remained away from him, fingers twisted together on her knees, her back straight and stiff. Her stillness aggravated him. He wanted to yank the chair from under her, to throw it over the balcony, hear it clatter and crash on the paving below. His nostrils flared as his breath came in short, sharp stabs of indignation.

The breeze plucked at Jimmy's hair and ruffled his shirt. He moved into Sarah's line of sight, blocking her view of the beach, of the ocean. He needed her to see him, to see the roiling turmoil in his heart, rather than the crashing waves of the sea.

Sarah blinked. A bead of perspiration on her forehead glistened in the moonlight. The lighthouse beam blinked on and off, her features stark and two-dimensional in its glare. She licked her lips, bent forward as though about to speak.

"No, Sarah. No." Jimmy held up his palms, shielding himself from whatever she was about to utter. It was his turn now. He'd spent half his life listening to everyone else, being told how he should feel or what he should do. Today, a switch had flicked inside, which wasn't about to be turned off with the same casual ease as a bedroom light. "Do not tell me one more time that you understand, that you get how I'm feeling or how it affected me." His throat ached as he forced the words through clenched teeth.

"You don't. And you never will. You weren't there. And before you say it, no, neither was I. Not at the ground. But my friend was. And other friends. And neighbours. We lived it." A ragged inhale. A dimming of the rage, a chink in the armour. "You didn't. You're not from Liverpool. You'll never know."

Percy

Cape Town, South Africa
Tuesday 14 November 1899

Flo stood with her face turned away from him, copper hair swirling in the wind blowing in from the river. Her pale blue dress, the one which best highlighted her ivory skin, billowed around her ankles, revealing a pair of worn button-boots. Percy called out, willing her to turn and see him. Why couldn't she hear him? If only he could reach out, tap her on the shoulder, attract her attention somehow...

"Talking in your sleep again, old boy?" Flo faded into a distant haze at Arthur's nasal tones.

It was the third time this week Percy's dreams had transported him to the banks of the Mersey. He groaned, rolling over on the hard, narrow bunk. The activities of the day — the drills, the target practice, the developing camaraderie between himself and the men of his unit — suppressed his longing for home beneath the weight of busyness. At night, with nothing to distract or occupy, the dull ache of missing floated to the surface with unbidden images.

"Sorry. Didn't mean to wake you." Percy opened a sleepy eyelid. Arthur's face loomed close, inches from his own. He jerked backwards, both eyes wide, banging his head on the iron railing of his cot. He rubbed the spot with one hand, pushed Arthur away with the other. "Oof, thanks for the wake-up call, mate. What time is it?"

The others in the dormitory still slept. Miller, on the bed opposite, lay on his back, arm flung out to one side, mouth open. The greyness of early dawn tinged the edges of the single windowpane. Nailed shut, it allowed no air in to refresh the stuffy room and dissipate the accumulation of sweaty socks and sweatier bodies. Percy wrinkled his nose.

"About five o'clock, I think. Couldn't sleep." Arthur jumped down from his bunk, perched on the edge of Percy's bed. Percy shifted his feet out of the way. "This is worse than the sea voyage, I reckon. At least we knew the destination, expected it to take an age. We've been stuck here in Cape Town for two weeks. If I have to strip another rifle and reassemble it with some bossy Sergeant timing me on his stopwatch, I swear I'll go mad. Brother Boer will be sipping tea in the houses of Durban before we get there, the rate we're going."

Percy raised himself up onto his elbow. "Mm. I thought they were in a desperate hurry to get us to the Front. But I suppose they know what they're doing."

Arthur frowned, lines creasing his forehead. He stroked his chin, making a rasping sound as his fingers scratched at the growth of overnight stubble. "Perhaps..."

Percy waited for Arthur to continue. He didn't. A ripple of alarm lifted the hairs at the back of his neck. Arthur never expressed doubts or displayed anxiety.

"What? Do you know something we don't?" A brief recollection of Arthur absent on some unknown errand the day before. Was his concern connected to that?

"No, no, it's nothing, I'm sure." A shake of the head — but a tone of voice lacking conviction. Arthur puffed out his cheeks, letting his breath escape in a long, slow sigh. "Well, sort of. But don't say anything. Not yet."

Someone coughed. Miller shifted on to his side, muttering. Soon, everyone would be awake and the chance for further revelations lost. Arthur, a finger on his lips, jerked his head toward the door. Standing up, he strode off without a word. If anyone opened an eye, they would see a man hurrying to the lavatory.

Percy paused for a couple of seconds. The coughing subsided. Miller snored into his pillow. Percy shoved away the blankets, swivelling to the floor in a single swift, silent movement. His toes curled in protest as bare skin encountered the cold tiles. Ignoring the sensation, Percy tiptoed across the room in pursuit of his friend.

The windowless corridor was dark. Percy blinked in the gloom.

"Psst. This way." Arthur, somewhere to his left. Percy followed the shadowed figure along the passageway and down a flight of stairs. A door creaked and a glint of light illuminated the hallway. Arthur slipped outside. Percy hurried after him. He nudged the door closed behind him, finding himself in an open courtyard he'd not been in before.

"What's all the secrecy for?" Percy shivered in the morning air. A hadeda ibis greeted him with a dreadful screech. He may have been in Africa for only a few days, but Percy already hated the bird's cry.

"Sorry, didn't want the lads to hear. In case I'm wrong." Arthur licked the corner of his mouth. "Swear you won't tell anyone, PP. I'd be in hot water, if word got out I've passed on information."

"Information? What information?" Percy's heart fluttered. This sounded serious.

"You remember I was sent on a special errand yesterday?" Percy nodded. Arthur had disappeared in the middle of their training exercise, a jaunty grin plastered across his face. "They asked me to carry a message to General Buller's HQ. In his rooms at the Mount Nelson Hotel. You know it?"

Another nod.

"Dunno why they chose me, but anyway. The reception desk was unattended when I arrived. No one around to pass the message to." Arthur linked his arms behind his back, pacing the perimeter of the courtyard. "So, I checked on the board which rooms Buller was using. Alright, I should have waited, but the sergeant told me it was urgent and not to waste any time delivering the note.

"From the top of the stairs, I could hear voices from further down the hallway. Old Redvers was talking — you know how unmistakable his voice is — and I...I wasn't eavesdropping. I couldn't knock and interrupt him mid-flow. So, I listened."

He ducked away, his cheeks a blush of shame. Percy chose not to add to his discomfort, despite the litany of disapproving comments marching through his mind.

"Well, I heard him. And that's all there is to it." Arthur paused his pacing, lifting his chin and straightening his shoulders. "And I'll tell you what he said. They're going to split us up. The army in general, I mean, not the Lancs in particular. One half is to go inland to sort out the problem at Kimberley. Apparently some rich diamond man is holed up there and insisting he's —"

"Cecil Rhodes. He was the Prime Minister of Cape Colony. Before. Moved on under a bit of a cloud, I understand…" Percy's voice trailed away at a glare from Arthur. He never did like his stories being interrupted.

"Hm, whatever you say. Anyway, we're being split into two groups. The second group is setting sail again. Up the coast to Durban, deal with Kroojer and his pals from that side. Give them a hiding, send them packing out of our territory."

Percy's stomach lurched. Please, not another journey out to sea. After a week of dizzy nights trying to stop a stationary room from swirling each time he lay down, he was loath to leave firm ground so soon.

"Which group are we?"

Arthur shrugged. "No idea." Now he'd shared his adventure, any further interest waned. "No doubt we'll find out soon enough."

A shaft of sunlight dappled the courtyard.

"Think we'd better get back before we're missed." Arthur spun on his heels, heading for the door to the dormitories. He tapped a finger against his nose. "Not a peep, mind. Let's see how things unfold."

Percy

Durban, South Africa
Wednesday 22 November 1899

P ercy pressed his forehead to the cold ship's railing. Events had unfolded at quite a pace. Within less than a week of Arthur's revelations, the Lancashire Fusiliers marched to the docks and up the gangplank of another ship. With far less fanfare and excitement than either their departure from England or their arrival at the Cape, the vessel departed for Durban. Dogged by howling gales and turbulent waters, Percy lay pinned to his bunk for the first two days of the voyage.

Lapsing in and out of fitful sleep, voices floated in a confused muddle of concrete news and wild speculation.

"If we'd been there, that scrap at Dundee would have been over before it began." Arthur's grumbling tones.

"You can't say that, Houltram. By all accounts, it was a beast of a battle with little hope of a positive outcome." Mickey, more considered, thoughtful. "Although the dash to escape to the garrison at Ladysmith seems somewhat rash. Now everyone's under siege and we've got to rush to rescue them…"

"Brother Boer won't keep them held down for long. They'll get bored. Besides, the general in charge there — fellow by the name of White — is a capital chap. He'll regain the upper hand, you mark my words."

Another wasted voyage then, no sooner arriving in Durban than to be scuttled back to Cape Town. Percy groaned into his meagre pillow at the thought.

And then a new voice. A visitor to their cabin. Speaking with authority and cigarette breath. Miller. "Buller didn't want it to go down this way. He planned we stay together, march through Natal and on up into Boer country, and so to Pretoria. Should have been simple." Suck and puff on a cigarette. "He kept saying they shouldn't cross over the main river up there. The Tug-something-or-other. Stay south, at least until the rest of us arrived. He knows the lay of the land, you see, been here before. But he's stuck with half a force and double the job."

So, they'd get to fight, then. That is, if Percy could believe Miller. Where did his information come from? The cousin he'd mentioned once or twice. Did he work at headquarters? Percy couldn't remember, his mind fogged with nausea and dehydration.

By the time Percy recovered from seasickness, queasiness of a different sort assailed him. Battle nerves, Miller called it. Weakness, scoffed Arthur.

"We've travelled halfway around the world to fight, man. Why wouldn't you want to, now we're so close? Can't wait to bag me a Boer, I can tell you." Arthur, sitting in the dining room for supper, waved his fork over his plate.

Percy stabbed at a lump of under-cooked potato. He forced it down, gulping from a cup of water when it wedged somewhere behind his rib cage.

"You alright there, old chap? You've gone bright red, you know." Arthur's fork remained suspended between his plate and mouth. "If you're having trouble with those spuds, I'll happily take them off your hands. I'm starving. Could eat them raw if I had to."

Percy pushed his dinner over. Appetite lost for another meal. His trousers hung on him, held up with a piece of string he'd found in his kitbag. His tunic sagged at the shoulders. Beneath his shirt, hidden from view and any murmurs of concern, his ribs were a bone xylophone. When last he'd shouldered his rifle, its weight surprised him. His arms shook as he tried to focus on a target positioned on the deck. Sweat dribbled down his forehead. How could he possibly hope to manage in a real battle against real people? Maybe there'd be time to build his strength, increase the fitness training, once they got off this wretched boat.

"I pity those poor creatures." Mickey sucked on a pencil before marking a couple of lines in his sketchbook. "It's not like they chose to sign up for this, is it?"

"What?" They stood on the quayside after disembarking from the ship in the early hours of a still, muggy morning. Percy leant against a stationary wagon while his system adjusted to solid ground once more. Preoccupied with his churning stomach, he wasn't sure what his friend was on about.

"The horses. Look. They can hardly walk." He pointed the end of the pencil towards their ship.

Horses skittered down the gangplanks, weak and woozy from the days spent propped into stalls on board the ship. Blinkers hid the worst of the activity from their view, but the sounds of men shouting, trains whistling, and wagons clanking had them bucking and shivering in obvious fear. Cavalry officers cajoled and cursed the animals onto the armoured railway carriages used for transporting men and beast alike to the battleground.

"I'm not sure I signed up for this either." Percy wiped a sweating palm on his trousers. "I thought we were coming here to wage a war, not travel the globe. We're miles from the Front. Miller reckons there's still plenty of Boers to bag, but what his sources are, I don't know."

"His cousin, I heard…I've decided to save all these drawings. Show people at home what we went through." A pink blush coloured his fair complexion. "I send them with my letters, ask Ethel to store them somewhere safe until I get back."

Percy blinked in surprise, both at the confession and the confidence. "Clever you. And I promise I'll keep that a secret from the others. Crosby will laugh you to kingdom come and back if he finds out. Speaking of, we'd better rejoin them and find out where we're being shunted to next."

The day was a frantic, chaotic affair, as ships disgorged soldiers and cargo in a frenzy of frontline preparations. Naval officers hitched their guns to makeshift wagons, shouting instructions and cautions as they organised the artillery for further transportation by train. A constant threat of thunder hung in the air, dull grey clouds blanketing the sky and trapping the heat in a stifling humidity so different from the fresh sea breezes of the Cape.

The soldiers trudged through the streets of Durban to a nearby barracks, where they awaited further news of their upcoming deployment.

They didn't have to wait long. Within days, the Lancashires, in full field uniform, marched to the railway station to be herded onto an armoured train. The same train now steaming across the vast countryside of the colony.

Percy's shirt clung to his back, sweat gluing the fabric to his skin. He took a sip of water from the canteen at his waist, grimacing as the lukewarm liquid — not warm enough to persuade himself it was tea; not cool enough to be refreshing — slid down his throat with little success at slaking his thirst. The train jolted before he had the lid on the bottle. Water sloshed over him.

"Oi, watch it PP. Keep your water to yourself." Private Alfred 'Alfie' Street. Close cropped dark hair, untidy moustache. Three inches taller than Percy.

"Sorry, Alfie." Percy made a show of screwing on the lid. "See, won't happen again."

"Make sure it doesn't." Alfie wiped his face with the sleeve of his jacket. "This heat is something else, isn't it? Feels as if someone left the oven door open in my mam's kitchen after she's cooked the Sunday roast."

"I don't fancy your mam's dinner, if it smells like this, Alfie, mate." Jimmy Crosby, wedged against the corner of the carriage, wrinkled his nose.

Percy glanced around at the converted cattle truck. The lack of windows made the interior dull and stuffy. Straw lay strewn across the wooden floorboards as though the rail company wished to provide some cushioning for its guests. Peeling brown paintwork curled from

the sides and roof of the simple structure. The odour of overheated
bodies cramped together outdid an underlying whiff of cow as soldiers
from the Lancashire Fusiliers and the Irish Brigade sat shoulder almost
touching shoulder on their journey inland. Those lucky enough to have
positioned themselves close to the doors leant out, hats abandoned, and
hair ruffled in the breeze of motion. For the rest, they perched on kitbags
or lounged against each other in red-faced sticky discomfort.

Percy fanned his field hat over his face. Perhaps that would cool him.

"PP, can you not sit still, man?" A sharp pain in the ribs from Alfie's
elbow. "We're all too hot. Quicker we find Mr Kroojer and his brother
Boers, quicker we leave and get on the first boat home."

"Give over, Alfie." Gordon Jackson, squeezed in between Percy, and
Mickey on his other side, yawned. "We should take a kip while we have
the chance. I reckon it'll be all action stations when we reach wherever
we're going."

"Oh, hark at you, Gordy. Fount of all knowledge." Alfie always
wanted the last word.

The train jerked to a halt. Steam and smoke poured in through the
open doorway. Men coughed and spluttered, covered their mouths with
handkerchiefs and elbows.

"What the...?" Crosby stepped over — or on — everyone as he peered
out.

"Everybody out. Welcome to Frere, gentlemen." A heavy thud on the
outside of the truck. The voice moved on, calling to the next carriage in
line. "Stop your dawdling, men."

Percy swallowed the sudden flutter of nerves jumping in his chest. So,
this was it. Another step in their war against the Boer. The Front.

Pins and needles prickled his left foot when he stood. Wiggling his
toes inside his boot, he hefted his kitbag and took his turn in the
shuffle towards the exit. Polished buckles and buttons flashed in a hazy
afternoon sunshine as he emerged from the gloom of the truck.

An officer with white-blonde hair, freckles and a peeling, sunburnt face barked out orders as the new arrivals jumped out onto the platform. "Lancashires to my right; Irish to the left. Come on, form up, lads. This isn't a holiday camp anymore."

"He's not wrong there." Arthur's eyes shone with excitement. "Time for some real fun, boys."

Percy agreed. He'd begun to despair of ever seeing any action. Limping to his place while his sleeping foot recovered, he wondered if his weak legs and feeble constitution would be up for the fight.

The men faced forward, waiting for their orders.

"Wonder if we're billeted there, then?" Arthur twitched his head to a large building at the side of the station.

Percy squinted to read a sign over the door. Hotel.

"I'd wager not. Think we have reservations at the *hotel de tent*, mate." Beyond the hotel and one or two tin-roofed shacks, the camp at Frere spread out before them in row after row of white bell tents.

"I hope the food is good." Arthur chuckled at his joke. "You need a bit of fattening up, PP."

Before he could compose a suitable retort, the order filtered through the ranks to march away from the railway line and into camp. Heavy boots clumped forward in a unified beat of British control and discipline. Percy squared to attention, pride filling his chest. With an army like this, a ragtag collection of farmers didn't stand a chance. Did they?

Percy

Frere, South Africa
Wednesday 29 November 1899

"Dratted flies." Percy flicked his handkerchief in front of his face. The insect buzzed out of reach. Seconds later it returned, tickling at Percy's ear. "Can you see anything?"

Miller lowered the binoculars, his head tilted to one side. "There's a camp over there. Near that tree. I think. They're well-hidden, the blighters."

He passed the glasses to Percy. Raising them to his eyes, Percy winked and blinked until the distant hills came into focus. He scanned the scrubby landscape. Other than the buzzing fly, the stillness was complete. Heat shimmered from the tin roofs of the few buildings grouped around the station. A bird, hidden from view, chirped its distinctive melody. A type of robin, Mickey had said. The answering whoop of a second bird foretold oncoming rain. According to Mickey.

Hot dust scented the breathless air.

"See that white road? Follow that to the row of trees. Got it?"

"Uh-huh."

"Just beyond the red hill you can see. That's the camp, I'm certain of it."

Percy held the binoculars steady. Was that movement he saw? Or just a trick of the light? A dark shape shifted. The new angle revealed the unmistakable outline of a man. A Boer.

The shape moved again. Gone.

Percy's hands trembled, his pulse racing. His first sighting of the enemy.

A bugle sounded below. Another train arriving, to be offloaded, the cargo stored ready for what Percy hoped was an imminent deployment to flush out the Boer from their holes. New recruits, fresh from the boat in Durban, pasty faced and doing their utmost to hide their nerves would no doubt also be on board.

Scrambling from their observation post, Percy chuckled at the memory of his arrival at Frere; the bewildered march to their regiment's location, the hurry to erect tents and stow kitbags before a threatened thunderstorm ripped the sky open and deposited a deluge of rain heavier than anything Percy had ever experienced.

"Some hotel, this. It leaks." Arthur lifted a hand, catching a persistent trickle of water as it dripped from the roof.

"It's your own fault, Art. You didn't pull your side ropes tight enough." Alfie hadn't stopped arguing since being billeted away from his cronies. He patted his bedding roll. "If this gets wet, I'm taking yours tonight."

Percy busied himself pretending to search for something amongst his belongings. Alfie's animosity soured the possibility of establishing any sort of friendship with the man. If they went into battle together, Percy doubted if he could trust him to have his back. Another of the disconcerting thoughts keeping Percy awake throughout the long nights.

Smoke from the train's stove pipe charted its progress up the valley. Percy quickened his pace. He jogged down the dusty path, skipping over rocks and boulders, skidding on loose shale. He reached the bottom of the slope, breathless and laughing.

"Come on, old man. Hurry up." Behind him, George Miller still picked his way down the steepest section, his binoculars dangling from the strap around his neck.

"You're a mountain goat, PP. No hope of me keeping up with you." He reached Percy's side, grabbing hold of his shoulder as he bent over to catch his breath.

Percy grinned. Camp activity suited him far more than constant travel on boats and trains.

"Race you to the station!" Percy shook off Miller's hand and sprinted along the path without a backward glance at his companion. He sucked in the dry air, chin down, nostrils flared. Fixing his eyes on a patch of bushes ahead, Percy surged forward, arms pumping in time with his legs, heart rate creeping higher as he pushed onwards. One more bend and he collapsed in the shade of the trees. Gulping for breath, he wiped the sweat from his eyes.

Percy bounced on his toes as he waited for Miller, coughing and wheezing, to lumber up to him. His friend's facial scar glowed white against his beetroot cheeks.

"You should pack in those cigarettes, you know." Percy thumped Miller between the shoulder blades as he spat phlegm into the dirt. "I reckon they'll kill you before the Boers get their hands on you."

"Very funny." Miller straightened with a groan. "We'll walk the rest of the way, if you don't mind."

The train puffed into the station just as Percy and Miller reached the platform.

Arthur beckoned them over.

"Where have you been? You run a marathon, Miller?"

"No, just a sprint with Light-foot here." Miller huffed a breath.

Percy shrugged his shoulders. "Dunno what he's talking about. Was a gentle jog to base, that's all."

A piercing whistle from the approaching train silenced further talk. The engine screeched to a halt, clouds of steam billowing across the platform.

"What do you think we've got today?" It was their daily game.

"It's a hospital train. Look." Miller pointed at the red crosses stamped in white circles emblazoned on the side of each of five trucks.

No one spoke as a man dressed in a neat civilian suit, head bare, alighted onto the platform. He gripped a leather briefcase in one hand. With the other, he shielded his eyes from the sun.

General Clery, as officer in charge, stepped forward in full dark blue regalia. Knee-length black boots shone from a recent polish, all evidence of the persistent dust that plagued the camp, wiped away. For now, at least. He extended a hand in greeting.

"Dr Treves. Delighted you made it. Welcome to Frere." His lilting Irish voice carried over the hushed group of waiting soldiers. "I see you've brought supplies with you. Let's hope we shan't need too many of them!"

The doctor shook the offered hand, eyes darting from left to right. Percy strained to hear his reply to General Clery, but the doctor spoke in tones too low to catch.

"Well, men, what are you gawking at? This train won't offload itself." General Clery turned to face the assembled soldiers. His shaggy moustache and magnificent, bushy side whiskers never failed to inspire awe in Percy, whose upper lip hosted little more than thin fluff. Clery waved at the wagons. "Let's get started. We can't take all day. Dr Treves, I will leave you to direct things here."

General Clery stalked off. At his departure, the soldiers sprang into action, organising themselves into parties of six or seven, each group tackling a different truck.

As Percy shifted crate after crate containing an unknown number of bandages or vials of morphine, his thoughts skittered from one question to the next. Who would the surgeons wrap in these bandages? When would they be crying out for morphine, pain searing through limbs? He glanced around at his fellow soldiers, many his closest friends, carrying stretchers or pushing small ambulance carts. Who would find the roles reversed, their broken bodies lain across the items they now conveyed? Whose flesh would return home intact, whose mutilated beyond recognition?

Shaking his head to dispel the horrors of his imagination, he grabbed another crate, back straining under its weight as he carried it to a waiting ox wagon. The African driver held the leading pair of oxen by the harness, clicking and muttering in his native language, an exotic, singsong tone to the unfamiliar words. Percy suspected they grumbled against their British masters.

The driver of the offloaded hospital train shunted the carriages off the main track. Percy, back aching, scooped his discarded tunic from where he'd draped it over a fence post, and headed with the others for the mess tent.

Lunchtime a distant memory, his stomach growled at the sight of a black cooking pot steaming over an open fire. Flames caught the edges of a log the chef's aide, Private Masterson, pushed in amongst the glowing coals. "What's for dinner, Smokey?" Percy's mouth watered at the aroma of stewing meat wafting in his direction.

Private Masterson — Smokey — straightened. A smudge of soot streaked his cheek, his shaven head glistening with sweat. Shirt sleeves rolled up over wobbling biceps revealed a tattoo of a snake wrapped round a heart. "Stew, PP. Beef stew." He dusted his hands. "What do you expect? It's the dish of the day every day. Or some variation of it."

"Smells good, anyway, even if it is the same." Percy stepped closer, sniffing the air.

"Not what I expected when I joined the catering corps, I can tell you." Smokey lifted the lid of the cauldron, dipped a spoon into the simmering liquid. "I thought I'd be entertaining officers with my fine dining skills, cooking in the smartest kitchens in the plushest London clubs. Here, have a taste."

Percy took the offered spoon, blowing on its contents. He slurped the gravy, burning his tongue and scalding his throat as he swallowed. "Tastes good enough for one of those clubs, at any rate." He handed the spoon back.

"You only say that because you're hungry and there's nothing else on offer. You should try my dumplings with it. Better than any your ma ever made."

"What's going on here, then? You trying to eat before anyone else, PP?" Arthur strolled across the scuffed grass in only his vest and trousers, the braces dangling at his hips. He banged a spoon against his metal bowl. "Grub's up everyone. Best you get served before Percy here finishes the lot."

"Help me with this, then." Smokey gripped the handle of the cauldron, a rag wrapped around his hand. He tossed a second rag at Arthur. "We'll move it off the fire. Put it on that patch of ground."

A line of men formed, dust and dirt smearing their faces. Smokey ladled stew into bowls, while an aide handed out chunks of bread.

"Thanks, Smokey." Percy stretched out his bowl. "Slip a friend some extra meat, there's a good chap."

Smokey rolled his eyes, moved on to the next in line.

Percy shrugged, grabbed his bread, and found a camp stool next to Arthur, Mickey, and Alfie.

A train whistle sounded before he'd swallowed his first mouthful. Percy groaned.

"Eat up, old chap. More work has arrived." Arthur soaked up the last of his gravy with a morsel of bread.

Percy guzzled his meal. His hunger satisfied, he spat a half-chewed piece of gristle back into his dish. "I'll save that for Bonnie later."

"That stray mongrel that keeps following you?" Alfie curled his lips. "You don't want to go encouraging it."

"Ah, she's harmless enough, Alfie." Percy enjoyed the company of the little dog. He'd found her, quivering and shaking beside the fence of the ransacked stationmaster's house. He'd taken a piece of biscuit from his pocket, holding it out on his open palm as he moved towards her one small step at a time. She'd sniffed, her ears pressed against her head, eyes darting from the treat to his face and back again. Percy encouraged her with slow, quiet words. Now, she trotted around camp with him by day, slept at the door of his tent at night. Her curled tail wagged in greeting whenever he returned from practice manoeuvres or reconnaissance work; her sand-coloured fur bristled as she growled her alarm at everyone else's approach.

Alfie threw a crust into Percy's bowl. "Don't say I didn't warn you." He strode away, whistling.

"Thanks. I'll tell her the bread's from you."

Alfie waved a farewell.

The last train of the day rumbled into the station. A squad of naval men disembarked, their beards trim and neat, their uniforms crisp and clean.

Percy rubbed at the stubble prickling his chin. How nice a shave would be. Or a chance to wash his clothes in something other than the muddy trickle of river at the edge of camp.

Pushing aside offers of help, the sailors hurried to the rear of the train where a wrapped crate occupied the end truck. Hauling on ropes and pulling back layers of tarpaulin, they uncovered a huge spotlight. Impressed, Percy hung around to watch.

Before he could investigate further, the sound of boots running down the platform, of raised voices and concerned calls, distracted his attention. Arthur, Crosby, Alfie, and several others stood in a huddle at the other end of the station, their backs to him. Miller ran to join the group, followed by two men from the Indian ambulance corps. White bands decorated with a red cross circled their upper left arms.

The hairs on Percy's neck prickled. He jogged towards the commotion; his feet leaden as though his boots had become too heavy to wear.

"Make way. Clear some space." Arthur tugged on Alfie's sleeve, moving him to one side. A gap opened in the gathering crowd through which the stretcher bearers shuffled, arms bulging under the weight of a burden added to their canvas stretcher. Percy's pulse quickened. Who was injured? And how?

Breath coming in heavy puffs, sweat pouring from their foreheads and glistening in their dark, close-cropped hair, the medics made slow progress along the platform. A silent, immobile figure lay on the canvas between them, eyes closed in a pale, lifeless face. A stain spread across the thigh of the figure's khaki trousers, the fabric ripped and torn. Percy glanced at the exposed flesh, pink and unrecognisable. His throat closed against the taste of bile. He looked away.

Another soldier trotted alongside, his hand resting on the figure's shoulder. "You'll be alright, Gunner. Just a scratch, mate." An anxious glance at the wound.

So, they were from Major Elliot's exploration team, returning after another day mapping the river, on the other side of which lay the besieged town of Ladysmith, focus of whatever future action General Buller intended when he eventually reached the Front.

"It's the Boers. Hiding away in their trenches, taking pot shots whenever they have the opportunity." A third gunner, voice shaking, face streaked with dirt. "It's not a fair fight with them. You can't see them. And their rifles shoot without smoke. So, you never know their position."

His listeners muttered their disapproval.

"I should have been watching. Too preoccupied with drawing some rock formation. Edwards wanted a closer look. I didn't even tell him to wait. We'd scouted the area earlier, no sign of the enemy anywhere. That crackle that you hear when their guns go off? That was the only warning we got. One minute Edwards was scrambling down the slope, the next he was on the ground. He screamed." The man's lip trembled. "I'll never forget that scream. Never."

Percy lay on his back, staring at the canvas above him. The imagined scene played over and over in his mind. A sharp crack, like a whip. A man falling. A scream.

Everything was about to change. General Clery met the sombre return to camp of the injured gunner's entourage with an announcement. General Sir Redvers Buller was at that moment steaming up the line from Durban to the Front. He would be with them by morning. No more time for preparations.

A train whistled in the distance. General Buller had arrived at Frere.

Percy

Frere, South Africa
Monday 11 December 1899

General Buller trotted through the camp. Ironmonger, his steed for the day, tossed his head, snorting. His ears and tail flicked at the constant irritation of flies.

As horse and rider approached, the men beside Percy became silent. They straightened, shoulders squared and eyes forward. Bonnie, asleep at Percy's feet, opened an eye. A warning growled in her throat. Percy nudged her with his foot.

"At ease, gentlemen." The General's Devonshire twang sounded so far from Percy's expectation of a high-class officer. Together with his square jaw, red face, and sturdy bulk, he looked like a farmer from a picture book Mother used to read to him.

The men relaxed. Miller puffed on his cigarette. Alfie slurped from his canteen of water.

"You boys know anything about last night's 'foraging expedition' to the local farms?" Buller leant closer, dropping Ironmonger's reins so he could snuffle the ground. Little hope of any grass there.

Percy shook his head. Others murmured their innocence.

"Very well, then. If you say so." Percy resisted the urge to shuffle his feet at the intensity of the General's stare. "But I want it known I'll have no more of it. Those farmers may have harboured Boers in their first foray into Natal, but that's no excuse for going on the rampage and stealing from them. Or their workers."

He gathered the reins, pulling Ironmonger away from a patch of dusty weeds.

"Pass the word on, be good fellows." He trotted to the next group of lounging soldiers.

"What was that all about?" Arthur slumped into his chair.

"Search me." Percy shrugged.

Alfie fiddled with the laces of his boots, avoiding eye contact.

"Alfie?" Arthur grabbed at Alfie's arm. "What's the story? It wasn't you, was it?"

Alfie's chin jerked up, his eyes flashing defiance. "No! Of course not. I'm not that stupid." He wriggled free from Arthur's grip, folding both arms across his chest. "Even though we are half-starving here. Or hadn't you noticed?"

Percy's stomach rumbled in agreement. Food supplies lagged supplies of men, as the base swelled with each new train load from Durban. Four infantry brigades, divided into sixteen different regiments, now camped on the arid fields around Frere. Not to mention the cavalry regiments and other mounted troops, their poor beasts still feeble and undernourished from weeks at sea. Percy felt a degree of sympathy whenever he saw them out on exercises.

"It was the Durhams." Alfie sulked like a child caught stealing sweets from a shop. "I'm mates with a couple of them. It was just for fun, no harm done. And they asked me, but I didn't go. Besides, their commander already dealt with it. Lyttleton, you know? Dunno why Old Buller has to stick his oar in."

He uncrossed his arms, challenging them to dispute him.

"The colonials were at it the other day." Mickey looked up from yet another drawing. "I heard them talking yesterday. They're locals, they don't think they need to follow the same rules as us. They just want their country back, I suppose."

"It's London's fault. They sent us out here, plucked us from the four corners of the Empire. But forgot to feed us." Miller, cigarette dangling from his lips. He fingered his scar. "Every war's the same. We're cannon fodder to them."

Percy squatted down next to Bonnie, fondling her ears to hide the confusion Miller's words caused. Miller, the hero career soldier, charging into battle to defend Queen and Country, speaking with unexpected bitterness. Most evenings, he regaled his friends with stories of his exploits on previous campaigns; the popping and crackling of the campfire the sound effects for his rapt audience. They heard tales of bravery, of courage under fire, of line after line marching in unswerving formation towards the enemy, bayonets fixed, and rifles cocked.

His stories helped quell Percy's niggling doubts about the war; questions that resurfaced in the darkness of a quiet night, regardless of how he pushed them aside during the day. He'd assured Flo and his parents, that this would be a short tussle with a simple opponent of farmers incapable of withstanding the might of the British Army. They had offended the Queen with their demands and would be taught a lesson. He would return to them victorious, a cheerful participant in securing calm in the furthest reaches of her Empire.

The delay in getting started on that path to victory had eroded much of Percy's confidence. Miller declared this all part of the normal progression of events, false starts and the boredom of preparation making eventual success all the sweeter.

Percy glanced at Miller, silent after his outburst. He'd stepped out of the circle of chatting comrades, his back turned to them. Alone, he sucked at the tobacco, long, slow breaths. He held his shoulders stiff and rigid, his gaze fixed on the distant purple hills beyond the camp. His fingers continued to pick at the scar.

He didn't seem to notice Percy approach.

"You never talk about it." Percy kept his tone low, not wanting the others to hear. "The scar."

"No. I don't." Miller's hand fell to his side.

"Cannon fodder?"

"Something like that." Miller dumped the cigarette, grinding at it with the toe of his boot. He exhaled smoke on a sigh. "Didn't mean to unsettle you, Percy. Ignore me. War makes me melancholy."

The naval searchlight flicked out a message in Morse code, its beam penetrating the dense cloud of a rain-swept evening. At each flash, the interior of the tent lit up, revealing the slumbering shapes of Percy's companions. Droplets pattered on the roof, dripped through the canvas above the door flap.

Another flash, bright, intense. Drip, drip. A crack of thunder shattered the sleeping night. Percy jerked wide awake. Bonnie, curled on the floor beside him, whimpered.

"We're under attack." Alfie scrambled out of his cot.

Arthur settled deeper into his pillow, his arm pressed against his exposed ear. "Thunder, mate, thunder. Go to sleep."

Alfie sat on the edge of his bed. He leant his elbows on his knees, hid his face in his hands. In the flickering light from the continuing Morse communication, he reminded Percy of the moving pictures captured by the Biograph on their sea voyage south. Jerky, in and out of focus.

Percy rolled the other way, taking care to ensure his movements didn't make the bed squeak. A stab of sympathy — tinged with guilt — pierced Percy's usual dislike of Alfie. Too often the butt of his jokes and teasing, it was a surprise to realise the bully struggled with the same fears as all of them.

The next day dawned sunny and washed clean. Birds sang from the bushes and trees. Pale white clouds scudded across the sky, driven along by a fresh, southerly breeze. The distant peaks of the Drakensberg Mountains rose in grey solidity from the surrounding landscape. Closer to camp, the rolling hills on the other side of the Tugela beckoned.

Percy breathed in the morning air, the bones in his back cracking as he stretched loose the stiffness of another restless night. Alfie emerged from the tent, dark, puffy circles, like bruises from a prize fight, rimming his eyes. He muttered a hasty greeting to Percy, then hurried towards the latrines.

"What's the urgency?" Arthur, hair tussled, lines from his pillow marking his cheeks, scrambled through the open tent flap. "Didn't even shout at me for snoring. Is he sick?"

The image of Alfie's huddled, rocking figure flashed into Percy's mind. If he told Arthur, Alfie would never hear the end of it. That would bring him down a peg or two, make him keep his ribald, opinionated comments to himself. *He's sick with fear.* Percy's mouth formed the words.

"Dunno. He didn't say anything to me." No, he wouldn't expose Alfie's secret. Father O'Brian spoke from his Merseyside pulpit about loving enemies, covering the shame of others with kind remarks and understanding. Perhaps now was the time to try.

"Oh well, so long as he doesn't give us all the Clap , I don't care what's wrong with him."

The note of a bugle, sharp and insistent, sounded through the stirring camp.

A frown added further lines to Arthur's forehead. "Surely that's not a train arriving so early? It would have had to travel overnight. Too risky."

A second bugle joined the first. This was no ordinary wake-up call.

Miller came running from behind a row of tents to their left. "It's started." All traces of the previous day's gloom were gone from his face, replaced with excitement gleaming in his eyes. "We're moving out. Buller's decided we should attack."

Men scrambled from their tents, shrugging into tunics, and pulling on boots as they gathered around Miller.

"Remember all those comings and goings down at the stationmaster's house?"

"Buller's HQ, you mean." A voice from the growing crowd.

"Yes, yes, the HQ then. Well, General Buller, Clery, French, all the other bigwigs, have been planning for us to deploy for ages." He raised a hand, warding off a barrage of questions. "No, don't ask me how I know. I just do."

He winked at Percy.

"Anyway, since he arrived two weeks ago, Buller's wanted to break camp and cross at a point along the river. Potgieter's Drift, the locals call it. The scouts reckon there's nowhere else suitable for a pontoon. Elliot told me that much. But then a crisis in the Cape diverted his attention and Buller couldn't put his plans into action. But now he can."

With slow, deliberate movements, Miller pulled a packet of cigarettes from his tunic pocket. He tapped out one of the tobacco sticks, rolling it between thumb and forefinger. Ignoring the clamours for him to continue with his news, he lifted the cigarette. Patting his pockets, he found matches, lit one and held the flame to his cigarette. Squinting through the smoke, he dropped the match to the ground. He took a drag, inhaling deep into his lungs.

Percy chuckled at his friend enjoying the drama of the moment, the rugged hero on a London stage.

Come to think of it, both the searchlight and the heliograph on the hill had flashed and winked with messages and instructions from Buller to General White — trapped in Ladysmith and awaiting rescue — more than any time over the last week.

"What plans then, Miller-Knows-All? You're bluffing. You don't know any more than the rest of us." Crosby shoved his way to the front, his fists clenched as though readying for a fight. "C'mon, lads, let's not waste our time. Breakfast's waiting."

"We march to Colenso at first light tomorrow." Miller's comment was so quiet, Percy almost missed his words as Crosby's challenge gained a few more followers. "Stopford is an old family friend. He's Buller's Private Secretary, did you know? Of course you did. Got it straight from the horse's mouth, Crosby, old thing."

A dark flush stained Crosby's face. A vein in his neck bulged. His fingers curled into an even tighter fist, the knuckles white. Without a word, he spun around and strode away from Miller's adoring audience.

Percy watched his departure, nerves fluttering in his stomach. Whether from Miller's disclosure or the prospect of a humiliated Crosby partnering him in battle, he was unsure.

Either way, he spent the day in a heightened state of tension, snapping his replies when spoken to, nibbling at his bread, or abandoning his tea after no more than a few sips.

Bonnie followed him, her tail between her legs, irritating him further with her constant presence and sad eyes.

"Get away, Bonnie. I'm busy." He lifted a vest from the pile of clothes on his cot. Pushing it to the bottom of his kit bag, he nudged the dog with his foot. She retreated to her bed with a dejected whine.

"She might as well come, PP. She can be our mascot." Arthur bowled a rolled-up ball of socks at Percy. It landed with a soft thud beside him. "Howzat!"

"A battlefield is no place for a dog, Arthur."

"Neither is an abandoned village. And is a battlefield really a place for anything?"

He had a point. Percy glanced over at Bonnie. Her head rested on her outstretched front paws, her eyes following his every movement. Her tail thumped against the floor.

"We'll see. No promises, Bonnie." The tail swished back and forth.

"You made the right decision. Now, pass me those socks. I'm not marching barefoot through the Tugela."

Wilhelm

Dundee, South Africa
Friday 20 October 1899

Wilhelm tugged on the reins, bringing Flooi to a standstill.

Throughout the days and nights of riding southwards towards Natal, General Joubert's commissioning ringing in his ears, nervous anticipation gripped Wilhelm. The torrential spring storms, the biting wind blowing down from the Drakensberg; nothing dampened his spirits. When, on the morning after yet another miserable night spent huddled amongst rocks with only a blanket for protection, the sun emerged to shine on a glistening Buffalo River and the fresh green plains of the territory beyond, memories of hardships melted with the rain.

High clouds chased across a wide blue sky, driven by a brisk, southerly breeze. Swallows dipped across the sky in their search for morning nourishment. A red-chested cuckoo trilled its repetitive greeting; "Piet my vrou, Piet my vrou". A shrike responded, piercing the quiet with its high-pitched song.

"So there it is." Jacobus reined his horse in beside Wilhelm. Hat removed, hair stuck up at odd angles, reminding Wilhelm of their schooldays when they'd raced round the playground together. Jacobus sat several inches taller in the saddle. Wilhelm pitied his pony. "I can almost smell the ocean."

Wilhelm shook his head. "You never were much good at geography. You know we're not so close, don't you?"

Jacobus scratched his cheek in a parody of confusion. "Really? And I thought it was just over that hill."

Other riders trotted up beside them. One gave a whistle of delight. Frederik Prinsloo, the commando leader, slid out of the saddle and onto his knees in the wet grass. He removed his slouch hat, damp and misshapen, bending his head in prayer. His rifle rested on his lap.

Willhelm caught the whisper of words — a gentle breeze rustling leaves on a tree.

"...your divine protection...guidance...victory over the enemy of us, your chosen people...Amen."

"Amen." Wilhelm fidgeted, his legs jiggling in the stirrups. His hand strayed to the pocket with the carving from the bedroom at home. A vision of Ma and Isobel rose in his imagination, seated at the kitchen table, fingers entwined as they blessed the meal before them, and their men who were not.

The commandant, wet patches circling the knees of his dark blue trousers, stood with hands on hips, gazing at the landscape. His jacket hung loose and unbuttoned. Two bandoliers of bullets criss-crossed his chest. Another served as a belt at his waist. Slung at a jaunty angle from his shoulder, his Mauser rifle.

Prinsloo treated Wilhelm with the same respect he accorded the older men, freeing him from being under Pa's shadow. He sent him to ride on ahead of the rest of the group, complimenting Flooi on her speed and agility, his startling blue eyes on Wilhelm as he listened to reports of the trail ahead or the actions of the other horsemen. Trotting alongside him, Prinsloo discussed battle tactics and farming practices, asked about his dreams, or teased him about Katryn. And always he spoke of the Lord, quoting passages of Scripture or breaking off mid-sentence to pray as a new idea arose from their conversation.

As the General faced his troops, pink-rimmed eyes glistening with emotion, Wilhelm vowed to follow wherever Prinsloo, and the Lord, might lead.

The field gun's aim flew high over the town, missing its mark.

Wilhelm tugged at his pocket watch. 5.35am. How would the British react? Not half an hour earlier, he'd glimpsed his first sighting of the enemy, standing to attention in the central square, the persistent drizzle smudging their outlines. They all wore identical outfits of khaki tunics and trousers, sturdy-looking leather boots and dome-shaped helmets. Patting the damp fabric of his dripping hat, Wilhelm considered himself under-dressed for any upcoming skirmish. Pa's Sunday jacket also displayed the dirt and rips of weeks. Ma wouldn't be pleased.

The military drill finished, the soldiers wandered off in different directions. One or two strode towards a large tent where others milled around, drinking from steaming cups. A red flag, bright spot amidst the gloom, hung from a pole beside a second tent.

"Must be the officer in charge." The Carolina post office clerk, Christiaan Meyer, scorn curling his lip. "Good of them to show us where to aim."

A rustle behind where Wilhelm crouched amongst the rocks and aloes of the hillside announced the arrival of more Boers. Prinsloo grunted a welcome. Below, a man gesticulated in their direction, spotting their movements. Wilhelm froze, every muscle taught. A second man emerged at the entrance of a tent, field glasses trained on their position. Dropping the binoculars to swing on the strap around his neck, he raised the alarm in a silent pantomime of urgent panic.

The next shell landed a few yards beyond a group of men wearing — was he seeing things? — skirts. They scattered to right and left. The watching Boers laughed and jeered.

"They're bringing out the artillery, look." Jacobus pointed at several soldiers straining to manoeuvre wheeled gun carriages into position.

Three batteries of six guns, each aimed at the hillside where General Lucas Meyer's troops waited. Within moments, the air danced with flashes and puffs of white smoke as shells burst from the loaded weapons. The ground shook with each explosion, thudding against Wilhelm's ribs like a monstrous heartbeat. Memories of long-forgotten thunder storms while under bedclothes or hiding beneath a table resurfaced. The same taste of fear filled Wilhelm's mouth.

"Hold steady, men. They don't know our exact position, so we aren't in any danger." Wilhelm's racing pulse slowed at Prinsloo's reassurance.

Wilhelm checked the time again. How long would the bombardment continue?

By seven thirty, a mute stillness settled on the town, as thick as the smoke swirling in the air.

Wilhelm squinted through the mist. Infantrymen, rifles poised, marched in brisk formation towards a collection of white farm buildings hugging the slopes of the hill. A dried-up stream snaked alongside the property, stone walls demarcating the homestead from the surrounding wilderness.

"They'll attack from that copse of trees, Frederik." Pa spoke with a calm Wilhelm hoped he felt. "Be ready to shoot as they come over the edge of that river bed. Do you see?"

"Yes, Oom Marthinus. Prepare your weapons."

Wilhelm wedged his rifle against his shoulder, its muzzle balancing on a rock. With one eye closed, he watched for the first figures to crawl over the lip of the bank.

"Fire!"

Wilhelm squeezed the trigger once, twice, three times. Bullet casings pinged off the rocks. Pa grunted as his shot hit its target and a British soldier crumpled in the dust.

"One less to worry about." Another shot. A spurt of dust. Reload. Shoot again.

Khaki-clad soldiers lay pinned in place, unable to shift their positions or aim their rifles in retaliation. A hail of bullets rained down on their prone figures, shattering the branches and scything through the eucalyptus leaves of the trees behind them, lacing the cordite-scented morning with a medicinal smell.

"What is he doing?" Jacobus paused reloading his Mauser. A man stepped forward, conspicuous in the gap in a low stone wall. "Doesn't he know we can see him?"

"He's their general. That red flag? It's like the one in the camp. I've seen that assistant of his carrying it everywhere he goes."

"Easy target, then."

"Yours, boy." Prinsloo whispered out of the corner of his mouth.

Wilhelm inhaled a deep breath, stilling his hands where he gripped the stock. The beat of his slowing heart pulsed in his temple. He squinted down the barrel, lining up his prey as Pa had taught him as soon as he was old enough to fire a gun. He squeezed his finger against the tension in the trigger, increasing the pressure in a quick, even movement. Crack. The gun recoiled into his shoulder. His muscles, accustomed to the kickback, absorbed the impact.

The general remained standing. Had he missed? Wilhelm was sure he'd aimed straight for him. After a few seconds' delay, the general turned, retreating in stiff, jerky movements. Helped by his aide, he navigated through the wall and struggled into the saddle of his horse. Within seconds, the woods obscured him from view.

Adrenalin surged through Wilhelm's veins. As though returning to the surface after diving into deep waters, men's voices, the continued barrage of shots, birdsong and the tickle of the breeze, burst over him.

A clap on the back in congratulation. A grunt from Pa as he released more shots, his attention fixed on the farm and wood below.

"No time to rest, son. They're making a break for it."

Something glinted as the sun made a brief appearance through the thick grey clouds. Metal spears on the end of the British rifles.

"Bayonets. They want to slash us to death." Jacobus' voice trembled.

"Back over the hill. Retreat." Prinsloo's command carried over the continuing din of rifle fire.

Crawling backwards, stones and thorns catching at his trousers, Wilhelm fired a few last rounds. Once away from the front edge, he scrambled to his feet and, crouched low, slid and tripped down the slope towards his waiting pony.

He unhooked the reins from a tree branch and hauled himself onto Flooi's back. She leapt forward as he pressed his boots into her side.

"Gallop, Flooi, gallop."

Horse and rider galloped over the plain, Wilhelm's heart pounding in unison with Flooi's thudding hooves on the rain-soaked earth. The plain rang with the shouts and cheers of the retreating Boers; their first foray into the opponent's territory a success, despite the dash across the veld.

Slowing as he approached the crossing over the Buffalo River, Wilhelm heard the British guns firing a barrage of shells. Or was that his imagination? Who were they firing at? He glanced behind him. Nothing except fleeing horsemen. No shrapnel flares. No explosions. Were the enemy attacking their own men?

Wilhelm

Dundee, South Africa
Sunday 22 October 1899

The next morning dawned cold and misty again. Wilhelm , the sodden grass squelching as he ambled over to the Carolina men. Christiaan Meyer poked at the grey embers of last night's fire. A flame flickered, disappeared, reignited. Wilhelm steepled a few damp sticks around the infant blaze, blowing soft puffs of encouragement until the kindling fizzled then caught with a leap of jubilant orange and yellow.

He sat on his haunches, mesmerised by the flames dancing through the cradle of twigs. Someone threw on a thicker branch, sending sparks flying and smoke billowing. Wilhelm blinked stinging eyes.

"What do we do now?" Meyer, dusting his hands, asked as though unconcerned with the reply; a throwaway comment added to the flow of conversation, like one of his sticks to the fire.

Wilhelm held his breath, waiting to hear if anyone would answer. Were they to trek back across Talana Hill and resume the battle started yesterday? Or was their position hopeless, a retreat to Volksrust their only option?

"A messenger rode in and went straight to General Meyer's headquarters early this morning. Soon after dawn." Pa stroked at his beard. "I imagine he carried instructions from General Joubert. Perhaps we're to combine with the other commandos on Mount Impati."

Where did Pa get his information? Once everyone had finished breakfast, orders from General Meyer to break camp and trek north filtered through to each commando. Petrus packed up Pa and Wilhelm's belongings and brought their horses, saddled and prepared for the journey.

They travelled in silence, alert for any sounds of nearby enemy activity. Wilhelm guessed there were more than a thousand men riding over the plain, winding their way along the trail or resting their animals — and themselves. In the occasional breaks in the floating mists and rain, he glimpsed the garrison of Dundee below.

Night fell as they reached the site behind Mount Impati. Petrus hurried to stretch the canvas sheet which served as their shelter between two stumpy trees. Disappointed by the lack of action and tired from hours in the saddle, Wilhelm glugged his canteen of water and unrolled his bedding mat.

Pa shook him awake after what seemed like mere minutes.

"Up, son. General Joubert is going to attack the garrison before dawn."

"Isn't it Sunday today? The Lord's day. For resting, not fighting."

"Some of us have said our prayers already." Pa sucked in his cheeks. The single wink softened his disapproval. "It seemed a shame to wake you. But now, you must hurry. The 'Long Toms' will sound the alarm for anyone still sleeping."

Wilhelm's eyes widened. "The guns are here? All the way from Pretoria?" He'd seen the cannons on a visit to Pretoria, silhouetted high on the walls surrounding the city, symbols of defiance and protection. "How did they do that?"

Pa shrugged. "I don't know. Nor do I need to. The fact is, they are. And the British will soon discover that."

Eager not to miss the upcoming action, Wilhelm searched for Flooi. A few yards from camp, he spotted not his pony, but a black mare tethered to a bush. Its owner puffed at a cigarette, his back to Wilhelm.

"Hendrik? Is that you?"

The man, startled from his reverie, dropped the cigarette, then shouldered his rifle, turning to the intruder in one swift movement.

Recognition dawned, and he lowered the weapon to his side. "Wilhelm Olivier of the Carolina Commando. Don't sneak up on people like that. You could get yourself shot."

Wilhelm stepped forward, hands raised in surrender.

"Don't shoot. Yes, it's me, Wilhelm." He paused, unsure whether Hendrik welcomed his presence. The man's eyebrows were drawn together in a scowl. A muscle flicked at the edge of his mouth, making his moustache twitch. His shirt was grubby and torn, the neat blonde hair so noticeable at their previous meeting now a thatch of untidy straw. "Sorry, I didn't mean to disturb you. I came to find Flooi. We must saddle up and ready ourselves for battle."

Was it his imagination, or did Hendrik's face pale, his body shudder, at the mention of battle?

"No, no, you didn't disturb me." The scowl lifted. He extended a hand in greeting. A crimson patch darkened his sleeve.

Wilhelm took the hand in his own, surprised to feel it limp and trembling. "Are you injured, Hendrik? Is that blood...?"

Hendrik snapped back his hand, shoving it into his trouser pocket. With his other, he hid the stain.

"It's nothing serious. A scratch, really."

"Were you at Talana on Friday? I didn't see you. But then, everything happened at once. I hardly noticed anyone, even if they stood alongside me." Wilhelm tried to keep his tone light, to hide the growing concern stealing over him like a winter wind.

"No. I rode with friends from Johannesburg for a couple of days. I returned a few hours ago, looking for my commando." He drew a shaky breath. "Have you hunted before, young Wilhelm? Yes, silly question, you're a farmer's child. Of course you have. I think I told you, I'm a clerk, an office man. I sit behind a desk. I read reports. I record transactions. I don't hunt. Never have..."

His words trailed away. The mare tossed her head, ears flicking. Wilhelm turned to leave.

"They were supposed to stay with General Joubert, on this side of the mountain." The words came out in a rush, halting Wilhelm before he could escape them. "It was foolhardy. We rode to a place further south. Elandslaagte. We had some fun posing for photos next to a train at the station. No one seemed to be there. But someone must have alerted them. The British, I mean. General Kock moved us to the top of a nearby hill and set the guns to work. It was too sudden to take it all in.

"Nothing stopped their advance. No matter what we did. We kept shooting and so did they. We retreated; they climbed up after us."

His experience at Talana fresh in his mind, Wilhelm nodded his silent understanding.

"I deserted them." A blush as dark as the mark on his shirt spread up his neck. "I ran down the hill, found my horse and rode here. I don't even know what happened to them."

The man was as broken as his voice.

Wilhelm avoided eye contact, kicking at a stone. He'd never run from anything; he'd teased the kids at school who did. Pa taught him to stand his ground against fear, to stare it in the eyes and conquer it with courage. And prayer. Lifting a surreptitious glance at Hendrik, watching him fiddle with a second cigarette with clumsy fingers, a prick of doubt niggled. Perhaps he hadn't experienced real fear, the kind this hollowed-out man before him spoke of.

"You'd best leave. Your people will be looking for you, thinking the enemy has captured you." Hendrik barked a forced, mirthless laugh.

"But...will you be alright?" Wilhelm hesitated. Men's voices floated through the mist, accompanied by a faint aroma of coffee. The clatter of pots, the clink of bridles, the clicking shout of a servant; the camp was awake and preparing to muster for the day's action. "Come with me. You can join your commando when we catch them."

Hendrik shook his head, squinting against the smoke rising from his dangling cigarette. "I appreciate your kindness, young Wilhelm. But no. I will only be a hindrance. Perhaps I shall fight alongside you another day. But not today."

He turned away.

Wilhelm

Dundee, South Africa
Monday 23 October 1899

Wilhelm gulped for breath, his shoulders heaving and his heart pounding from the dash down the hillside and into town.

The white flag of surrender fluttered its shame atop the hospital tent in the centre of the abandoned military camp. Wilhelm hadn't seen the British medical officer trudge up the hill with a second white flag for delivery to General Erasmus, but news of his visit carried to all the men occupying the mist-shrouded hills around Dundee. Later that day, two field cornets saddled up and trotted past him, sent as emissaries to accept the town's handover to the Boers.

After days of tension, of being exposed to the miseries of the elements, the excitement of foraging through the abandoned tents and houses of a routed enemy spread like a fever amongst the men on the hillside.

"They've left everything behind. Guns, bullets, food. And liquor." A Boer with matted beard and bushy eyebrows grinned as he shoved Wilhelm aside. "It's ours for the taking."

A group from another commando emerged from a tent ahead of Wilhelm, laughing and clinking beer bottles together in self-congratulations. Others rummaged through a trunk they'd dragged outside, clothes and papers tossed into the mud with careless disinterest.

Not wishing to draw attention to himself and be forced into joining them, Wilhelm hurried past, head down. The further into town he ventured, the worse the destruction from the continuous bombardment of shells from the Long Tom guns positioned on the slopes of Mount Impati. Shell craters scarred the streets. The skeletons of homes and buildings stood in twisted brokenness, their roofs a jagged mess of metal and timber. A shredded curtain, white flowers printed on yellow fabric, flapped in the breeze. Smoke rose in wisps from a pile of charred rubble.

Wilhelm stamped it out with his boot, grinding his toe with the force of shock coursing through his muscles. Hendrik's haggard expression flitted into his mind. This wholesale destruction of buildings and homes, of towns and streets, wasn't something he'd expected.

It was then he'd noticed the body. Thinking it an assortment of rags, he wandered over to make sure the fire hadn't spread. The hum of insects and the distinctive metallic tang of blood, so familiar from hunting expeditions at home, quickened his pulse as he approached. The man lay near the gate into the garden of what remained of a simple, white-painted cottage. A bougainvillea vine crept in pink profusion beside a plain wooden door. To the left, a window overlooked the street; to the right, only crumpled stone and wood. A corrugated roof sheet dangled over whatever room should be there.

Wilhelm gagged and retched, unable to tear his eyes from the prone figure sprawled at his feet. Unseeing eyes stared into the sun. A fly crawled over his upper lip. Another buzzed near the wound where his chin and neck ought to be. A sick regret settled on Wilhelm, as disorienting as the early morning fog through which the cannon's shells had fallen on the unprotected town.

The sound of raised voices from around the corner startled Wilhelm. An urge to cover the man's hideous wounds, provide some sort of dignity until his own people found him and gave him a proper burial, propelled him inside the ruined property. The gate still hung on its latch in the wall, the absurdity catching in Wilhelm's throat as he clicked it open — like visiting for Sunday tea with the neighbours. He scrabbled amongst the ruins in search of a section of untorn fabric he could use as a temporary shroud. A glint of something shiny caught his attention. He flicked the dirt aside to uncover it. A picture frame. The faces of a young couple smiled up at him. The lady wore a long pale dress and a broad, floppy hat decorated with flowers and feathers. Behind her, a man with a short, severe moustache dressed in a dark suit, a hand resting on the woman's shoulder.

Wilhelm dropped the frame as though the metal burnt his fingers. A crack shattered the protective glass, splitting the image. Still the faces

smiled. Wilhelm stumbled away, tripping in his haste to escape the
couple's happiness. His ankle buckled under him. He steadied himself
against a lump of masonry, gritting his teeth against darts of pain, and
hauled himself upright. Testing his twisted ankle, he hobbled to the gate.
A soiled carpet he'd found would cover the remains of the man from the
photograph. Had the woman escaped? Or did she lie crushed beneath
the weight of her destroyed home? Wilhelm buried the question under
the rubble of his horror.

Jeers and taunts in Afrikaans; a voice of command, speaking English.
The scuffle of feet.

Wilhelm limped towards the sounds, relieved to break the
condemning silence of the shattered body lying under the coarse rug
taken from his life.

He stopped in his tracks as he rounded the corner. A large white tent
occupied the end of the street. Printed on the canvas sides, a red cross.
The hospital.

Debris lay strewn across the ground where another shell had exploded,
leaving the earth pockmarked and seared black. Mud splattered up the
white canvas. A smell reminiscent of the carcasses hung in rows at the
butcher's shop at home lingered in the air.

A man stood at the flapped entrance, bloody apron tied at his waist,
shirt sleeves rolled up. He bounced on his toes, his fists clenched, and his
cheeks coloured with angry red blotches.

"Stop this immediately. Do you understand? This is a hospital."

Two Boer men — unknown to Wilhelm — brandished pistols.
Ignoring the order, they ran past him into the makeshift hospital.
Outraged English cries of someone inside, the crash of a table falling.
A faint moan from an injured patient? The canvas wall bulged with the
outline of a figure pressed against it. Another shout. The bulge moved.
The first of the men staggered from the tent, one eye closed against
the blood oozing from a gash in his temple. He limped past Wilhelm,
his breathing laboured and heavy with alcohol fumes. The second man

paused at the entrance, glancing from side to side with wide, staring eyes. His opponent disappearing into the next street, he let out a cry and dashed off in pursuit.

The Englishman in the apron wiped at his forehead, shaking his head. His lips moved, but his muttering didn't reach where Wilhelm stood motionless in the shadows. As though sensing his presence, the man squinted down the street. He took a step forward.

Wilhelm spun away, his heart racing, boots splashing through puddles as he ran past the broken house and the motionless figure of the dead man, away from the cracked glass and the smiling face of a pretty woman.

"They fled south. To Ladysmith." Meyer's voice rang hoarse with disappointment. "We missed them."

Wilhelm lounged in the grass, chewing on a piece of dried meat. He didn't reply, images of the shattered garrison and the funeral for its general tumbling through his mind. The man he'd shot at the battle over at Talana, the one whose red flag singled him out as general, lay buried in the graveyard of the English church near the site of his mortal wounding.

"We will follow. Tomorrow, we ride to Ladysmith and settle in the hills." Commandant Prinsloo strode into the midst of the huddle of disgruntled conversation. Wilhelm swallowed the biltong in a gulp, its salty tang lingering on his tongue. "I've met with the other generals — Maroola, Erasmus, Joubert. We're to encircle the town and remain in place until the British surrender."

It sounded simple. And dull.

"If we rode hard now, surely we could catch them before they make it into the safety of Ladysmith?" Jacobus Malan perched on a crate of beer someone had hauled up to the camp, English writing stamped on its top. Wilhelm held his breath, expecting an explosion of outrage from Prinsloo at being questioned by a subordinate.

Prinsloo stared at Malan through narrowed eyes. He tugged at his beard. A rumble of laughter and a grin burst like sunshine in his dark features. "So, the young pup is eager for more action?" He spread his arms wide, embracing them all. "Anyone else?"

Wilhelm fixed his attention on a patch of mud in front of him. His ears burned. He longed for the adrenalin surge of another successful chase, at shooting the enemy and watching him fall. His stomach lurched at the thought of the dead man, at the sombre funeral of the general, at the undignified burial of other, lesser soldiers.

"I would like nothing more than to reinforce our advantage. The British army is in a state of confusion. Striking now would deal them a significant blow." Prinsloo shrugged. "I've received intelligence reports from the Cape. Reinforcements are arriving, led by a General Buller. Some of you older men may recall him from previous skirmishes with the natives?"

Pa nodded. Wilhelm recognised the look of alarm at mention of the unfamiliar name. He must question Pa later about him.

Prinsloo continued speaking. "We will ride out and pursue them at first light. Ladysmith is a poor choice of refuge. If we can secure the hills, we'll surround the town and besiege the garrison until it is forced to surrender. So, secure the hills we must."

Not waiting to hear his men's response to the instructions, Commandant Prinsloo turned and strode out of the camp.

Wilhelm

Ladysmith, South Africa
Monday 30 October 1899

"You can see them there, on top of that flat hill."

Wilhelm squinted against the rising sun, searching the area Christiaan Meyer pointed out. Figures piled stones into a protective wall while others — officers, perhaps? — bent over a map or something similar. Behind them, a third group draped a tarpaulin between two scrubby thorn trees as a shelter from the weather.

"Do you think they know we're here?" The unhurried preparations indicated an army in blissful ignorance of the enemy's proximity.

"I'd say so. Didn't you notice the forts and redoubts on the heights as we rode through from Dundee yesterday?" Meyer waved back along the route they'd ridden the previous day. "And it isn't as though we kept our presence secret. Us galloping towards them *en masse* must have made them shake in their boots."

Wilhelm grinned at the memory of thousands of horsemen charging up the final hills surrounding the garrison at Ladysmith. A sweet scent rose as Flooi's hooves crushed the swishing green grass, refreshed by the continual rain of the last few days. A couple of shrikes accompanied them, their song piercing through the clink of bridles and the chatter of riders.

"Did you hear shots early this morning? Before dawn?" Meyer ran a dirt-stained hand through his hair, blonde tufts clumping together in a wild tangle. "I wasn't sure if I dreamt it. You know, reliving Talana..."

His face flushed a deep crimson. So, Wilhelm wasn't the only one affected by the sight of man — not beast — suffering under a hail of bullets.

"I don't think I heard shots. But people were moving around somewhere close by." Wilhelm considered some more. "Although maybe the gunfire woke me first."

Before Meyer could respond, shots sounded to their left.

Wilhelm ducked. Realising the firing came from their own lines, he sat up, cheeks warm with a flush of his own.

Meyer laughed. "Our boys are getting bored. Look at the effect on the British over there."

The men working on the shelter dropped the tarpaulin and reached for their rifles. An officer folded the map with quick, jerking movements, while his companions pulled on helmets and jogged along the path leading to the hilltop, pursued by puffs of dust as the riflemen found their range.

Within minutes, the repeated pops and snaps of sustained rifle fire carried on the wind from the other side of Ladysmith. The battle had begun.

Column after column of khaki-clad infantrymen advanced across the plain, guns raised and bayonets flashing in the sun. Behind Wilhelm, the unmistakable fizz of the Creusot gun being lit announced the main Boer defence. The shell landed amid the marching soldiers below. They scattered to either side. Some remained sprawled in the dust, immobile. Others returned to formation beyond the crater, not stopping to check on their fallen comrades.

Wilhelm swallowed, his mouth dry. He'd expected the barrage of shells from the cannons to deter the British soldiers, sending them into disarray. Instead, they seemed even more determined to push forward. Like a river in full flood, infantrymen surged onward. After them, the mounted battalions galloped into position. Those hauling the gun carriages to within range of the Boers followed at a lumbering pace as wheels caught in the sucking mud of the rain-soaked valley.

The first shell soared high over Wilhelm. Pebbles and earth cascaded over him as it exploded on impact a few yards from where he cowered, arms flung over his head as protection against the falling debris. Beside him, Meyer's lips moved, his eyebrows raised in a question which Wilhelm couldn't hear above the shrill ringing in his ears. He waggled his head as though emerging from a pool of water.

"What did you say? I didn't hear you." The ringing eased.

Meyer patted Wilhelm's shoulder, smiling and nodding. "I can't hear you, but I'm fine otherwise."

A second shell scythed through the air. Wilhelm winced, holding his hands over his ears and his breath in his throat. It missed the mark, plummeting to ground several yards beyond him, far from harm's way.

The Boer gunners responded, and the men hunkering behind rocks and in deep trenches raised their rifles to stop the enemy's advance. The din bounced and echoed around the hills like a hundred highveld storms, flashes of gunpowder the lightning. Exhilaration coursed through Wilhelm's veins in a rush of blood flooding any remaining fear. He grabbed at his rifle, firing without aim into the faltering ranks of the khaki rows.

Wilhelm lowered the weapon, eager to witness the retreat of the British army. To his surprise, rather than fleeing in retreat, figures dropped to the ground, sheltering behind the ant heaps dotted throughout the landscape, or flattening themselves into whatever hollows they could find. Wilhelm couldn't help but compare their behaviour to his helter-skelter race from the summit of Talana Hill. Half-embarrassed, half-impressed, he picked up his rifle and took aim at a head poking over a boulder a thousand yards away.

Crack! The helmet rolled from the man's head. A thatch of red hair, easy target in the brown dustiness surrounding him.

Crack! The soldier ducked.

Wilhelm laughed.

"Do you want some more fun, young Wilhelm?" A voice shouted above the noise.

Wilhelm twisted around. A man seated on a black mare smiled down at him. Hendrik.

Scrambling to his feet — although bending low for fear the red-headed soldier may wish to seek revenge for his damaged helmet — Wilhelm hurried to his friend, the gaunt, haunted look of their previous meeting gone from his expression. The eyes twinkled. A full moustache bristled and twitched at his approach.

"You see that ridge over there?" Hendrik leant forward over the mare's neck, making it possible for Wilhelm to hear him above the continued clamour of the ongoing battle. "Pepworth Hill. Our guns are there. And they're taking a beating. Want to come and help relieve them?"

Wilhelm didn't need further persuasion. He glanced around, checking to see Pa's whereabouts; he would disapprove of such an adventure away from the Carolina commando. Wilhelm discovered him squatting below the ridge, facing down into the valley below. Satisfied his absence would go unnoticed, Wilhelm skidded down the bank in search of Flooi.

He found her tethered with the other horses belonging to the fighting men, her saddle on and reins looped over her neck. Petrus sat on a felled log in a patch of shade. A long blade of dry grass hung from his lips.

"Petrus, I'm taking Flooi. Don't tell Pa I've gone, will you?"

White teeth in a dark face, brown eyes dancing with mischief. "Perhaps I come too? Make sure you are safe."

"No, Petrus. Stay here and wait for Pa. Tell him I — I felt sick. Or scared."

Petrus nodded. "I will say I know nothing about anything."

His chuckle followed Wilhelm as he galloped with Hendrik in pursuit of adventure.

They were too late. The twisted and shattered limbs of the artillery men repulsed Wilhelm more than the glazed eyes of the man in Dundee. He perched on a rock, head in hands, waiting for the dizzying bout of nausea to subside.

Snatches of Dominee Fourie's sermon floated through Wilhelm's mind; assurance of God's protection, promises of victory against those seeking to occupy the land of the covenant. He couldn't recall mention of bodies ripped to pieces, lying in tangled confusion under the blistering sunshine of the African veld.

An ambulance van rocked over the uneven surface of the lower slopes of the hill towards a group of injured artillerymen laid out on a square of canvas. A doctor hurried between the prone figures.

"Dr Ferdinand Holz. German." Hendrik slid from his saddle, tossing the mare's reins to a native helper standing nearby. "I met him once before. Do you know him?"

Wilhelm shook his head as he jumped off Flooi. A wrinkled brown hand took her reins and led the two horses to where other animals awaited their riders. Wilhelm wondered which would return to camp unburdened at day's end.

"Are you coming? I'm going to check on the guns." Hendrik grabbed Wilhelm's arm.

As he spoke, a shell burst overhead. Shrapnel rained down in searing shards of metal, tearing into the ground. Wilhelm raced to shelter under the protection of the ambulance van. Hendrik followed.

The Boer guns continued firing, twenty, thirty shells aimed at the still-advancing British troops. The air was bitter as wreaths of cordite smoke mingled with the familiar smell of shed blood. Wilhelm tried not to breathe through his nose.

In a pause in the returning volley of rifle fire, Hendrik ventured out from under the ambulance wagon. Wilhelm crawled after him. One of the mules had been hit by the falling shrapnel and stood, lifeless, in its traces. The remaining team snorted and stamped their hooves, their native driver clicking and muttering at them in a quiet whisper as he tried to calm them.

Wilhelm stumbled up the incline, crouching as he ran from stone to stone between bursts of gunfire. Once at the top, he crawled forward to the gun emplacement, his trousers snagging on thorns and clumps of dried grass. Unseeing eyes of dead men watched his progress. The injured groaned in mournful agony.

The remaining gunners lay behind a low parapet at the edge of the hillside. Hendrik reached them before Wilhelm. He knelt beside two of them, gesticulating to the comparative protection below. Wilhelm guessed the gist of the conversation. He waited, not wishing to push on and expose himself to more danger than was necessary.

Hendrik slithered towards him. "They won't come with us." The excited bravado had left his face, his eyes pink-rimmed and his skin pale. A sheen of sweat glistened on his forehead. "I admire their bravery. But feel they are wrong."

"Let's get back before we're missed." Wilhelm squeezed Hendrik's forearm to express his sympathy for the man's dilemma. "We can't do anything more here."

Hendrik huffed a sigh, plucking at his moustache. "You're right." He gave himself a shake. "There might be more adventure elsewhere."

They retreated to the field hospital, bullets pinging off the rocks as they darted and tripped down the slope.

"Oh..." Hendrik, leading the way, stopped with such abruptness Wilhelm collided with him.

"What? I almost knocked you over. Oh..."

The doctor lay in a crumpled heap amongst his patients.

Wilhelm buried a hand in his jacket pocket, his fingers seeking the rough comfort of the wooden ornament from a bedroom wall a hundred lifetimes away.

Wilhelm slumped in his saddle, eyes closed and fingers loose on the reins. Flooi plodded along, picking her way on the pathway to the Carolina camp. Hendrik rode alongside in silence. The familiar high-pitched call of a rock pigeon rang out at their approach. Wilhelm opened one eye, seeking to locate the bird. Instead, he jerked awake at the sight of Petrus hastening towards him.

"Your father is looking for you. He noticed you were missing about half an hour ago." Petrus jigged from foot to foot, agitation lining his features. "Hurry. I'll take Flooi."

Wilhelm jumped from his pony. Hendrik seemed recovered from the shock of their outing. He lifted his hat in farewell.

"I'll see you again, young Wilhelm. My people will start worrying about my absence if I don't reappear soon."

He galloped away, the black mare flicking her tail and snorting.

"Goodbye, Hendrik. And thank you, Petrus. Do you know where Pa is?"

"Behind the hill, last I saw him."

"Right. I'll go and find him."

Wilhelm jogged towards the commando's camp hidden in a clump of trees beyond the ridge where he'd last seen Pa. Half a dozen men stood in a group, their heads bowed in prayer. Pa's unruly curls bobbed amongst them.

Not wishing to disturb them, Wilhelm held back and waited for the prayer to finish. He removed his hat, running his hands through his hair, tried to calm his racing heart. What would Pa say?

"Amen." Pa's deep voice sounded loud, authoritative. Everyone dispersed, walking away in groups of two or three. "Son, show yourself then."

Wilhelm stepped forward, heat rushing to his face. He kept his gaze fixed on the ground, scuffing his boots in the dirt as he moved.

"Sir, I — I'm sorry. I shouldn't have gone —"

Pa drew him into his arms, squeezing the breath from him. The steady beat of Pa's heart thumped in Wilhelm's ear, the wool of his jacket tickling his nose and making him want to sneeze. Pa's shoulders shook, his chest rising and falling with short, sharp breaths.

"You're laughing." Wilhelm pulled out of the embrace.

Mischief danced in Pa's eyes, like when he'd brought home a jackal puppy and presented it to Ma. "The poor thing is sick. Abandoned by its pack. I'm sure you'll nurse it back to health," he'd said. Ma hadn't spoken to him for the rest of the day. But she had taken care of the pup, crying when they released it into the wild.

"So, you thought it time to venture out by yourself, did you? Find a different battle to fight?" Pa cocked his head on one side. "Where did your adventure take you?"

"Sort of over there." Wilhelm waved a vague hand. "I was with Hendrik. You know, the man from Standerton?"

"I know him. A reckless individual, from all I've heard." Wilhelm glanced up, surprised Pa remembered Hendrik from their previous introduction at Volksrust. "I hear things, son. So, you went to try the guns, did you? How was that?"

He shrugged. "Alright. I suppose."

Pa rested his hands on Wilhelm's shoulders, his expression becoming serious. Wilhelm squirmed under his scrutiny.

"I'm relieved you were at Pepworth Hill. I worried you may have wandered over to Nicholson's Nek."

"Nicholson's Nek? No. Why? What happened over there?"

"Of course, you wouldn't have heard. The British generals sent their soldiers on a fool's errand, that's what. They intended to capture the heights, establish a base to protect the town." He stroked at his beard. "Meyer rode over at the first sound of rifle fire. Wanted a bit of the action himself, instead of listening to it. He returned a few minutes ago."

"And?"

"You'll hear the story from him, I've no doubt. But the scenes he started to describe? Well, let's just say he couldn't finish." Another pause. "The British surrendered in the end."

"But that's good, isn't it?" An image of the doctor's fatal wounds swam across Wilhelm's vision. Rage flickered, the need for revenge smouldering somewhere deep inside. "They deserve whatever they get."

"War is not the noble — simple — fight our leaders would have us believe." Pa's voice softened. "I'm sorry you are realising this. I wished to protect you from the knowledge until you are older. Much older."

"Pa, I'm fine." Wilhelm chewed his upper lip. "But it was horrible. Bodies and blood and flies. So many flies. The doctor got hit. Died while working to save his patients. How is that right? How is that —" he flung his arms at the distant hills " — God moving on behalf of His people? I don't understand, Pa."

He stopped. His throat tightened. Stinging tears pricked at the corner of his eyes.

"Neither do I, son. It is easy for Dominee Fourie to stand in his pulpit and preach to us about the will of God, about His victories and our service." He paused. "It is less easy to see the damaged bodies, to smell the spilled blood, of men whose lives are ended before they truly start. Young men from both sides…"

Pa lifted a hand from Wilhelm's shoulder, resting it instead on his head, caressing his scalp; the calming gesture of his childhood.

"We can only pray, son. Pray to the Lord for mercy. For us all."

Wilhelm

**Ladysmith, South Africa
Thursday 9 November 1899**

"We should have taken them when we could." Jacobus Malan flicked at a fly crawling across his leg. "This is no way to win a war. Sitting here playing cards, and hoping they surrender."

"Commandant-General Joubert thinks differently. The Lord has extended His finger; we should not seek to take His arm." Cornelius Grobler, a farmer from the outskirts of Carolina, switched his attention from the Bible in his lap. He had eyes the colour of a summer sky, a fleshy nose, and thick lips. Hands which reminded Wilhelm of tree branches rested on the pages of the book.

"Admirable theology. Poor military strategy..." Wilhelm hoped none of the others heard Pa's muttered comment.

"It is not our place to question those in authority —" a sharp glance in Pa's direction "— but rather to seek the Lord for His strength to carry out our duty. Whatever that duty may be." Grobler smoothed the page of his Bible, his lips moving, demonstrating his instructions. "Besides, the pause does at least allow our horses to recover, our injured to heal."

Wilhelm agreed with that point. The hard, overnight rides in the appalling spring weather had tested Flooi and her resilience to its limit. Despite Petrus' best efforts, she had grown skinny, ribs showing through the dullness of her coat. Days of nibbling at the fresh grass around the laager had already begun to restore her.

"But half the men have left. Returned to their families and farms. And the others have brought them here." Malan pointed at the circle of wagons in a dip below them. Smoke curled upwards from a campfire. A woman sang a lilting melody, her voice carrying on the still morning air.

The first transport arrived a week after the British abandoned the fight and retreated into Ladysmith. After the Boers destroyed the railway line and cut the enemy's lines of communication, there was little action for the fighting men. Only the gunners remained occupied, sending shells crashing into the town on a regular basis as a deterrent to escape.

At each new arrival lumbering into camp, Wilhelm hoped to see Ma and Isobel. Or Katryn and her family. But he suspected Pa had sent a message home, telling them not to come. He wouldn't approve of their presence, and would worry for their safety as they travelled.

Trying to ignore his disappointment, Wilhelm trotted around on Flooi, visiting the other commandos or foraging for food to supplement their dwindling supplies. He'd joined Hendrik on an expedition down the valley, calling in at secluded farms for gifts of coffee, or eggs and vegetables from suspicious farmers and their wives.

"They have ordered the train company to only accept passengers with home passes." Pa spoke with the usual mix of knowledge and authority which Wilhelm now expected.

"A wise idea." Grobler nodded his approval.

Pa rose from the stool where he sat. He pulled his pocket-watch from his waistcoat, squinting at the dial and tapping its face. "Commandant Prinsloo has requested my presence at the headquarters over at Modderspruit."

Wilhelm, lying in the grass and dozing as the conversation flowed above him, snapped awake. He pushed himself up onto his elbow. "Why, Pa? Are they discussing our next move?"

"Perhaps." Pa attempted to sound vague, but Wilhelm recognised excitement in the thin line of his lips. "British troops have landed in Durban and are travelling towards the Tugela. General Buller has them massing for an assault to cross the river and shake us from our positions here at Ladysmith."

"You said you knew him?" Out of the corner of his eye, Wilhelm saw Grobler close his Bible. Malan swivelled around to hear.

"Not personally. I haven't met him or fought him in battle. But my father did. During the native wars, the British and the Boer joined forces against a common enemy." Petrus, standing on the edge of the circle, clicked his tongue. "Sorry, Petrus. It was a different time. Anyway, Buller learnt our way of life, our way of fighting. He knows we can shoot. And he knows we can ride."

"And?" Wilhelm plucked at a blade of grass, confused. "What does it matter if he knows how we do things?"

"Because to beat your enemy, you need to know your enemy." Cornelius Grobler stroked his Bible. "Isn't that so, Marthinus?"

"Yes, Oom Cornelius. You are right." Tucking his watch in his pocket, Pa left the words hanging. His eyes no longer gleamed with excitement; instead, they glistened with sadness.

"Can I go with you? To the generals' camp, I mean?" Wilhelm doubted Pa would agree.

"Why not? You'll have to stay with the horses. I'm not certain who will be at the meeting. Your presence may not be welcome. Or mine, come to that."

The encampment buzzed with activity. Leaders of each of the commandos ranged along the ridge of hills surrounding Ladysmith greeted each other with shouts of recognition as they arrived. Dismounting, they tossed horses' reins to native attendants, hurrying to join the conference.

Snatches of conversation buzzed like bees swarming their hive.

"We lost half a dozen yesterday. Said they were needed for the early harvest. Nonsense, of course, but you can't blame them. Kicking their heels and watching the British scurry about like ants all day."

"I hope they make some decisions here. Old Joubert must stop dithering and order another attack before it's too late."

"He's too sick of the whole thing…"

"Buller won't waste time, I'll guarantee that. We should strike now, before he has chance to organise."

"Any news from home? Maria arrived with some of the other wives last week. I reckon this is no place for a woman, and sent her away.

Although it was good to see her. Hear about the farm, and the children, that sort of thing."

"My Susanna is here. There's no harm in it. Nothing happening that would distress her."

Pa tapped Wilhelm on the shoulder. "Lead the horses down to that stream. Over there, look."

Wilhelm opened his mouth to plead that he be allowed to stay.

"No, son. I'll find you when we're done."

Wilhelm gathered the reins of the two horses and led them from the bustle towards the stream. Its waters ran brown and muddy, more rain having washed sand down from the hillside. Wilhelm's feet squelched through the marshy grasses along the bank, the horses' hooves making a sucking sound as they trod.

Weaver birds flitted in and out of a clump of swaying reeds, their ball-like nests hanging from the slender stalks.

"This isn't what I had in mind for this expedition, Flooi." Wilhelm nudged the horse nearer the water's edge. "Drink quickly, then I'll take you back. You can wait with the other animals, and I'll wander over to that big tent we saw. Must be Joubert's headquarters."

As though understanding her master's instructions, Flooi dipped her nose to slurp at the water. Pa's horse remained alert, his ears flicking as he listened for any sound of approaching danger. Still wary, he bent forward and drank.

Deciding they'd drunk enough, Wilhelm tugged on the reins and pulled them up the bank. Urging them on, he jogged to the camp. He paused at its edge, scanning the group of men chatting. Pa wasn't one of them.

Tying their harnesses to a sturdy bush, he patted Flooi's rump, and bid his farewells. "I'll be back before you know it, Flooi. Just want to check on what's happening."

The smell of smoke and damp wood hung in the air as Wilhelm approached the tent. Men huddled, arms folded, in the shade of the trees. Outside, no one spoke; inside, raised voices competed for attention.

Ignoring the watchful stares as he passed, Wilhelm edged closer to the tent's entrance. Finding a gap, he squatted down, blinking the sun from his eyes as he tried to make out the speakers in the interior's gloom.

He located Commandant-General Joubert, seated in the centre of a table at the front. Wilhelm hadn't seen him since the party at Volkrust. Then, he sat tall and proud on his horse, a resolute expression on his face as men streamed past him, declaring victory in the upcoming war against the impudent British invaders.

The man at the table looked neither proud nor victorious. The blue fabric of his uniform was dusty, the brass buttons no longer gleaming. His eyes flicked from one speaker to the next, his lips parted. His white beard was unkempt, the mop of bushy brown hair streaked with grey.

The young man to his right sat upright in his chair, his posture rigid. Blue eyes stared out over the assembly, his lip curling each time someone new voiced his opinion. A neat moustache and trimmed beard framed his stern features. Fingers drummed on the table. This must be General Louis Botha, Joubert's second-in-command, according to Pa.

On Joubert's other side, Wilhelm recognised the bulky frame of General Meyer from the battle at Talana Hill. He kept his head lowered, a cigarette smouldering in his fingers.

Wilhelm scanned the rest of the crowd. In the first row, his back to Wilhelm, Commandant Prinsloo leant forward; beside him, Pa. Wilhelm ducked behind the canvas as Pa twisted in his seat, as if looking for someone. Had he guessed Wilhelm would disobey his orders and leave the ponies so he could listen in on the debate?

"I see no reason to abandon our positions around Ladysmith." A man unknown to Wilhelm stood. He wiped his forehead with his shirt sleeve before continuing. "The British will have to weaken, eventually. And when they do, we must be ready for them. We will march into the main street and seize the town with hardly a bullet fired…"

"Nonsense. They will starve to death before allowing us to take them. They'll burn all the provisions, fire their remaining ammunition so we can't get our hands on it, butcher their horses." A second man rose. He waved his hat, emphasising his words. "We should ride into Natal, meet Buller face to face. Fight on our terms, not his."

Cheers greeted this suggestion. Men clapped, and stamped their feet in approval.

"The men grow fat and lazy — those that haven't deserted and headed home." The second man shouted above the hubbub. "Our horses are well rested. We could leave tomorrow."

Another burst of raucous applause.

A third, older man rose. He lifted his hands, quietening the assembly with a slow turn of the head and an unblinking stare from under raised eyebrows. "You young things don't understand what you're saying. I was at Majuba —" a collective gasp at mention of the great defeat from an earlier conflict. Wilhelm held his breath, waiting for the war veteran to continue. "We have not seen the best of the British army yet. We have won the battles thus far, with much thanks to their generals' mistakes and incompetence. Those steaming inland on trains from Durban are better trained, more prepared. They'll have native scouts and local spies mapping the ground and reporting on our movements. I advise caution and proper planning before we proceed into what is, after all, their territory."

A few muted claps from the older men in the group. Most muttered under their breath, shaking their heads.

"We could try a combination of both. You know, keep some positioned here, maintaining the siege. Then send others to investigate the position south of the Tugela." The speaker remained seated, as though not wishing to draw attention to himself and his idea.

Wilhelm fidgeted, the muscles in his legs cramping. He ought to check on the horses. He turned to crawl away and leave the men to their endless discussions. A commotion from the front of the tent stopped him. General Joubert rose from his seat.

Only the breeze rustling through the trees outside broke the silence. Every man focussed their attention on their leader. Pa leant over and whispered in Prinsloo's ear. The Commandant nodded.

Joubert cleared his throat. "Men, I wish to thank you for your comments and suggestions. More, I wish to thank you for your service to the volk and to the Lord. We have experienced some successes over recent weeks, and some setbacks." Some muttering from the burghers huddled in the shadows. Joubert waited for their attention to return to him. "I am not unaware of our losses, and indeed pray for all who have suffered. I believe it would be foolish to storm the garrison at Ladysmith at this point — I understand an attempt to do so earlier today met with stiff resistance — and waiting for the British to surrender is a fool's errand."

As Joubert continued, his voice lost its initial apologetic tone. He squared his shoulders, glaring across at those daring to speak their minds.

"We will ride to the Tugela. And cross into Natal. We will meet General Buller and his army wherever they have reached, and we will send them back to Durban." Those in disagreement shook their heads, half-rising from their seats in protest. Joubert waved them down. "We are more mobile than they are. They rely on the railway line and the bridges to transport them inland. We have our horses. They need their vast camps of equipment and supplies, their tents, and their champagne." Laughter rippled through the tent. "Men, we have our coffee and our cooking pots. And we know our land. For this is our land, promised to us by God Himself and protected and defended by Him."

Men rose to their feet, waving their hats and cheering again. Wilhelm's skin tingled as the mood shifted from complaining defeat to exuberant optimism. Pa remained in conference with Prinsloo in their seats at the front. The tips of his ears and his neck were red. Whether from anxiety and anger or excitement, Wilhelm would have to find out later.

"And finally, we have our Mausers!" General Botha leapt out of his chair, brandishing his rifle above his head. "The British are no match for our bullets and our marksmanship. They won't see us coming, and won't know what hit them after we're gone."

Wilhelm scrambled to his feet, shouting until his voice was hoarse. A hymn broke out. Rough-edged voices formed the melody and the harmonies in an uprising of praise and prayer to the Almighty.

"What are you doing here, Wilhelm?" He hadn't noticed Pa elbowing through the crowd. "I told you to wait with the horses."

"But Pa, this is wonderful. We will cross into Natal and find the British and — and —" Red spots high on Pa's cheekbones warned Wilhelm to stop talking. He ignored the warning. "We will fight, and we will win. You heard the Generals. The advantages are all ours."

Pa grabbed Wilhelm's arm, pulling him away from the men and out into the open.

"Do you still think it's that simple, child?" Wilhelm clenched his jaw at being called a child. He'd shot a man, hadn't he? "What you saw at Pepworth Hill, in Dundee, even what your friend Hendrik claimed he witnessed at Elandslaagte. That's only the beginning."

"But, the Lord —"

"The Lord may be on our side, but He is not on these hillsides, fording these rivers or stumbling through these valleys, is He? It is not His flesh being mutilated, His life being extinguished." Pa let go of Wilhelm's arm. He sounded weary, the words rasping as though he were coming down with illness. "And before you say it, yes, the Lord Jesus has experienced those things. That cross you carry with you everywhere reminds us all of that. But I am not a father who can willingly sacrifice my son, Wilhelm. I am too selfish in my love for you to manage that."

Wilhelm's hand strayed to his pocket. He pulled out the ornament, rubbed the wood with his thumb. Turning it over, he traced a finger over Isobel's inexpert carving.

"Pa, I —" His voice cracked. He coughed, started again. "Pa, you won't have to. I'll stay safe, I promise."

Pa turned to face him. He brushed a hand over his face. "Son, that's a promise you can't make." He stepped closer. "We can only promise to commit ourselves to the Lord, and trust Him to guard all our steps. And do our utmost to defeat the enemy with our wits and our rifles wherever we find him. Agreed?"

Wilhelm nodded, not trusting himself to speak as he swallowed his constricted throat.

"Now, where did you leave those horses? I hope they haven't wandered off. Otherwise, we have a long walk home."

Jimmy

**Durban, South Africa
Sunday 12 April 2015**

Jimmy flopped into his seat. "Of all the days we have to be up with the birds."

"What?" Sarah turned from looking out of the coach window. Dark sunglasses hid the puffy eyes of their argument.

His explosion, more like. Where had that aggression lurked all these years? He hadn't physically punched her, but his words left their mark as clearly as any fist. They'd sat on the balcony until long after midnight, the sporadic beam of the lighthouse illuminating her tears, probing his pain. Words exhausted and emotions depleted, they'd retreated to bed, Sarah curled on her side. Away from him.

He listened to her jagged breathing, wishing for the courage to reach out and draw her to him, until the waking day shimmered over the ocean.

"The early start, that's all. I'd have liked a bit of space this morning..."

"We'll be fine. At least we both know how you feel. We can work with that." Sarah reached for his hand, pressing her palm against his. His fingers curled over hers.

"Thank you. And I'm sorry. I —"

"Oo, look at the lovebirds again. Second honeymoon, is it? Not missing the kids then, Sar?" Des poked his head through the seats, a toothy grin flashing his amusement. A waft of aftershave accompanied him. Yesterday's despair cleansed.

"Mind your own business, Des. Haven't you got a phone call to make or something? You usually do." Jimmy scrunched a piece of damp tissue from Sarah's lap and pinged it into Des' face. "Goooaaallll."

The smile twisted into a grimace. Teasing eyes flashed in anger.

"Watch it, Jimbo. Or should that be Jumbo? You've enjoyed the steak and chips since we've been here, that's for sure. Not to mention the ice cream..."

"Boys! No, Desmond, I'm not missing the kids. You two squabbling more than makes up for their absence."

"Touché." He reached over the seat and ruffled Jimmy's hair. "Just a bit of morning banter, right, mate?"

"Right." Jimmy jerked out of Des' reach. "Anyway, why are we up at the crack of dawn, only to be sitting here going nowhere? What's the delay?"

"I'm not sure." Sarah kept her hand in his. "Maybe we're waiting for someone."

"I dunno who. Our tour party's all here. Well, in body anyway. Perhaps not in mind." Des chuckled. "Some of us sampled too much of the local brew at last night's match."

Jimmy leant out into the aisle, twisting around to look down the bus. One or two of the party gripped cups of steaming beverages. Kevin Strepley glugged a bottle of water, the liquid spilling from the corners of his mouth. Greying curls framed a sunburnt face in an unruly bedhead mop. Bethany, his wife, winked at Jimmy and giggled. Despite the hour, make-up decorated her eyes and lips. Long silver earrings flashed as she moved her head, her short, dyed-black hair accentuating their gleam.

Jimmy hadn't known the couple before the trip. But a long-haul flight and several coach excursions proved a great way to develop new friendships. Similar in age to him and Sarah, they'd sat at the same table at their first meal in the hotel, and hit it off straight away.

"Hi, Kevin and Bethany." Kevin had extended a hand in welcome.

"Jimmy and Sarah." Jimmy returned the greeting. Calloused fingertips rubbed against his skin. "You play the guitar."

"I do. How did you guess?" Kevin peered at his fingers. "Clever. Do you play?"

"A little. I'm more a drum man myself."

"No way. Where? You in a band?"

Jimmy, absorbed in the conversation, ate his meal without tasting the rich tomato of the pasta sauce, drank a juice without knowing its fruit. Beside him, Sarah seemed as involved in chatting with Bethany. Since that evening, they'd sought each other's company most days, walking together along the beach, grabbing a coffee or lunch at one of the nearby restaurants.

It made a pleasant change from always having Des with them. Although they were friends from childhood, Jimmy hadn't stayed more than a couple of nights away with him. He could understand why Sarah complained he was such hard work. His moods ranged from cloud high to plummeting depths at least once a day. Despite claiming to be desperate for a proper holiday, exhausted to the point of near breakdown, he spent hours tapping at his laptop or fielding calls from clients. And his meticulous personal grooming drove Jimmy mad with impatience. It took longer for Des to be ready than Sarah.

Beyond the Strepleys, the group slumped into seats in varying degrees of wakefulness. Jimmy imagined the alcohol fumes wreathing like smoke around them.

"Oh, someone's coming." Sarah nudged him in the ribs.

He leant forward, peering past Sarah. A blue Citi Golf lurched to a halt, its indicators flashing. Its driver tooted the horn twice, eliciting hungover groans from the occupants at the rear. The passenger door opened and a woman in her mid-twenties bundled out of the car. Her dark hair hung in tight plaits, the ends decorated with red and yellow beads. She wore a red top with an outline of Africa printed in a rainbow of colours on the front. Black jeans, white trainers, and a denim bag slung over her shoulder completed her outfit.

She yanked open the boot and tugged out a cream canvas holdall almost as big as herself. Slamming the door and waving a hurried farewell to her driver, she jogged across to them.

The coach driver waited, taking her bag, and ushering her inside. She burst up the stairs in a riot of clacking beads and laughter.

"Morning, morning! Sorry I'm late everyone. Couldn't find a lift."

A few grunts to her cheery greeting. Jimmy ducked to avoid her glance, embarrassed at her vibrancy so early in the morning and his own sluggish start.

"I'm Thandi. And I'm your guide for the visit to the Battlefields." She beamed at her audience, appearing unfazed at their lack of response. "Once we're on our way — and you're all more awake — I'll give you the rundown on what's in store for the next few days. But for the first part of the journey, I'll be quiet and let you sleep."

Sarah giggled. "She's fun. I'm excited about the trip now."

"Weren't you before?"

"The memorial will be special, of course. But the war stuff? You know history's not my thing. And does it matter to me, a conflict fought over a hundred years ago in a country I've never visited?" She shrugged. "I'm not convinced it does."

Jimmy took a sip of his drink, swallowing his surprise at her comment.

"But Thandi might be just the person to help me appreciate it all."

"You never said anything. When we were planning all this." Jimmy rested the cup on his knee.

"I didn't want to spoil your fun." She patted Jimmy's arm. "I've seen you researching things on the internet. And that book you bought from Amazon before we left. That's not light holiday reading."

"Well, no, it isn't. But Packenham — the author — is an expert."

"As you will be after this. Here's Charlie back."

The bus driver puffed up the steps and into his seat, his blue uniform bulging and straining at the seams with his bulk. Cheerful Charlie, his round features always lit with a smile and crinkled eyes.

"Everyone ready?" Not pausing for a response, the doors swished shut. The engine stuttered into life. Charlie revved the accelerator. The stench of diesel fumes wafted in through the ventilation system.

Jimmy stretched up and closed the fan above them. "I'll open that again later, I think."

With a roar and a final belch of exhaust smoke, the vehicle lurched forward. Half-hearted cheers broke out. The tinny sound of music playing through cheap headphones buzzed from the seat in front.

The driver nosed the coach into the road. A minibus, operating as a taxi, honked its impatience. Waving his hand out of the window, a deep-throated chuckle rumbling, Charlie hauled on the wheel and swung left, out of town.

Jimmy

Road to Ladysmith, South Africa
Sunday 12 April 2015

"We'll take a comfort break in about five minutes." Thandi's voice jerked Jimmy out of his doze. She stood wedged against the panel dividing the passengers from the driver. A lapel mic looped around her ear hovered a few centimetres from her mouth. "But while we get there, let me introduce myself and give you an idea of what you're in for on our tour."

"Welcome, Thandi. We're delighted you're with us." Bethany always seemed to say the right thing at the right time. Must be the teacher in her.

"Thank you. I'm excited to be here." Thandi bent to the seat in front of her. "I'd love to get to know you all, so I want help with names. Here's my list —" she brandished an A4 sheet of paper "— but I need to put faces to it. I'm sending around some stickers and a koki, sorry, felt-tipped pen. Local expression creeping in there. Take a sticker and write your name on it. We'll use those until we reach the hotel. I've got proper lanyards for you all then."

She passed the stack of labels to Sean, the teenager with the headphones. Travelling with his dad, Brian, the lad asserted his independence at every opportunity, refusing to sit with his father whenever possible. Jimmy, thinking it must be lonely to be the only one of his age, chatted to him whenever he got the chance. He was a pleasant kid, smart and relaxed in adult company.

The tap-tap of the music stopped as Sean hit the pause button, then stretched for the stickers. Within a few seconds, he shoved the sheet and a black pen through the gap between the seats.

"Thanks, Sean." Sarah grabbed the page before it fell. Jimmy retrieved the pen.

"You first." He handed Sarah the pen.

She wrote in neat capitals, all the letters the same height. She doodled a flower and butterfly in opposite corners of the page, a tongue of concentration licking her lips.

"Come on, she didn't ask for a work of art."

"Everything I do is a work of art, darling." She pulled off her sticker. It curled up at the edges. She pressed it onto her shirt, patting it in place. "Here you go. Try not to smudge the ink as you write..."

"Thank you, Mam, I'll do my best." Exaggerating the hook of his left hand, frowning in mock concentration, Jimmy scrawled his name. "There. Perfect. Des, on your head, old son."

He tossed the pen behind him. He heard it clatter to the floor, followed by Des' muffled swearing.

"What d'you do that for? Couldn't you pass it like a normal person? Give me the labels. Here." Des waggled his fingers.

"Just making sure you're awake, mate." Jimmy grinned as he passed over the stickers.

"I am, thanks."

"Right, then, so that's your temporary name badges sorted out. At least I hope you have yours before we stop. The front row are taking their time with the task." Thandi laughed. "As I said earlier, I'm Thandi. Thandi Cele. I grew up in a township outside Durban, but was lucky enough to attend a great school. My favourite teacher taught History. And so, my favourite subject became History, too."

"Same with me. Mr. Green was the best. Do you remember him?" Sarah shook her head. "Shh, don't interrupt."

Thandi continued speaking. "With Miss Zondi's help, I got top marks in my final school exams and was awarded a scholarship to study History at university." She paused, flicking a bead in her hair. "I finished my PhD at Oxford in August last year."

The passengers burst into a round of applause, a few whistling their admiration.

"Whoa, no way, Miss Thandi. You're far too young to have achieved so much." Blood rushed up Jimmy's neck and into the tips of his ears at Des' comment. Surely, he wasn't about to sweet talk their tour guide, was he?

"Thanks for the compliment, er, Desmond. But really, I am quite old enough. Ask my husband and kids. They'll tell you exactly how old I am." Thandi smiled, belying her assertion of age.

Jimmy snorted at the put-down. The rules firmly established there, then.

Thandi continued her speech, undaunted by the interruption. "My doctorate centred on the role of indigenous communities in predominantly white, colonialist wars around the world. In particular, here in South Africa. The Anglo-Boer war became my obsession."

"I think you've met your match, darling." Sarah whispered in Jimmy's ear, her hair tickling against his cheek. "She's even more of an expert than you."

"Let's have a quick show of hands. Do any of you know about the area we're visiting?"

Sean's arm shot up, much to Jimmy's surprise. Their conversations gave no clue of any interest in history. Jimmy lifted a tentative hand, while shrinking back in his seat, half-hoping Thandi wouldn't notice him.

Thandi clapped, her bracelets jingling. "That's marvellous. Two here in the front and five or six further along. I look forward to chatting some more with you while we're together. As for the rest of you, I assure you, you won't be bored. In fact, you might just find you'll enjoy yourselves."

Des snorted. "Or maybe not."

Thandi ignored the comment. "Our first visit today is the town of Ladysmith. After being effectively routed out of Dundee by the Boers, the British army under General Yule — the garrison leader, General Penn-Symmons having succumbed to his earlier battle wounds — retreated to Ladysmith. The Boers —" She held up her hands, palms outwards. "No, wait up. I'm getting ahead of myself. You need a bit more background. Make yourselves comfortable, I'm going to tell you a story."

"The year is 1899. Queen Victoria is on the British throne. Chamberlain is her Prime Minister. In South Africa, one Albert Milner is the governor of the British Cape Colony. In the country's north, the

Afrikaner people live in two independent republics — the Orange Free State and the Transvaal Republic. President Steyn leads the Orange Free State; President Paul Kruger, a veteran of the long-ago Great Trek out of the Cape, leads the Transvaal."

Jimmy relaxed against the headrest. Tinted windows shaded the interior of the bus from the brightness of the morning sunshine. Cheerful Charlie crunched through gears as the coach growled up a steep, winding hill. They overtook a lorry laden with crates of what appeared to be cabbages. Cars sped past on their right.

A grassy bank followed one side of the road; trees lined the other. Beyond, the view stretched over miles of undulating hills and deep valleys.

"It's pretty, isn't it?" Sarah craned forward.

"What? Oh, yes, very impressive scenery."

"I loved the beach and everything, but I'm glad to see the countryside, too."

"Me too. Ssh, you must listen to Thandi. She's a fantastic storyteller."

"I am listening. I'm looking at the same time."

"The British, based in the south and here along the eastern coast of Natal, lived in relative peace with the Afrikaners in the north. That is, until diamonds were discovered in Kimberley, a town in what was the Free State, and gold around Johannesburg in the Transvaal Republic. Foreigners poured into the country in search of riches and fame. The Free State welcomed the new arrivals. In contrast, the Transvaal government tolerated the outsiders, or Uitlanders, enjoying the wealth they generated, but denying them any political voice."

"Sounds like a recipe for disaster." All the talk about diamonds and gold and the rights of businessmen seemed to interest Des despite himself. Jimmy peered through the gap in the seats. His friend gave him a thumbs up. "You might be onto something with your nerdy hobby, Jimbo."

Thandi bobbed up and down on her toes. "Yes! That's it exactly. Influential Uitlanders began demanding citizenship rights, including the vote. President Kruger refused. The British amongst them appealed to the government back home to intervene. You may have heard of some of the most prominent campaigners — Cecil Rhodes, Albert Beit? Oh, and do any of you know the book 'Jock of the Bushveld'? A few of you.

It's a cute story about a man and his dog. Anyway, the author, Percy Fitzpatrick, played a major role in — shall we say? — stirring up trouble."

"Really? That's disappointing." Bethany sounded indignant. "I read that to the children at school. I'll think of it in a different light now."

"Yes. Perhaps the most surprising aspect to this war is the significant characters involved who later become prominent on the world stage. As you'll discover." Thandi winked. "Anyway, back to Johannesburg. Albert Milner, rather than mind his own business in the Cape, inserted himself in the argument, spearheading a campaign to take over the independent republics and expand the economic and cultural empire of Britain."

"Bet that went down well." Kevin spoke up. The tour group was warming to their guide.

"Not well at all. To cut a long and complicated explanation short, President Kruger, supported by President Steyn of the Free State, issued an ultimatum to the British government. Its terms would never be accepted, as I suspect President Kruger calculated. And so, the British declared war."

Thandi rummaged in her bag. Retrieving a plastic water bottle, she snapped open the cap, took a couple of sips. "I'll leave it there for now. Keep you in suspense!"

A stab of disappointment surprised Jimmy. Thandi brought to life the detailed account of the war contained in the pages of the Packenham book. It was a good read, packed with information, but slow going. Especially when they were constantly on the move and hustled from one activity to the next. Thandi offered a shortcut to knowledge.

"It's your turn, Jimbo. You can tell us the next bit." Des poked between the seats again.

"Nah, I'm alright thanks, Des. Wouldn't want to show up your ignorance."

Des swatted him on the head. "Boffin, that you are! I wonder where we're stopping? I need another coffee."

Thandi must have overheard. "Almost there, Desmond. You can buy drinks and food — pies and muffins, that kind of thing — at the top of this hill. We'll have lunch in Ladysmith."

Jimmy

Ladysmith, South Africa
Sunday 12 April 2015

"So, Ladysmith?" Jimmy, crumbs cascading onto his lap from the croissant he'd bought for breakfast, was eager to continue the story.

"Give the poor woman a chance to catch her breath." Sarah broke off a piece of the giant muffin she'd chosen. "They chose a lovely place for us to stop, didn't they?"

"Did you notice the mountains in the distance?" Des slurped at his second coffee. The caffeine hit had restored his amiable nature. "I think I saw snow. Or did I imagine that?"

"The wind was pretty bitter. Not what I expected." Jimmy, leaving his jacket behind, had shivered at the drop in temperature. "Different to Durban, that's for certain."

They relapsed into silence, focusing on their 'baked goods', as the shop referred to them. The landscape rose and fell in grass-covered hills. Pockets of water glistened in the hollows, birds floating on the surface or pecking around the edges. Brown cows grazed under leafy trees. In the far distance, away to their left, the purple-grey outline of a range of mountains loomed.

"The Drakensberg." Wiping her hands on a paper serviette, Thandi resumed her storytelling position. "They form a sort of spine up the length of the country. We're staying at the Drakensberg Mountain Hotel in the foothills tonight."

"Now that sounds like a place we could go for a run, Jumbo."

"Maybe." Jimmy brushed at his shorts. A mountain run sounded a bit extreme for the laid-back jog he had in mind.

"Let me tell you about Ladysmith, where we're headed." Paper bags rustled as everyone finished their breakfast, then settled in to listen. The back row, rejuvenated after swallowing a couple of aspirins with their coffees, clapped their encouragement. "With the war declared, Britain needed to appoint a general they could send to lead the troops. They chose General Sir Redvers Buller. A great name, don't you think?

"Anyway, Buller had been in South Africa before, fighting alongside the Boers against an uprising of the natives." Thandi wrinkled her nose as though assailed by a bad smell. "But that's for another day. He knew the land, and he knew the enemy. The one thing he implored the generals already stationed here was not to venture across the Tugela River, where the terrain suited the mobility of the horse-mounted Boers."

The bus passengers sat in rapt silence, the only interruption to Thandi's lecture a cough from somewhere near the back.

"No one took Buller's advice. They pushed forward to Dundee, only to be routed by the Boers in a humiliating defeat from which they retreated to the town of Ladysmith. Ringed by hills, the garrison, led by General White, found itself in the unenviable position of being surrounded by commandos of Boers. A single battle later — known to the British as the Battle of Ladysmith, and to the Boers as the Battle of Modderspruit — and the might of the British army lay under siege." Was that a sneer on Thandi's lips, or did Jimmy imagine it? "With the railway line broken and the telegraph communication lines destroyed, General White had little option but to wait to be relieved."

"Let me guess, by General Buller?" Des sounded like an eager schoolboy wanting to earn extra points from the teacher.

Thandi nodded, grinning. "Yes. The poor man had to shelve all his plans to overcome the Boers in favour of relieving both Ladysmith, and, in the Northern Cape, the diamond town of Kimberley. Where an irate Cecil Rhodes — yes, the same Cecil Rhodes who some argue helped instigate the whole war — demanded he be rescued first."

"And did he? Relieve and rescue Cecil Rhodes?" The seat in front of Jimmy squeaked as Sean leant forward.

"Ah, now you're the boy who always skipped to the back of the book to find out the ending, aren't you?" Thandi held up a hand. "I'm not going to spoil the story by getting ahead of myself, but let's just say by the time Buller landed his troops in Cape Town and Durban, the situation demanded action."

Sean exhaled a loud sigh. His seat sighed in reply as he slumped against his chair.

Jimmy reached over and patted him on the shoulder. "All will be revealed, Sean. It makes the tour more exciting, to watch events unfold in the places they happened. Much better than listening to a lecture or reading a textbook."

Sean's red hair and freckled nose appeared in the gap between the seats. Blue eyes blinked from under pale lashes. "Mum says I'm too impatient, that I don't enjoy the moment." He grinned, revealing teeth encased in wire braces. "And Thandi's right. I did always skip to the end of the book."

The face disappeared.

"That was kind of you, to encourage him like that." Sarah rested her palm on Jimmy's knee. "Getting a bit bored with Packenham, are you?"

"How dare you? It is a work of great scholarly expertise." Jimmy squeezed the hand. Peace restored. "But Thandi is more engaging, I'll give you that. And perhaps it's a teeny bit more interesting to get the potted version with a few sights thrown in..."

Sarah laughed. "Caught you. I noticed you reading with your eyes closed yesterday afternoon. I rescued your precious book from falling to the floor, actually."

Thandi finished the coffee she'd been sipping. "As we drive through the area on our way to Ladysmith, notice the change in the landscape. It'll give you a clue as to General Buller's insistence that the army not venture over the river and into this territory."

Jimmy leant over, wanting to see out of the front window. The distant hills, hazy in the mid-morning sunshine, grew larger, each becoming more distinct, as the coach roared along the motorway. The road cut its way through steep-sided rock formations, pale brown boulders dotted amongst the stunted bushes and small trees.

"Plenty places to hide out and wait in ambush." He pointed out a hollow to Sarah as Cheerful Charlie wrestled the gears up the incline.

"Mm, I'm sure you're right." Her head rested against the window, eyes closed.

A blast of air, as if from an opened oven door, hit Jimmy as he stepped from the coach.

"Phew, it's hot out here." He fanned his face with the paper information sheet Thandi handed out as they pulled into the parking area in the middle of Ladysmith. Heat shimmered from the surface of the car park. Pools of melting tar glistened like puddles of water.

"I'm enjoying it. It's nice to be warm, for a change." Sarah's sunglasses no longer in place to hide her from enquiry, but rather to shield her from the sun's glare. "Not sure I could live with it, mind you. Let's go stand under that tree while we wait."

They moved into the shade. Des bounded down the steps, surveying the scene from behind Top Gun inspired Aviator Ray Bans. His black polo shirt and jeans made Jimmy sweat just to look at.

"Des. Over here." He shuffled over for Des to join them. "Aren't you boiling, all those black clothes?"

"Black skin, black clothes. It's all the same to me, mate." He pulled a handkerchief from his pocket, lifting his sunglasses and wiping it over his face. "Not exactly England though, is it?"

Thandi, hovering midway between the coach and where they stood, took a step towards them. "And remember, this is April. This phase of the war started in October, our spring. Then, the temperatures might range from upper thirties to snowing within a day. Many of the battles we'll discuss were in December and January — the height of the South African summer. Can you imagine the men arriving off the boats in their winter uniforms into this climate?" She chuckled. "I think President Kruger knew exactly what he was doing when he issued his ultimatum in the last months of our winter and the start of yours!"

She clapped her hands, attracting everyone's attention as they grouped beside the bus, faces as red as the Liverpool shirts several of them wore.

"To me, please, everyone. We'll visit the Ladysmith museum in a moment, which you'll be relieved to discover has air-conditioning."

Cheers and sighs of relief. "But first, I want you to look around, get a feel for where you are. We'll talk some more outside the museum's entrance."

She strode away, expecting her charges to follow her without question. They did.

"We're a bit of a sight, aren't we?" Sarah took Jimmy's hand.

"We don't blend in, I'll say that."

Thandi led them around the corner. Dingy shop facades lined the streets on either side; a bed shop, a bank. The 'Mad Price Family Store' intrigued Jimmy, wondering if it was the price or the family deemed mad. Music blared from a speaker on the pavement next to the bed shop.

Pedestrians choked the pavements. Women in bright headscarves, weighed down with shopping bags, their sandals slapping on the concrete as they walked, strolled in groups of two or three. Snatches of conversation floated past, the clicks and consonants of their unfamiliar language fascinating Jimmy. Men in tatty trousers and faded T-shirts, heads exposed to the glaring sunshine, sauntered along. Children darted amongst everyone, Sarah gasping each time one hopped into the road or scurried in front of a car.

"Liverpool will win the league, right?" A young man with Indian features, in a tight-fitting striped shirt and ripped jeans, attached himself to Jimmy and Sarah.

Taking a while to understand his accent, Jimmy frowned. "Oh, the Champions League? Yes, definitely. You a fan?"

The man nodded, a gold-capped tooth glinting in his smile. "Always have been. Steven Gerrard, he's a great player. Not a bad captain, either. Pity his contract ends at the close of the season."

"He is. Had a shocker game last Saturday though. Did you watch it?"

Sarah tugged on his arm. "We're getting left behind." She sounded nervous.

Groups of shoppers filled a growing distance between them and the tour party. Jimmy tried to identify Des, or Kevin and Bethany, but couldn't see them. Even Nick's tall figure had vanished.

"Oh, sorry, mate. Would love to chat, but we'd better catch the others. Don't want to get lost."

"No problem. Nice meeting you."

"Likewise."

Giving a backwards wave to his new friend, Jimmy led Sarah towards their group, weaving between the pedestrians, stepping into the road to pass more quickly. A car hooted, rattling past them in a blast of music. They jumped to the paving, palms slippery with sweat.

"That was close. Didn't they see us, or what?" Jimmy released Sarah's hand.

"We weren't exactly walking where we should be..."

"He could at least have slowed down. Look, there they are. Next to that gun." The pavement widened into a square, edged with raised flower beds. Stubby plants with thick, silver-grey leaves surrounded by one or two taller, spiky trees.

A wheeled cannon stood in the centre, painted white with black trim. Thandi beckoned them over.

"Sarah, Jimmy, I was worried we lost you there for a moment."

"No, sorry, just got chatting. About football." Jimmy shrugged. "What can a man do?"

A few of the group chuckled.

Sean, off to one side, leant against the gun's protruding barrel. "Is this real? Like, used in the war and everything?" Awe tinged his voice.

Jimmy stepped closer, a flutter of excitement tickling in his stomach.

"Yes, Sean. It was located here at Ladysmith. And behind us, this beautiful building is the museum. It's quite something, isn't it?"

A grand entrance portico spanned the front of the dark grey brick-built structure. Decorated brickwork in pale stone criss-crossed the frontage and framed the rectangular windows. Angled lintels mirrored the style of the porch. A magnificent white clock tower, complete with belfry and domed top, rose from the red-tiled roof.

Des whistled. "Wouldn't be out of place near the Liver Building, would it?"

"No, it wouldn't. Built in 1884, it served as a ration post for besieged civilians. The Boers surrounded the town for four months. You can imagine the conditions by the end of that period. Many residents — civilian and army alike — were sick or starving. Or both. And don't forget, this was summer." Thandi pointed up at the cloudless sky. "You'd have days like this, only heavy with humidity. Most afternoons, there'd be a thunderstorm, maybe with hail the size of small rocks. Water was scarce and food in short supply. Add to that regular shelling by the Boers located on the hills surrounding you. And an army general undecided as to the best way forward."

"It sounds awful." Sarah shivered as if a sudden breeze blew over her, despite the air being still and breathless.

"It was. When we go inside, you'll see diary excerpts written by the besieged. It's a lot to take in, but I encourage you to at least read a couple of them. They give a fascinating insight into what people endured. The collection of memorabilia and displays depict daily life here. There's also a section explaining the siege in the context of the wider war. I hope you'll find it as helpful as I do." She beamed at her party. "Oh, and something else of particular interest."

She paused, teasing her audience.

"Yes? What's that then?" Des, fidgeting.

"One regiment caught up in the siege was the Liverpools." She stretched out her arm, encompassing the group. "Your city. There are several diary extracts and pictures inside. Who knows, perhaps you'll hear of someone you or your family know."

Sarah turned to Jimmy. "Your Mam's grandfather? Do you think he was here?"

Jimmy sucked on his lip, trying to remember what he'd heard about Grampy Percy, as Mam called him. He shook his head. "I don't know. Nothing springs to mind. But then, I didn't listen much when Mam talked about him. I saw a photo of him once. Everyone said I look just like him."

"Wouldn't it be fun if we found him here? Maybe we'll discover more about that ornament thing, too."

"I'm going to ask Thandi about it when there's a chance. Perhaps this evening, if we don't find any clues here."

Thandi waved her arm. The excited chatter stopped mid-flow.

"I see that's got you interested." She beckoned towards the museum. "Shall we move on?"

Jimmy

Drakensberg Mountain Resort, South Africa
Monday 13 April 2015

S arah sat on the cane chair on their hotel balcony, the complimentary gown, white and fluffy, draped over her shoulders. A book lay in her lap, her hands resting on its pages. Jimmy clicked open the door, tea sloshing from the cups he carried.

"Here you go." He handed a cup to Sarah. "Do you want one of these rusk biscuit things they left out for us?"

"No, thanks. I'll wait for breakfast. We never seem to stop eating on this tour."

"You're right. It's wonderful." A chunk of rusk sploshed into Jimmy's tea. "Ugh, that'll be all soggy now."

"Sean tells me that's how they eat them here. Dipping them into their hot drinks." Sarah clinked the teaspoon into her saucer. "Though how he found that out, I'm not sure."

"How that boy knows anything is a mystery to me. He's always plugged into his headphones." Jimmy settled into the second chair. "Did you hear him at the museum, chatting with Thandi? He recounted the names of half the generals, and not only the British ones. And he's an expert on weapons and artillery."

"Where did he learn all that? Certainly not at school."

"Brian has a military background or something. I overheard him and Kevin the other day. That's part of the reason he came on the tour. More than the memorial, he said."

"Talking of school, I wonder how the kids are getting on? And your mam?" Sarah cradled her cup between both hands. "It's funny not having them here. I keep thinking it's far too quiet and they must be up to mischief."

"There's certainly more hours in the day without them, somehow." Jimmy tried Sean's method, dunking his rusk. "Mm, that is better, dipping it. Less dry. And we get to finish our full sentences before they interrupt us."

"I miss them, though. Don't you?"

"Of course I do. Maybe we'll be able to phone them later. At least there's only an hour time difference, so we can catch them before bedtime."

They relapsed into silence. Birdsong filled the air, some twittering in the tree overhanging the balcony, others bobbing about on the expanse of lawn below, searching for grubs and worms. A bright, two-toned call rang out louder than the rest.

Beyond the grass, a pathway meandered through shrubs, benches dotted at convenient spots for admiring the view of the mountains circling the valley. The rockface reflected the golden tones of the early morning sunshine, waterfalls glistening like silver ribbons in the crevices. A wisp of cloud decorated the peak.

"It's magnificent, isn't it?" Sarah spoke almost in a whisper.

Jimmy stretched out his legs, absorbing the peace. He inhaled a deep breath laden with the scents of damp grass, wood smoke, and a flowery perfume he couldn't identify. Better than any incense in church. A few lines of a hymn drifted through his memory. 'How great thou art, Lord. How great thou art.'

"Do you think Des is alright?" Sarah's tone was light, but Jimmy recognised the worry in her words.

A cloud flitted across the sun, throwing their seats into sudden shade. Jimmy blinked.

"What do you mean?" He put his cup on the small round table between them. "I thought we weren't to concern ourselves too much with him. Aren't you wanting to distance ourselves from him a bit?"

Sarah abandoned her drink. Jimmy supposed it would be cold. "I thought so. But all this talk of war and casualties and so on…"

Jimmy waited for her to continue.

"He went off by himself today. Did you notice?" Jimmy hadn't. The museum had fascinated him. Travelling through time, he didn't notice anyone else's movements. "I don't think he realised I saw him. There was a display in the corner where the lighting wasn't so good. Did you go in there?"

"That one with the models dressed in uniforms? No, I meant to. But I got distracted with reading everything."

"Mm, I noticed. Anyway, the room was a reconstruction of a field hospital, complete with a model of a medic. With a white apron and a red cross stamped on it. Injured 'soldiers' lay on the floor at his feet, you know, all wrapped in bandages, blood painted on them in lurid splotches. It was gruesome."

Jimmy grimaced in sympathy.

"I think it affected Des. He just stood there, rocking on his heels, staring at it. I walked in to have a look, but he can't have heard me. I wanted to say something. But nothing seemed right." She stroked the page of the book. "I was trying to see if anything in here might help."

Jimmy squinted at her reading material. A Bible. "And did you?" He tried to keep the scepticism from his voice. It was one thing to sing a hymn to yourself; quite another to begin the day with Bible study.

"No, I didn't." She hung her head, her hair curtaining her face. "Megan gave this to me before we left home. She goes to the church down the road from ours. The happy-clappy one."

Jimmy grunted. They'd visited for a couple of services. Special occasions. He'd enjoyed the music, and the preacher spoke well. But the informality put him off.

"We chat over lunch sometimes. She mentions God — Jesus, to be exact — like she knows Him. Not as if He's a character in a story, but a person you meet and talk to, and..." She gazed over at the mountain. "I'm not making sense, am I?"

"No, carry on, I understand. Sort of."

"I love Father O' Brien, and our church. But it's lovely to experience something more. More than following a pattern and saying certain prayers at certain times." Her eyes shone, lit by an internal sunshine. "This Bible. It has easier language than we use. Well, perhaps not easier. More modern, more real, I suppose. She suggested, I should ask Jesus to come and meet me while I read. And, maybe it's my imagination, but I think He has."

She wrinkled her nose, pursing her lips. The shining eyes hid behind half-closed lashes. "You must think I've gone mad. I promised myself I wouldn't go all weird and I have. Haven't I?"

Jimmy leant over and kissed the lips. He chuckled. "No, darling, you could never be weird. Perhaps slightly odd, difficult to understand, a little alien. But weird? No, never."

She swatted him away, laughing. "And you're just rude!" Taking his hand, a serious expression returned. "But back to Des..."

"Sar, you said not to worry about him so much." Her talk about Jesus and the Bible made a kind of sense, and if it meant her attitude to his friend softened, then perhaps it was a good thing. But she'd been so adamant before. And they had their own issues to deal with, if the outburst in Durban was any indication.

"I know, I know. But I might be wrong." She tapped on the Bible with her free hand. "Jesus talks about being released from heavy burdens. There was a woman He healed — I'm sure we've heard the story a hundred times, but I've only now paid attention to it — who was all bent over and twisted. He touched her, and immediately she stood up straight. A burden lifted from her.

"Des is similar to that woman. Not physically, I don't mean. But he's so bent double and twisted on the inside. Isn't he? He carries a weight around with him, everywhere he goes. And nothing he tries will free him from it. Perhaps only Jesus can."

Jimmy swallowed, his throat tight and eyes stinging at her words. He squeezed Sarah's fingers, unable to speak.

Jimmy

Drakensberg Mountain Resort, South Africa
Monday 13 April 2015

Jimmy's stomach rumbled at the smell of fried bacon and sweet pancakes as he walked into the dining room hand in hand with Sarah. A griddle station sizzled and smoked where Brian and Sean waited, plates laden with beans and sausages. Behind the counter, a woman dressed in a starched white chef's jacket click-clacked a metal spatula through a mound of eggs. A tall hat perched on top of her gelled-back hair.

"I heard that, Jimmy. How can you be so hungry? We ate a huge dinner last night."

"That's the problem. Makes my stomach expand, expect more at the next meal."

"Oh, look, there's Kevin and Bethany. There's space at their table. Shall we join them?"

"Sure. Let me collect my first round of breakfast, though."

Sarah patted his tummy, her dimple on full display. "First round? I'll have some juice for now. Can you pour me a glass? Apple if they have it. Or orange. Only not that horrible pink one. What do they call it? Guava?"

"Uh-huh." Focused on the row of silver cloches ranged in front of him, Jimmy released her hand. "Yep, you want guava juice. I'll bring that."

"Never mind, I'll sort myself out. I'll say hi, bagsy our place."

Jimmy wandered along the buffet display, deciding whether to start with fresh fruit and yoghurt, or dive straight into the cooked stuff. A dish of mixed fruit, diced into chunks and swimming in juice, appealed.

He ladled a spoonful into a bowl, careful to avoid the bright red cherries bobbing amongst the apple, melon, and pineapple.

"You missed something, mate." A brown hand plucked a cherry from the dish, plopping it into Jimmy's bowl with a splash.

"Morning, Des. Thanks for that. I really love the cherries. Can't imagine why I didn't fish one out myself." Jimmy scooped out the offending fruit.

"I'll have it then." Des rescued the cherry from Jimmy's spoon, licking his fingers after he swallowed it. "Delicious. Don't know what your problem is."

"Mm. What are you having? Besides my unwanted contributions, that is."

"A strong, black coffee. I'm not much of an early eater." Des sounded gruff, his voice hoarse as though suffering from the scratchy throat at the start of a cold.

Jimmy glanced at him out of the corner of his eye. Droplets of sweat glimmered on his forehead. Red-rimmed eyes looked puffy and swollen. The usually clean-shaven chin sported a rough stubble.

"You alright, mate? Not coming down with something, are you? You don't sound too good." Or look it.

Des laughed at his worries. Alert to Sarah's concerns, Jimmy thought it sounded false, a forced attempt to make light of a turmoil his friend didn't want anyone to see. Or was he imagining things? The guy could be sick.

"Nah. Stayed up too late. Watched a rubbish film on TV." Whiskey fumes carried on his breath as he draped an arm around Jimmy's shoulder. "But thanks for caring. Where's Sarah?"

Jimmy wriggled free. "Over there. With Kevin and Bethany."

"Oh, the saintly duo."

"What? They're not like that. They're great. Why don't you like them?"

"I don't not like them. They're not my kind of people, that's all." Des dropped his arm, sounding huffy. The little boy not getting his own way. Again.

Jimmy bit down on a surge of irritation. "No one is your kind of people, Des." He stepped away from the counter. "I'm going to eat my breakfast. You can join us if you want. Or don't, if you don't."

Jimmy wove through the tables to where Sarah already sat deep in conversation. Des turned, leaving the room.

"Hi, Jimmy. That looks healthy." Kevin half-rose from his seat in greeting.

"Just the starter, Kevin, just the starter." Jimmy pulled back a chair, the wooden legs scraping on the tiled floor. "Sorry, that's a horrible noise. Morning, Bethany. You had anything?"

"Tea and toast. I'm not keen on a fry-up. But your fruit looks good."

"Come with me, Bethany. I haven't seen what's there yet." Jimmy winced as now Sarah's chair scraped. "And I want a glass of *orange* juice." She dug an elbow in his ribs.

The melon was hard and the apples bitter. The yoghurt tasted sour and watery. Des had a way of spoiling things. Jimmy pushed the half-full bowl to one side. A waiter in black trousers, white shirt and a purple waistcoat whisked it away.

"Thanks." Maybe the eggs and bacon were better.

Sarah and Bethany returned, smiling at some joke or other.

"What's so funny?" Des had infected his mood, and he knew he sounded grumpy. Sarah gave him a look, eyebrows raised. "Sorry. Bad starter. What did you get?"

"Waffles." She grinned. "Isn't that naughty first thing in the morning?"

Jimmy inhaled the aromas of toasted vanilla and sugar wafting in his direction as Sarah resumed her place.

"What's with it? Surely not ice cream?"

"No. I was tempted, though. But I've got crispy bacon, banana, and maple syrup." She popped a forkful into her mouth, cheeks bulging. "Want to try some?"

"No, thanks. I saw someone walk past with an omelette the size of a dinner plate. I'll have one of those. Kevin, what you having?"

Kevin shook his head, sipped from a cup of frothy cappuccino. "This is enough for me. I'll pinch a piece of Bethany's fruit. If she'll let me..." He reached over, plucking at a slice of apple.

"Oi, get your own."

About to go in search of his omelette, Thandi's arrival stopped Jimmy before he could make his move.

"Hello, everyone." Her cheery tones silenced the hum of chatter and the clatter of cutlery.

"She's better at controlling her students than any teacher I ever had at school." Jimmy whispered out of the side of his mouth. "You a sergeant-major yourself, Bethany?"

Bethany lifted a serviette to wipe her smile.

Sarah frowned. "Ssh. Thandi might hear you." The frown lines shifted into a grin. "But you're not wrong."

Thandi stood alongside the buffet counter. Today she wore jeans and a lime-green blouse of some floaty material which billowed with the movement of the ceiling fan above her. Dangly earrings swung and clacked each time she moved her head. Clumpy boots completed her outfit.

Were they going hiking? Jimmy breathed a silent groan. He hoped not.

"Sorry to disturb your breakfast. But I wanted to give you a heads-up ready for today." She rummaged in a bag at her feet, retrieving a sheaf of papers, which she placed on the table next to her. "We've got quite a full day ahead. I can't wait to get started."

A ripple of laughter as the group responded to her enthusiasm.

"Once you've finished eating, please bring all your bags here to the reception desk. Cheerful Charlie will load everything onto the bus, and tonight we'll stay in our next hotel." A few groans. "Yes, I know it's lovely here. But it's too far from the sights we're visiting, and I'd rather not waste our time driving back and forth. But don't worry. We'll return for a couple of days of R and R before you leave for Johannesburg, and your flights back home.

"Also, please make sure you have your lanyards — your name badges — with you. If there are other groups out and about today, I don't want to lose any of you to another guide!"

More laughter.

"She really is good at her job, isn't she?" Bethany fiddled with an apple pip.

"Very." Sarah nodded. "We're very lucky to have her with us."

"Our first stop is the town of Colenso. From here, General Buller launched his initial attempt to cross the Tugela and march north towards Ladysmith." She tapped the papers. "I've created a simple map for you, to help you find your bearings and understand the lay of the land.

It's more detailed than anything the British army had at their disposal, believe it or not. As you'll see, the topography presented Buller with a near-impossible challenge..."

"She gets better and better. Leaving us on a cliffhanger, keeping us interested." Kevin nodded his approval.

"Can I ask you to be ready in, say —" Thandi adjusted the watch on her wrist, "— forty-five minutes? We'll meet at the reception area. With your luggage and lanyards. Right?"

Everyone sprang into action as though waking from sleep. Questions and instructions erupted, each voice vying to be heard in the confusion. A queue re-formed around the buffet, last-minute breakfast orders placed, and final choices piled onto plates and into bowls.

Sarah laid her knife and fork across her empty plate. The purple-waistcoated waiter appeared at her elbow, removing the crockery. "That was delicious. But goodness, I'm full now. Jimmy, I'll go to the room, finish packing my things. Are you having more food?"

"Yes, I want that omelette." He stood from the table. "I've put everything of mine in the suitcase. Except my jacket. I'll keep that with me on the coach. It's sunny at the moment, but the weather might change..."

Sarah gave an exaggerated stare out of the window. Leaves hung limp on the trees, undisturbed by even the slightest breeze. Birds flitted across a blue sky devoid of the earlier clouds. Heat shimmered from the concrete path curving around the hotel garden. "Indeed, it might even snow." She patted Jimmy's arm. "Kevin, Bethany, see you in a bit."

Jimmy stowed his jacket on the parcel shelf. The chair wheezed as he sat, settling into the coarse upholstery. Sean's earphones already emitted their metallic tick of music from in front.

Des appeared at the top of the stairs. He paused, glancing along the rows of seats. His eyes flicked over Jimmy. Nodding at someone further behind, he strode up the aisle, coffee cup in hand, aftershave strong enough to cause Jimmy to sneeze following in his wake.

"Bless you." Sarah's automatic response. "Isn't Des sitting with us, then? Have you fallen out or something?"

"I dunno. I didn't think we had." Jimmy refused to twist around and see who Des sat with.

He didn't need to.

"Brian! That seat taken? No? It is now." Des guffawed a false laugh.

"Des can't stand Brian, can he?" Sarah's brow crumpled in a frown.

"No, he can't. He's obviously making a point. For some reason." Jimmy sighed. "He probably didn't like my tone at breakfast. He was going on about the Strepleys, teasing me about them being too nice. You know how he does."

"Mm, I do."

"So, I told him he could join us at breakfast if he wanted to. Or not, if he didn't. I think he left the dining room then." Jimmy shrugged. "Oh well, I can't do much when he's in a mood like that."

"He'll come around. He always does. I keep remembering this is the only time we've been away together for so long. He must be hard to live with. Anyway, here's Thandi. I hope that means we can get going now."

Thandi bounced into the aisle, her smile wide. "Righto, everyone. My History lecturer always began his talks that way. Very English, isn't it? That's all of you, isn't it? Unless one or two of you have decided to stay here by the pool for the next few days? Do a quick check to left and right of you to make sure your partner's still here."

A chuckle rippled through her charges.

The door swished closed behind her. Cheerful Charlie revved the engine and rolled down the hotel drive.

Jimmy relapsed into silence, gazing out at the gum trees and fields speckled with flowers, the bus throwing them from side to side as it navigated the turns and bends of the valley road. His breakfast churned and flipped with more than motion sickness; the minor confrontation with Des and his subsequent snub niggling. Jimmy would end up apologising, as usual, striving to keep the peace between them despite never fully understanding the offence he seemed to have given.

Once, when they were in their thirties, navigating early marriage and young kids, he'd been determined to hold his ground. Wait for Des to blink first. They'd not spoken in a month. Eventually, over beers in the local pub — initiated and paid for by Jimmy — they'd reconciled, albeit in a false, pretend-as-if-nothing-happened way.

"You didn't ask Thandi about the carving last night, did you?" Sarah broke in on Jimmy's uncomfortable memories. "I was disappointed we didn't find anything like it in the museum. Mind you, amongst all those exhibits and reading boards, we could have missed it."

Relieved at the chance to hop off the hamster wheel of his thoughts, Jimmy straightened. He rubbed at the dull ache in his temple. "That's very true. I've never seen so much memorabilia collected together in one place. Very impressive. And no, there didn't seem to be a suitable opportunity to chat to Thandi." He'd decided against taking the carving in to dinner, instead leaving it on the bedside cabinet. "I'd prefer to ask her about it in private, without all the others chipping in with their ideas."

"Without Des, you mean."

"Not only Des. It just feels, well, too personal. You know, part of the family."

Sarah pulled a crumpled sheet of paper from her handbag. Smoothing it on her lap, she pointed along the squiggles and arrows of Thandi's map. "Did you see this? It's very helpful. Look, this is where we're going."

Jimmy leant over. Lines criss-crossed the page. Jagged triangles showed a range of peaks, around which a blue squiggle of river curled.

"Here be dragons, right?" He tapped a finger in the centre of the hills, marked 'Boers'. "So that's Ladysmith, all the way up there. It's far north of the river, isn't it? No wonder Buller was so upset when he heard what had happened."

"It's wonderful to visualise the landscape like this. I'm glad Thandi gave us the maps. I was losing my bearings a bit. I enjoyed the museum, and it was good for background. But I left more confused than when we arrived, to be honest."

"Mm, it was quite heavy, wasn't it?" Jimmy squinted at the small, neat writing. "Colenso. That's where Thandi said we're visiting today. Maybe we'll learn something about the ornament there."

"I overheard Thandi talking to Cheerful Charlie while waiting for you. She said something about taking a bit of a detour to show us where they camped before moving out to Colenso."

"Oh, do you mean Frere? That's here, look." Jimmy pointed at the map. "Not exactly *en route*, that's for sure. I wonder why it's so important?"

"Well, she also went all whispery and secretive. Hinted at a famous prisoner of war capture nearby. Any idea who that was?"

"I might well know..." He tapped the side of his nose with his index finger and winked. "But I won't spoil the surprise for you."

Wilhelm

Chieveley, South Africa
Wednesday 15 November 1899

The locomotive shunted forward, smoke billowing from its funnel. British soldiers stared out of the windows, many with binoculars raised.

"They make it too simple for us." Prinsloo shaded his eyes with his hand. "The train's travelling no faster than a man can ride. We can storm it with ease."

Wilhelm paused in cleaning his rifle. Would anyone respond?

"We should proceed with caution, Frederik." Pa. Of course. "After the victory at Modderspruit, we should be wary of further, unnecessary action. The British are on high alert for any attack by us."

"They don't look on their guard on that train, though." Prinsloo gestured towards where the engine had stopped. "They do the same journey, at the same time, every day. Steam out of Estcourt to just beyond Chieveley station, then back, either all the way to its starting point or stopping in Frere until nightfall."

"Indeed, they do. But how would capturing it be to our advantage?" Pa had a point. They could hardly steal a train and return with it to Pretoria.

"Prisoners, Marthinus. We'll capture those army men and have them interrogated about their plans. Use them as bargaining tools later. Plus, we commandeer whatever weapons and ammunition they have. We are in short enough supply ourselves."

Pa pulled on his beard. "I'm not so sure..."

"Well, General Botha is. We're to lay an ambush first thing tomorrow."

Wilhelm suppressed the cheer rising in his throat. If he showed too much enthusiasm, Pa may deny his participation. Since Commandant-General Joubert's council of war, Pa kept Wilhelm on a short rein. He watched his comings and goings from under drawn eyebrows, waiting by the fire or beside the tents for Wilhelm to return from work parties or reconnaissance rides. He asked questions about his day, frowning if Hendrik Venter had been his companion.

The train whistled, swaying into motion, returning to Chieveley.

Wilhelm fidgeted in his saddle. The train chugged onward, five wagons curling through the grass-covered, rolling Natal hills like a picture in a children's book. The early sunshine glinted on the sheet metal of the armoured carriages.

"Ride, men, ride. We'll meet them as they slow up that incline, below the ridge there." Prinsloo waved his hat in the air, tugged on his horse's reins, and galloped away.

Whooping with delight, Wilhelm dug his heels into Flooi's side. The pony leapt forward, ears pricked and tail swishing, snorting as though echoing her master's contagious excitement. Together, they plunged down the hillside. The scent of fresh-cut grass filled Wilhelm's lungs as horse and rider crushed the spring growth beneath the pounding hooves. A plover flew from her nest on the ground, screeching and dive-bombing their passing.

"Silly place to lay eggs." Wilhelm's shout carried on the wind. He twisted the reins in his left hand, his rifle held at the ready in his right. Pa might speak of death and sacrifice, of blood and war, but Wilhelm had never felt so alive. The hunt for game was often slow and cautious, days spent tracking an animal culminating in a silent stalk on foot through the veld. The hunt for the British — chasing their transport as it steamed, undefended, through the countryside — tingled in excitement down his arms. His breath came in the short, even spurts he practised when running. The hammering of his heart eclipsed all other sounds.

The commando surged toward a rocky outcrop overlooking the railway track. They waited. Appearing around a corner, the train slowed in preparation for the uphill climb to Frere. The sides of the carriage bristled with protruding weapons. So, the British knew of their presence.

"Make way." The line of watchers moved aside as the Boer artillery drivers hauled their guns to the hill's summit. Grunting with effort, jackets discarded, and shirt sleeves rolled up, they shifted the carts into position.

Flooi stamped her hooves, ears pinned back. She tugged on the bridle. "Whoa, girl. Don't get scared on me now." Wilhelm patted her neck as he pulled her steady.

"Come this side of me." Meyer created space for Flooi. "She won't like it when that thing explodes. It's not just the noise; they can't stand the smell either."

"Thanks." Wilhelm nudged between Meyer and Cornelius Grobler. "What about your horse?"

"He's used to it." Wilhelm raised his eyebrows. When had Meyer taken his horse into battle before? "My father's ride at Majuba. He's old, but he's faithful. And he wants revenge against the British for their victory that day."

Wilhelm understood. Pa was involved in that campaign. He didn't speak of it. But the bitterness in his voice if anyone suggested defeat at the hands of the British expressed more than any fireside story.

The train below them paused, as though contemplating its next move. A scurry of activity in one wagon attracted Wilhelm's attention.

"Look, they also have a gun with them." He pointed at the four men, shifting the weapon into position. It aimed in their direction.

"We're well beyond range of that old pea shooter." A soldier bent to light the fuse. "Wait for it."

Wilhelm tightened Flooi's reins as a succession of yellowish-white flashes roared from the Maxim's barrel. The horse bucked and whinnied, but maintained her ground. Further along, the second field gun joined the action, then the third.

The explosion shattered the morning quiet. The figures below scrambled to light their own weapon. Too late. The Boer shells crashed into the advancing train.

"Now!" At Prinsloo's command, Wilhelm slid from Flooi's saddle, then wriggled to the edge of the ridge. The others did likewise. "Fire."

Wilhelm released his first volley. The bullets rained down on the disabled train, pinging off the metal like hail on the tin roofs of farm sheds.

The driver must have opened a valve in the engine as steam billowed from its pistons. The carriages jerked at the sudden movement.

Answering fire blazed from rifles poking through the wagon's loopholes as the British infantry worked to defend their transport as it hurtled down the line, shrouded in smoke from the exploding shells. It raced around the curve of the hill, wheels clanking and screeching.

"The plan is working." Meyer, breathless, stood in his stirrups. "Quick, we need to secure the other embankment."

Jangling the reins and kicking with his heels, he spurred the animal on. "They'll not escape this time."

Wilhelm, slow to react to Meyer's sudden departure, fired a couple of shots before joining everyone in their dash over the hillock and down into the valley beyond.

Under cover of darkness, the commandoes had manoeuvred a large boulder onto the tracks at the point they predicted the train would go at its fastest. The thud of impact and the crunch of twisting metal confirmed they'd chosen the correct location. The first truck, flung from the track, landed on the far embankment, its wheels turning in air. No one emerged from the wreckage.

Behind it, the second carriage continued for another few yards, gathering momentum as it went. It lurched and shook, tipping from the rails and onto its side. Figures crawled from the disabled truck, coughing, or clutching at bleeding injuries. The third wagon careered into the debris, remaining upright but twisting half-on and half-off the track.

The pops and pings of hot metal soured the air. Steam hissed and men groaned. They limped away from the accident. Some ran across the fields, fleeing the scene before they were captured or shot.

After a dazed pause, the soldiers manning the artillery let off three rounds from the top of their open truck. The shells thumped to earth with a spray of dirt and stone, falling several feet short of the watching Boers. Wheels crunched as the Boer counterparts wheeled the Maxim and field guns into new positions. From the opposite hill, the flash and whizz of a third gun sounded. Unable to locate the shell as it descended, Wilhelm cheered at its landing; it hit the barrel of the small British gun, smashing the weapon into pieces.

No time to enjoy the moment.

"Fire!"

Wilhelm swung from Flooi, dropping into the grass in one swift movement. He propped the Mauser on a convenient boulder. Volley after volley peppered the train, some bullets skidding off the armoured plating, others penetrating through its thin protection. The Boers encircled the cowering British on three sides. Their only rescue lay in clearing the line and pushing on to Frere. First, the locomotive needed disentangling from the mangled remains of the front carriages.

Wilhelm halted his firing. A man scuttled out from behind the iron shield of the middle, intact wagon. Bent low, he hurried forward, dodging a stream of bullets cascading around him. As he grew level with the engine, a shell burst overhead. Smoking shards of shrapnel fizzed to the ground. The man ducked for shelter. A second figure jumped from the cab, running, with his hands pressed to his cheek, towards the overturned trucks in front. He dived into a gap, safe from further attack. Not dressed in the usual khaki of the soldiers, Wilhelm guessed he was a civilian forced into driving the train for the British. A flicker of sympathy. At least without the driver, the chance of freedom for everyone else was lessened. Wilhelm's frown creased into a smile.

Fascinated by events unfolding below him, Wilhelm abandoned his post, edging closer to watch the next act in the drama. The man dashed, body low to the ground, to where the driver sheltered in the shadows. They exchanged words; the latter shaking his head, pointing at the wound on his cheeks. The man gripped the driver's arm, seemed to give him a shake. A few moments later, the driver slunk from his hiding place and returned to his cab. He clambered inside.

Wilhelm's heart skipped a beat. They would escape, after all.

The man waved at the reinvigorated civilian. Weaving past twisted metal and splintered wood, dodging in and out to avoid the bullets still firing at him, he reached a company of men sprawled beneath their upturned truck. Another conversation, more hand gestures.

"What's so interesting? You should take a shot. They're so close." Wilhelm jumped at Meyer's approach.

"No bullets left." It was half true; he had only those left in the magazine, his bandolier hanging limp from his shoulders. "Besides, I want to watch what happens. See that man there. He seems to in charge of everyone."

Meyer squinted through the haze of dust and smoke. "I don't think he's in proper uniform, is he? Maybe he's one of the Natal Volunteers. He won't be in command if he is a local." Meyer spat into the grass. "He should fight with us, not the British. Defending his land, not handing it over."

"Uh-huh." Wilhelm wasn't listening. The man in question ran to the rear of the train. He jumped aboard an armoured wagon, more rifles on display. They remained silent.

After a few seconds, he re-emerged onto the track. A flash of musketry illuminated the carriage windows, their aim directed at the field guns on the hillside above.

Wilhelm grabbed his rifle, squeezing the trigger and returning a volley of fire.

"Thought you'd run out of bullets." Meyer shouted above the crack of rifles.

"I had a few left." Wilhelm glanced sideways, grinning.

"The luck's with them. For now. See, shells just went right through their shields, but they're still firing. What's that man of yours doing now?"

"He's trying to clear a way through."

Steam rose as the reinstated driver nudged forward. Releasing the tension from the coupling which bound the sideways wagon from its derailed counterpart, the man preoccupying Wilhelm succeeded in detaching one from the other. With a screeching sound that penetrated through the continued storm of gunfire, the engine reversed, hauling the truck far enough along the line to straighten its position. The man ran to a group of recovering soldiers, urged their help with gesticulating arms. They rocked the carriage back and forth, toppling it off the rails in a cloud of dust and hopeful cheers.

"They're getting away." Wilhelm half-rose to his feet.

Meyer plucked at his jacket, preventing him from racing down the hill. "Wait, Wilhelm. Look. They're not going anywhere. They're still stuck."

The engine chugged on, the line ahead open. But as it reached the derailed wreckage, the fender caught on the corner of the toppled wagon. The driver reversed, paused, accelerated. Would he bump the obstacle out of the way? It didn't budge.

"Let's have some sport." Meyer aimed his rifle. He tossed a pouch of ammunition to Wilhelm. "Here, take a shot at your mystery man."

Ears ringing at the din of hissing steam, the ricochet of bullets off metal, the whizz and thud of shells targeting the stricken locomotive, Wilhelm fired into the chaos. With a tearing of metal, the engine burst free and clattered away. Within moments it reversed, perhaps realising it pulled nothing along with it.

Laughter gurgled in Wilhelm's throat as the comedy unfolded. Injured soldiers struggled into the cab or hung from its sides. Steam billowed. The locomotive lurched along at a walking pace, the uninjured trotting alongside for protection from the continued efforts of the Boer artillery and infantry.

And then the final blow. A shell landed in the path of the straggling convoy. Fire leapt from splinters of shattered wood. Men tumbled from the cab, lying prone in the grass. Those still in possession of weapons dropped to their knees, taking aim in a last desperate attempt against their attackers. But the effort was useless. Too much firepower ranged against them on all sides.

"He's waving his handkerchief. Look. That one at the far end. They're surrendering."

"Hold your fire. Hold your fire."

Wilhelm peered around his rifle. Commandant Prinsloo stepped forward, gesturing for the men to follow him. British bullets continued to skim past Wilhelm's ear like angry insects.

"Are you sure that was a surrender? None of them seem to know about it." Wilhelm ducked. Clods of earth leapt up, inches from his sprawled legs.

"I think they've realised." Meyer's hoarse shout sounded above the racket. "Now what?"

The men below lowered their weapons. At what looked like a signal from one, they rose from their knees and, slinging their rifles over their shoulders, they bolted into the field alongside the line. Escaping.

"Stop them." Commandant Prinsloo, already halfway down the slope, beckoned to his men. "We mustn't let them get away."

Wilhelm screamed with all the breath in his lungs as he hurtled towards the wreckage, his rifle thumping against his thigh. The man he'd been watching, the man coordinating the salvage operation, making his escape. Changing direction, Wilhelm raced off in pursuit.

Ahead of Wilhelm, two Boers in flapping black overcoats made chase.

A backward glance. The man swerved to the left. Caught in a siding with no route out except into the arms of the approaching Boers, he scrambled up the bank. The Boers raised their rifles. Wilhelm kept his distance, fingers wrapping around the cold metal of the Mauser's trigger, should the man make a dash towards him. The man paused, seeming to assess his options. His pursuers fired. The ground danced at the fugitive's feet.

Raising his hands in surrender, he slid down the bank. The Boers continued to point their weapons.

Wilhelm leant on his rifle, curious to understand the exchange passing between the three men. The Englishman, a head taller than his captors, wore a slouch hat similar to Wilhelm's, rather than the helmet common amongst the other British soldiers. His tunic and loose-fitting trousers, tucked into scuffed knee-length boots, gave him the appearance of a local. But his accent as he declared his innocence belied that appearance.

Wilhelm frowned in concentration as the trio approached. The man's words tumbled out in a rush of unfamiliar language. Wilhelm picked up one or two phrases. Something about not being a soldier. And being exempt from capture.

The men on either side shrugged. They escorted the man to the waiting commandant.

"Good day, sir. I am a reporter. With the Morning Post. I should therefore be released as a civilian." The man lifted his chin, glaring at Prinsloo. "My name is Winston Churchill."

Wilhelm

Ladysmith, South Africa
Monday 11 December 1899

"It's not fair." Wilhelm grumbled to anyone who would listen.

"I might as well return to my post office for all the good I'm doing here." Christiaan Meyer agreed.

Following the council of war at Commandant-General Joubert's tent, the idea to advance into Natal developed into a firm plan. A little under half the commando units were instructed to protect the hills overlooking Ladysmith, ensuring the British General White could neither escape nor open his gates to reinforcements. The rest would ride, under the leadership of General Louis Botha, towards the Tugela River and on to Natal. God willing, as everyone added.

The Carolina Commando were to be amongst those remaining at Ladysmith.

"No, no, we should stay. The garrison is a prize we mustn't lose. It is our duty to honour and obey the instructions of our leaders." Jacobus Malan avoided eye contact with Wilhelm.

"You've never shown regard for authority before, Malan." Wilhelm scoffed at the suggestion. "How many lessons did you miss at school, going hunting or fishing rather than sit with your books?"

"I've grown up since then." A blush spread over Malan's tanned face.

"You mean you've grown scared…"

"Wilhelm. Enough." Pa strode from behind a tent. "The generals have ordered us to remain here, so here we shall remain. End of discussion."

Malan beamed, delighting in Pa's intervention.

Wilhelm hid his face, blinking hard, swallowing the humiliation of being rebuked by Pa in front of others.

"I think I'll check on Flooi." He'd walked away, his fists shoved into his pockets. Pa didn't follow.

Finding Flooi tethered with the other horses amongst the trees below the camp, Wilhelm had jumped on her bare back, entwining his fingers in her mane. He needed action, to feel the wind in his hair, to hear the thud of the horse's galloping hooves loud in his ears. Bending low, his cheek pressed to the warm softness of her neck, he'd urged her faster.

They skirted along the edge of the hillside. Ladysmith spread out like a map beneath them. Distant figures scurried across the market square, eyes raised to the sky as though wary of an unexpected bombardment from the Boer guns. On an opposite hill, the remains of the gunnery tower, stark and abandoned after its storming by a party of Boers, scarred the landscape.

Flooi, her hooves skimming the rough surface, caught a foot in a tree root. Her sudden halt catapulted Wilhelm to the ground. The breath whooshed from his lungs. Stars exploded across his vision. Flooi, sweat foaming on her back, tossed her mane and trotted away.

Rolling onto his side, his head swirling from the impact and loss of oxygen, Wilhelm vomited into the grass.

"Alright there, young Wilhelm?" A pair of brown boots swam into view. "I've got your horse, in case you're wondering."

Wilhelm groaned. Pain burst in his ribs.

"Up you get. You're winded, that's all." A hand reached out. "Good job I saw you. Riding like an idiot. And that's coming from me."

Wilhelm grasped the offered hand. Holding his head with the other, he staggered to his feet.

Hendrik Venter grinned.

"What were you thinking? Trying to be sure the British don't kill you by doing it yourself?" Venter released Wilhelm's hand, held out his water bottle. "Here, drink some of this."

Wilhelm sipped at the cool liquid. "Bored. Wanted to get away." His voice croaked.

"Then it's destiny we met." Venter took the water bottle, gulping with noisy swallows. "We're moving on. Being sent to Colenso. The enemy is gathering there for a big assault across the river. They want Ladysmith back."

"Pa said we're staying here. Guarding Ladysmith." Wilhelm sank onto the grass, his legs shaking. Venter dropped next to him.

"That's your commando. Not mine."

"But…"

"Do you want some real action? Or would you rather hang around here, trotting about on that pony of yours?" The words were bitter, angry. "Men shift from unit to unit all the time. I've seen them. They find a cousin or an uncle from a different town, then join with him for a few days. But stay if you want to."

He took a step.

"I need to be going. Have to pack up camp."

"No, wait. I'll come. When do you leave?"

"First light." Venter's eyes glinted with something like triumph. "Don't be late."

Percy

Colenso, South Africa
Thursday 14 December 1899

Percy tugged at the laces of his boot. Encrusted with dried mud, they were glued together into a tight knot. He picked at the worst of the claylike clump, until, with a sigh of relief, the tangle eased. Pulling his foot from the shoe, Percy wriggled his toes, the biggest showing through a hole in the fabric.

"Some darning to do there, old son." Arthur flicked a pebble towards Percy. It missed him by inches.

"I've got blisters on my blisters." Peeling off his sock, Percy inspected his damaged feet. Angry red sores coloured each toe. Blood oozed from his heel. "I didn't know we signed up to walk across Africa."

Miller's intelligence proved correct. Again. They'd broken camp in the mist of early morning. Although only twenty or so miles to Colenso, the trek from Frere had taken two days. Lumbering ox wagons, led by native drivers, carried the baggage, tents and provisions. Becoming stuck in the rain-softened terrain, the soldiers paused their march to help dig the wheels free of mud, or push the laden carts out of a ditch or over a hillock. Those not engaged in helping with the supplies were sent ahead on reconnaissance missions.

Percy joined Major Elliott's map team, spending his days clambering over rocks and reporting on the view seen through a pair of binoculars. He measured distances between bends in the river or from a grove of trees to the next. Bonnie trotted alongside him, learning to heed his commands of "stay" or "lie down" through rewards of pilfered bully beef, wrapped in a scrap of paper from Mickey's notepad and kept in Percy's pockets for obedience training.

Occasional shots fired from the Boer side sent the team scurrying for cover under scrubby bushes or cowering behind boulders. His hands caught against thorns or pieces of dagger-sharp rock, leaving his fingertips and knuckles scratched and bleeding. Worried he wouldn't be able to wield his rifle and shoot when needed, he'd discharged himself from the surveyor's team, returning to the mundane task of trekking alongside the wagons, with some regret.

"Walking in a heatwave at that." Arthur's tunic flapped open, the vest underneath untucked from his trousers. "Pass me that water, won't you? I'm parched."

Percy tossed the bottle over, the liquid sloshing about inside. He went to work on his other boot. Bonnie raised her head as though contemplating whether to chase after the bottle. Her tail flicked in the dust, but she shifted her front paws and settled her chin between them.

Arthur gulped at the drink. "Ah, that's better." He wiped his mouth with the back of his hand, discarding the empty canteen in the grass. Its lid rolled against a stone. "Old Buller's as mad as blazes about that train being blown up last month. You know, while out on patrol?"

"I heard about that. Wasn't that reporter chap on board? The one who was on the Dunottar with us. Son of a Lord, or something."

"Winston Churchill. Silly fool, tried to help clear the line, and ended up getting himself carted off to Pretoria for his troubles. Anyway, Buller wants to press on with pushing to Ladysmith, stop any more of that kind of thing happening again. I hear there'll be action tomorrow. Or maybe even tonight.

"How do you know that, then? You've been with the same people I have, and I've not heard any rumours like that." Percy examined his second foot. It looked worse than the first.

Arthur tapped the side of his nose, winking. "I have my sources, PP." He laughed. "Miller again. Who do you think? Bumped into him earlier in the mess tent. He knows more than the generals about what's going on, I tell you."

"True." Percy stretched for the water. "Oh, you finished it. Thanks."

"Sorry. Mine's on my bed. You can have that." Arthur made no move to fetch it. "I reckon Miller is a spy. He sneaks around gathering information, picking up snippets here and there."

"And who does he report to, then?" Percy scoffed at the idea. "Hardly to Brother Boer. They'd shoot him before he got close enough to speak to them."

"Maybe he's an informant for Buller. Tells him what the other officers are thinking and planning. Then passes their ideas to Sir Redvers so he can claim the credit for a successful scheme. And deny all knowledge if it goes wrong."

"You talk rot, Arthur." Percy hobbled off in search of a drink. He winced as he stubbed his damaged toe against a stone. "Ow. Do you see these Africans? They walk everywhere in bare feet. I don't know how they do it. Must have skin like leather."

Percy leant against a tent pole, waiting for his vision to adjust to the relative gloom inside. Four cots filled the space, bedding rolls at the foot of each. Kit bags, propped against the metal bed frames, awaited their owners. A sketch pad lay open on one cot. Mickey's bed. He'd dashed off somewhere almost as soon as they'd returned to camp after the day's field training and reconnaissance. Percy would question him later as to his whereabouts.

The smell of damp canvas and sweaty clothes hung in the stuffy air. A fly buzzed near the roof. Percy searched for Arthur's water bottle in vain. Bending down to check the floor, he found it discarded, lid off, under Alfie's cot. Empty.

Percy flung the canteen aside. It bounced along the rutted ground, ending up in the far corner. Anger burned his dry throat. Alfie's rudeness, his disdain for his tent mates, was one thing; the petty theft of belongings — whether water, or food rations, or socks — was intolerable. Would he take their bullets when in battle, exposing his fellows to unarmed danger against the enemy? Would he even remain at his post, or would he slink away, like he did during training manoeuvres or during camp set-up and break-down?

He hadn't mentioned anything to the others, hoping they didn't pay too much attention to pieces of missing kit. Perhaps Alfie would change as they approached the Front, as they fought Brother Boer rather than practise for war. But his pilfering grew worse; Percy found his pocketknife amongst a pile of Alfie's clothing the day before. It had to stop. Resolving to discuss the matter with Arthur while anger usurped caution, Percy backed out of the tent.

A scuffle of feet and the authoritative voice of Colonel Blomfield stopped Percy in his tracks, all thoughts of confrontation with Alfie vanished from his mind.

"As you were, men, at ease..." This could mean a confrontation of another kind was in the offing.

Percy stepped from the tent. Soldiers in various stages of relaxed undress surrounded the colonel. A quizzical glance at Arthur received a shrug. Blomfield stood in full uniform; his expression shaded by the peak of his helmet. His thick, dark moustache curled upwards, waxed in place.

"Our orders are in." A cheer erupted from the men, all bored with preparations, itching to commence the real fun of battle.

"About time." Crosby lounged against a tree on the other side of the tents. Shirtless, his trousers rolled up to expose white ankles and dark, hairy legs. He flicked the stub of a cigarette into the grass. "Thought we'd never get a chance for more than target practice. Maybe we'll have a war after all."

Blomfield scowled in his direction. He may favour informality, but Percy guessed he still expected his position of Officer Commanding to be marked with respect, a certain etiquette.

"We're to begin active engagement with the enemy. Starting tonight."

Tonight? Percy clutched at the tent pole as a wave of dizziness washed over him.

Blomfield paced up and down, his hands clasped behind him. The officer instructing his subordinates. "General Buller has outlined his proposal to establish a lodgement on a portion of land in the curve of the river. Once the ground is secured, troops will take up position opposite the Boer camp, so protecting the rear — the supply wagons and so on — as they cross the river into enemy territory." The plan sounded simple enough. Percy wondered if there was a catch. "We will then march north, straight up to Ladysmith, and so relieve the garrison who've got themselves into a spot of bother, by all accounts."

Laughter. A ribald joke at the expense of the regiments holed up in a town everyone was sure should have been easy to defend. Percy cringed.

He'd missed out on signing up to volunteer with the Liverpools, unable to travel home from Salford in time to enlist. But for a boss too stubborn to allow Percy to quit before he finished a job, he would be amongst those currently sitting out the war in the besieged garrison.

"There are two possible locations for an attack against the Boers. Deliberations are continuing as to which is best. Once I'm informed of the detailed strategy, I'll return and issue final instructions before leading you into battle." Blomfield halted his pacing. He removed the helmet, taking a handkerchief from his pocket and wiping his forehead. "Men, prepare well for the fight ahead. Ensure your weapons are in good working order and your bullet and ration bags packed. Full water bottles are essential. The guns are the first to leave at midnight, regardless of the exact plan of engagement. They will provide us with sufficient cover to advance over the drift — the ford — whichever one that turns out to be."

He replaced his helmet, snapping the strap under his chin. He balled the handkerchief in his fist. The men shuffled about, getting to their feet, or doing up the buttons on their tunics. Conversations broke out between them as they discussed the plan for today and on into tomorrow.

A swirling breeze lifted the dust at Percy's feet. He coughed as it billowed up and caught in his throat. He realised he still hadn't had a drink. Remembering the discarded, empty water bottle, he scanned the groups of men until he found Alfie surrounded by his gang. He watched Percy looking at him and winked. Folding his thumb and fingers into a pistol shape, he mimed taking aim and shooting at Percy. Blowing the barrel of his imaginary weapon, he winked at his mates, head thrown back in laughter.

Percy turned away, crimson shame spreading up his neck and across his cheeks, his ears burning.

Colonel Blomfield clicked his heels to attention. The men hurried to salute before he gave a departing nod, striding away toward Buller's tented headquarters.

They remained beside the campfires until long after sunset, speculating about the orders they waited for.

"They hadn't intended us to cross here at Colenso. Old Buller preferred somewhere further north. Potgieters, I heard them call it." Crosby sounded certain.

"He's right." Miller, rejoining them for the evening meal, spoke in low tones, his voice not carrying beyond the immediate circle of Percy's group. "There was bad news from the Cape. Battles gone wrong, men captured or killed. Buller's regiment is the only mobile company left in Natal. And Potgieters runs too far from the railway line. So, if there's heavy fighting, he'd be hard pressed to call for reinforcements, or even communicate his position."

Arthur twirled his moustache. "Sounds reasonable. But this place? Colenso. Aren't we in line with the Boer positions here?"

"They believe so, but can't be certain. Brother Boer keeps himself well hidden."

Percy chewed the stub of pencil he held poised over a sheet of notepaper. He wanted to write to Flo before experiencing his first major battle, but the flickering firelight, the swirling questions about tomorrow's advance, the doubt and uncertainty clouding his thoughts, prevented the words from flowing. The couple of sentences he'd managed sounded stilted and unreal. He scrubbed a line through them.

Dearest Flo

He started again.

He got no further. Colonel Blomfield appeared from the shadows. Percy hastened to his feet, his pulse quickening. He raised his chin, holding his arms to stiff attention at his side. The others scrambled to do likewise. Alfie squeezed the tip of a burning cigarette between a finger and thumb, his hand shaking as he tucked the extinguished smoke behind his ear.

"Saving it for later, PP." His eyes darted from side to side, a few beads of sweat glistening in his moustache. Afraid?

"Men, we march at first light. The cavalry are to precede us, leaving at midnight sharp. One party, under the command of General Burn-Murdoch, will secure our left flank; Colonel Lord Dundonald's mounted infantry and local irregulars are to take to the right." He paused. "Our mission is to ford the Tugela River at points south of here, where, it is believed, the river's flow has sufficiently abated for us to proceed. The artillery will prepare our approach with an early bombardment, and cover us as we advance."

The clink and rattle of bridles, the snort and snuffle of horses, disturbed the usual night sounds of wind rustling in the trees, or men snoring under canvas. Percy peered at his watch; the light too dim to discern the time. But he could guess. Midnight.

Time for the cavalry brigades and mounted infantry to ride out to their positions.

"Now for some fun, boys."

"It'll all be over before these sleeping beauties wake up and start with the day."

Bonnie growled from outside the tent's entrance. Footsteps shuffled past.

Percy rolled onto his side. He wasn't much of a sleeping beauty. The belt buckle of his trousers dug into his waist. Fully clothed, he would be ready at sunrise to assemble on the square patch in front of the tents, and march with the other infantry brigades into who knew what?

He closed his eyes, willing his muscles to relax and his thoughts to quieten. He tried to recite a psalm, the one Flo loved, about shepherds and green pastures. But whenever he reached the part about quiet waters, his mind lurched to images of a river, hurtling between gouged-out rock walls on either side. He saw the twisted remains of a metal bridge, observed on an earlier reconnaissance trip. How would they ever get across? And where were the Boers?

Wilhelm

Colenso, South Africa
Thursday 14 December 1899

Wilhelm leant on his spade, pausing for breath. The grunts of men digging, the ting of metal as it hit stone, continued around him. A slight breeze disturbed the knee-high grasses along the riverbank, passing over the vegetation like a ripple of water.

"Do you really think we're hidden from the British?" He looked at the steep sides of the trench cut into the fertile sides of the bank. Behind him, the enlisted teams of natives raked the dug-out soil away, dispersing it amongst the grasses and bushes.

"We won't be if you stand there chatting." Venter stretched, massaging the small of his back. "We've got the low walls to build up with stones next."

Glugging a cupful of water from a nearby bucket, Wilhelm returned to his task. Jumping in beside Venter, he shovelled at the ground beneath his feet. Bending backwards, the angle awkward in the confined space, he flung the spadeful of dirt over the lip of the trench. Half of it rained back down, showering them both with pebbles and grit.

"Hey, watch it. Maybe you're better up top, spreading this muck around. You're good at that." Venter wiped his face with his hand. Smudges of dirt mingled with the sweat dripping from his hairline.

Wilhelm laughed. He flicked a clump of earth at Venter. It hit him on the cheek.

"Why did I think it was a good idea to bring you along? You're such a child." Venter bent, rolling damp soil between his fingers to form a ball. He swung his arm upward, releasing the mud ball so it collided with Wilhelm's shoulder. "Got you!"

"Now who's the child?"

A head appeared over the trench. The supervising Field-Cornet of the Standerton Commando. "What's going on here? You're building an ark, a lifesaver for you and your comrades, not playing in a sandpit like children."

"Yes, sir." Wilhelm glared at Venter.

"Yes, Olivier, this is a serious business. No more messing around." Venter shook his head in mock disapproval.

The Field-Cornet disappeared, admonishing another wayward labourer. "No, no, not over there. He'll have your hat off with your head still in it, if you entrench there."

Wilhelm and Venter finished digging in silence.

The muscles in his shoulders aching and hands blistered, Wilhelm sprawled on the grass, fanning himself with his hat. The sun shimmered in a clear blue sky. A buzzard wheeled overhead, rising and dipping on the thermals above the river.

"No time to rest." The returned Field-Cornet prodded him with his foot. "Get the sangars in place and scope your field of fire. General Botha believes the attack will happen tomorrow."

"Tomorrow?" Venter rose, his voice excited. "Do we know where they'll try to cross?"

"There's a fordable drift to the west of the town where they're stationed. And, of course, we left the old wagon bridge intact. Perhaps they'll be unwise and attempt to cross there." The Field-Cornet shrugged. "We'll see soon enough, I suppose. But in the meantime, your defences won't build themselves..."

Wilhelm knocked the last stone into place. He patted its rough surface before jumping over to examine his handiwork. He wandered down the riverbank, pulling at clumps of reeds, collecting fallen branches and twigs. Arms full, he retraced his steps. Dumping the vegetation on the ground, he stepped back a pace or two. Head tilted, he scanned the wall for any exposed areas. The left end of the trench seemed well hidden; an overhanging tree branch cast a dappled shape, camouflaging the packed stones. The right needed work.

Shoving reeds into the gaps between the boulders, Wilhelm did his best to blend the stones in with the long grass. He laced twigs and branches across the stonework, pushing more greenery in amongst the damp wood.

"Now, to test you out."

Ducking behind the sangar, he rested his right arm on the low wall as though it were the barrel of his rifle.

"Can you see me?" He lifted his head, checking that Venter was looking.

"Well, I can when you do that. Keep your head down." The grass twitched. "That's better."

"The problem is, I can't see to aim. Everything is in my line of sight." Wilhelm sat up. "Locating the bank of the river is hard enough, never mind anything moving on the other side."

"I don't think you need worry. If the British enter the loop, they'll be packed in so tightly, you won't need to aim. You'll hit something — someone — for certain."

"I hope so." Wilhelm wiped dirty palms on his trousers, ignoring the sick feeling stirring in his stomach. Perhaps it would be better, not seeing the enemy's eyes as he released his shot.

"We're being mustered to the hilltop over there." Venter pointed. "They're building a decoy gun post. We need to help, make sure it's finished by nightfall."

Audible hunger grumbles shouted Wilhelm's reluctance to continue working. He had hoped they'd be returning to base, a pot of stew bubbling on the fire and waiting to be enjoyed. He dug in his pocket, retrieving a chunk of dried beef he'd saved from the morning. Chewing, he collected his jacket, rifle and water bottle and followed in Venter's wake.

They tramped through the grass, sticky burrs attaching themselves to trousers and boots. Wilhelm wished he could ride Flooi across the floodplain and up the hill, but the horses were left at camp, under the care of the wagon drivers. A path criss-crossed the fields, broadening into a wider track as it snaked behind some trees.

The sun dipped in the sky, shadows lengthening as Wilhelm and Hendrik crested the hilltop. Swallows flitted overhead in search of insects. In front of them, men busied themselves with the final touches on the gun emplacement General Botha had ordered they build.

"Surely they won't fall for this, will they?" A mule dragged a felled tree trunk across to the structure. Wilhelm's eyes widened. "Is that supposed to be the gun?"

"Yes, it is. Help us manoeuvre it into position." A broad-shouldered man, dark beard speckled with grey, ordered Wilhelm over.

His back muscles already stiff and sore from the hours of trench-digging, Wilhelm bit his lip to suppress a groan as he strained under the weight of the log. Knees bent, he shuffled alongside the team of six as they worked the tree through a hole in the wooden structure of the gun tower.

"Steady. Lift it higher on this side." Grunts and a splintering sound as they wedged the 'gun' in place.

"It needs wheels. If they look through binoculars, they'll expect to see the gun carriage." Venter drew a round shape in the air with his hands.

"And what do you suggest we use for those?" The bearded man leant against the trunk.

"Don't you have any damaged wheels from the mule carts?" Venter looked around as though two sets of wheels would magically present themselves.

Bearded Man scowled. "We don't. We take care of our belongings…"

"What about these?" Wilhelm held up the discarded branches. "We can just prop them up, maybe tie them together so they look like spokes."

Bearded Man folded his arms across his chest. "I'm not sure even the British are that easily fooled."

"But we might as well try." Venter hurried over to Wilhelm, grabbing the sticks. Frowning with concentration, he twisted the twigs around in a rough circle, their stems bending and cracking under the pressure from his fingers. "There. What do you think?"

Wilhelm held the wheel aloft. "It's perfect." He propped the decoy wheel next to the trunk while Venter worked on one for the other side. "Where did you learn to do that?"

"My grandfather was a woodsman. He taught me all kinds of things. How to prepare the wood for carving, the best knives to work with. Most of which I've forgotten." He bounced the second wheel along the ground, ducking under the log. "There. They'll never suspect it's not real." He dusted his hands together.

Bearded Man acknowledged his efforts with a brief salute. "That's it until morning." He sauntered over to the others, packing away their belongings and preparing for the trek to camp.

Wilhelm wandered in the opposite direction. The valley stretched out below him, Boer territory forming a triangle between the rocky hills and kopjes on one side, and the winding river looping back on itself as it meandered through the landscape. He traced the series of trenches spread the length of the bank, hard to identify from the lush vegetation of the water's edge.

A dark smudge painted the distant horizon, smoke drifting upwards in the still air of evening. The British camp.

A footstep crunched on the shale beside him. Venter, puffing on a cigarette.

"What do we do now?" Wilhelm's question was almost a whisper.

"We wait, young Wilhelm. We wait for the British to come."

Jimmy

Colenso, South Africa
Monday 13 April 2015

"G eneral Buller faced a dilemma."

Thandi stood on a small incline in the road, her group gathered around her like a brood of fussing chicks.

"Shh, I'm trying to hear." Jimmy frowned at the chatter. He took a step closer to Thandi.

"How would he cross the river from Colenso into Boer territory? General Botha had dynamited the railway bridge spanning the gorge." Thandi indicated further upstream. "Where we're standing was the only recognisable crossing intact. But could it be a trap?"

"They could wade across. It's hardly deep, is it?" Des leant on the railings, peering at the water below.

He had a point. Trees crowded both banks, their branches dipping into the water. Long grasses and a tangle of flowers, delicate white butterflies flitting amongst them, grew along the water's edge. The river flowed in a sluggish, lazy stream. It looked an ideal spot for a picnic rather than an impassable raging torrent.

"That's how it is now, I agree. But all this vegetation is recent. Although the topography of the area is the same as back then, the landscape and overall appearance aren't. You'll see why that's important as we continue.

"Anyway, so Buller had limited options. Do you have your maps with you?"

Sarah waved hers aloft. Sean and a few others did likewise.

"Good. Perhaps you can gather around those with maps. It will help you understand Buller's predicament, give some insight into why he chose the routes he did." Clusters formed around the organised few with their maps. Jimmy strained to see. He saw a few squiggles, but the text was too small. He'd check on his own later. "You'll see four possible crossing points marked. You'll also see the way the river twists and turns around Colenso, rather than flowing in a straight line through it."

A few "uh-huhs" and nods of acknowledgment.

"We're at the point marked Old Wagon Bridge. Before returning to the bus, be sure to read the engraving on the wall over there. The bridge has been here since 1879. Buller and his scouts knew of its existence. What they didn't know was if the Boers had booby-trapped it with explosives, ready to detonate when assured of the most casualties.

"So much for the bridge. Now, trace along to the left. There are a couple of drifts — fords. These presented viable crossing places. The problem was, no one had been able to assess conditions. Was it in flood after the recent rains? Where could they erect the pontoon bridges needed for the supply wagons to cross, without being exposed to the Boers? And, more pertinent, where were the Boers?"

The question hung in the air. A teacher prompting her pupils to think beyond the obvious.

Sean raised a hand. More familiar with the expected response than his elders. "Um, the map says here, on the right. On the other side of the river. I think those are hills, aren't they?"

"Yes, you're correct. They're the hills you may have noticed on the drive down from Ladysmith." Thandi beamed at her star student. Jimmy felt a twist of disappointment that it wasn't him. "But Buller and his aides didn't have the knowledge we do; he couldn't be certain of General Botha's whereabouts. Nor of their numbers. This area was uncharted territory. There were a few maps, drawn up by the land registry, but these were deemed incomplete at best, and inaccurate at worst."

Ah, Sean hadn't thought of that. He hung his head, ears burning red. Jimmy folded his arms, torn between feeling sorry for the boy and smug that he didn't have all the answers after all.

"Some of his officers suggested they first take the heights on the east. Hlangwane Hill. From there, they would have a view over the whole plain, and so direct the action. Buller agreed in part, sending a cavalry detachment there. But he kept his main forces centred around the village of Colenso.

"So, where did Buller cross?" Des, impatient to get to the point. As always.

"He decided on two locations, protected on each side by his cavalry. He sent one company, the Irish regiment under the command of Major-General Hart, towards the Bridle Drift. It's beyond Colenso on your maps, a little further downriver. The second company he despatched to cross right here, at this bridge. General Long's artillery force would support an advance of infantry troops, led by Colonel Hildyard."

"And did it work?" Sean, eager to earn favour with the teacher once more.

"Not exactly." Thandi's expression changed, her lips pressed together in a thin line of pink lipstick.

Intrigued, Jimmy hoped she would continue.

The smile returned. "But I'll show you that at the next stop. I'll give you five minutes to wander around here, take a few pictures, then I'd like you back on the bus."

The party milled around in small groups. The smokers all collected a discreet distance apart, sharing lighters and matches as they dragged on their cigarettes. Des held court, waving his arms in authoritative gestures while pulling smoke into his lungs. A roar of laughter as he told a joke.

"...Jumbo..."

Jimmy hurried away, his ears burning.

Sarah, Kevin, Bethany, a few others gathered at the far end of the bridge. Sean squatted in front of them.

"It's the plaque, darling. It's quite hard to read though, so Sean here's helping with his young eyes."

Another slight. Jimmy frowned. His eyes could read words carved into an old stone.

THIS BRIDGE
EREC... ... ... COST OF
19 000 POUNDS
WAS OPENED FOR PUBLIC TRAFFIC
AND NAMED
THE BULWER BRIDGE

ON THE 3RD DAY OF
OCTOBER 1879

Sean read out the inscription before Jimmy finished deciphering the first two lines.

Brian snatched a photo of Sean pointing at the inscription stone. The boy kept his eyes fixed on the ground, not looking into the camera.

"Smile, Sean. You're on a trip of a lifetime." Jimmy squeezed Sarah's hand, acknowledging her gift to speak gentle encouragement to those he would have snapped at in his irritation. The boy should show some gratitude to his father for bringing him to South Africa.

Sean lifted his face. He gave a lopsided smile at the camera, tousled hair falling into his shy eyes. Brian retook the photograph, stepping forward to show Sean the image in the camera's small screen.

Jimmy tugged Sarah to one side. "That was kind of you."

"Not really." Sarah tucked her arm into Jimmy's. "He's like how I imagine Tom could be one day. Full of enthusiasm, but in need of someone noticing him."

"Brian notices Sean." Jimmy paused in his protestations. "Are you saying I don't notice Tom?"

"No, silly, that's not what I'm saying at all. Quite the contrary, actually. Tom won't be like that because we — you — do notice him. He's very lucky." She gave his arm a squeeze. "Isn't this place amazing?" Sarah fell silent. She leant against the balustrade, staring down at the water. "You can just imagine them, can't you?"

Jimmy glanced at the stream, keeping an eye on the rest of the group. Several already hovered beside the coach, waiting to clamber back on. "Imagine who?"

"The soldiers. General Buller and his men. Marching across this bridge. Hearts in their mouths, not knowing where the enemy would shoot from. Boots thudding on the stones. The mighty Tugela racing underneath."

"Sweltering to death in the heat. Plagued by flies. Eaten alive by mosquitoes..." Jimmy swatted an insect as it landed on his forearm.

Sarah pushed off the parapet, her mouth twisted somewhere between a frown and a laugh. "You know how to spoil the moment, don't you?"

"Just being realistic, that's all. Come on, let's go. Everyone will be waiting for us."

Jimmy

Colenso, South Africa
Monday 13 April 2015

The bus crept along the track, twigs and branches scraping the sides. Charlie looked less than cheerful.

Jimmy held on to the headrest of the seat in front, pushing himself back into his seat as they lurched and bumped through potholes and over boulders.

"We could have walked down here in less time." Des raised his voice against the strain of the engine. There was a thump on the window. "Ouch. My head. I'd have kept myself free from breaking my neck, too."

"And died of heat exhaustion." Jimmy braced against another jolt. "It's not getting any cooler out there. Or hadn't you noticed?"

"Too busy concentrating on not falling out of my seat, mate."

"Almost there, everyone." Thandi shouted in snatched bursts, pausing each time Charlie braked or hauled on the steering wheel. "Sorry...state of the road...heavy rain a few weeks back...lots of damage."

"Road? Is that what they call it? Donkey track more like." Des grumbled in a not-so-quiet voice.

Jimmy breathed through flared nostrils. "If he doesn't stop going on..."

Sarah touched a restraining hand on Jimmy's arm. "Leave it. He'll be fine. All this shaking probably isn't doing that hangover much good."

Jimmy suppressed the chuckle gurgling in his throat. "No, it wouldn't."

"Aren't the views spectacular? Much nicer than in the town or around Ladysmith."

Farmland stretched on either side of the track, a tall, dark green crop growing in neat rows. Maize? Cows grazed in the other fields, standing in groups, or lying in the shade of trees. Growing along the fence-line, a mass of pink and white flowers bobbed slender necks in the draught of the passing vehicle.

Glimpses of the river sparkled in the mid-afternoon sunshine, willows draping their branches like delicate curtains. The cool, unreachable scene stifled Jimmy, unable to breathe in the stuffiness of the bus. He reached up and fiddled with the air vents. Hot air blasted down on him. He clicked the vents closed.

Beyond the farmland and the river, hills rolled over one another in waves of tree-covered grassland, dotted with rocks and boulders in shades of browns and yellows.

"I wonder where exactly we are. It feels like we're in the middle of nowhere, doesn't it? I don't recognise anything from the map."

"I'm sure Thandi will tell us as soon as she can. Oh, that looks like a clearing up ahead. Maybe we're stopping there."

They did. With a sigh of brakes, Charlie returned to his usual cheerful self. The doors whooshed open. Overheated air rushed into the bus's interior.

Thandi stood, turning to face everyone. She gave them a wobbly smile. "Well, that was quite the trip. I'm sure you'll all be glad to climb out onto firm ground. You didn't realise you were coming on an ocean cruise, did you?"

She waited for the jabber of conversation to subside. "Once off the bus, please move over to give everyone enough room. The road is pretty narrow and overgrown, as we discovered, and I want to fill you in on the background to where we are before we move on to view the battle site itself. I suggest you bring your maps if you've got them handy. You're more likely to get your bearings." She waved a sheaf of papers. "I have one or two spare, if you need. Let's get off this ship then, shall we?"

She hitched her bag over her shoulder and disappeared down the stairs.

Everyone hustled to follow her, reaching bags down from the luggage shelf or collecting bottles of water from seat pockets.

Sarah dug around in her bag. "The map. Did you take it? I thought I'd put it back in my bag, but I can't find it."

"No. You had it out earlier. Maybe it fell to the floor." Jimmy half-bent to feel along the floor. "Here it is. It's a bit dirty, I'm afraid. Looks like one of us stepped on it."

"I'll ask Thandi for another one. I'm going to keep it, make a few notes, you know. Feel like I'm understanding the story."

"Really?" Jimmy paused before stepping into the aisle. "I thought you didn't like all this war stuff? That's what you said the other day."

"I still don't, not particularly. It's just that when Thandi tells it, and then seeing the costumes and memorabilia in the museum yesterday, standing on the bridge, I don't know, it became less — less history and more real. About real, ordinary people, instead of photographs in a textbook."

"I know what you mean. Like some of those diary pages. Did you read any?"

"Hurry up, Jimbo. I need out of this torture chamber to stretch my legs. And I can't get past with you half in and half out of your seat." Des nudged Jimmy in the ribs.

"Hold your horses. I'm moving, I'm moving." Jimmy stepped off the coach. Sweat ran down his forehead almost as soon as his feet touched the ground.

"Right then, everybody here?" Thandi donned a white wide-brimmed hat, but remained standing in the sun. "You can probably make out the river through those trees. We're now downstream from Colenso and the wagon bridge favoured by Buller for his attack. On your map, we're almost at the place marked Bridle Drift. To the left of that large loop you can see. Got it?"

Jimmy leant over Sarah's shoulder. A loop in the river resembled a hangman's noose. "I don't like the thought of that as a battleground."

"You're right not to, Jimmy. We're on the edge of that loop. As we move along in a moment, you'll understand its significance. As I mentioned at the bridge in Colenso, the Bridle Drift was the second location where Buller wanted to cross. Once again protected by the calvary ahead, the reconnaissance teams felt it was a reasonable crossing point for a well-organised infantry force.

"But look around. This is such flat ground, distances are deceptive. Is the river running close by, or does it dip behind that incline there? Is it easier to see up into the hills surrounding you, or to look down from the hills onto this plain?"

Jimmy imagined being somewhere in the hills. He would have a bird's eye view of the entire area, wouldn't he? Whereas here, the closeness of the trees, the thick grass, the rough ground — even the sun in his eyes — made it impossible to see more than a few metres ahead.

"Maybe they used binoculars to compensate for not being able to see very far?" Kevin lifted imaginary field glasses to his face, his fingers forming the circular eye pieces.

"Would they have had time once the advance got underway?" Claire, a woman with season tickets in the same row as Jimmy at Anfield, spoke from the back of the circle.

"But surely the commanding officer, or whoever, would have some way of seeing ahead?" Ron, Claire's husband, joined the discussion.

The group, earlier somewhat bored and eager to check-in at the next hotel, were drawn into the puzzle by Thandi's expert leading. She made the history tour more fun than Jimmy expected. How would she approach the memorial? He glanced over at Des. He stood with his hands in his pockets, distance between himself and the rest of them. His jaw worked up and down as he chewed on some gum. His habitual post-smoke routine.

"Some of the officers carried field glasses, yes. Or even telescopes. I'm not sure Major Hart was one of them. By all accounts, he was a courageous man. But perhaps not suited to the peculiar circumstances of a bush war. To be honest, this early in the war, not many of the British were. Most didn't realise the tactics and strategies had changed.

"Unfortunately, the Major took a wrong turn — blamed on a local African guide who disputed the findings of the mapmakers and instead led Hart towards a point used by the local community." Thandi sucked in her cheeks. "It's easy to cast blame on those with no voice to refute the accusations. Or who disappears from the scene when events don't turn out as planned."

Jimmy avoided eye contact as she waited for her audience to respond. He kicked at a clump of grass in the path.

"Anyway, let me not spoil the story. Come and see for yourselves."

The path followed a line of trees before opening into a railed clearing. A collection of weathered headstones stood within the railings.

Unlatching a gate, Thandi stepped to one side, allowing the party to pass. A shiver tickled along Jimmy's spine at the sensation of stepping into a cemetery. He checked for Des. He lingered away from the group, filing in a few seconds later with a Liverpool cap pulled low on his forehead. Jimmy knew Des didn't hide from the sun under the hat's peak; since they were teenagers, a hat — or scarf, or hoodie — always kept others from seeing Des displaying the intensity of emotions he struggled to control at times.

Sarah was right. Des needed help. And compassion. Jimmy waited at the gate for his friend, pushing aside the irritations and humiliations of the last few days.

He muttered under his breath as he took Thandi's place at the entrance. "Lord Jesus, I don't know much about the kind of praying Sarah's talking about. But I do know I don't like to see my friend struggling. And I could use your help."

He laid a hand on Des' shoulder as he entered the clearing, his shoulders hunched and hands still in pockets.

"Alright, mate?" Jimmy clicked the latch closed behind them.

"What? Oh, yes, fine thanks, Jimbo. And you?" Des cast a wild glance around the clearing, his eyes darting from monument to monument. "What is this place?"

"Not too sure. Thandi said she'd explain it. You coming?"

"I think I'll hang around out there. Enjoy the view." Des backed into the gate.

"It might help." Jimmy lowered his voice. Half-hoping Des wouldn't hear.

He did. "What will help with what, Jimbo?" He stepped from the gate, a snarl curling his lips. "You got something you want to say."

"No, Des. It's just..." Jimmy kept his attention on the clenched fists. Preparing to duck if necessary. "This must be quite hard, that's all. You know, all the reminders of terrible events, that sort of thing."

It sounded lame, even to Jimmy. Des' nostrils flared. Jimmy waited for an outburst.

Des let out a long, whistling breath. The fists unclenched, hid inside trouser pockets again.

"To tell you the truth, Jimbo, you're not far wrong." Des slumped against the gate. It creaked in protest. "I didn't expect it to be like this.

Dunno why. It's battlefields, after all. I thought we'd have a bit of fun in the sun, y'know? Hang out at the beach, watch some footie. Do the...the memorial thing up at the African Kop. Then head back home. Nothing too heavy, right?"

"Des, I ... "

Des raised a hand. "No, let me finish. Now you've got me started. Just don't tell the others." He indicated the group wandering amongst the headstones. Brian had his camera out, Sean posing near one of the memorial stones. "It's all these memories. Although they're not mine, they're real. In the museum, the diaries and the saved treasures. That bridge. You could almost feel the soldiers marching across."

A shiver passed through his body, even though the sun shone high in a cloudless sky.

"Funny, that's what Sarah said, too."

"Astute woman, your Sarah. Do you know, I can't even support Poppy Day? I buy the things, but can't bear to wear them. I must have hundreds stashed in a drawer somewhere."

With a jolt of surprise, Jimmy realised he'd never seen Des at a Remembrance Day service in church. Or the lapel of his expensive jackets sporting the paper flower of national remembrance.

"Maybe I shouldn't have come. I just wanted to honour..." He stopped talking, his words forming instead a whispered moan.

All coherent thought fell from Jimmy's mind at the sound of Des' distress. He caught Sarah watching them. He mouthed a silent appeal. "Help!"

She excused herself from Thandi and Bethany, shaking her head and shrugging. The three women laughed, heads back, enjoying whatever the joke was.

Sarah approached with short, quick strides; not quite running, but seeming to read Jimmy's sense of urgency.

She raised her eyebrows, quizzing Jimmy.

"Everything alright, boys? You got lost after the gate, did you?" She kept her voice light. Unflustered. Unconcerned. She pulled a water bottle from her bag. "Phew, this heat is something else, isn't it? Here, Des, have some water. Sorry, I don't have anything stronger."

Des appeared not to have heard. His chin hung low against his chest, almost as though he'd fallen asleep on his feet. His one fist remained in his pocket, the outline of his bunched fingers imprinted on the stretched fabric. He kneaded the back of his neck with his free hand, as though massaging a knot of muscle.

Sarah reached for the hand, drawing it away from his neck in a slow, gentle movement. "Jimmy, could you pick up Des' cap? It's there in the grass."

Jimmy retrieved the cap, its bright red colour garish and out of place. He dusted off the sand.

Taking the hat, Sarah held it out to Des. "Here, put this on against the glare. You'll feel better."

Des obeyed without looking up or commenting.

"Come on then. Let's join the others and see what's going on."

"Shouldn't we take him to the bus? I think he's had enough history for one day."

Sarah shook her head. "No, he needs company. His adoring public. If we hide on the bus, they'll bombard him with a million questions he won't know how to answer. Look, they're already getting curious."

A few of Des' friends stood around, feet shuffling in the dirt. They chatted amongst themselves, glancing back at the gate.

"You're right. Of course." Jimmy planted a kiss on Sarah's cheek. Des' posse whistled in appreciation. "Des, come on, your fans need you."

He linked his arm through Des' as Sarah took the other side. Des moved like lead through treacle, each step slow and deliberate. Sarah chatted away — about the weather, the birds, their lunch — ignoring the stares and muttered comments of the onlookers.

Kevin and Bethany greeted them with looks of concern, but no questions.

"Thandi's about to start her next lecture." Bethany giggled. "Sorry, story. Des, stand over here with us. We've found a spot with a bit of breeze, although there's no shade."

"Now, can anyone tell me what's wrong here?"

The field widened out from the memorial site, beyond which the hills dominated the skyline.

"You can't see the river very well, can you?" Sean pointed to a line of trees edging the field. "Is that it there?"

"Yes. You can just make it out. Bear in mind, the trees are a new addition to the landscape. Then, it was a grassy flood plain. What else?"

"If that's the river, it bends back on itself, doesn't it? Would they have known which bit to ford?" Ron again, him and Claire standing closer to the front this time.

"You're right. This is the loop shown on your maps."

"Oh, so they didn't cross here then? You said the Bridle Drift was to the left." Sean held his map out. "Can we see it from here?"

"No. And that's the point." Thandi paused, allowing the importance of her words to sink in. "This is where the African guide supposedly led Hart and his Irish forces."

"What? How many of them were there?" Jimmy scanned the area. "It's not very wide, is it?"

"It's about one thousand yards across. And there were about four thousand men in his infantry brigade."

"And the Boers were...?" Jimmy's question hung in the air.

"In the hills." Thandi extended her arm to encompass the ring of high ground surrounding their position.

Jimmy closed his eyes, trying to picture the scene. Grainy black and white images from old war films paraded through his mind. Was it like that? Or was that too neat — too Hollywood — for what took place?

"And the monuments behind us?" Jimmy's eyes snapped open as Des spoke, his voice so quiet, Jimmy wondered if Thandi would hear.

"They are a poignant reminder of the mistakes made in war." A wobble of emotion crept into Thandi's reply.

"So, the men were funnelled into a space too small for their number. Is that right? And they paid for it with their lives." Des's expression hardened, the muscles around his jaw tight. Self-pity and despair replaced with the burning anger never far from the surface. "Yes, I understand."

Percy

Colenso, South Africa
Friday 15 December 1899

P ercy resisted the urge to fidget. New recruit on the parade ground
again, rather than seasoned private on the battlefield. But then, all
he'd done was march and camp and reconnoitre, so perhaps he wasn't the
experienced soldier he fancied. Miller stood to attention an arm's length
away, eyes facing straight ahead. The shadows of pre-dawn masked his
scar. If he was nervous about the upcoming action, he hid it well.

Giving up on sleep, Percy had slipped from the tent as the last of the
cavalry rattled past. He prodded at the campfire, hoping for the grey
embers to spark into flame so he could boil water for a cup of tea. In the
east, the dark blue of night softened to a pale purple. Almost sunrise.

The fire didn't respond to Percy's efforts. Abandoning the attempt,
he wandered over to the edge of camp. Spread before him, the tents
sprouted like mushrooms from the dry soil. How many others lay awake
under the fading stars of near dawn? How many dreamt of glory and
military honours? And how many would taste death before the day's
end? Two days of artillery bombardment against the Boer positions, and
still not a shot fired in retaliation. Were they even there? Perhaps today
would be nothing more than yet another exercise in futility.

Percy sat on a tree stump. He retrieved Flo's pictures from his pocket
— the photograph taken in Liverpool and the portrait sketched by
Mickey. He ran a finger over her face, tracing the outline of her hair as
it curled into her neck. He painted the pale blue of her dress, the green
of the garden in the background, with his imagination. He smiled at the
laughter in her eyes.

Searching his other pockets, Percy found a stub of pencil. He should write to Flo, tell her he loved her, ask her to wait for his return. He flipped over the portrait, licking the lead while he composed his opening words.

Florence...

No, too formal.

Darling Flo...

Too soppy. He'd called no one darling in his life.

My dearest Flo...

Better.

It is with a heavy heart I pen these words to you, knowing if you are reading them, I can no longer voice them aloud...

Percy shook his head, banishing the notion of imminent death. This was the best army in the world, conqueror of India and Sudan, marching against a ragtag bunch of farmers and wild men cowering in the hills.

My dearest Flo,

I write this to you on the morning of our first major offensive against the enemy. I am excited and nervous in equal measure, yet remain confident of our victory over the inexperienced Boers. I shall give you a full account of the battle, and the part I play in it, on my return to Liverpool, where — dare I hope? — to find you waiting.

Until then

Yours, Percival

"Miller?" Percy turned to his friend, away from the others. This wasn't something he wanted them to witness.

"Mm?"

"Could I ask a favour of you?"

Miller peered at him in the hazy light. "A favour? Yes, if it's in my power to carry it out, I'd be more than happy to. What is it?"

Percy propped his rifle against his thigh as he fumbled in his pocket. Heat rushed into his cheeks. "Could you keep this? In case..."

"In case it needs delivering to a young lady at home, perhaps?" Miller winked. "It would be my honour."

He took the folded page without a glance, stowing it in his breast pocket.

"Although I believe I'll be returning it to your care before the day is out, PP." He patted Percy's arm. "We're under orders."

Percy hefted his weapon and clicked to attention. His heart fluttered as his breathing quickened.

He peeked at his watch after half an hour. They still hadn't left camp; Major-General Hart demanded more manoeuvres on the makeshift parade ground before permitting anyone onto the battlefield. As if the Boers would be dazzled by the beauty and discipline of the British army's advance.

Percy's shirt stuck to his back, where his ammunition belts rubbed against his shoulders. His feet throbbed inside boots whose laces were too tight. A golden sun rose in the sky, swallowing the gentle pinks and oranges of dawn.

"How many more of these drills are we doing? It's a clever trick to give Brother Boer a fighting chance. Wear us out before we reach them." Arthur prodded Percy forward with his rifle butt. "Come on, PP, you're falling out of line."

Percy scuttled into place.

A heavy thud, repeated in quick succession, prevented his reply.

"Are those our guns? I thought Blomfield said Buller sent them further around. That sounds nearby." Confused, Percy concentrated on not catching his foot on a loose stone.

"I know nothing about that. But at least it means the game's about to start." Arthur gave a clap. "About time."

He was right. Orders filtered down through the ranks. They were to march in close formation, defeating the enemy by the sheer sight of their presence as they headed for the drift to the west of the one remaining bridge at Colenso.

Already the front lines, led by the Irish Fusiliers, had picked up the pace. After them, the Connaught Rangers, their kilts swinging with every stride. At the rear, the Lancashire Fusiliers assigned to the Irish contingent for the day.

"Glad I don't have to wear a skirt into battle." Alfie marched on Percy's left side. "Funny way to fight, if you ask me."

"Nobody did, Alfie old boy." Arthur's voice carried across the small gap between the rows. "We're awfully tightly packed in here, don't you think? Miller, you've done this before. Is this normal?"

Percy marched in silence, focused on keeping time with Miller and Alfie, while not bumping into Crosby in front of him.

"Well, it was successful at Omdurman. And it's how they train at Aldershot." A hint of alarm flickered in Percy's chest at Miller's doubtful reply. "This terrain is different, though. And the enemy is better hidden."

"We're probably not close enough to see them." Percy could hear the shrug in Arthur's response.

They tramped in silence for the next mile. Percy's palms grew slippery with sweat where he held his rifle. Thirst burned his throat as dust swirled under the disturbance of thousands of feet pounding the ground. His vision blurred, grit flicking into his eyes despite the peak of his helmet. He carried enough water for the day's engagement. Unwilling to dip into his reserves so early in the proceedings, he chose to wait, rationing it until desperate.

Alfie whistled a jaunty music hall song Percy disliked. He tried to tune it out, occupy his thoughts with calculations about bullets and ration packs. But that brought a rush of panic as he wondered if he had sufficient supplies. He focused on the nicks and cuts of the barber's razor, the welts from nibbling mosquitoes, showing above Crosby's collar. Scratching at his own neck, he pitied Arthur's view behind him.

"Halt." The command rippled down the columns.

"Now what? More practice?" Alfie stopped whistling.

Percy stood on tiptoe to look over the sea of khaki helmets. It didn't help.

"I think they'll be looking for the crossing point. It's one thing to mark it on a map. Another to pinpoint it for real." Miller rested on his rifle. "Take a break, PP. All this paraphernalia weighs a ton after a day in the field. Grab the chance to rest while you can."

Percy slung the rifle from his shoulders, rolling his head from side to side to relieve the build-up of tension in his muscles. He considered removing his helmet to cool off. Glancing at the hills, closer than at the start of their march, he thought better of it. Rather safe — and hot — than sorry.

"Attention. March."

Muttered swearing greeted the order. Percy hefted the rifle. He risked a sip of water. Lukewarm, it tasted of metal. He grimaced, screwing on the lid. Maybe not so hard to ration, after all.

The column moved on, veering aside from their previous path.

Without warning, the double thud-thud of field guns sounded ahead. And again. Within minutes, Percy choked on thick, swirling dust. Cries of surprise drifted on the wind. Scanning the horizon in search of Brother Boer, Percy spotted a structure built on the top of a hill overlooking their position. A dark shape protruded from its front.

"A gun tower. There, to the right." Percy tapped Crosby on the shoulder. "See. Over there."

Crosby shook Percy's hand off. He twisted around, confronting Percy with a sneer. "It can't be, PP. Too far away. They'd never reach us from there."

"They've duped us." Miller shielded his eyes. "Led us to believe they're further off than they really are. It's quite the ruse."

Another thud of shell fire forced the end of the conversation. They marched on, rifles poised.

Percy froze. Ice cold terror pulsed through his veins as shrieks from the front of the column pierced the bass crump of the guns.

Arthur bumped into him.

"Private Percival. Onward march." Miller's stern command broke into Percy's terrified brain.

Percy's legs moved as though through thick treacle. His heart pounded, his breath laboured like a man running uphill. The continual thudding grew louder, more intense, now joined by a strange popping sound.

"Is that...?" Something whistled past his ear.

"Shots!" Miller ducked, one hand holding onto his helmet. "Keep low."

"But where are they coming from?" Percy strained to locate the telltale puffs of smoke through the clouds of dust. If only he were taller.

Alfie swerved into him, his rifle thumping into Percy's ribs. "They're firing on us." The whites of his eyes gleamed, panic pouring in the sweat down his forehead. "What do we do?"

"Keep going." Arthur grunted, jostled against Percy. "Sorry, PP. Trying to avoid being shot back here."

"I can't see the guns, the bullets. Where are they?" Why would no one answer him?

"Smokeless ammunition." Miller scurried forward, crouching with his knees bent, rifle at the ready. "New. Didn't realise they had them."

"What? So, we'll get no warning?" Percy's throat closed on a scream. His eyes darted back and forth. A commotion a few rows ahead. Men crumpling. Groans.

The soldiers parted, like water flowing around an obstacle. A crumpled heap of flesh and fabric lay before Percy. He clenched his jaw against the acrid taste of bile. Worse than any seasickness. He staggered past the stricken man.

Something glistened in Percy's peripheral vision. Turning for a proper look, Percy choked in horror. The river sparkled in the mid-morning sunshine. Not straight ahead of them. On the left.

"Miller." He coughed away the croak. "Miller. We're in the wrong place."

"What? Stop talking, PP. Save your energy. You're going to need it."

Percy tugged on Miller's sleeve, forcing him to pay attention. "We're in the wrong place. That's the river on our left. And there — " he pointed to a slight incline on the right, " — that's also the river."

Miller's face paled. "How do you know, PP? You don't know this area."

The whistle and crump of falling shells. A sound reminiscent of hail on a tin roof. More cries from up ahead.

The beat of a frightened heart.

"I went out with them at Frere." The words came in rushed gasps between breaths. "Know what to look for. Water. River banks. Greener. Thicker grass. Trees. Like over there."

"We've missed the drift." Miller spoke with certainty, stating a fact as if reporting on the weather.

Percy gripped his rifle until his fingers ached, his knuckles gleaming white through the sunburnt flesh of his hands. They were marching into a loop in the river. With no space to spread out, no way to avoid the barrage of bullets raining down on them. And no means of retreat.

He stumbled on something soft. A soldier's outstretched arm. Blood pouring from a wound in his chest.

"Leave him, PP. You can't help him without getting yourself killed. Or one of us." Arthur shoved him forward.

"We can't carry on. We must retreat." Alfie stopped walking. He shook his water bottle. "I've got no drink left."

"Here, have some of mine." Percy handed Alfie his canteen. He grabbed it, tipping his head, glugging the liquid. He returned the bottle, the remaining few mouthfuls of water sloshing in the bottom.

"There'll be no talk of going back." Miller sank to his knees. "But you're right, we can't go on. We'll have to sit it out until nightfall. Look, they're thinking the same."

Across the plain, men lay prone, unprotected. Some writhed and groaned. A few propped rifles on stones or boulders, aiming at the invisible enemy.

Percy dropped next to Miller. His exposed neck prickled under the sun's unrelenting rays. Flies crawled over his skin. Dust and pebbles spurted upwards each time he raised his head or tried scrabbling for his water. A strange, sweet smell lingered.

Alfie moaned, his face buried in his arms. Percy wanted to reach out, reassure him somehow, but daren't move an inch. He could try praying. Phrases of liturgy flitted through his mind. But this was no church pew, no grand cathedral. Anything else? Nothing the Lord Almighty would want to hear. It was like trying to compose that letter to Flo, searching for words and finding only platitudes.

Flo. Would she remember him when he was gone? He glanced over at Miller, still alert, rifle poised. Although how he could use it against the Boers lurking on the other side of a field of prostrate British soldiers, Percy couldn't fathom. The bullet would hit one of their own before reaching halfway to the river. Let alone beyond.

How were the Boers remaining so hidden? No sign of life stirred on the opposite bank, no one marched in tight formation or galloped into view on horseback. The grass waved undisturbed. Lengthening shadows and a shimmering heat haze played tricks with Percy's imagination. A tree became a soldier advancing with a rifle, bayonet fixed. The call of a bird swooping overhead was the whistle to advance, blown by a fallen commanding officer.

Percy licked his lips, his tongue tearing at the dry flesh. He tasted the salt of blood. An internal gun pounded at his temples. His leg spasmed with cramp. He shifted position. The whizz and spurt of a bullet. He flattened himself into the grass, his breath rasping in his burning throat.

Why hadn't he tried harder with the letter? To tell Flo he cared for — loved? — her. That he fell asleep at night to dreams of her, that his waking moments were filled with thoughts of her. That he'd looked at her picture so often, he knew the number of freckles decorating her nose. Thirty-seven. That...

Miller grunted. Percy peered through the grass at his companion. A dark patch spread along his upper arm.

"George! You're shot." He wriggled closer.

"Just a graze." Sweat beaded on Miller's moustache. His scar slashed a red, angry mark across his pale cheek.

Percy eased a handkerchief from his trouser pocket. Keeping low, he inched next to Miller. Stretched to wrap the white fabric around the wound. It soaked crimson in seconds.

A crackle of paper in Miller's tunic as he rolled onto his other side. The letter. Would Flo ever get to read it?

Wilhelm

Colenso, South Africa
Friday 15 December 1899

U nease rippled through Wilhelm. The Standerton commando rode out of the camp at Fort Wylie — without either Hendrik Venter or himself in their ranks.

Days of silent waiting in the hills surrounding Colenso — ordered to hold their fire until the British were within range of Boer Mausers — grated on already stretched nerves.

The men grumbled and complained. "We've left our farms, our families, for this. To watch the invaders from a distance. Might as well go home."

A few did just that, slinking away under cover of darkness.

Wilhelm considered riding back to Pa and the Carolina commando. Perhaps watching Ladysmith wasn't such a bad idea after all. At least he'd be with his friends, like Meyer and Malan, instead of tagging along with Venter. He wasn't popular with the Standerton men. They excluded him from their card games or left him to ride ahead of them, alone.

Two days previously, reports of the humiliating retreat of exhausted Boer soldiers further unnerved the bored men. A well-timed telegram from Oom Paul read to his wavering troops, strengthened weak knees and feeble resolve with its pious rebuke.

Gentlemen, I have received reports that you gave up your position. Understand please, if you give up position there, you give up the whole land to the enemy. Please stand fast, dead or alive, each man at his place, and fight in the name of the Lord. The Kop on the other side of the river must not be given up because then all hope is gone with it...And fear not the enemy, but fear God...if you give up position, and surrender our country to England, where will you go then?

Reinvigorated, the generals had drawn lots to decide who would bear the honour of marching into enemy territory and recapturing the abandoned kopje. Cheers broke out as the lot fell to the men of Standerton and the Wakkerstroom commando. They spent the afternoon packing kit bags and supplies ready for the night-time expedition.

"I'm not going." Lolling against a boulder, Venter smoked a cigarette while watching the activity.

"What? We must. You heard what President Kruger said."

The instructions to retake the kopje at the far end of the Boer encampment, on the opposite bank of the river, were clear.

"President Kruger is away in Pretoria. He won't know which hill a man from Standerton rides up." He shrugged. "You can go, if you want."

"But I don't know anyone. I'm here with you. Maybe I should go back to Ladysmith..."

Venter bolted upright, cigarette ash spilling on his shirt with the suddenness of his movement. "No. You can't do that. Not without me. I'll need to explain to your pa." He pinched the bridge of his nose. "If you get into trouble, it's because of me. You mustn't take the blame."

"But..." Wilhelm couldn't see sense in that argument. Venter hadn't thrown him over the saddle of his horse and kidnapped him.

"I'm glad you came. I...I needed your company." A shadow passed across his face. "I still do."

Venter waved his comrades farewell, assuring them they would ride out in the morning.

"We'll bring updates on any developments. If there's anything more exciting than a bombardment of shells aiming at the wrong place."

The commando rode into the night without a backward glance.

Venter stoked the fire, boiling a pot of coffee on its glowing embers. Unconcerned by his insubordination.

"It'll be alright, Wilhelm. Your Pa won't suspect anything." The mask of confidence restored, he handed a mug of the steaming liquid to Wilhelm.

Wilhelm sipped the aromatic drink, scalding his lips and tongue. He'd always done as he was told growing up. When his friends avoided helping with harvest or the cattle or chores on their homesteads, sneaking out before dawn laden with fishing tackle or hunting rifles, he couldn't bring himself to join them. He knew disappointment would etch Ma's face on his return, her sighs heavy and her talk minimal. Pa would fetch the leather switch and give him a hiding his backside would regret.

Disobedience didn't seem worth the reward.

He glanced around the deserted camp. Discarded tins and empty boxes of bullets lay strewn across the trampled grass. A worn-out boot, the laces removed, lay on its side next to the blackened earth of the smouldering campfire. Staying here wasn't an option.

A nightjar called its haunting melody from a grove of trees nearby. Stars sprinkled the velvet sky with diamond dust. Wilhelm had lain back, his head resting in his hands. No need to decide anything right now.

"What are they doing?" Hendrik Venter faced into the sun, his tone incredulous. "Are those their guns at the front?"

A cloud of sandy earth enveloped the plain below. More men than Wilhelm could remember seeing in one place marched as a single body towards the river. He imagined the earth trembled beneath his feet at the thud of their boots.

"What do you mean? What guns?"

"Over there, near the bridge. Field guns. About, say, fifteen, sixteen. No, more than that."

"Yes, I see them. What of it? Will they fire on us?" Nerves fluttered in Wilhelm's stomach.

"They can try. But I'm sure they're in the wrong place. Behind them — those are the marching troops. Doesn't the artillery usually follow the infantry, not lead it? That's how Joubert and Botha do it."

"I suppose so." The horse-drawn gun carriages advanced to within a few yards of the bank, the foot soldiers still lagging behind.

The man at the head of the artillery brigade halted. The drivers leading the horses paused, then began a coordinated series of manoeuvres, wheeling the wagons so the field guns faced across the river. Into Boer territory.

"They're going to attack!" Wilhelm's eyes widened, his voice a high-pitched, pre-teen screech.

Venter snatched up his rifle. "Come on! We'll join the others in that trench, make the British pay for their mistake."

"What? But you said we'd follow the others to that hill, Bos Kop or whatever they called it. Wasn't your commandant given orders to defend it against the British?"

"Yes, those were the orders. And that's what I said. But where's the excitement in defending a hillside no one is attacking when there's action right here?"

Boom!

The air reverberated with the discharge of Botha's Krupp howitzer. The corresponding thud of its shell landing on the ground made Wilhelm's decision for him. He couldn't reach Bos Kop now, even if he wanted to. And a retreat to Ladysmith was impossible.

He hoisted his rifle and followed Venter, bouncing along a path below the deserted camp. Two or three native servants sat on their haunches in the shadow of the wagons. Wilhelm felt their eyes track his departure. Skirting the river, away from the iron wagon bridge spanning its flow, Wilhelm ran in a crouched position, scuttling between patches of dappled shade from the overhanging trees.

He kept one eye on the way ahead, the other watching events across the water. Dark figures scurried beside a dozen gun carriages, arrayed in a line facing Boer territory. The man Wilhelm saw from their earlier vantage point continued to direct the gunners' positions, striding from one group of men to the next, gesticulating with waving arms. At his instruction, they adjusted the barrels, pointing them across the river. But their aim was high. Had the decoys — the tree trunk guns in their improvised placements on the top of the surrounding hills — really fooled the British?

Wilhelm hurried on, catching up with Venter as a second round of artillery crashed overhead.

A flash burst in the sky on the British side. They were returning fire. Wilhelm braced for impact. The shell landed yards off target, far from the entrenched Boers. It exploded in a harmless shower of red sand and tree roots. The draught from the detonation twitched the leaves of the bushes nearest him.

"Hurry. Look, there they are." Venter urged Wilhelm onward.

A row of men lay a few feet from the riverbank, only their rifles showing above the sand and rock piles they hid behind. Venter jumped in beside them, disappearing from view. Wilhelm crawled forward, unsure of what to do next.

"Here, Wilhelm. Jump down and find a place."

Wilhelm slithered over the lip and into the dugout. A cascade of soil followed him. Venter nudged aside a man in a blue waistcoat, a dusty brown hat pulled low over his forehead, making a space for Wilhelm.

Blue Waistcoat acknowledged the newcomers with a grunt, unperturbed by their unexpected presence.

Pebbles and loose sand trickled into the dugout. Another shell.

"Men, it's time to protect our land, our home, our destiny." A shout from the commando's leader from deep within the trench line. "Fire!"

Wilhelm wedged his rifle barrel in the crack between two rocks. He closed his eyes, holding his breath.

"Three, two, one. Yaaaaahhhhh!" His eyes snapped open. Squeeze the trigger.

A bullet storm, held at bay for days, deluged the exposed British gunners. The leader fell first, collapsing onto the ground.

Flashes as they relit the guns. Thuds and booms as the shells landed — still far wide of the Boer's position. The Africans responsible for the horses left their posts, scurrying away from a war that wasn't theirs. The animals in their care remained in their traces, tethered to the gun carriages as the artillery blazed around them. They bucked and reared, their cries of panic adding to the crackle and thunder of the rifles and guns.

Wilhelm paused for breath, his chest heaving. He wedged the rifle in the crook of his arm, shaking the stiffness from his hands. Venter, his face red and sweating, winked across at him. Wilhelm grinned but didn't speak; Venter wouldn't hear the words above the tumult.

At a slight lull in the flashes and thuds of the guns, Wilhelm risked looking into the crater. Prone figures littered the ground, some in the stillness of death, others writhing in the agony of injury. Six or seven wagons loaded with crates nudged their way toward the front, their drivers sheltering behind their cargo as they bumped over the uneven ground. Men darted out, emptying the wagons of their contents. Fresh supplies of shells.

Wilhelm ducked below the trench. He raised his rifle, releasing a volley of fire into the midst of the activity. He didn't look to see its effect. The shouts and screams told enough.

The British gave up their guns, fleeing into whatever dips and hollows they could find to shelter from the onslaught of a thousand Mauser rifles. Wilhelm pressed his back into the cool soil of the trench wall. The muscles in his arms twitched and shook under the weight of his rifle. He rubbed at a blister on his thumb. Blue Waistcoat rested against the trench wall, his breathing laboured with exhaustion. Venter leant on his rifle, chin slumped onto his chest, eyes closed.

Smoke and dust hung in a cloud over the battleground, a shroud over the dead and dying. Wilhelm breathed in through his mouth, the stench of war burning his nostrils.

"Is it over?" He licked dry lips.

"The guns are ours. I told you they'd pay for their error." Even through his exhaustion, Venter spoke with triumph.

"Horses and riders approaching." An urgent cry from further down the line. "To arms, men."

Blue Waistcoat snapped to attention. Wilhelm resumed a fighting stance. Cramp spasmed in his shoulders. Venter aimed his rifle.

A horse cantered forward, the rider urging it on. A second rider galloped behind.

"They're coming for the guns. Fools. Don't they know we're still here?" Blue Waistcoat lined up his rifle. Bullets spat from the barrel.

The first horse skittered sideways as bullets sprayed dust. The rider bent over his horse's neck. Along the trench, Boer marksmen hunted the would-be rescuer of the artillery. He jerked once, twice. The horse reared. Its rider slid from the saddle, feet slipping from the stirrups as the horse bolted.

The second rider, further to the right, galloped on until the bullets found him. He flung backwards from the saddle, his arms flailing.

Through the haze of heat and smoke, a new rescue cart lumbered forward. More gunfire met its advance. It halted, wheeled around, retreated.

"They're trying again." Venter nudged Wilhelm in the ribs. "They don't give up easily, do they?"

Three teams of horses plodded towards the guns. Within moments of them being noticed, shots rang out from the trenches. The animals plunged forward, collapsing against the traces as the bullets hit their mark. A soldier crumpled to the ground. Lifeless. Four or five others fell alongside him, limbs shattered and wounds bleeding. The officer in charge raised an arm. His men abandoned the horses and retreated to safety.

The afternoon sun burned through Wilhelm's shirt. He didn't recognise any signals to abandon their post, but a stream of bedraggled, limping khaki staggered away from the guns. The neat formation of the morning, the bravado with which the guns advanced, in disarray.

The men in the trench alongside Wilhelm cheered. One shouted a prayer of thanks to the Lord for his victories. Venter patted in his pockets for his cigarettes.

Wilhelm

Colenso, South Africa
Friday 15 December 1899

A coucal called from a tree somewhere behind the trenches. The Rainbird. Clear skies belied its declaration.

Wilhelm fidgeted, battle energy draining from him as a dull quiet settled over the trench. They wouldn't withdraw from their positions until darkness fell, safe in the knowledge the British would spend the night attending to their wounded.

"They're hiding over there. In that donga." Blue Waistcoat pointed across the river. "We should take them prisoner."

Wilhelm stirred himself to look. He could make out shapes huddled in the natural trench. As he watched, one shape became a figure bent low over the ground. He hurried to the stricken rider shot from his horse earlier. Dragging him over the rough terrain, the man — dressed in a different uniform to the usual drab khaki — called to his comrades for help. Two dashed from their makeshift bunker. Together, they hauled the wounded man from the battlefield.

"Why bother now? They won't go anywhere. Let them enjoy the African sun a while longer." Venter sounded half asleep.

"And wait here to dry out like biltong?" Blue Waistcoat's beard quivered with its owner's outrage. "I'm going over."

He heaved himself out of the trench. Running towards a grove of trees, he returned mounted on a roan pony.

"Easier to ride across. Who's with me?"

"Hold on, we're following you." Venter stretched. "You are coming, young Wilhelm?"

"Flooi isn't..."

"Don't worry about that. We'll wade through."

By the time Wilhelm clambered from the trench, several men trotted along the river's edge. The horses skidded down the bank and into the river, their riders holding rifles high above their heads.

Wilhelm plunged into the water, the sudden cool taking his breath away. His boots slipped on mud and loose stones, and he lurched forward. Venter grabbed his shirt, pulling him upright.

"We're not here for a swim, you know." He laughed, letting go of Wilhelm's sleeve. "This is better, though, isn't it? I couldn't bear another minute hanging around back there. Perhaps we'll catch fish for supper when we're done with our captives."

Wading through the murky water swirling between his legs, Wilhelm doubted they'd find any fish today.

Blue Waistcoat approached the edge of the donga. Wilhelm hung back, unsure what he should do. A khaki jacket shaded the head of the retrieved officer, his body motionless beneath. The other rider lay on his back, his face burnt and blistered. A third man, pale and shivering, Wilhelm recognised as the officer leading the gun battery at the start of the day's proceedings.

"Surrender or we shoot." Wilhelm whirled around in surprise at the accented English spoken by Blue Waistcoat. "The choice is yours."

"Never." A voice floated over the donga's edge. Its owner rose from amongst the assembled refugees. "I am Colonel Bullock, Commanding Officer of the 2nd Devons. And I can assure you, we will never hand ourselves over as your prisoners. Death is a nobler end."

Blue Waistcoat shrugged. He tapped his horse's reins and trotted back fifty yards. The others did likewise.

"Is he giving up?" Disappointment and relief fought against each other as Wilhelm joined the apparent retreat.

Blue Waistcoat pulled his horse up. He twisted around in the saddle, firing in quick succession from the rifle at his hip.

The British returned fire.

Two of Blue Waistcoat's companions collapsed to the ground. The hairs on Wilhelm's arms and neck tingled at their cries.

"They will pay for that." Blue Waistcoat delved into a pocket, retrieving a grubby white handkerchief. He waved it aloft, urging his horse around, returning to the donga. Shoulders slumped and hat removed. The picture of dejected surrender.

Sliding from the saddle, he walked to the steep-sided edge.

"Two, three wounded. One fatally. How do you intend to escape?" He could be asking about the weather. Or the general state of their health.

Wilhelm drew closer, eager to watch the exchange unfold. Movement behind the donga caught his attention. He stepped back, horrified. A hundred or so Boers, those he had fought alongside throughout the day, sprang from their hiding place in the long grasses, brandishing their rifles. A dozen British soldiers found themselves at the wrong end of a barrel.

Before the commanding officer could react, Blue Waistcoat raised his rifle. He slammed the butt into the officer's face. Blood gushed from his mouth.

"No!" Wilhelm's legs gave way under him. "This isn't how it should be."

Wilhelm splashed water over his face, gulping for air. Bent double, he retched the contents of an empty stomach.

He pushed up from the stream, staggering on shaking legs, far from the drunken laughter of men celebrating the capture of a British officer and his troops. He collapsed onto a boulder, the valley spread beneath him. Clouds drifted across a sky tinged pink by the setting sun. Ambulances and stretcher bearers criss-crossed the battle site under the watchful gaze of a handful of Boer commanders, dark figures in the twilight.

Wilhelm held his head in his hands. He rubbed at his eyes, trying to wipe away the scenes of earlier. The defeated prisoners, defiance blazing from angry eyes. The brown-skinned stretcher bearers, turbans wrapped around their helmets in an exotic display of heritage. Their matter-of-fact collection of the groaning wounded, the silent dead. Blue Waistcoat's triumphant return to the Boer side, a British helmet balancing on his bloodied rifle butt as a trophy. Venter's arm tight at his waist, supporting him through the water and onward to a resting place.

Wilhelm rocked back and forth, a moan rising in his throat and escaping into the night air. He should have stayed with Pa, with his friends from Carolina. Men he knew and trusted. Men who honoured others, no matter which side of a river they found themselves. An image of Dominee Fourie, his hand raised in blessing, swam into his mind. He spoke of duty and pride, of defending the volk and protecting the homeland. But he also preached of loving enemies, of vengeance from the Lord, rather than the action of man.

The wooden cross from his bedroom dug into Wilhelm's flesh. He retrieved it from his trouser pocket. Resting it on his knee, he pressed his palm into its contours. The peace he sought evaded him.

A rustle of grass, footsteps. A sigh. Venter lowered himself beside Wilhelm. He stretched his legs, lounging on his elbows. Blue eyes searched Wilhelm's face.

"Are you alright, young Wilhelm?" Wilhelm remained silent. "No, of course you're not. I'm sorry. Truly. It shouldn't have ended that way."

Wilhelm stroked his fingers over the carving.

"What have you there?"

"Something from home."

"Can I see?"

Too worn out to argue, Wilhelm passed the ornament to Venter.

He examined the piece, caressing the wood. "It's well crafted. Who carved it?"

"My mother's father." Wilhelm's heart squeezed at the mention of family. Tears pricked. He dashed them away, hoping Venter didn't see.

Venter peered at the back. "And the writing. That's less expert."

"My sussie did that. Before we left." A cloud lifted as Isobel's remembered sunshine dawned. He turned to Venter. "She's only ten."

Venter's softened expression threatened the return of tears.

"Would you mind if I...?" Venter drew a penknife from his pocket. "I'd like to add a few words of my own."

"Is there space?"

"I'm neater than your sister."

Wilhelm's gaze returned to the view. The scrape of Venter's knife through wood calmed his agitation.

"There." Venter blew away any loose shavings. He handed back the cross.

Aan my vriend Wilhelm Olivier van die Carolina Kommando. Om naas jou te ry, is 'n eer en voorreg. Hendrik Venter. Standerton.

To my friend Wilhelm Olivier of the Carolina Commando. To ride alongside you is an honour. Hendrik Venter. Standerton.

Jimmy

Spionkop Lodge, South Africa
Monday 13 April 2015

C heerful Charlie stretched an arm out of the driver's window and pushed the buzzer on a post beside the gate.

Nothing happened.

He pressed again.

The barrier slid open, its motor whirring loud enough to hear over the idling engine.

Jimmy tapped Sarah on the knee. "We're here."

She lifted her head from his shoulder, blinking the sleep from her eyes. She yawned. "Where's here?"

"I couldn't tell you. But wherever it is, we're here."

The bus bumped along a rough track, winding through trees and bushes looming out of the darkness. Moths flickered in and out of the glare of the bus' headlights.

Cheerful Charlie slowed to a walking pace. Caught in the spotlight, a deer straddled the narrow track. Its deep brown coat reminded Jimmy of a shaggy carpet. White markings dotted its face, lined its belly. Two magnificent horns curled upwards behind large, flapping ears.

Thandi jumped up, pointing. "A male nyala."

"Oo, let me see." Sarah leant over Jimmy, craning her neck past Sean's seat in front.

The nyala blinked in the headlights, standing his ground. His tail flicked. Cheerful Charlie edged forward. The deer twitched its ears, bolting into the undergrowth.

"There it goes. Keep a look out for more animals." Thandi, ever the teacher, encouraging her students.

"I don't see anything, do you?" Sarah had her forehead pressed to the window.

"I see a beautiful bird with slightly bedraggled feathers..."

"What, where?" Sarah whirled around. Jimmy winked. "Ah, you're such a tease. Do I really look a fright, though?"

"Nothing a quick comb won't fix."

"I haven't one handy. I'll have to tie the feathers out of the way." She snapped a hair band from her wrist, twisting the curls into a loose bun on top of her head. "That'll have to do. I can't wait for a shower after such a hot day."

Jimmy wiped sticky palms on his shorts. "Know what you mean."

The engine revved as Charlie navigated a sharp incline. He brought the vehicle to a shuddering halt in the centre of a large, flat area. The doors swished open, bringing the scent of cut grass in on a cool breeze.

Before anyone could rise from their seats, Thandi leapt up. "Welcome to Spionkop Lodge, ladies and gentlemen." She glanced at her watch. "We're a touch later than expected, so can I suggest you make your way to the bar for pre-dinner drinks while I get you checked in? Charlie will offload the bags and drop them at your rooms so you can freshen up before supper."

"You hear that, Claire? I could murder a pint." Ron's voice carried down the length of the bus.

"Me too!" A ripple of agreement from all the passengers.

Jimmy twisted in his seat to look through the gap. "You keen for a beer, Des? My shout."

Des continued to stare out of the window. He gave no indication he'd heard Jimmy.

"Des? You awake, mate? We're at the hotel. Time for a drink."

Des turned his head in slow, jerky movements. Dark, swollen smudges ringed his eyes.

"Not thirsty, Jimbo. I'll grab my bag, find my room. Thanks, though. You and Sarah have one for me." A lopsided smile disfigured his features. He retreated to his reflection in the glass.

"Come on, Des..."

Sarah pulled on Jimmy's sleeve. "Leave it, Jimmy. He's had quite a day. Let him compose himself before he has to deal with everyone again."

Des remained in his seat, face to the window, as Jimmy collected his jacket and left the bus. He glanced back as he followed in the wake of Thandi, Sarah, and others. A flicker of concern at Des' slack expression, his eyes half-closed. How would he cope with the memorial programme, when an event from decades ago — an event he'd never attended — had such a profound effect on him?

A fire crackled in the grate, flames dancing amongst the logs and lumps of coal. Jimmy rubbed his hands in its warmth.

"I wasn't expecting it to be this nippy. Not when it's been so hot all day."

Kevin approached, laden with pints of beer and two Cokes. "Here you go. For those observing Lent." He passed a Coke to Jimmy. Liquid sloshed over the rim and onto the floor. "Oops, mind the spill. I know mate, talk about extremes in temperature. I wonder if this is usual? Or laid on specially for us?"

Thandi, standing close by, leant over. "No, it's not just for you. We're up quite high here, and far from the coast. So, the weather does its own thing. The dam here makes it even colder. But, of course, you've not seen that yet."

"Oh, there's a dam, is there? I don't remember seeing one on that map you gave us?" Sarah sipped her drink. Bubbles decorated her upper lip. Jimmy wiped them away with his thumb. "Thanks, darling. What would I do without you?" The dimple winked.

Thandi stepped closer, joining their circle. "No, it wasn't there then. In fact, the second of General Buller's key strategic crossing points lies right in the middle of it." She smiled. "Well, under it."

"Thandi, you don't have a drink. Can I order you something?" Jimmy wanted to prevent her from wandering to another group. Perhaps a chance to mention the ornament would present itself while they relaxed before dinner.

"Thanks, Jimmy, but I don't drink. Alcohol, that is." She pulled her battered water bottle from the handbag. "I'm happy with this."

"We can do better than that. Go on, what would you really like? I'm buying."

"Well, if you insist, a passion fruit and lemonade would be lovely."

Jimmy blinked. He'd never heard of it. "A...?"

"Passion fruit. It's a cordial. Very refreshing with lemonade." Thandi smiled. "Don't worry, the barman will understand."

Jimmy elbowed his way to the counter. "Something with lemonade, please. A something fruit."

"Passion fruit." The barman reached for a bottle of yellowy-orange syrup. Splashing a centimetre into the bottom of a glass, he added a few ice cubes. He flicked open a can of lemonade.

Jimmy juggled his and Thandi's drinks, the barman adding the half-full can to the collection. Concentrating so he didn't trip or spill anything, the first he knew of Des' appearance was a raucous slurring.

"Jumbo. One of those for me?"

Conversations dropped to an awkward whisper as Des stumbled across the threshold, grabbing for the backs of chairs as he made his way over to Jimmy's group. His untucked shirt gaped at the neck, his top two buttons undone.

Jimmy placed the drinks on a round table to the side of the fireplace. He gripped Des by the elbow, steering him towards the door.

"Don't mind us folks, carry on and enjoy your drinks. Everything's fine, don't worry." The tips of his ears burned with more than the reflected heat from the fire. He caught Sarah's eye. "I'll take him to his room. I'll be back in a sec."

Jimmy tensed against Des' weight, his face turned away from the whiskey fumes as they staggered across a carpet of lawn to another stone-clad building housing the guest suites. A door swung open, light spilling out onto a low veranda.

"Yours, I presume?"

Des burped in reply. He slumped against Jimmy's chest, giggling.

"Great." Jimmy wound his arm around Des' waist, half-pulling and half-pushing him into the bedroom. A ceiling fan whirred at full speed, a helicopter preparing for take-off. Jimmy flicked the switch. A flying beetle-like insect buzzed, bumping against the walls. "You don't look suited for flight, buddy." Talking to insects. Is this what it's come to?

Jimmy flopped Des onto the bed. His foot kicked against something rolled underneath. He bent to retrieve it. A silver hip flask. Engraved. *To Des. From Jimmy and Sarah.*

"Oh, Des, mate, you've not drunk all this since you got off the bus, have you?" He swung Des' legs onto the bed. Fumbled with the laces of his Nike trainers. Giving up, he pulled the shoes off, threw them to the floor. A patterned blanket draped the end of the bed. Jimmy shook it out, covering Des as though he were one of the kids sick with fever.

He turned off the lamp. Moonlight flooded through the open door. Des snored. Jimmy replaced the cap on the hip flask. Should he take it? No, that would enrage Des when he woke. He put it on the bedside table. At least it was empty. For now.

The keys dangled in the door lock. Another dilemma. Should he lock Des in? Or would that terrify him, stuck in a room he wouldn't recognise through the fog of alcohol? He left the keys in place, closing the latch with a click.

A wooden bench occupied space on the veranda outside the bedroom. Jimmy sank onto its cushions. He needed a moment before returning to the bar.

He looked up at a soft footstep on the tiles. Sarah. She hovered above him for a few seconds, then sat down beside him. She tucked her arm through his, rested against his shoulder.

"It's getting worse, isn't it?"

"Maybe this trip wasn't a good idea. It's stirring up too much. By association." Jimmy exhaled a breath. "And the memorial is still a couple of days from now."

"But perhaps it will make it easier. Bring everything back into perspective again." Doubt filled Sarah's whisper.

"I don't know. I wish we knew how to help him."

"Thandi was asking about him. After you'd gone."

"You didn't say anything, did you?" Jimmy pulled away from Sarah. Des would be furious if he thought they gossiped about him.

"No, I didn't." Jimmy relaxed back into the seat. "Kevin and Bethany did."

Jimmy groaned. "Oh, no, what did they say?" He wasn't sure he wanted to hear.

"Did you know they're Christians too? Like Megan from work. I think they're at the same church, actually."

"Des said something about them being too nice. Yesterday, when I got mad with him."

"They said they'd been praying for him. For Des. Said they felt 'the Lord' — their words — was working deep in his heart, and we should give him all the space he needs. And the love."

Jimmy jiggled his leg in protest at the soppy language.

"I know, it's not really how Father O'Brien talks, is it? But their motives are kind." She rose from the bench. "Let's go for dinner. There's nothing more we can do right now. He'll sleep it off and forget it ever happened in the morning. Then when we're up on Spionkop — I think that's the plan for tomorrow — we'll be able to keep an eye on him. See how he is."

Jimmy allowed her to pull him to his feet. He wrapped his arms around her, tasting the smell of her shampoo as she snuggled into him. "He might not quite forget everything. His headache will remind him."

"Friends, I'd like to introduce you to our hosts for the next few days." Thandi tinkled a spoon against the side of her glass. A man in chinos and a checked shirt, and a woman in jeans and a blue blouse smiled at everyone. "This is Raymond and Lynette Heron. They are experts on the Anglo-Boer War in general, and the battle of Spionkop in particular. You'll learn more from them than any number of readings of Thomas Packenham's weighty volume."

"Welcome to Spionkop Lodge, everyone. We're delighted you are here." Raymond raised a hand in greeting. "Tomorrow, I'll take you on a tour of the area, visiting Mount Alice after breakfast and Spionkop in the afternoon. The memorial's scheduled for the following day."

"Mount Alice...?" Sean held a pencil poised over his notebook. "I've not read of that."

"General Sir Redvers Buller's headquarters. From where he watched the whole battle unfold." Raymond spread his arms, encompassing the dining room and the dark night beyond the floor-to-ceiling windows. "This is it, young man."

"Well, we're at the foot of Mount Alice." Lynette corrected her husband.

"Are you saying General Buller stayed here, then?" Sean's eyes gleamed with excitement. He glanced around, as though half expecting his hero to appear in a doorway.

"Yes, dear. Not in this exact room, but hereabouts." Lynette beckoned to the restaurant staff hovering near the kitchen to her left. "Raymond, we should leave these people to their meal. Mary, you can come through. Enjoy your supper, everyone. And goodnight."

A chorus of goodnights filled the room. Raymond waved farewell and the two of them disappeared into the kitchen. Mary summoned her waitresses and placed bowls of a thick vegetable soup in front of each diner. Jimmy's mouth watered at the rising aroma. He lathered butter on a piece of warm seed bread, dipping it into the soup.

"Delicious. Better than at yesterday's fancy hotel." He dipped a second time.

"Is Des alright, Jimmy?" Bethany held her spoon ready to plunge into the starter.

"Oh yes, he'll be fine. Tired from the day's excursion, that's all." He licked butter from his fingers, avoiding her searching look.

"It must be hard for him. Do you think he'd be open to us talking to him at all?"

"No!" Jimmy covered the near shout with a cough. "Sorry, went down the wrong way. I'm not sure he wants to talk, to be honest. He's done a lot of that over the years. Not that it seems to have helped." Swallowing a spoonful of scalding soup, he knew he'd said too much.

Bethany lowered her spoon into the bowl. "Of course, I understand. You're right, this is wonderful. Very tasty. Definitely homemade. You'll let Des know we're concerned for him, though?"

"Uh-huh." Desperate to change the topic, Jimmy tried to get Sarah's attention. Have her help with the small talk. She was deep in conversation with Thandi. "Have you enjoyed the tour so far? You didn't find today too, um, depressing?"

"No. Not depressing. Moving, yes. Awful for all those young men, don't you think?"

Mary approached the table. He exhaled with relief at not having to respond to Bethany.

"Have you finished, sir?" Mary's hand hovered over his bowl.

"Yes, thank you. That was delicious."

The bowl disappeared.

The rest of the waitresses bustled between the tables, collecting one set of dishes, and delivering the next. Servings of lasagne, a neat square on each plate, accompanied by a salad platter, made up the main course.

Jimmy tucked in, stabbing his fork into the layers of pasta, mince, and sauce. Thanks to the pause between courses, Bethany seemed to have forgotten about Des.

"Sarah here was telling me about a family heirloom you have, Jimmy?" Thandi leant across the table. "You think it may have originated here, from the Boer war?"

Kevin held a fork of lettuce midway between his plate and mouth. "Do you, Jimmy? That's fascinating."

Jimmy glared at Sarah. It was up to him when, and how, he mentioned the carving. She gave a slight shrug.

He pushed his empty plate to one side. No salad for him, thanks all the same. "Um, yes. It's nothing grand or anything. Certainly not valuable. Just a simple wooden cross. We've had it hanging on our wall for as long as I can remember." He tried to sound nonchalant, disinterested, but at Thandi's fixed gaze, her chin resting on her fist, Kevin and Bethany's wide eyes and silent chewing, Sarah's smile, a flutter of excitement quickened his pulse. "My mother persuaded me to bring it along, see if I could find out more about it. It came from her grandfather."

"Is it here with you?" Thandi relaxed the fist, her fingers fluttering. A child expecting a rabbit from a hat.

He shook his head. "No, it's in my bag. In the room. I can get it though…"

"No, no, it's late. I'd love to see it tomorrow…"

"Tell her about the writing." Sarah interrupted the goodnight speech. "I didn't tell her about that."

"Writing? That might help you trace its origin, then?" Bethany drank a sip of water. "Why haven't you mentioned it before? This is so exciting, isn't it, Kev?"

"Shh, let the man talk." Kevin leant on his elbows. "Carry on, Jimmy."

Jimmy cleared his throat. Excitement tinged with a hint of embarrassment. "It's only a few words. Well, two sets really. Scratched into the wood on the back. The initial lettering is quite faint, a bit clumsy. As if a child did it, maybe. But the rest is clearer, perhaps more expertly done."

"Jimmy! Don't keep us in suspense. What do they say?" Bethany blew a strand of hair out of her eyes.

"That's the thing. I have no idea. They're in a foreign language."

Jimmy

Spionkop Lodge, South Africa
Tuesday 14 April 2015

"Did I make a fool of myself last night, Jimbo?" Des sidled up to Jimmy, dark glasses shading his eyes. Jimmy could only imagine what he looked like beneath them. "Found myself under a blanket, fully clothed, at about two this morning. You?"

"Mm, that was me. Think nothing of it, mate. It was a tough day." Jimmy kept his attention fixed on the ground. An ant scurried across the veranda's crazy paving.

"Here's your coffee, Jimmy." Sarah appeared in the doorway of their room; a steaming mug held in each hand. "Oh, hello, Des. Here, you have mine. I'll pour another."

"No, no, that's yours, Sarah. There's a kettle in my room, I'll make one for myself..." His voice trailed away. He fiddled with his watch strap.

"Des, sit down, have a coffee." Sarah pressed the mug into his hands, guiding him towards their bench seat, similar to the one they'd sat on the previous evening. "You're with friends, Des. Relax."

Des took the cup between shaking hands. He lowered himself to the seat, his sigh the sound of an old man struggling for breath.

Sarah disappeared into the room. She dragged a chair from the dressing table to the door, the legs scraping on the tiled floor.

Des winced.

"Oh, sorry, Des. That must have sounded awful. Jimmy, can you carry it?"

Jimmy balanced his cup on the wide windowsill, lifted the chair from Sarah.

Retrieving his drink, he settled beside Des.

"I did make an idiot of myself, didn't I?" Des stared into the cup cradled in his hands. "What's wrong with me, Jimmy?"

Jimmy sipped his coffee. Now for the post-drinking recriminations, the apologies, the promises to change. It was always the same.

"I think this trip is making you confront a few things you'd rather forget about, Des." Sarah squeezed onto the bench next to Des, a cup in her hand. It looked like the tooth mug from the bathroom. "Perhaps you need a different type of help this time."

Jimmy choked on his drink. She wasn't going to talk about Jesus, was she? Or, even worse, offer that they pray for him?

Des pushed the sunglasses up onto his forehead. Swollen eyelids covered watery, bloodshot eyes. It looked painful to blink. "I don't know, Sarah. What else is there? You know I've tried everything. Nothing works."

Here we go, the self-pity thing again. Jimmy put his cup down with a clatter. He rose from the chair, began pacing the balcony. Movement the only way to contain his irritation at a cycle he'd been stuck in since he was fifteen.

Sarah reached for Des' hand. "Maybe this time you'll let us help. Your friends."

What was she going on about? He'd been helping Des all his life. So it seemed.

"You've been to all the outsiders, the professionals. They've given you the tools. Tools you need to start actually using, instead of accumulating." Jimmy paused in his pacing. Des would explode at that comment. He didn't. He nodded, giving Sarah's hand a squeeze. "But they don't know you like we do, Des. You can pretend with them. You can't with us."

Jimmy wondered where this was going.

"Jimmy's known you since you were a kid, Des. He's been there, part of it, from the day it happened."

"No, Sarah, he hasn't." That triggered a reaction. The belief he suffered in some unique way — that no one could understand or share — Jimmy knew was core to Des' version of events. He'd heard him say it often enough. "Jimmy wasn't at the match, Sar. He stayed home, watching on the telly like it was a movie. I was there. Seeing everything. Hearing everything."

Jimmy could no longer keep quiet. "And you won't let me forget it, will you? As though it's my fault, we couldn't afford the tickets. Or that Dad couldn't be off from work for the whole weekend." The words tumbled over themselves — a dam on the inside shimmering in the morning light, bursting, emptying, to reveal hidden secrets. He clenched his fists, willing himself not to shout or scream. Like he wanted to. "You've no idea how I felt, waiting to hear from you. Wondering which stand you were in. Wondering if I'd ever see you again."

He wiped at the tears streaming down his face, too undone to be embarrassed.

"Driving down to Anfield. Not understanding what had happened, hoping for news." He drew a shaky breath. "And then years of listening to you describing what a narrow escape you had. Telling me over and over and over. And despising me for not being there. For not being dead."

There. He'd said it.

Sarah's hand over her mouth, liquid diamonds caught in her eyelashes.

Des bent double, folded in on himself. Knuckles pressed into his eyes. Birdsong. The whisper of the wind.

"Jimmy..." Sarah fumbled for his hand. He swayed out of reach.

"Forget it." Every muscle taut, ready to run.

Had to get away, escape their scrutiny, their questions. He stumbled off the veranda, crossing the lawn to the end of the garden. Shrubs crowded the flower beds, a riot of colour and smell. Hands in pockets, he breathed in deep gulps, a drowning man gasping for air.

A cushioned step on the lushness of the grass. A hand touching his arm. Holiday perfume.

"Jimmy, you never told me."

He squeezed his eyes closed against the leaking tears. "I'm not sure I told myself."

Brian's camera flashed. Ror
wandered aside from the grou
He stroked her hair, resting hi
beyond the garden with glassy

Jimmy couldn't watch. Mo

"We also want to celebrate t
with the tassels of her scarf. "F
determination to live as norm:
injuries, is an inspiration to us

Jimmy always noticed And
front row of the Kop in his wl

Small groups formed on th
low voices, hugging, or holdir
Individuals stepped forward,
standing alongside or sitting c

"Jimmy." Des strode towar
a bear-hug embrace would fix

"Desmond." Jimmy steppe
front of him, awkward at the

Lowering them to his side, I
"That bench looks amazing. I

He examined the plaque o1
plastic bottle he carried. Repl
the carvings, his fingers tracir

"We should take a picture.
over, beaming. "Jimmy, you s

Sarah pushed Jimmy into r
her voice low, making sure no

Jimmy stood, tense and av
bench, reaching out. Jimmy d
unsmiling. A gulf of ninety-si
he'd always called friend.

"What kept you?" Brian, jovial. A blob of yellow egg yolk dribbled down his red Liverpool shirt.

"Just fancied a slower start, Brian." Sarah kept her arm hooked in Jimmy's. "Coffee and a relax in this beautiful garden. Really, what more could I want?"

"Breakfast, perhaps?" Brian laughed at his joke. Sean shuffled his feet. The teenager embarrassed by his dad. "Well, you're here now. They're about to unveil the bench for us to see."

Everyone stood in a semi-circle in front of a shape shrouded in a white sheet pushed against the wall. A plaque decorated the stonework above, the Liverpool emblems in the top corners; two eternal flames in the bottom. Writing filled the centre. Jimmy looked away. He didn't want to know.

"Des not joining us?" Kevin's eyes flicked from Jimmy to Sarah.

"He'll be along in a minute. Just getting changed, I think. I'm sure we can carry on without him."

"We can." Jimmy disentangled himself from Sarah. "Let's get on with it, shall we? Thandi, over to you."

Thandi frowned, gave him a quizzical look. He stared back, unblinking.

"Good morning, everyone. How did you sleep?" Thandi beamed at her charges.

"Like a log."

"No, like a baby."

"Great, thanks."

Jimmy's sigh attracted some stares, a few whispers. He didn't care.

"Good, good. Now, gather around. We've got a full day today. Before we go out on our tour with Raymond, there's someone I want to introduce to you."

A woman hovered beside the covered object. Short, dark hair curled around her face. She wore a Liverpool shirt and scarf over jeans and white trainers.

"This is Sue. As you can see, she is also a Liverpool fan." Laughter, calls of welcome. "She's one of the group behind the memorial and annual commemoration of the Hillsborough disaster here at Spionkop."

Sue smiled.

"Tomorrow, you'll meet t
afternoon's events. But I wa
give you a chance to chat to
forward. "Sue, why don't yo

Sue cleared her throat. "H
here." No trace of Liverpool
dad introduced me to soccer
experienced many changes,
the one constant has been L

Cheers and nods of agree

"So, when, in 1989, I wat
television in a house in Joha
She pulled a tissue from her
less to Liverpool or Anfield.
the street next to you."

A sniff from someone in

"As the years went by, m
supporters — most notably
Walters — realised we need
injustice, in solidarity with
her words. "We wanted to
much discussion and inspir
we commissioned this…"

She tugged at the sheet.
slatted bench. Claps. Murr

Curious despite himself,
featured a pair of phoenix
and the date, *15th April 19*
decorated each armrest. Jim
woodwork. He shoved his

Now he was closer, he c
bench. Names. The 96. He

Sue, her hand stroking t
admiring chatter. "You'll r
expect? That's because the
back here. One for each vi

Jimmy

Mount Alice, South Africa
Tuesday 14 April 2015

"Welcome to Mount Alice." Raymond Heron wore a white, wide-brimmed hat in addition to the chinos and check shirt. He gestured for the group to enter the small enclosure where he waited. In its centre, an obelisk-style monument caught the dappled sun filtering through the trees. At the edge of the clearing, two more headstones and a stone plinth. Beyond, a view over a wide valley. In the distance, a series of steep hills rose like a wall.

Jimmy hugged the shade, a headache gnawing at his temples. His stomach gurgled, suffering from both lack of food and emotional turmoil. Des hovered close by.

"You want some water, mate? You're looking a little peaky." He held out an unopened water bottle.

"No. I'm fine, thanks." Jimmy would have to speak to the man sometime. Clear the air after his outburst. But this wasn't the time. Civil monosyllables would have to do.

Des nodded. "Well, shout if you do…"

Sarah walked alongside Bethany, deep in conversation. About him, probably. Jimmy rubbed at his forehead.

"Spread below us is the view General Sir Redvers Buller saw in the early hours of 24 January 1900."

"He was here? Right here?" Sean almost jumped up and down.

"Yes." Raymond smiled. "He stayed at the Lodge following the disastrous attack at Colenso. Of course, it wasn't a hotel then. More a simple farmhouse."

Sean nodded, scribbling in his notebook.

"Anyway, Buller's campaign to relieve Ladysmith was in tatters. He still needed to find a way to cross the Tugela River and march north to relieve the besieged town. Which, by this point, was riddled with disease, its citizens and soldiers alike starving, and its leading general, White, about to surrender to the Boers. Add to that the pressure Buller was under from the War Office and the politicians in England, and really, circumstances couldn't be much worse."

Jimmy sympathised with the general. His foray into battle left him with a pounding head, a strain in his marriage, and anger between friends. He would, like Buller, have to forge a new crossing over the gorges he'd dug.

"Now, if you'll look behind me here, you'll observe the river challenge confronting Buller. He needs to organise his troops to cross the river while being overlooked by the Boers from the heights over there. There are only one or two fordable places, and, thanks to days and nights of heavy January rains, even these options were hazardous.

"Buller reverted to his original plan of crossing at Potgieter's Drift, postponed earlier due to complications down in the Cape. The second location he chose now lies under the Spionkop Dam. That was Trichardt's Drift. The problem? The distance between them prevented him from commanding both advances from this, his central location. He would need to divide his forces."

Divide and conquer? Divide and fail? Jimmy, caught up in events of over a hundred years previously, didn't notice Des step into the tree's shade alongside him.

"Buller therefore felt he had little choice but to send the main body of his force to cross at Trichardt's, under the command of General Warren. Unfortunately for him — and his men under him — Warren had only recently arrived in South Africa. He knew nothing of the Natal terrain, nor the conditions of this new warfare against an invisible, mobile enemy."

"That doesn't sound as if it leads to a great outcome." Kevin joined Jimmy and Des under the trees. "Phew, it's getting hot already, isn't it?"

"Mm." Jimmy didn't fancy engaging in small talk. Besides, he wanted to hear what else Raymond had to say.

"Before we move on, I need to point out a couple of landmarks, so you have your bearings when we go up Spionkop this afternoon. You see that hill? The one with the lone tree on the top?"

Jimmy shielded his eyes against the sun, focusing on where Raymond pointed to the left.

"That's the summit of Spionkop. Lookout Hill. Or Spy Hill, as the Boers called it. From here we have a good view of both sides of approach to the top. With binoculars and field glasses, Buller and his aides could watch events unfolding from this vantage point. Tragic events, as it turned out." Raymond swivelled around, pointing in the opposite direction. "Beyond there, Warren and his troops were positioned. You'll understand why that's important later."

Voices coming up the path behind the clearing made Jimmy turn. Two African men trudged along, a large cooler box carried between them.

"Ah, lunch." Raymond rubbed his hands together. "When you're ready, come over to that area under the shade, grab a chair, and we'll serve you some food and drinks. Lynette said it's quiche today." He strode through the group, everyone parting to let him through. Pushing through the gate, he followed the men over to a second clearing. A green fabric, hung from a wooden framework, offered shade for the tables and chairs grouped beneath it.

"I'm starving. All these history lessons make me think I'm back at school! Did you enjoy history as a youngster, Desmond?" Kevin draped an arm over Des' shoulder, drawing him away from Jimmy.

"Wait up, I'll come with you." Bethany tucked her arm into Kevin's other side.

"That was nice of them, to give us some space." Sarah twisted her fingers into a cat's cradle. "Jimmy, I'm sorry..."

"No, I'm sorry." Jimmy, awkward, not yet ready to draw her to him, plucked a leaf from the tree. He tore it into pieces, scattering it like confetti. "Let's just leave it, shall we? For now, anyway."

"But..."

"We'll talk. I'll talk. I promise. Just not today. Not right now. I need time to...to understand for myself first." He clamped his mouth shut, feeling he'd said too much already. The pain in his head pulsed. "You don't have a paracetamol in that bag of yours, do you?"

"Of course." She rummaged in her bag. He knew he'd upset her by not responding in the way she wanted. But really, at this moment, he had nothing to offer in explanation. It was all too jumbled and confused, a collection of memories and thoughts and feelings knotted into a giant tangle. A ball of Ma's knitting wool dropped to the ground and played with by the cat. "Ah-ha, here they are. Have you got water?"

"No, but I'll swallow them as they are." Their fingers touched as she handed him the blister pack. "Give me some time, Sarah. It's all a bit much…"

"Uh-huh." She bit her lip, blinking tears.

Jimmy swallowed the last of the quiche. Crumbs cascaded onto his lap. He dusted them off as he stood from his chair.

"I want another look from over there. That was a map, wasn't it? I didn't have a chance to look at it properly. You coming?" He smiled at Sarah. A truce between them.

"Yes, alright. Not for long, though. It's too hot in this sun."

Thandi stopped them before they could leave. "Hold up, both of you. I wanted to chat to you." She pulled up a spare chair. Jimmy sat back down, perched on the edge of the seat. Where was this leading? "Jimmy, that heirloom we chatted about last night. You don't have it with you, do you?"

Jimmy relaxed against the chair's backrest. Was that all? After all the drama of the morning, he'd forgotten about the carving. "Oh, no, it slipped my mind. When we return to the hotel later…"

"Ta-da! Here, it is." Sarah pulled an object from her bag. "I…I hope you don't mind, Jimmy. I thought we might be able to show it to Thandi while we're out and about."

He smiled. No more exploding shells. "No, I'm glad you did. There's not much opportunity to chat in the evenings, it seems." He took the ornament from Sarah, turning it over in his hands. "We've had this hanging on one wall or another at home since I was a child. Mum uses it as a talisman, touching it whenever she goes out or comes home. Or when something bad happens." A memory of a football game and a phone call. Jimmy pushed it aside.

"That's wonderful. Very special." Thandi held out a hand. "Could I look at it more closely? I want to examine the writing you mentioned."

"Yes, it's there. Quite faint. Hidden under years of dust, perhaps."

"Jimmy! Don't let your mam hear you say that." Sarah swatted his arm. Peaceful relations resumed.

"Ssh, said what?" Jimmy widened his eyes in innocence. "Only joking. Here, Thandi. We've never been able to decipher what it says."

Thandi cradled the wooden cross in her palms, twisting it to catch the light. "It's beautiful." She stroked the wood. "Cherry, I think. See what a deep red tinge it has? And the pattern in the grain."

"Do you have a PhD in wood as well as warfare, then?" Jimmy hoped he didn't sound patronising.

"No. My husband is an artist. He likes anything beautiful. Especially natural wood. I've learnt a few things along the way." She smiled. "The wood gives us a clue as to its origins. Cherry isn't grown everywhere in the country, only on the higher plains, which experience cold, frosty winters. So not Natal. Now let me see..."

Squinting at the scratchings on the back, she gave a sharp intake of breath. "Oh — "

"What?" Sarah leant forward, her hair falling around her face. She tucked it behind her ear.

"Raymond, could I disturb you a minute? I want to ask your opinion on something." Thandi was on her feet.

Those gathered around Raymond frowned at her interruption.

"Excuse me for one moment. Hold that thought, young Sean. I'll be back as soon as I solve Thandi's problem." He wove his way through the picnickers. His abandoned audience grumbled. "What's that you've got there, Thandi?"

Jimmy wanted to snatch the carving back, bury it in the depths of Sarah's bag again. As Thandi and Raymond chatted together, the tour party fell silent. Curious stares flicked between the experts and Jimmy. His cheeks grew hot. He'd told Sarah she shouldn't have spoken of it with Kevin and Bethany. Thandi wouldn't realise it was a private family thing, would announce their findings to the entire group. Telling everyone Jimmy had carted a chunk of driftwood halfway around the world.

Hostilities recommenced?

Raymond and Thandi returned to sit beside Jimmy. Raymond held the ornament. "So, this has been in the family for as long as you can remember?" Jimmy nodded. A light gleamed in Raymond's eyes. Here it comes. He's having a good laugh. It's a pretty trinket, but nothing more. "I'm certain you have a unique piece of history here. Thandi, you tell him."

"So, the wood first. As I said, cherries don't grow everywhere. You mainly find them growing near Cape Town or in the Free State. A few farms cultivate them in the Gauteng area. The old Transvaal." She took the cross from Raymond. "Someone might carve a piece of wood found on their own land, or from nearby. I suppose it provided a kind of hobby during the winter. They wouldn't go to the expense of buying and transporting it from elsewhere, as perhaps they would nowadays. You understand?"

Jimmy nodded. Sarah reached for his hand.

"And then there are the words. And this is where it gets exciting." Thandi licked her lips. "You may not recognise the language, but Raymond and I do. It's Afrikaans. The language of the Boers. But that's not all — " she hurried on, preventing Jimmy from interrupting, " — some of the specific words are no longer common. But they were in use at the turn of the last century."

Jimmy and Sarah exchanged looks. "So...?"

"So that means you're right when you said you think it returned with your mother's grandfather from South Africa." Thandi leant back, beaming.

Jimmy felt a stirring of disappointment. He sort of knew that already. He had hoped for more.

"The names, though, are the most significant." Raymond spoke in the tones of a magician, saving his best trick until the audience began leaving the auditorium. "I have something to show you when we're on Spionkop."

Percy

Spionkop, South Africa
Tuesday 23 January 1900

Percy blew into his hands, wriggling his fingers to restore the blood flow to their frozen tips. Rain dripped from his helmet.

"This is worse than a Sunday afternoon picnic on the banks of the Mersey in midwinter." He stamped his feet in an effort to stimulate circulation.

"I wouldn't know." Crosby's sour response. "Some of us don't have the privilege of living at the beach."

"It's not exactly the beach…"

"Don't bother, PP. Crosby's missing his mum and his bed back home. No point arguing with him." Arthur flapped his arms around his chest. "But you're right. They could have warned us about the cold."

"When do you think we're leaving? I hope not in another two days." Alfie's turn to complain. "Why we took that long to skirt the bottom of a few hills beats me. That Warren fellow — too cautious for sense, I'm thinking."

For once, Percy agreed with his tentmate. The previous couple of months had taught him one thing; speed and agility were needed against the Boers. Lumbering along with laden ox wagons and gun carriages, proceeding at the pace of the slowest animals, halting whenever it rained, gave the enemy plenty of opportunity to follow their movements. Guess their tactics. Decide on their defensive strategy.

He greeted the order to fallout from the base at Colenso with relief. A relay of the wounded in and out of the surgeon's tent — many exiting minus at least one limb — punctuated the day; mutterings and terrified screams from the hospital disturbed the night.

Once rested after the disaster that was the attempted crossing of the wagon bridge, the Lancashire Fusiliers joined Major Coke on forays along the river, engaging in brief but exhausting skirmishes with the hidden Boers. The recovering Miller greeted their return each evening with demands for news of the action, swinging his lame arm in the vain hope the medics would give him permission to join the fun the following day.

"Look, I can hold my rifle steady. I'm ready, doc." His pleading eventually yielded the results he wanted. Whether because he was truly recovered, or whether the medical orderlies couldn't bear any more of his begging, Percy couldn't tell.

An officer on horseback rode down the line. "Get ready to leave at sunset, men. Only your day's ration packs, a water bottle, and one hundred rounds of ammunition required. Plus your rifle, of course." The soldiers laughed, waving their weapons. "No need to carry much. The supply wagons will follow us up. We'll have lunch on the top, take it in turns to fire potshots at Brother Boer."

Cheers. Percy fiddled with the strap of his ammunition pack, securing it in place. He wasn't sure it would be as easy as the officer promised.

"Sunset? We haven't had sunrise yet today, have we?" Arthur tipped his head skywards. Black clouds hung heavy over the skyline. The summit of the hill, subject of tonight's attack, drifted in and out of focus as sheets of rain obscured it from view.

Percy shuffled into position between Miller on one side, and Arthur and Mickey on the other. General Woodgate, returning to lead the Lancashire Brigade despite the pronounced limp Percy noticed when he'd inspected his troops, had ordered the fours formation until single file became necessary.

"Did you see he put the local boys in at the front?" Arthur settled his rifle over his shoulder. "That huge fellow with the red hair — he's their CO. Prickly, Thorny, something like that."

"Thorneycroft." Miller offered the correct name.

"Clever move, I should think. They'll know the lay of the land better than us, won't they?" Percy had seen the giant in camp a few times.

"You'd hope so. And something else...." Arthur paused, making certain he had the full attention of his audience. "You know that reporter who got taken at the train wreck? What's his name?"

"Churchill. Winston."

"Thanks, Miller. You really have a splendid memory, don't you? Anyway, he's with Thorneycroft."

Percy almost expected him to call for a drum roll at the announcement.

"So?" Nonplussed, he didn't want to puncture his friend's enthusiasm.

"So? He escaped. From the prison in Pretoria. That's so." Percy shook his head, unimpressed. "Oh, where is your sense of adventure, PP? I heard he jumped over a wall and hid aboard trains travelling from Pretoria to Delagoa Bay, avoiding the Boers the whole time. He caught a steamer bound for Durban from the harbour. And then rushed here so he wouldn't miss any more of the hunt."

"Where did you hear that, Houltram? You talk such nonsense." His friends laughed at Crosby's scoffing.

"It's true." Miller's quiet voice.

The jeers fell silent.

Arthur thumped Miller on the back. "Thanks, mate."

"Cigarettes out. Silent march, please, boys." Blomfield maintained manners even when issuing commands. Much to the amusement of his men.

The convoy started out, boots sloshing in the mud or clinking against unseen rocks. Percy had sodden socks within minutes, his toes numb until he stumbled into a boulder or lost his footing on the loose shale. The braying of the mules as they carried the extra supplies of water, their drivers clicking and urging them onward, accentuated the night's eeriness.

Within less than half an hour, the path narrowed to a single file track. Percy puffed his way up the steep incline, grabbing handfuls of slippery grass to pull himself over the largest of the boulders strewn across the terrain.

A sudden clatter behind him provided the rest his burning lungs and wobbling legs demanded. Leaning with hands on hips, he turned to investigate the commotion.

A stretcher carrying, not a lifeless comrade, but the paraphernalia required — picks, shovels, and spades — to protect life-filled bodies from Mauser bullets, had spilled to the ground. If the Boers could dig trenches, so could the British. Percy scrambled down the hillside to retrieve anything the others had missed, certain there must be more than the dozen or so implements he counted.

There weren't.

Once the diggers stowed the tools on the stretcher, Percy recommenced his climb. In the dark and the persistent drizzle, he lost his bearings. A figure loomed out of the gloom ahead. Percy, heart beating from more than exertion, reached for his rifle. He crept closer. The figure remained motionless.

A rock? The rock snored. Stepping closer, Percy found a khaki-clad soldier curled in the wet grass, fast asleep. He shook him awake.

"Come on, mate, you can't stay here. You'll catch your death…"

"Good joke." The man's words slurred. Drunk on exhaustion. He allowed Percy to haul him to his feet. "What time is it?"

"I dunno. About one, I suppose. Hard to tell with the moon lost behind the clouds."

The soldier swore, twisted out of Percy's grasp, and collapsed against a rock. "Leave me here. I need to sleep."

Percy hooked an arm around his waist, half pushing and half dragging the man until his legs regained their strength and he could walk unaided.

"I grew up in the Fens. Never walked up anything steeper than an anthill before this." He cursed as he stubbed his toe. "I've discovered muscles I never knew existed until now. Was quite happy not knowing about them, too."

Percy smiled into the darkness.

They toiled onward. Stars penetrated the drifting clouds, glimmers of light decorating the rainswept night. Far below, campfires glowed across the plain. Brother Boer enjoying his evening.

Wilhelm

Spionkop, South Africa
Tuesday 23 January 1900

Wilhelm blew on the dying embers of the fire. A crackle of orange sparks flew into the air.

"You never could resist playing with fire. Your Ma always wanted to stop you, but I told her to let you be." Pa slurped on his coffee. "I'm glad I found you, son."

Wilhelm nodded, a sudden lump in his throat preventing speech.

He'd ridden away from Hendrik Venter and the Standerton Commando, sickened and exhausted after the capture of the guns at Colenso. Wandering the hills with only Flooi for company, he'd taken the route to Ladysmith. To Pa.

With only half the distance covered, he met a contingent of riders under the command of General Schalk Burger galloping in the opposite direction.

"We've been ordered to join Botha's forces on the Tugela. Repulse a second attempt at crossing."

"The Carolina commando? What of them? Have they stayed in Ladysmith? Or are they also coming this way?" Wilhelm's heart had raced. How would he ever find Pa?

"Small group? Under Prinsloo? They're a few miles behind us."

Wilhelm reined in beside the road, under the shade of an acacia tree.

Pa rode out of the cloud of dust sweeping down the valley at Prinsloo's side. Percy kicked Flooi into a canter.

"Pa!"

"Wilhelm? Is that you?" Pa slowed his horse to a trot. "Venter abandoned you to find your own way, did he?"

"No, Pa. I left."

Pa's face relaxed, his eyes searching Wilhelm's face. "It's good to see you, son. I was worried. We heard about Colenso…"

Wilhelm hid the surge of emotion — the rawness of recent memories, the relief at hearing Pa's voice — by bending over Flooi to pat her neck.

"No time to waste, though. Turn around and ride with us. You're retracing your steps."

Shouts of alarm shattered the night-time calm. Two men clattered into camp, their horses snorting from exertion.

Pa dropped his cup to the ground, hurrying after Prinsloo as he strode with the newcomers to General Burger's tent.

Wilhelm stamped out the last of the smouldering twigs. He recognised the signs of an impending battle.

He collected up the tin mugs, stowing them under the tarpaulin they used as shelter against the persistent rain. Petrus shuffled over.

"I have your rifles ready. And your bandoliers are full."

"It might not be anything, Petrus." The quickened pulse belied the feigned disinterest. "They've been bombarding the range with their shells for the last two days. No doubt it's more of the same."

"The guns prepare for something more. That much I have discovered. Don't think me a fool, young Wilhelm." Petrus busied himself with tying down the canvas covers, his usual contented whistle silent.

Wilhelm wandered off in search of Flooi. He'd check on her in case they needed to ride out in the morning. The horse sheltered under a tree, rain dripping from its branches. Her head hung low, reflecting Wilhelm's mood. He ran his hands along her body, feeling the xylophone of ribs through her coat.

"You've done me proud, faithful friend." He pulled a carrot top from his pocket. She raised her head, nuzzling his palm, dark eyes staring into his. "We've worn you ragged, haven't we, old girl? Maybe Petrus should take you home. Back to Ma and Isobel."

Wilhelm rested his head against Flooi's neck, leant into her warmth as a chill settled over him from more than the dank weather. Petrus' strange mood; waiting for Pa for news — or orders; thoughts of the farm; icy fingers sending shivers up his spine.

"Wilhelm, where are you?" Pa strode out of the twilight. "Our scouts have seen the Khaki's approaching Spionkop. They seem to think we can't see in the dark. General Burger needs someone to mount a defence. Prinsloo volunteered us."

Wilhelm gave Flooi a final rub before turning to Pa. "When do we go?" Heart in his mouth.

"Now." Of course, using the darkness against the British. "Petrus has our things. We leave immediately."

Wilhelm jogged to catch up with Pa as he disappeared amongst the tents. Petrus handed him the rifle and bandolier without a word. Wilhelm flung the weighted strap over his shoulder.

"Wait." Petrus had a hand on his arm. "You forgot this."

He held the carved cross out to Wilhelm.

"Oh, I didn't forget. It's too cumbersome, too heavy, especially when I'm not riding Flooi. You hold on to it for when we return."

"No." Petrus jerked open Wilhelm's overcoat. He shoved the ornament deep into the inside pocket. "You must take it. Isobel gave it into your care. She'll want to know you didn't leave it behind."

Percy

Spionkop, South Africa
Tuesday 23 January 1900

They rounded a bend — and bumped into a young bugle boy leading a white spaniel on a length of thick twine towards camp.

"What the...?" Percy rubbed his eyes. He must be hallucinating. He'd left Bonnie curled up on his kit bag, hadn't he? Whose dog was this?

"Evening, sir. Got to take this mutt out of the way. For 'is own safety, sir. They wanted to wring 'is neck, stop 'im . But someone had a bit of old rope and used it to make a leash." The boy ruffled the dog's ears. "Nice boy, 'e is. Not 'is fault 'e's wandering around up 'ere, lost. Anyways, I must leave you gentlemen. Oh, and not much further, sir. See them bushes? Just the other side, you'll find everyone else. Waiting for you, sir."

"Thank you — er — your name?"

"Jack. Jack Pearson, sir."

"Well, thanks, Jack. And good luck with your dog there."

Jack skipped on down the hill. A child from another world.

Percy pushed on, stopping every few yards to ensure his companion remained with him.

It took an age. Percy's calves cramped on every step. He imagined he felt the blisters ballooning inside his boots. After an hour or more of climbing, they reached the thorn-covered shrubs pointed out by Jack.

Beyond, a gentle plateau flattened out. The rain had eased off, leaving in its wake a dense, swirling mist. In the pre-dawn fade from pitch black to darkest blue, Percy made out a few shapes ranged along the ridge. He paused, arching his back, massaging his aching spine with balled fists. The man with him sank to his knees.

"Looks like we're in the right place. I'm going in search of my company." Percy gave his companion a prod with the toe of his boot. "C'mon, you've come this far. You need to join your men."

The man raised his head. "I will. Give me a minute. Don't worry about me." He reached up a hand. "And thanks. Raymond Eaves. Ray."

Percy shook the hand. "Percival Barnes. Percy." He let go. "Better dash. Good luck!"

Percy fumbled his way through the mist to a group crouching beside the bushes. How would he find his company? He didn't recognise anyone amongst those he passed.

"PP, is that you? Where on earth have you been?" A harsh whisper drew Percy's attention.

"Crosby? Are you with the others?"

"Course I am. I don't drag my feet, get left behind. Like some I could mention. Good news, everyone. PP's arrived."

Percy exhaled a sigh of relief, grinning at the slight. "I stopped to help someone. Thank goodness I've found you."

"Thank goodness indeed. Now bob down here before Brother Boer notices you and uses you for target practice."

"Are they up here, then?" Percy slithered down a bank until coming to a halt beside Crosby.

"Welcome back, PP. Thought we'd lost you for a moment." Arthur waved in mock welcome. "We've not seen any sign of them. But that doesn't mean..."

A volley of rifle fire interrupted him. The fight at Colenso flashed into Percy's mind. Boers.

Above them, the scrabble of boots and a few pops from a British gun. Silence.

The attackers chased away. Or killed?

"Wish I could have a puff." Alfie held an unlit cigarette between his fingers. He held it to his lips, sucking on the end, inhaling imaginary smoke.

They lapsed into silence. Percy's eyelids, heavy with sleep, drooped.

The sound of metal clinking against stone jolted him awake. The sapper's shovels.

"We'll beat Brother Boer at his own game. Hiding in holes in the rocks. It's not sporting of them, is it?" Alfie tucked the cigarette into the pocket of his tunic. "I'll save that for later. After we win."

No more digging. Cheers burst out from the men on the summit, invigorating those resting before the final push to the top. Spionkop was in British hands.

Jimmy

Spionkop, South Africa
Tuesday 14 April 2015

The road wound up the hillside, flanked on either side by flowering bushes and waving grasses. A cluster of white crosses behind a metal fence marked the start of the battlefield.

"Boer graves. From a small contingent of soldiers posted as lookouts. In case the British sprung a night attack. They were taken by surprise." Thandi spoke from her usual position at the front. "But Raymond will tell you more. When we catch up with him."

The white Toyota Land Cruiser ahead disappeared around a corner.

Cheerful Charlie wrestled the gear lever. At the top of the climb, the track opened into a wide parking area. Raymond leant against the bonnet of his car, already waiting.

Jimmy hurried from the bus. Ever since the museum at Ladysmith, he'd been looking forward to this visit. It represented the climax of the war. Or perhaps the tipping point was a better description.

He wandered to the edge of the car park while everyone clambered from the coach. The landscape spread out below him like a three-dimensional map.

"Isn't it spectacular?" Kevin crunched across the sand and loose stones. "Especially in this light. Brian's photos should be amazing from up here."

An afternoon haze blurred the outlines of the distant hills. A river meandered through a patchwork of green and yellow fields.

"Oh, that's the Tugela again, isn't it?" Kevin traced the river's path with a pointing finger.

"I honestly don't know, mate. All those twists and turns, I've completely lost my bearings." Jimmy spun around in a slow circle, searching for any landmarks by which to fix his position. "Where were we before lunch? Mount Alice. I thought we could see this summit from there?"

"Raymond's calling us over. He must be about to start his talk. Hopefully, he'll make everything clear." Kevin rested a hand on Jimmy's arm, preventing him from marching over to the rest of the group straight away. "Before we join the others, I just want to check. You and Des — everything okay between you?"

Jimmy shook off the hand. "Of course. Why wouldn't it be?" Kevin continued to look at him, unblinking. "Alright, it's not great. Thanks for asking. But I'm sure it will work out. He's working through stuff, I suppose."

"I think you are too, aren't you?" Kevin held up his hands, palms facing Jimmy. "I don't want to pry, stick my nose in where it's not wanted. And before you go jumping to conclusions, no, Sarah hasn't mentioned anything. To either of us. I had a — well, a feeling, that's all."

Jimmy focussed on the view laid out below, avoiding eye contact. If only he could unspeak this morning's outburst. Put the worms back in the can.

Kevin thumped him on the back. "Anyway, I'm here if you need to chat, that's what I wanted to say. About you, I mean, not about Des." His hand remained between Jimmy's shoulder blades. "Come on, we'll be missing some vital nugget of information, I've no doubt."

"Thanks, Kevin." Jimmy cleared the croak from his throat. "Appreciate it."

They strolled to the group, Kevin whistling as he walked.

"...and as you can see, we've crossed the river..." Raymond paused at their approach.

"Sorry." A flush of embarrassment prickled Jimmy's cheeks.

"No, no, you haven't missed anything. I was just explaining where we are relative to this morning. Where General Buller was in relation to unfolding events.

"Now, see that tree over there? The one with the split trunks?" Everyone turned, nodding. "That's the landmark I pointed out earlier.

But from the other side. We're a good few metres below it, would you agree?"

He didn't wait for their reply.

"If you look behind you, to that hill over there — " another gesture, more shuffling of feet " — at the base of the slope. General Warren established his headquarters there."

A few nods. One or two snapped a photo.

Sean looked up from his notepad. "No, but...but that doesn't make sense." He scratched his head with the pen.

"Why not, young man? Anyone else? What's wrong with what you're seeing?" Blank faces stared back. "Come on, think strategy, think leadership. What does a general require when leading his troops into battle?"

Jimmy looked down the valley, then at the tree on the skyline. If Mount Alice was beyond that... "Wait, was this the primary site of all the action? You know, where most of the fighting took place?"

"No, it wasn't." Raymond folded his arms, the teacher waiting for the star pupil to catch up.

"You told us General Buller watched events unfold, didn't you? But you also said Warren was in command of those assigned to crossing the Tugela at this point." Jimmy hesitated. He glanced at the faces all turned in his direction. All fans of football, not war. "A good manager needs to see the field of play to direct his team to win the match, doesn't he?"

A few mutters of agreement.

"But from down there, Warren wouldn't have seen a thing, would he?" Ron stepped out of the circle, facing the valley. "That's like Brendon managing Liverpool from the Everton ground."

Delighted laughter broke out. "Or better still, Martinez managing Everton from Anfield."

"Perhaps we should suggest it for the next derby."

"Nah, we don't need to. Martinez can't organise his team even when he's at the same ground."

More laughter.

Raymond raised his hands for quiet. "That is exactly the problem. General Buller gave command of the troops to General Warren. And remember, I said he was newly arrived in South Africa. He hadn't yet experienced the new style of warfare the Boers employed — mounted commandos, able to come and go with ease, hiding in the hills or in their trenches. Smokeless bullets and artillery.

"So, Warren set up camp there below us. General Buller planned for him to strike quickly, not give the Boers any chance to mount a defence. But Warren was cautious, unsure. If any of you watch cricket, you'll know it's when the batsman feels trapped and uncertain, that he's at his most reckless."

"Or when Rickie Lambert gets tied up by the defence and kicks a flyer for goal from outside the box. And misses."

"Yes, that sort of thing. Harried by Buller into making his move, Warren abandoned the agreed plan to cross through Trichardt's drift, skirting the hills, while protected by an artillery bombardment from the naval guns situated over there —" Raymond pointed out a hazy summit in the distance, " — and instead decided he needed to secure the high ground overlooking the drift first. This high ground.

"So, let's find out how that plan worked, shall we? We'll take a short walk along that path there, then we'll discuss the first act of the day's play. The first half, if you like."

Percy

Spionkop, South Africa
Wednesday 24 January 1900

The morning artillery bombardment began while the cloying fog still shrouded the hillside. The signal to advance.

Before Percy could gather himself, a corresponding thump split the air.

"Brother Boer. He knows we're here." Arthur flinched, as though expecting incoming shrapnel to descend on their unsuspecting heads.

"That's miles from our position. They're probably trying to take out our guns, but their peashooters don't have the range." Had Crosby forgotten Colenso already? "They're tired of us waking them up so early, that's all."

"We made quite a racket last night. Perhaps they heard." Mickey sounded nervous. A more appropriate response than Crosby's scoffing.

"Well, whatever. We must secure this hill and prepare a way for the 15-pounders to come up." Miller spoke with calm practicality. His arm fully healed, he seemed as eager as ever to engage with the enemy. Percy wondered why he kept going in for more. Perhaps the competition between him and the cousin? The one with all the inside information.

"Up and at 'em, men. Wakey, wakey, rise and shine. Brother Boer's waiting for you." The order carried down the line.

A staccato pop, pop punctuated the thud and rumble of the shells. Colenso again.

"Gunfire. From above us. What the...?" Crosby's bravado vanished.

"Are we in the wrong place?" Mist blurred Percy's vision. Only the shapes of his fellow soldiers, murky and indistinct, showed themselves.

"Boers. On our right flank." A shout from the furthest edge of the ridge where the officers encamped. General Woodgate insisted his staff should remain close by, able to receive orders the moment they were issued.

A commotion as someone went in pursuit. More pops.

Percy pressed his forehead against the cold steel of his rifle barrel. Fear slithered through his empty stomach. It was happening again. This invisible enemy everywhere and nowhere at once, a will-o'-the-wisp hiding in the shadows and flitting through the mists and fogs of this hostile outpost.

"Come on, lads. For Queen and Country. We've got business to do today, and no Mr Kroojer is going to stop us." Miller surged forward, his rifle held at the ready.

Arthur leapt up, scampering up the hillside, a cascade of stones and pebbles tumbling down onto Percy. He dodged out of the way, grabbing for purchase as he tried to gain his footing and follow his comrades. He slipped down a yard or two. His knee collided with a rock. Pain coursed through his leg. Blast this mountain. And blast this war. He wanted to be at home, far from the cracks and whistles of gunfire and shelling. Far from the blistering sun, the freezing rain.

"PP. What you doing down there?" Mickey's voice spurred Percy into action.

He shook his head, banishing thoughts of Flo and the Mersey, and the ring he would buy, and the proposal he would make. Ignoring his throbbing leg, he scrabbled up to Mickey.

"Where to?" He found himself shouting above the increasing din of guns and explosions, bullets pinging off rocks, or shrapnel shattering those same rocks to smithereens. Could he hear screams? Or was it birdsong, and his imagination playing tricks on him?

"Up there. You were right. We're not where we should be. At all."

Percy realised he was shaking, every muscle jangling and twanging with an anger he hadn't known was possible to experience. He'd trusted that those in authority knew what they were doing, understood the implications and consequences of their decisions. He believed they sought his good, not his harm. Four months, and everything he'd ever thought stood on its head, laughing at him for his naiveté. Crosby was right; he was a young fool.

He pushed up from the ground, a roar spilling from his throat. If they — his comrades, his regiment, his friends — were being sent to their deaths by the orders of the far-away, they wouldn't go alone. He would be at their side.

He scuttled forward. His foot caught against something. Not a rock. Too soft. Maybe a tree root. He glanced down. An arm. Sliced from a bleeding torso. He recognised the man from camp. He'd never asked his name.

Percy, clenching his jaw until his teeth ached, pressed on, Mickey close by.

"You should draw this, Mickey. Show people what really happened."

"It would put them off their breakfast eggs and kippers, PP." Mickey raised his rifle. Released a shot. An instant reply from their right. Percy ducked as bullets ricocheted past. "Oof..."

"Mickey, you're hit." Blood oozed down Mickey's face, dripping over his collar. Percy attempted to reach his friend, assess the injury, and stem the bleeding. A second volley of rifle fire pinned him in place.

"Just my ear. Nothing serious." Beads of sweat glistened on his forehead. "Let's get those..." The crump of an exploding shell swallowed the expletive.

Percy rose from behind the low wall of a trench too shallow to protect his body. He aimed his weapon. And fired into the blinding glare of the rising sun.

Wilhelm

Spionkop, South Africa
Wednesday 24 January 1900

Wilhelm crawled through the damp grass. He'd ridden on the back of Pa's horse, arms hooked round Pa's waist; Flooi too weak for the two-mile gallop. Petrus had waved them away, his fingers twisted through the pony's mane. Two pairs of sombre brown eyes watching their departure.

Leaving all the horses tethered to trees and bushes in the plain below, Prinsloo gathered his commando around him.

"Burghers, we're now going to attack the enemy. We won't all return. Do your duty and trust in the Lord."

Wilhelm felt the weight of the cross in his pocket. Would the Lord come to their rescue tonight?

Prinsloo continued speaking. "General Botha has called for reinforcements to join us from amongst the other, larger commandos. The burghers from Pretoria, Krugersdorp, Standerton — all who can be spared — will accompany us, of that I am certain." Standerton. Would Hendrik Venter be amongst them? "We must attack this side of the hill and stop the British from establishing an artillery presence on the summit. Should they succeed, all will be lost, and our brothers will be hard-pressed to defend the Tugela line against the Khaki's advance. There is no time to lose, and we can't wait for fighters to arrive. We go alone. Alone, except for the Lord."

Wilhelm grinned at Malan and Meyer next to him, certain his expression shone with the same pride as theirs. A mere ninety men from the small town of Carolina were tasked with taking the twin peaks looming ahead. Snatching victory from the hands of the Khakis.

They set off, spreading across the hillside. Pa went ahead beside Prinsloo. Scouting the terrain, alerting their followers to danger.

The first barrage of artillery from the British position startled Wilhelm. Although the same every morning, somehow this seemed closer, more menacing.

A familiar thump responded. Botha had brought the Creusot guns into action.

"Sounds like ours this time. Bet the Khakis weren't expecting that." Malan trudged alongside Wilhelm. "They probably thought we didn't notice them trying to sneak over the river. More fool them."

The pounding continued, the distant British guns competing with the closer Creusots and Boer field guns, the mist dulling the sounds of impact. Wilhelm's wet fingers slipped on the barrel of his Mauser. He dried them on his overcoat. The steady incline dragged at his lungs, his breath puffing as he climbed. Settling into a rhythmic plod, he could almost imagine himself out on the open veld at home, hunting down an elusive prey. Would he stumble upon it, frighten it caught in a thicket? Or would he follow its spoor throughout the day, patience winning over stealth?

Prinsloo paused a few yards below a cluster of boulders and scrubby trees. He gestured for his men to lie low to the ground. The hunter in charge of his team.

"We must split up, spread out along the ridge ahead." Wilhelm strained to hear the whisper above his own breathing, the continuous clatter of shellfire. "Some to the left. The picket they attacked last night was on the steeper part of the slope. We think the British are dug in somewhere near there."

"I overheard one of them talking. Said one minute he was dozing off, dreaming of dinner. The next the Khakis were over the top and onto them." Meyer spoke out of the corner of his mouth. "Doesn't know how he escaped with little more than a scratch."

"Not everyone did." Wilhelm wished Malan didn't feel the need to complete the story. Pa had already filled him on the details.

"Marthinus, you cover that side. I'll take the front with this group here." Wilhelm fell under Prinsloo's command.

Pa hesitated, counting those he'd have with him. His gaze held Wilhelm's for a few seconds, then he resumed with his tally.

"That looks a good compromise." He nodded his satisfaction.

"Men, with me." Prinsloo gestured forward.

Wilhelm's legs refused to move. He loosened his shirt collar, hands trembling. He waited for a wave of dizziness to subside. Not trusting himself to stand without fainting.

A hand massaged his shoulder. "Son..." Pa. Wilhelm inhaled the smell of damp coat, of coffee and woodsmoke. Of comfort. "Be strong and courageous, child."

The Bible phrase preached by Dominee Fourie before they left home. Wilhelm lifted his head, mute.

Pa moved his hand to cradle his cheek. "You heard the Commandant; trust in the Lord, son. Trust in His promises of protection, His assurance of victory." He pressed his lips to Wilhelm's forehead. "And go with my blessing. We'll meet beside the fire when this is all over."

Wilhelm leaned into Pa's embrace, still unable to speak. Perhaps it was the drifting mist, the size of their force or Prinsloo's speech, but this parting differed from before.

A rattle of rifle fire. The moment passed.

Pa released Wilhelm, pulling his rifle around. He gave a final, long stare and crept into the paling grey of the morning light.

Wilhelm wiped his face with his sleeve. Energy surged through him. He clambered up to the edge.

As the sun broke through the clouds, warming his neck, he raised his head. To look straight into the eyes of a blinded Khaki.

He fired.

Jimmy

Spionkop, South Africa
Tuesday 14 April 2015

"The Boers positioned their artillery over there — " Raymond pointed to the right " — and on the opposite hillside, there."

The group gathered beside the path, the car park out of sight. Jimmy stepped up on a rock, straining to see over everyone's heads. Here, the slope down the valley seemed less severe, despite being strewn with gullies. He didn't fancy trying to hike up here in the dark.

"Were they within range?" Ron looked doubtful. "Surely their guns weren't as powerful as our naval ones."

"You're right, they weren't. But distances are deceptive, partly because of the relative heights of the hills. And, also bear in mind, the British artillery were focusing their attention on the range further east, believing the Boers were concentrated in that area." Raymond turned and pointed directly down the hill in front of them. "When, in fact, Botha's men were here, sent to defend Spionkop against the British infantry.

"Can you make out those white roofs in the distance? Surrounded by some trees?" Jimmy thought he knew where Raymond meant. "That's Ladysmith."

"No way. I thought we were miles from there." Claire raised a pair of binoculars.

"No. It really wasn't a vast undertaking to reach there. A river in flood and a few thousand Boers did present a problem, though!" Raymond chuckled.

"Only a few thousand? Surely the British outnumbered the Boers, then?" Brian lowered his camera. "Their fire power must have been superior, their military know-how. It should have been a walkover. Well, this bit anyway. I can understand things going awry at Colenso. Wrong maps, that sort of thing."

"You're forgetting the Boer's superior knowledge of the terrain. And their added mobility. Most, if not all, rode on horseback. Contrast that to the lumbering war machine of the British, who relied almost solely on the railway network or ox wagons to move around." Raymond sipped water from a bottle. "And the reconnaissance was possibly worse for this second campaign than it was at Colenso. You recall where Warren was based?"

Some nods.

"It wasn't possible for him to observe events unfolding here, no matter how strong his binoculars were. And yet he was officially commanding the battle. As opposed to Buller. Now, from here, you don't overlook Mount Alice. But if we stood where Botha had his guns, we could. Which means Buller could see Botha's guns. And their devastating effect on his troops as they summited the kopje."

"At what point did the Brits realise they were in the wrong place? You know, on that false top?" Jimmy indicated the path behind them.

"Almost as soon as it grew light. The first casualty was Woodgate himself — the Lancashire Brigade's general. He went to investigate reports of Boers on the right flank of that first trench. The Boers shot him for his efforts, and he was invalided back to base with an injured eye."

"Carried down from the battle site in damp, treacherous conditions by the Indian stretcher bearers. They were local volunteers from Durban, descendants of the indentured labourers brought to South Africa in the 1860s by the British to work on the newly-developing sugar plantations. Men who, at personal cost to themselves, chose to serve their imperial masters in the Ambulance Corps rather than take up arms." Thandi curled her lip, as though recoiling from a foul smell. "Although why they felt the need to be involved at all is a matter for a whole other debate."

"And the Africans? You said you'd researched their involvement too?" Des, hanging around at the edge of the party, joined the conversation. Jimmy didn't need to turn to imagine the aggressive stance of hands on hips, chin jutting forward.

"I have, Des." Thandi pulled on a braid. "You'll hear lots about the inadequate trenches that the Africans dug for the British. Or how, like at Colenso, the African guides led the British officers to the wrong crossing points. You'll even read commentaries stating this was a 'white man's war', that British and Boer alike kept to a gentleman's agreement to not involve 'the natives'."

"But?" Des, as if accusing Thandi of writing the history books.

"But, it simply isn't true." Raymond answered for her. "Without the help of the African and Indian populations, neither British nor Boer could have waged war for longer than a few months, much less the years it dragged on for. And the price paid by the indigenous people was as high..."

"More so, if you consider it went unrecognised." Thandi interrupted, bouncing on her toes as she talked. "Which is why I'm grateful to Raymond and others for campaigning to erect a memorial here at Spionkop in honour of these unsung heroes."

Her smile illuminated her face.

Des let out a low whistle. "There's a monument here? Where? I didn't notice anything."

"It's at the top. We'll go past it on the way to the bus. We'll give you some time to wander around the site before we return to the lodge for supper. But anyway, Raymond, sorry for interrupting." She laughed. "Please, carry on."

"No, not an interruption at all. It's important to emphasise the roles of those outside the limelight, remembering their sacrifice, as much as it is to focus on those we all know about."

Jimmy's heart skipped a beat. That comment hit home. He shuffled his feet, hoping no one noticed any reaction.

Sarah slipped a hand into his. So maybe someone had.

Raymond continued speaking. "Where was I? Oh, yes, Woodgate. So, with him absent from the field, the command of the Lancashires passed to Colonel Blomfield. Unfortunately for him — and his men — he sustained critical injuries and had to be pulled to shelter out of the line of fire."

"Doesn't sound like there were many substitutes left on the bench."

"That's a good way of thinking about it. Major Massey, the officer responsible for marking out the trench his sappers were to dig, fell dead within minutes of engagement. And the wonderfully named Captain Vertue, the Brigade's Major, was also mortally wounded."

"How do you remember all those names?" Sean sounded impressed, scribbling in his notebook as he asked the question.

"Ah, well, there are some that are so integral to the story, they're easy to remember. As to the others — that's why we strive to maintain this site in its present state. Each life lost is recorded on the monuments and memorials here. The British and the Boer. And, as Thandi mentioned, the Indian and African dead." He paused. Was it Jimmy's imagination, or did Raymond look straight at him? "I think you'll find the records fascinating."

"Okay, so everyone in charge has died. What happened next?" Des, impatient as ever. Perhaps he was thinking of another memorial, another list of names, found on a plaque above a bench with 96 wooden slats.

"A good question. Now the command rested with a Colonel Malby Crofton, of the Royal Lancasters. He recognised the need for reinforcements, but in the confusion of operations, found it impossible to heliograph to Warren with the request. Rather than send a written report by messenger and horse, however, he relied on the accurate signalling of a flagman to communicate his SOS. Once having dictated a brief message, he seems to have left the battlefield entirely. It was left to a Durban man, the commanding officer of the Natal Mounted Infantry, one Colonel Thorneycroft, to save the day."

Percy

Spionkop, South Africa
Wednesday 24 January 1900

"Men, with me!" Colonel Thorneycroft's command bellowed above the din.

He rushed over the patch of scrubby grass between the main trench and the new one along the crest, dug in a hurry as the mist lifted and exposed their actual position. His burly figure and shock of red hair made him an easy man to follow through the chaos.

Percy, inspired by the earlier heroic dash of a Fusilier lieutenant he vaguely remembered as called something-or-other-Charlton, took a deep breath and dived into the fray, much like a swimmer submerging himself in the choppy waters of the Mersey.

Bent low, he scuttled forward, weaving past mutilated figures in shredded khaki. Out of the corner of his eye, he saw Miller leap over a pile of rocks before flinging himself flat on the ground and crawling to the edge of the trench. He peered over.

In slow motion, Percy watched as Miller's head flicked back, his body arching before crumpling backwards. Blood soaked his uniform.

No time to stop, to cover him. To mourn.

Percy pushed on, sweat dripping into his eyes, blinding his progress.

A Boer shell screamed overhead. Shrapnel rained out of a smoke-filled sky. Percy lost his footing, the explosion propelling him forward faster than his legs could move. A cry from behind. Mickey, flung onto his back, the jacket ripped from his torso.

Propped against a rock, blood pulsing from two gaping wounds, an officer continued to shoot at the Boers. At a burst of returning fire, the officer slumped over. His rifle clattered to the ground, released from his grip.

Percy looked away. Another officer stood, exposing himself to the onslaught of bullets. He gesticulated to the right, mouthing words Percy couldn't hear. Thorneycroft turned around to where the man pointed. His foot caught on something, and he fell.

Percy hurried to his aid, unsure what injuries he would find.

"Ankle." Thorneycroft groaned, his foot at an awkward angle beneath him. No blood stained his trousers. "Tell the men to fall back."

Percy looked around. Only a few remained to carry out the order. About to run in search of help to haul Thorneycroft to safety, a shout from the left caught his attention.

Arthur. Percy abandoned the prostrate Thorneycroft and scuttled to his friend.

"What kept you?" Arthur twisted his lips into a lopsided smile. Dried blood crusted around a gash on his temple. "Come and join the fun. Brother Boer is over this hump. And putting up quite a fight. Watch out..."

He yanked on Percy's sleeve, pulling him down. Mausers rattled.

"I think they saw you, PP. Sending you a welcome message." He discharged a couple of rounds in reply. "You brought any spare ammunition with you? I'm all out."

"They're dead, Arthur. Miller, Mickey." Percy tucked in behind the trench wall, lying on his stomach, the barrel of his rifle resting on a mound of soil. Sharp stones poked through his tunic, scraping his flesh. Better than a Boer bullet. Without waiting to take aim, he pulled the trigger. "And no, nothing spare — " reload " — supply wagons can't make it — " fire, reload " — water run out."

No reply. Percy glanced to his side.

Arthur, helmet knocked from his head, limbs askew. His dark hair black against the white of his skin. "Shot, PP." His eyelids flickered, then closed.

Percy crawled to him, shaking his shoulder. "Wait, Arthur, I'll get the medic."

"Too late, PP." A rattle of breath. "Time's up."

Percy clasped Arthur's limp hand. Fingers fluttered at his touch. Stilled.

"We should give ourselves up." Percy jumped at the voice. Alfie. He dragged himself next to Percy, his arm hanging useless at his side. His eyes shone with a delirious brightness. "There're no officers left. It's just us. We should surrender."

"No." The word exploded from Percy. He laid Arthur's lifeless hand on his chest. Pulling a handkerchief from his pocket, he placed it over Arthur's face. He should pray, but there wasn't anything he wanted to say that God would want to hear. "Then all this — " he waved a shaking hand at the carnage " — is for nothing."

Alfie cradled his arm, rocking on his haunches. "It's for nothing, anyway."

A crackle of musketry. Alfie's deadweight collapsed into Percy's lap.

Percy tried to push the body off, to wriggle free from underneath it. He clawed at the loose earth, his boots slipping on bullet casings and shrapnel debris. Black spots clouded his vision. He slumped backwards, disentangling his legs at last.

He rolled away, curled in a heaving, retching heap.

Someone stood at the end of the trench. A white rag quivered in the breeze.

Wilhelm

Spionkop, South Africa
Wednesday 24 January 1900

"They're surrendering!"

Wilhelm collapsed to his knees, holding himself upright by leaning on his upturned rifle. His shoulders cramped, spasming from the exhaustion of being kept in one position for hour after hour.

Jacobus Malan flopped down next to him. He glugged at his water bottle. "I was about to run for home." He shook the bottle. A trickle of final drops dribbled over his beard. "Not such a fun hunt, after all."

Fun. Wilhelm could think of no word further from that morning's experience. With grudging admiration, he'd watched wave after wave of khaki figures repelling the Boer attack on the forward trench.

"Why do you think their main trench was on the other side?" The question had mystified him since the burning away of the mist revealed the true situation on the summit of the hill. "They were too low down."

"I don't know. Got lost in the fog, probably." Malan wafted his hat in front of his face. "I wouldn't mind it coming back. Or, even better, the rain."

Heat shimmered off the rocks littered along the slope. Pools of shade spread around the aloe plants, their spikey leaves reaching skyward.

A shell crashed into the kop behind them. A cloud of dust mushroomed in the air, obscuring the sun. Wilhelm coughed.

A round of rifle fire spilled over the crest. "I thought they had surrendered." Wilhelm scrambled for cover behind a rock.

"Must have been a false alarm." Malan grunted, rolling to his knees. "We should take a look."

They crawled to the edge of the commando's makeshift dugout. The British bullets had found their mark. Christiaan Meyer lay in a pool of blood, his rifle flung aside. Another of the Carolina men sprawled across him, his leg and foot smashed to a pulp. An old man Wilhelm recognised from previous skirmishes held his Mauser wedged in the crook of his elbow, his bloodied hand dangling from the wrist. Tucked alongside him, a boy four or five years younger than Wilhelm released the trigger. Soft brown eyes glistened in similar features. Father and son? Too apart in age. Grandfather and grandson, then?

"Doesn't look like surrender to me." Malan loaded his rifle from his bandolier. "Not many of these left. Better make them count."

He discharged the ammunition into the British trench just yards away. Malan turned to Wilhelm, grinning. A soldier appeared from behind the barricade, pistol raised.

"Jacob..." Too late. The man fired. Malan's eyes widened. He crashed forward, tumbling down the hill. He came to rest at Wilhelm's side.

Wilhelm jerked away, shivering as though doused in icy water.

"A white flag. I see a white flag." Wilhelm dragged his attention away from Malan as the cry echoed from above. He jumped up. This time, he wanted to check for himself.

Over to his left, a small square of fabric rippled white in a shaking hand.

Wilhelm didn't hesitate. He grabbed his weapon and ran towards the British trench. His boot caught on something hidden in the grass. Flying headlong to the ground, he lay winded, his eyes closed. Regaining his breath, he sat up, searching for the object he'd fallen over. A pair of lifeless blue eyes stared back at him. Matted hair the colour of corn.

Hendrik Venter.

Something between a scream and a roar exploded in Wilhelm's belly. He surged to his feet, heart pounding. He would be there to capture the British prisoners. He would see the fear in their eyes as they witnessed the pain in his.

Percy

Spionkop, South Africa
Wednesday 24 January 1900

"There will be no surrender." A figure hobbled into view, leaning on a makeshift stick made from a tree branch. Thorneycroft.

Too late. The Boers were already clambering out of their positions and storming their position. Percy wavered. Should he open fire, or rather lay down his weapon and raise his arms in defeat?

"Fire! Fire!" Thorneycroft brandished his stick, waving it at the oncoming Boers. "I am the Commanding Officer here; take your men away, as I will allow no surrender."

The Boers didn't halt their advance. A bullet whistled past Percy's ear. Thorneycroft's defiance had galvanised his troops into action.

Percy's decision was made. Abandoning all thoughts of surrender, his mind saturated with images of Miller and Mickey, of Alfie and Arthur, he hefted his rifle. A young man in a floppy hat ran, shrieking, straight at him. Percy flexed his finger. The lad spun around, a dancer on a stage performing a pirouette.

The shadows lengthened across the hillside. Percy shivered, a chill creeping over him. The aftermath of battle filled the air; the eerie stillness of silenced guns; the staccato pop of a few remaining tussles between enemies. Flies buzzed and crawled. Men cried out, or groaned, or screamed. Or lay in prone silence.

The crunch of boots on gravel as the Indian stretcher bearers wandered from group to group in search of those worth bearing.

Percy struggled to his feet. Blood crusted around a hole in his trousers where shrapnel had grazed his shin. He staggered along the trench, desperate to escape the butcher-shop stench, the carnage. No one stirred.

Dipping below the horizon — beyond the hills encircling Ladysmith — the sinking sun painted the sky in slashes of vivid orange and magenta pink. Percy recognised the familiar forked tails of swallows as their silhouettes flitted across the sky. Another creature far from home.

A boulder perched on the gently sloped hillside. Percy would hide there, watch the evening display. Pretend he was somewhere else. He crawled to it, his legs weak and his arms bruised.

He flopped behind the boulder, resting against its solid bulk as though it were the softest of pillows. His eyelids drooped.

A dull moan set his pulse racing. He snapped his eyes open, reached for his rifle. The waning light after the intense brightness of the day confused him. Was that a person lying near his feet?

The shape groaned again. A wounded soldier. Percy dropped the gun into the grass and scooted forward until he was level with the figure.

"You're injured. Let me look..." He removed the slouch hat from the figure's face. A sharp intake of breath burned his throat. The boy he'd shot stared back.

Percy recoiled in horror. A Boer. Then he noticed the hands twitching at the waist of a blood-soaked overcoat. What did it matter whether it was Boer or British? The lad needed help. Or company.

Percy reached for his water bottle. He had a few drops left. Unscrewing the cap, he wriggled down to the boy.

"Do you speak English?"

"Yes." The voice so faint Percy had to bend his ear over the lad's mouth to hear.

"I have water for you. Here, I'll help you." Percy cradled the boy's head. He dribbled the water onto his lips.

A tongue licked at the droplets of water. "Thank you."

"Here. Let's see if we can't make you comfortable. While we wait for help." Percy unlooped the straps of his haversack, letting them slide to the ground. With slow, clumsy movements, his fingers raw and puffy, he unbuttoned his tunic. Hitching his arms out of the sleeves, he folded the fabric into a loose cushion.

He lifted the boy's head again, wedging the pillow into place. "There, that should be better."

"It is." The boy sighed. Rousing himself, he rolled his head, blue eyes watching Percy. "You're British."

"Yes."

"And you're helping me." A gurgling breath. "Staying with me."

"Yes." Percy dripped a little more liquid on the boy's lips. "My name is Percy."

"And mine is Wilhelm."

"I'm pleased to meet you, Wilhelm."

"I came with my Pa. Lost him. Don't know where he is." Wilhelm shifted his position. He winced. "I'm afraid, Percy."

Percy grasped his hand. "I am too, Wilhelm." He took a shaky breath. "I'm sorry, Wilhelm. I think we shouldn't be here. In your country, in your land."

"No. But you are. I am sorry we fought you."

Wilhelm's chest rose and fell with ever-laboured breaths.

Moaning, he plucked at his overcoat. "Percy..." Nothing more than a whisper.

"What do you need, Wilhelm? Something in your pocket?" Percy pulled aside the overcoat. His vision swam at the sight of a mass of mangled flesh beneath its folds. Mangled by a bullet fired from his rifle.

He inhaled a shallow breath.

He reached into the coat's inside pocket. Touching a solid object, he eased it out.

A wooden cross. He examined it, stroking the surface with fingers numbed by a weeping heart. "It's beautiful." The words snagged in his throat.

A long silence.

"Take it home for me, Percy." A hand slick with blood wrapped around Percy's. "Promise me, Percy. You'll take it home."

Percy swallowed. "I promise, Wilhelm. I'll return it to your family."

Jimmy

Spionkop, South Africa
Tuesday 14 April 2015

Jimmy stared at the engraving etched into the shiny grey marble. It didn't mean much. However, he looked at it. Some of the words reminded him of the carving. How much longer would he have to wait before Thandi and Raymond revealed its secrets to him?

They'd been deep in conversation with each other, sidelong glances cast his way, ever since the official part of the tour broke up, everyone wandering around the graves and memorials in small groups. Des had disappeared, declaring in a loud voice he was off in search of the memorial erected to honour the Africans and Indians. He didn't speak to Jimmy or Sarah, seeming to avoid them since leaving Mount Alice at lunchtime.

Jimmy had noticed Kevin chatting to him, recognised the change in expression, the folded arms. No doubt he'd be gearing up for another night's whiskey drinking later.

Ron and Claire, Kevin and Bethany went out to the edge of the ridge overlooking the dam below. Bethany held onto Claire's hand, the two sniffing into tissues. The snaking lines of trenches, piled high with the local red-brown stones between white painted lines, unnerved them all. Raymond explained the carnage was so complete, the destruction so appalling, many of those killed remained buried where they fell. Buried in three-deep piles of bodies.

Jimmy swayed at the thought of it, his stomach churning with queasiness. His mind refused to imagine such horrors, instead focussing on the beauty of their final resting place. A sudden, unbidden thought flickered. Was that what Des meant when he accused Jimmy of not engaging with his experiences? Did he change the subject, chatting about the latest scores or the cloudiness of his pint instead of really listening to his mate describing the most terrifying day of his life?

"This monument is to the fallen Boer soldiers." Jimmy dragged himself away from his navel gazing, concentrating on Raymond's story. "The quote is from FW Reitz, the Former State Secretary of the South African Republic. Perhaps of more interest, he is the father of Deneys Reitz, a young Boer of sixteen who joined the war alongside his two brothers. He recorded an account of his involvement. I strongly recommend you read it if you want to extend your knowledge of what happened here."

It sounded a bit dry. Packenham was hard enough to get through; Jimmy didn't fancy a second book, this time in Afrikaans.

"It's fantastic, told by Deneys himself. Translated into English, of course. We wouldn't expect you to learn a different language just to read it. It's full of plucky adventures and daring deeds!" Thandi's enthusiasm made him rethink. "It also contains perhaps the most accurate description of the battle on Spionkop."

"We should buy that when we get home." Sarah's whisper echoed his own thoughts. "Not for the blood and gore — you can read that part. But to understand how it was for the other side. I suspect it makes for uncomfortable reading."

"Mm, I would think so." He lifted his hand a fraction. "Raymond, Thandi. What does it mean in English?"

Thandi cleared her throat. "I'll recite it as it's written first, in my best Afrikaans." She winked. "Seriously, it's worth you hearing it in its own words, if you see what I mean. We don't always need a translator to understand the meaning."

She dropped her hands to her side, her gaze fixed on the horizon.

"She must have memorised it." Sarah snuggled into Jimmy's side. "I'm crying already, and she hasn't said a word."

Jimmy kissed the top of her head, too mesmerised by the suddenly sombre atmosphere to speak. He closed his eyes, allowing Thandi's voice to transport him through time.

"Dapper en pligsgetrou aan volk en vaderland.

'Laat hulle nageslag hulle nooit vergeet nie, solank die mensdom bestaan.

Totdat selfs die hemel uitgeput is en die aarde wankel tot haar val.'

Eksodus 15: 18. Die Here sal vergewe vir ewig en altyd."

Thandi was right. He didn't need an interpreter to feel the heart. Sarah sniffed into his T-shirt. He blinked away tears.

Thandi paused, watching the reaction of her audience.

"And now the English...

Steadfast and loyal to nation and native country.

'Let their offspring never forget them, as long as mankind exists.

Until even heaven will be exhausted and earth staggers to its fall.'

Exodus 15:18. The Lord will reign for ever and ever."

"They really believed God was with them, didn't they?" Sarah spoke through a bundle of tissue.

"They did. And as the war ground on, their belief grew, rather than diminished." Raymond tucked his handkerchief back in his pocket. "Despite Britain committing some of the worst atrocities against civilians anyone had ever seen before. But that's for a different day. We have something to show you, Jimmy, Sarah. Come around this way..."

He led them along the path to the front of the monument. Jimmy shielded his eyes from the sun. A list of names was inscribed on a second grey marble surface.

He scanned the records. Nothing jumped out at him. Unless...but no, the initial was 'S'.

"Jimmy! There, under the list for Standerton." Sarah grabbed Jimmy's wrist. She dragged him a step closer to the monument, pointing. "Isn't that who carved the second inscription?"

Could it be? Beside him, Raymond and Thandi nodded, smiles beaming. Like proud parents waiting for a child to discover treasure.

STANDERTON. The fourth name. VENTER H.C.A.

Palms clammy, Jimmy gripped the railings. He checked through the inscriptions again. His breath caught. The third group from the top. The one with the most names. Under the heading 'Carolina'.

There it was. There he was.

OLIVIER W

Wilhelm Olivier. Of the Carolina Commando. Died on Spionkop on the twenty-fourth of January, 1900.

The owner of Grampy Percy's wooden cross.

Jimmy

Spionkop, South Africa
Wednesday 15 April 2015

The last notes of the bagpipe faded, carried on the breeze down a hillside and over a river.

The page shook in Des' hand, a faint rustle against the sniffs and coughs of emotion.

"John Alfred Anderson, age sixty-two.
Colin Mark Ashcroft, age nineteen.
James Gary Aspinall, age eighteen.
Kester Roger Marcus Ball, age sixteen."

Des recited each name. At each breath, Jimmy added an extra name in his mind.

"Kevin Daniel Williams, eleven..." Wilhelm Olivier, unknown age. " Wright, seventeen."

Wilhelm Olivier, unknown age.

Jimmy wandered away from the others, a new grief overlaying the old. A connection to Grampy Percy, one he'd never felt before, seemed to flow from the soil through his feet and up into his heart. How did Grampy Percy end up here, on this very hillside? Did he look over the same view, grieving the loss of his friends? Was he unsure how to continue as the living?

Jimmy stopped beside a twisted tree, its trunk split into three pieces. The one they'd seen from Mount Alice. Landmark of modern day Spionkop. Pulling the heirloom from his pocket, he fingered the smooth surface of a different tree.

"Do you know its story? The tree with three trunks?" He hadn't heard Des approach. "Raymond told me."

"No." He wasn't in the mood for stories. He wasn't in the mood for Des.

"A woman brought it from England, as a sapling. The mother of a young soldier who died in the battle." Des kicked at a stone. "She wanted to mark his grave, even though she would never find his remains."

He sighed.

"Lightning's struck it four times. It's nearly blown over twice as many. And yet here it stands." He draped an arm around Jimmy's neck. He tensed against the touch. "A crooked testimony to the power of life, Jimmy."

A crack opened in Jimmy's defences.

"I'm getting help when we get back. Kevin's putting me in contact with some people. From his church, of all places." A hollow, out of place, laugh. "Jimmy, I'm sorry. You've marked my sorrow since we were fifteen…"

Des' voice broke. His face crumpled.

"Des, it's…" Jimmy couldn't continue.

"Let me finish, Jimmy." Des gulped a couple of breaths. "You've been like that tree, and I've been the lightning and the wind. I wanted to tear you down, destroy you like I thought I was destroyed. Bury you with me."

The evening breeze rustled through the branches. A bird called from its shelter. Jimmy's shoulders shook, a fifteen-year-old's heart breaking through the brittle exterior of a forty-something-year-old's composure.

"But you wouldn't die, Jimmy. You just kept growing. Spreading your shade over me. Sharing Sarah and the kids with me. Sheltering me."

Jimmy choked on a sob. He squeezed the wooden cross until its edges bit into the flesh of his hand.

"It's alright, Des. It's the least I could do."

Jimmy

Midway between South Africa and England
Friday 17 April 2015

Sarah rested her head against his shoulder, her fingers entwined in his. The overhead lights extinguished, they sat in the soft glow of a sleeping aircraft.

"Are you alright, Jimmy?" A gentle probing now they were alone in the bubble of travel.

"I'm not sure, to be honest. It's been quite an...an experience, hasn't it?" Jimmy settled back in his seat. "I think it'll take a while to process, work through everything."

"And you're okay with Kevin getting involved with Des?" She chewed on her lip. "I'm sorry. I probably shouldn't have said anything to them. They just seemed to care, and have peace about a solution that I've not seen in anyone else."

Jimmy kissed her hand. "You did what I never could. Led Des to the help he needs. I always thought I should be enough, you know? Able to make up for not being there on the day, by being there forever after." He scrunched his face. "A crooked tree indeed."

Sarah lifted her head. "That story really moved you, didn't it? You and Des have been different around each other since the memorial. Calmer or something. Less tense."

"Mm, I suppose so. We'll see if it lasts."

She squeezed his hand. "It will."

They lapsed into silence.

"Will you follow it up?"

Jimmy had thought Sarah asleep. "What? Des going to counselling or whatever? No, you're right — I should let go. Be a mate, not his..."

"No, not Des, silly. The cross."

"Oh." He'd known that's what Sarah meant. His insides flipped from more than turbulence every time he remembered it, stowed in his luggage in the locker above their heads.

"You should, darling. Thandi said she'd help, trace his history, that sort of thing. Find out about his family."

"Yes, she told me that, too. Raymond mentioned he'd send me some of his contacts as well." Jimmy flicked the cup holder in the tray table in front of him. "I don't know, Sar. Maybe we should leave it. You heard what Raymond said. The second phase of the war was awful. He even used the term 'concentration camps' when he spoke to me about it."

"Thandi said that too."

"I'm not sure I want to open that particular can of worms. Dealing with Des over the next few months will be hard enough. I'm not ready for another drama."

"What would Grampy Percy want?"

"How would I know? He died long before I was born. And Ma doesn't remember him too well. Only that her ma had to promise not to throw away the wooden cross from his war trip."

"Doesn't that tell you all you need to know?"

"Hm? How?"

"It was precious to him, Jimmy. It held a value no one else knew about." She paused, searching Jimmy's face. "What if he met Wilhelm Olivier, rather than picked up a discarded trinket after the battle? What if he made Wilhelm Olivier a promise? To look after his treasure. Perhaps to return it to its rightful owners some day?"

"And what if I'm the one to carry out that promise?" Jimmy swallowed, his heart racing.

"Yes. What if you are?"

Author's Note

The Anglo-Boer War 1899-1902

Writing the story of British imperialism and her expansionist policies, as a British expat living in a former colony shaped by the outworking of those policies, makes for uncomfortable authoring!

I first visited the site of the Battle of Spionkop many years ago and was struck by the poignancy of a war fought by young British men on the foreign soil of a country they knew little about, and probably cared for even less. I pitied the soldiers arriving from a British winter to a South African summer; chuckled at the thought of woollen uniforms and un-sunned flesh turning pink under an African sky.

After subsequent visits and reading accounts from both sides of the Anglo-Boer War, I find my sympathies for the Boers equalling, if not surpassing, that for my countrymen. I cheer at the accounts of daring and determination told by Deneys Reitz; I groan and roll my eyes at the ineptitude and blundering of the British Generals as recounted by Thomas Packenham and others. I wince at the 'boys out on adventure' despatches of war correspondent-turned-honorary-officer Winston Churchill; I understand why Mahatma Ghandi, member of the Ambulance Corps and stretcher bearer of the broken bodies of combatants at the Battle of Spionkop, chose pacifism. I understand the simmering anger and bitterness driving Louis Botha's premiership of the finally-free Republic of South Africa.

On one visit to Spionkop, I noticed an unmarked gravestone. One dedicated to an unknown Boer soldier — similar to those found at countless war memorials around the world. And I heard that whisper of

God which stirs my heart. *He's not unknown to me. I know his story —*
who he loved, who loved him.

And so the idea for Remembered Lives was born. A novel of young
lives with big dreams, of the unnamed being known and remembered.

Private Percival Barnes wasn't a member of the Lancashire Fusiliers,
and only travelled to South Africa in my imagination; the soldiers he
served alongside, although sporting fictional Christian names, are listed
on the war memorial at Spionkop alongside the trench in which they
died and were, ultimately, buried.

Similarly, Wihelm Olivier and his father Marthinus, never left their
farm in Carolina to travel with their commando to the defence of the
Republic. But Commandant Prinsloo did deliver the stirring address to
his comrades at the foot of Spionkop before they rushed into the storm
of British bullets. They are equally remembered in a memorial at the site
of the battle. As is H Venter of the Standerton Commando.

A more recent addition to the memorials at Spionkop is that
honouring the heroism and service of the African and Indian personnel
caught up in what many believed to be 'a white man's' war.

In total, some three hundred to four hundred British soldiers lost
their lives atop a hill in a land at the bottom of the world; another
one thousand four hundred were wounded or in captivity. Boer losses
were considerably lower, with fifty-eight dead and one hundred and
forty wounded; these included fifty-five of the eighty-eight-strong
Carolina Commando. Little wonder contemporary reporter John
Atkins summarised the Battle of Spionkop as 'that acre of massacre, that
complete shambles'.

For this was a different war, fought not according to the traditional
set pieces of the British Army, but by the rules of a new, mobile
guerrilla force. The Boers dug trenches, mastering the art of surprise with
dummy gun placements and smokeless bullets. They travelled through
a landscape they knew well, on horses and ponies they'd ridden all their
lives. And they defended their land.

In contrast, the British relied on the railway network for movement of
both troops and supplies — a network which became an easy target for
the patrolling Boers. They lacked maps and surveys of the terrain they
occupied. Their soldiers arrived unprepared and inappropriately kitted
out.

Add to this rival factions within the British government and confusion over who was in command when and where, and it should be no surprise that the campaign lasted longer, was more costly, and bloodier than any since 1815. It cost more than two hundred million pounds, and twenty-two thousand British soldiers lost their lives. The Boer losses, both soldiers and civilians, totalled thirty-four thousand. More than fifteen thousand Africans were killed.

Commentator and historian Thomas Packenham powerfully states, 'It was the precursor...this Armageddon in the trenches under the African sun, of a greater one, fifteen years later, in the mud of Flanders'. The era of 'gentlemanly warfare' was over, replaced by the modern horror we are now all too familiar with.

Jesus' reassurance echoes throughout. 'Are not two sparrows sold for a penny? And not one of them will fall to the ground apart from your Father. But even the hairs of your head are all numbered. Fear not, therefore; you are of more value than many sparrows.'

The Hillsborough Disaster

It may seem strange to connect the story of a football disaster in 1989 with a war fought on the opposite side of the world almost ninety years previously. But there is a link!

On my first visit to Spionkop, I noticed the fans and photographs adorning the walls of the guard hut at the entrance to the site. My Dad was with us, and he declared, as though we all should know, "That's because of the Kop, at Anfield."

This was before my son became interested in football and a follower of Liverpool FC.

I decided to find out more.

Of all those engaged at the Battle of Spionkop, the Lancashire Fusilier's regiment suffered the highest losses; several of the men were from Liverpool. So strong ties already existed between the two locations. These were further cemented when, in 1906, the *Liverpool Echo* sports editor Ernest Edwards noted of a new open-air embankment at Liverpool Football Club's ground at Anfield, "This huge wall of earth has been termed 'Spion Kop', and no doubt this apt name will always be used in future in referring to this spot."

The use of the name for the stand was given recognition at Anfield in 1928 when it was extended to a twenty-seven thousand capacity, and a cantilever roof was added, which amplified the roar of the crowd to create an intense atmosphere. Traditionally, Liverpool's most vocal supporters congregate in this stand; all Liverpool fans are *kopites*. Such is the reputation of the stand that it was claimed that the crowd in the Kop could suck the ball into the goal, and it has become one of the most famous football stands in the world.

No telling of this story would be complete without recounting the full list of victims of the 1989 Hillsborough Disaster.

Ninety-four fans lost their lives on 15 April 1989 because of a deadly crush during the first minutes of the FA Cup semi-final football match between Liverpool FC and Nottingham Forest. Another died a few days later, and the ninety-sixth victim in 1993.

Andrew Devine, twenty-two, suffered life-changing crush and brain injuries at the match. Confined to a wheelchair, and cared for by family and teams of professionals, he died on 27 July 2021. At the inquest, the coroner ruled he was unlawfully killed because of the 1989 disaster. This makes him the ninety-seventh victim.

Stephen Whittle is considered by some to be the ninety-eighth victim. Having given his match ticket to a friend, the survivor's guilt was too great to live with. He committed suicide on 26 February 2011.

The families of the victims sought justice for their loved ones for over twenty years. Not until April 2016 were the deaths declared 'unlawful', rather than the result of fans' behaviour on the day. The findings heavily criticised the police operation, stadium layout and design, and local ambulance service. As yet, no one has been prosecuted for their role in the disaster.

Memorials were held each year at Anfield Football Stadium in memory of the victims of the Hillsborough Disaster. At the request of the families, the last memorial was held in 2016. I,

n 2007, a group of South African fans held their own service on the original 'kop' — Spionkop. Four of the supporters — Guy Prowse, Sioux Gijzen, Dave Walters and Jim Abraham — fundraised for a memorial bench. Guy proposed the bench should consist of ninety-six slats in the seat; he unveiled the finished bench at a ceremony at Spionkop Lodge in 2008.

In 2023, the group (without Guy, who had passed away) added a chair in remembrance of Andrew Devine, the ninety-seventh victim.

I was honoured to be able to attend the ceremony.

At any gathering of Liverpool fans, whether it be on match day or for remembrance, one song is on everyone's lips — *You'll Never Walk Alone*.

It began life on Broadway as part of the Rodgers and Hammerstein show, *Carousel*, which was premiered in 1945.

The song was an instant hit — perhaps because the song's message of triumph in times of adversity spoke to the wartime crowds of April 1945 — less than a month before the end of World War Two.

It remained popular throughout the 1950s, with artists including Frank Sinatra and Elvis Presley releasing covers. Then in 1963, a recording by Merseybeat band Gerry And The Pacemakers brought the song to the doorstep of Liverpool FC.

At that time, Liverpool's Anfield Stadium was one of the first football grounds to have a PA system, and the Top 10 in the charts was played over the speakers before the match, as a form of early pre-match entertainment.

This was also the time when 'Merseybeat' bands like The Beatles, and Gerry And The Pacemakers, dominated the charts, so the fans would have heard a lot of their local heroes over the tannoy. 'You'll Never Walk Alone' stayed at No. 1 in the charts for about four weeks in 1963, by which time it had become Liverpool FC's signature tune.

On the day after the tragedy at Hillsborough, thirteen thousand people gathered at Liverpool's Roman Catholic Cathedral; five thousand in the church, and a further eight thousand spilling into the streets outside. 'You'll Never Walk Alone' was sung by a lone choir boy, offering both comfort and hope to a city in mourning.

When you walk through a storm, hold your head up high
And don't be afraid of the dark
At the end of the storm, there's a golden sky
And the sweet, silver song of a lark

Walk on through the wind
Walk on through the rain
Though your dreams be tossed and blown

Walk on, walk on
With hope in your heart
And you'll never walk alone
You'll never walk alone

Walk on, walk on
With hope in your heart
And you'll never walk alone
You'll never walk alone.

Rather like the words of Jesus.

I am with you always [remaining with you perpetually—regardless of circumstance, and on every occasion], even to the end of the age. Matthew 28:20 (Amplified Version)

The ninety-seven

John Alfred Anderson (62)
Colin Mark Ashcroft (19)
James Gary Aspinall (18)
Kester Roger Marcus Ball (16)
Gerard Bernard Patrick Baron (67)
Simon Bell (17)
Barry Sidney Bennett (26)
David John Benson (22)
David William Birtle (22)
Tony Bland (22)
Paul David Brady (21)
Andrew Mark Brookes (26)
Carl Brown (18)
David Steven Brown (25)
Henry Thomas Burke (47)
Peter Andrew Burkett (24)
Paul William Carlile (19)
Raymond Thomas Chapman (50)
Gary Christopher Church (19)
Joseph Clark (29)
Paul Clark (18)
Gary Collins (22)
Stephen Paul Copoc (20)
Tracey Elizabeth Cox (23)
James Philip Delaney (19)
Christopher Barry Devonside (18)
Chris Edwards (29)
Vincent Michael Fitzsimmons (34)
Thomas Steven Fox (21)
Jon-Paul Gilhooley (10)
Barry Glover (27)
Ian Thomas Glover (20)
Derrick George Godwin (24)
Roy Harry Hamilton (34)

Philip Hammond (14)
Eric Hankin (33)
Gary Harrison (27)
Stephen Francis Harrison (31)
Peter Andrew Harrison (15)
David Hawley (39)
James Robert Hennessy (29)
Paul Anthony Hewitson (26)
Carl Darren Hewitt (17)
Nicholas Michael Hewitt (16)
Sarah Louise Hicks (19)
Victoria Jane Hicks (15)
Gordon Rodney Horn (20)
Arthur Horrocks (41)
Thomas Howard (39)
Thomas Anthony Howard (14)
Eric George Hughes (42)
Alan Johnston (29)
Christine Anne Jones (27)
Gary Philip Jones (18)
Richard Jones (25)
Nicholas Peter Joynes (27)
Anthony Peter Kelly (29)
Michael David Kelly (38)
Carl David Lewis (18)
David William Mather (19)
Brian Christopher Matthews (38)
Francis Joseph McAllister (27)
John McBrien (18)
Marian Hazel McCabe (21)
Joseph Daniel McCarthy (21)
Peter McDonnell (21)
Alan McGlone (28)
Keith McGrath (17)
Paul Brian Murray (14)
Lee Nicol (14)
Stephen Francis O'Neill (17)

Jonathon Owens (18)
William Roy Pemberton (23)
Carl William Rimmer (21)
Dave George Rimmer (38)
Graham John Roberts (24)
Steven Joseph Robinson (17)
Henry Charles Rogers (17)
Colin Andrew Hugh William Sefton (23)
Inger Shah (38)
Paula Ann Smith (26)
Adam Edward Spearritt (14)
Philip John Steele (15)
David Leonard Thomas (23)
Patrick John Thompson (35)
Peter Reuben Thompson (30)
Stuart Paul William Thompson (17)
Peter Francis Tootle (21)
Christopher James Traynor (26)
Martin Kevin Traynor (16)
Kevin Tyrrell (15)
Colin Wafer (19)
Ian David Whelan (19)
Martin Kenneth Wild (29)
Kevin Daniel Williams (15)
Graham John Wright (17)
   Andrew Devine — died 2021, aged 52

Further Reading

I used a number of sources when researching Remembered Lives. I recommend the following if you are interested in learning more about the Battle of Spionkop in particular, and the Anglo-Boer War in general.

The Boer War Thomas Packenham. Available in paperback and Kindle formats from Amazon.

Commando Deneys Reitz. Available in paperback and Kindle formats from Amazon.

The Boer War: London to Ladysmith via Pretoria and Ian Hamilton's March (Bloomsbury Revelations) Winston S Churchill. Available in paperback and Kindle formats from Amazon. An audiobook is also available from Audible — I listened to the audiobook, which added extra flavour to Churchill's despatches.

A video of the opening moments of the football match between Liverpool FC and Nottingham Forest is available at https://bit.ly/hillsboroughmatch should you wish to see how events on that fateful day unfolded.

The 25th Anniversary service held at Anfield Stadium is also available to watch at https://www.thisisanfield.com/2014/04/hillsborough-25th-memorial-service/

The Ripples Through Time series

Ripples Through Time is a series of novels telling stories of the past and showing how they inspire our present. Stories of how God takes the ordinary and transforms it into something extraordinary. The smallest of stones, tossed into smooth water, will create waves; concentric circles spreading outward to reach beyond the immediate or seen. So too, the seemingly insignificant actions of today can leave ripples that are felt into eternity.

There is the village of Eyam and her inhabitants' love and sacrifice which saved a generation, the Bletchley Park codebreakers' dedication to fight a war far from public praise, the adventure and ingenuity of diamond hunters settling in the impermanence of the Namibian desert, and the discovery of a 2000-year-old fishing vessel believed to date to the time of Jesus and his disciples. Campaigns and conflicts, castles and cottages – tales to uncover and histories to unfold.

These are the pebbles and the ripples they leave.

The *Ripples Through Time* series is dedicated to my personal mentor, author Marion Ueckermann, who sadly passed away on 25 June 2021. She included a devotion entitled *Reflections in Pebbles* in the multi-author boxed set, *In All Things* (a set which I also contributed to). I would like to leave you with this quote from Marion:

'God has chosen you to be His pebble in the sea of humanity. What ripples of hope could emit from the splashes of your life? What giants could tumble from the impact of one small stone, one random act of kindness?'

May you, like Marion, become a pebble in the hand of God, leaving ripples in the world as you pass.

Given Lives

SEPTEMBER 1665.

Plague ravages the English capital, London.

Thousands are left dead.

In the Derbyshire village of Eyam, 160 miles north of the London tragedies, Kitty Allenby is settling into country life. Encouraged by her Aunt Anne and Uncle Robert, she is excited for the year ahead.

That is until a stranger arrives from London, bringing a parcel of cloth for the local tailor – cloth infested with plague-carrying fleas.

Within weeks, Eyam is under siege.

By spring 1666, drastic action is needed to contain the spread of disease. What can be done?

The Reverend William Mompesson thinks he knows. For his plan to succeed, Mompesson will need the co-operation of the whole community, including his predecessor and rival, Thomas Stanley.

Will the two men be able to put aside the deep mistrust of one another for the sake of the people they are called to serve? How will the doomed villagers respond?

And what of Kitty? Can she learn to love a community not her own, perhaps paying the ultimate price alongside strangers she barely knows?

Based on true events, Given Lives is a story of bravery and sacrifice, of love that laid itself down for the sake of others. It is a whisper through time to each of us confronted by a modern plague, the global Covid 19 pandemic. Will we attune our ears and listen?

'My great aunt (nine times over) and ancestor, Margaret Blackwell, is part of this wonderful novel and, as a family survivor of this dreadful plague, I felt privileged to be asked to read Anna's novel.

The story unfolds as Kitty comes to Eyam to celebrate the annual Wakes Week and becomes isolated with the villagers as they try to contain the disease. It captures the real depth of sacrificial love, care and compassion and their heroism during the plague outbreak in 1665–66. The trust and hope the families had in God to bring them through this tragic time is a real testament to their fortitude, as Kitty constantly, with her family, looks forward to a brighter and happier future.

It's a great read. and my thanks to Anna for her factual insight and passion for our history.' — Joan Plant, Descendant of a Plague Survivor

Buy now from Amazon or scan the QR code

Secret Lives

Secret Lives
Two Women. Two Generations.
One World War.

Anna
JENSEN

Can you keep a secret?
February 1942

Alice Stallard, encouraged by her two friends, submits her entry to the Daily Telegraph prize crossword – a crossword she solves in record time. She thinks nothing more about it until called into the study of her Cambridge University professor where she's invited to an interview at the mysterious Bletchley Park near Bedford.

Once at Bletchley Park, Alice is confronted with the Official Secrets Act and months of training for a job no one will talk about. After being moved from one training centre to another, her final posting is to Station 53a of the Special Operations Executive – Winston Churchill's 'Ministry of Ungentlemanly Warfare'.

But what of when the War is over? Will Alice keep her promise of silence?

February 1998

A-levels loom on the horizon for 18-year old Rosie Mason. She had expected her favourite subject to be History but instead is finding it dull and lifeless. Perhaps the drama and romance she was hoping for can be found elsewhere – in her grandmother's memories. But Gran is reluctant to share any war stories, changing the subject at every one of Rosie's questions.

Determined to conquer Gran's reticence, Rosie decides to spend her long post-exam holiday with her grandparents. After days of trying, Gran agrees to show Rosie a few photos -- and the first edition copy of C S Lewis' The Screwtape Letters.

Only when Rosie stumbles on a handwritten note tucked between the pages of Screwtape does the silence of decades threaten to unravel.

Buy now from Amazon or scan the QR code

More from Anna

You'll find all of my books listed on my online shop at www.annajensen.co.uk/shop. Simply choose your store (*Amazon.com* or *amazon.co.uk* or the *books2read* link provided with each listing) or, if you live in South Africa, purchase signed paperback copies directly from me.

Prairie Roses - Maria

A Prairie Roses wagon trail story with a South African twist

Maria Steyn's life is characterised by goodbyes. From the dim recollection of long-dead parents to the farewells from an established life in the Cape Colony of South Africa, she has learnt to live with loss and sadness.

Joining the voortrekkers in their search for freedom and a land of their own, Maria embarks on a journey inland. But disagreements soon arise, breaking relationships and, once again, Maria's heart suffers loss.

When the dust settles after this final wagon trek, will Maria find the stability she longs for? Could her reunion with

Field-Cornet Christiaan Venter, hero of the Battle of Blood River, signal a new beginning? Or, is she destined for a life of upheaval and tragedy?

Buy now from Amazon or scan the QR code

Our House on Sycamore Street

Our House on Sycamore Street is a new multi-author, multi-genre series set in quaint and quirky Eden Cove, an English seaside town with plenty of spirit. With stories of redemption and salvation behind every door, you're sure to find a new tale of romance, intrigue, humour or heart. All you have to do is knock!

The Ferryman's Light

He has plans for the future. What happens when circumstances dictate those plans must change?

If you love an historical origins drama, you'll be sure to enjoy The Ferryman's Light

October, 1853:

Walter Ferryman's life is simple and predictable, running the Eden Cove ferry while his father works as gamekeeper to Castle on the Hill owners, the Wingfields.

That is until sweetheart Susan Wingfield reveals a dreadful secret - which puts all Walter's future hopes and plans into jeopardy. Will Walter find the courage to own his mistakes? How will he make good on his promise to Susan while remaining in Eden Cove?

Welcome to Our House on Sycamore Street

Our House on Sycamore Street is a new multi-author, multi-genre series set in quaint and quirky Eden Cove, an English seaside town with plenty of spirit. With stories of redemption and salvation behind every door, you're sure to find a new tale of romance, intrigue, humour or heart. All you have to do is knock!

Other books can be read in any order:

The Italian Musician's Sanctuary by Danielle Grandinetti
The Outsider's Welcome by Vida Li Sik
The Daughter's Truth by Claire Lagerwall
The Light Keeper's Wife by Jennifer Mistmorgan
The Key Collector's Promise by Donna Jo Stone
The Maestro's Missing Melody by Amy Walsh
The Niece's Aussie Patient by Meredith Resce
The Runaway's Redemption by Allyson Koekhoven
The Bookbinder's Daughter by Lynn Dean
The Widow's Request by Ashley Winter
The Lost Daughter's Irishman by Carolyn Miller
The Mother's Song by Caroline Johnston
The Wedding Planner's Predicament by Dianne J. Wilson

Buy now from Amazon or scan the QR code

OUR HOUSE on Sycamore Street

BOOK 1: THE FERRYMAN'S LIGHT *by Anna Jensen*
He has plans for the future. What happens when circumstances dictate those plans must change?

BOOK 2: THE ITALIAN MUSICIAN'S SANCTUARY
by Danielle Grandinetti
Hunted by one man, can she open her heart to another?

BOOK 3: THE OUTSIDER'S WELCOME
by Vida Li Sik
If you love women's fiction, you will enjoy The Outsider's Welcome, a tale of resilience, community, and a search for belonging.

BOOK 4: THE DAUGHTER'S TRUTH *by Claire Lagerwall*
Emmy Whitehouse is about to discover that everything she knows is not at all what she thinks.

BOOK 5: THE LIGHT KEEPER'S WIFE
by Jennifer Mistmorgan

They've come to escape their wartime secrets. But are some shadows too dark to shake off?

BOOK 6: THE KEY COLLECTOR'S PROMISE
by Donna Jo Stone

She came to warn her estranged mother of danger. But will the cost of unraveling family secrets be too much to bear?

BOOK 7: THE MAESTRO'S MISSING MELODY
by Amy Walsh

She is thrilled to apprentice with her fiddler hero—until his grumpiness knocks him off his pedestal.

BOOK 8: THE NIECE'S AUSSIE PATIENT
by Meredith Resce

Newly graduated in hospitality management, Stephanie Delafonte is looking forward to managing her aunt's guest house for three weeks while Lina takes a well-earned break.

BOOK 9: THE RUNAWAY'S REDEMPTION
by Allyson Koekhoven

A tragic event at work leaves South African paramedic Johlene Anderson reeling.

BOOK 10: THE BOOKBINDER'S DAUGHTER
by Lynn Dean

A war refugee is invited to live with an aging recluse but learns too late she's being used.

BOOK 11: THE WIDOW'S REQUEST   *by Ashley Winter*

Join Fiona as she unravels old family secrets, faces danger head on and uncovers the truth about her parents' deception...

BOOK 12: THE LOST DAUGHTER'S IRISHMAN
by Carolyn Miller

She wants to find a way to live again; he wants to close a deal and move on. Until sparks fly and these opposites attract in this contemporary romance filled with heart and humour.

BOOK 13: THE MOTHER'S SONG   *by Caroline Johnston*

Miranda McVitty, wife, mother and campsite owner. Miranda loves to sing as she goes about her work and this summer she's learning to sing her prayers as well as her to do list.

BOOK 14: THE WEDDING PLANNER'S PREDICAMENT
by Dianne J. Wilson

Cleo is done organizing weddings. James has a wedding to plan, and Cleo is his only hope.

St Saviours

Seasonal

Stories

The seasons of the church calendar are important to Richard, vicar of St Saviours, a thriving church community in the heart of London. Christmas, Easter, Advent and Lent — all have a special place in the Reverend's heart and actions.

Book 1:

A Candle for Christmas
Four candles. Four stories. One Christmas Day.

The vicar of St Saviour's is preparing for Christmas. Four Sundays, four services, four advent candles to light.

Richard loves Christmas. And he loves the ritual of the advent candles. Only this year is different. Memories and regrets threaten to spoil his favourite season.

Joelle is tired. Tired of the streets; tired of the weather. Tired of being unseen.

Could the preparations for Christmas at St Saviour's herald a new beginning?

Tamara knows this Christmas is going to be different. She's been planning for weeks. But will it be in the way she expects or is there a surprise in store?

Ellen realises her new-found freedom isn't as wonderful as she expected it to be. Can she retrace her steps and find restoration? Or is it too late?

Christmas Day. Richard ignites the final candle...

Book 2:

The Nine Readings of Christmas
Nine lessons. One Christmas story

Christmas is fast approaching.

The congregation of St Saviours is caught up with Christmas preparations and parties — not least amongst them their vicar, Richard.

The service of Nine Lessons and Carols has been months in the planning. Everything is in place for the evening to be the highlight of this year's church calendar. Until Richard receives a telephone call; his soloist has a sore throat. Can The Service still go ahead? Will Richard seek to find his own solution? Or will God have His way?

Marjorie is baking up a storm; containers full of every Christmas treat occupying all available space. When a Christmas card from afar arrives with unwelcome news — and a gift — Marj is forced to reassess the life she has chosen. Is she where she should be or has her focus on family and church been misdirected?

Ellen, studying and involving herself in the local community, is experiencing dreams of Africa. What do they mean? And does an email she receives have anything to do with them?

Tamara has made her peace with the single life she now leads. But is there more? Are a young girl, a homeless woman, and a Christmas party the key to her happiness?

Joelle has a new home, with a comfortable bed and two cooked meals a day. She also has a family — the family of St Saviours. Can she help Ellen decipher her dreams and discover her heart? Or show Tamara that they are more alike than she may think? Christmas at St Saviours. Nine lessons; one story.

Book 3:

One Passing Easter
Seven special days. And the lives they changed
Shrove Tuesday.

The annual St Saviours Pancake Relay is in full flip. Runners and spectators alike are wild with excitement.
Until an accident occurs and an ambulance is called.

Reverend Richard has a full schedule of services and events planned between now and Easter Sunday. Will he be able to continue as arranged, or will circumstances dictate otherwise?

Tamara, persuaded to go on a blind date by a friend and colleague, is desperate for change. Abandoning the shallowness of yet another meaningless relationship, she seeks something deeper this Lent. Can she find the love she longs for? Or will past experiences and hurts keep her in their grip?

Joelle harbours a secret. Does she have the courage to share it with Marjorie? Or is time running out?

Elsewhere, Ellen has found her calling. Or so she hopes. But when disaster strikes her community, bringing with it an unexpected confrontation, can beauty rise from the ashes?

After this one passing Easter, the lives of the St Saviours community may never be the same.

Buy the Box Set

But all three St Saviours Seasonal Stories in one complete ebook.

Poems and Devotionals

The '14 Days of Devotions' Series

A Seat in a Garden
14 days of reflections and poems from seven gardens of Africa

What better place to enjoy the presence of God than from a seat in a secluded garden? Take a moment to wander with Anna Jensen through seven of her favourite African gardens in this book of 14 daily devotions.

Discover with her the delights of quiet contemplation, finding glimpses of the Creator in every leaf and flower. Pause and rest for reflection on a 'bench' – a space created through poetry and prayer.

Rugged Roads
14 stories and poems from seven journeys in Africa

Take a journey off the beaten track and enjoy the drama on seven journeys of adventure and discovery through South Africa and beyond. Take the warned-against route from Harare to Victoria Falls, Zimbabwe, or discover the twists and turns of a mountain pass into Lesotho. Stumble through the sand of a Namibian desert or feel the adrenalin rush of being charged by a rhino or threatened by an elephant. In this collection of 14 daily devotions, reflect on the whispers of God heard when driving off-road. Through stories and Scripture readings, poetry and prayer, find the joy of choosing 'rugged roads'.

Poems and Prayers
14 reflections from a year of change
The year 2020 started like any other – full of promise and hope. Within a few months, it was clear this was to be no ordinary year. By March, the World Health Organisation had declared a global pandemic of the hitherto-unknown coronavirus Covid-19. For Anna Jensen, it was a time of bewilderment, but also an opportunity; an opportunity to press in afresh and hear all that God wants to whisper.

In this collection of 14 daily devotions, Anna reflects on those early months of the pandemic, articulating her thoughts through poems and prayerful reflections.

A Gratitude Challenge
14 days of choosing thanks
In November 2020, Anna Jensen embarked on her first 'gratitude challenge', a series of social media posts giving thanks on a daily basis.

Anna found herself being grateful for the serious and the silly, and everything in between (on one of the days, she was thankful for shoe shops, after her son climbed into the car from school with a 'flapping sole', which needed an urgent remedy).

This book of 14 days of devotions is the pick of Anna's month of gratitude, shared with you in the hope that you will see the delight in the daily and the mundane. There really is so much to be thankful for.

Other books by Anna

The Outskirts of His Glory

Join Anna Jensen and her family as they travel to seek out and experience the odd and unexpected of God's creation.

Captivated by the Creator (paperback only)
Be inspired afresh by the voice of the Creator through the beauty of His creation. Be guided by Anna Jensen as she describes her own journey of discovery through articles and poems. This beautiful journal contains pictures for you to colour and space for your own thoughts and prayers.

Twenty Years an Expat
Read about Anna's experiences when she left her native land and learned to embrace the different and the new as she settled in South Africa. At times funny, at others poignant, the one constant is God's love and purpose for Anna in all she experiences.
Find all my books on Amazon

About Anna

I'm a British expat who has lived in South Africa for a little over twenty years. My husband and I live with our two teenage children on the east coast, a few miles north of the city of Durban. We overlook the Indian Ocean where we have the privilege of watching dolphins and whales at play.

My first book *The Outskirts of His Glory* was published in May 2019. The book is a Christian devotional and poetry collection, exploring the many surprising ways that God can speak to us through His creation. I have drawn on my travels in and around South Africa, as well as further afield, to hopefully inspire each of us to slow down and perhaps listen more carefully to the 'whispers of His ways' (Job 26:14) that are all around us.

Since publishing *Outskirts*, I have had the privilege of speaking at a number of local churches and even have a weekly slot on a Christian radio station. I have also continued writing by contributing to a variety of blogs and online writing communities as well as developing my own website and blog.

Want to know more? Check out my website at www.annajensen.co.uk

Cornwall, September 1742

Tin mining is in Jem Pearce's blood. For as long as he can remember, the subterranean caverns of the Cornish mines have been his world — just like his father before him. Intimate knowledge of the maze of tunnels and passageways lights the way in the underground darkness, as sure as any lantern.

So why, when mine owner Mr Roberts announces plans for a proposed expansion project, is Jem so uneasy?

Compounding his anxiety is his son Edward's eagerness to experience the thrill of the blasting preparations.

Can Jem persuade the mine officials to change their plans, and so avert disaster?

Meanwhile, Mr John Wesley has returned to this remote part of the country with his vibrant Gospel crusades. Thousands gather to hear his simple, hope-filled teaching, including Susanna Pearce, Jem's wife. Can she help her husband discover the true light that shines in the deepest darkness — the light that is Jesus?

Make it easier to hear about all things Anna and sign up for my free more-or-less monthly newsletter. You'll receive a gift of the ebook, Seeking Light, a Cornish tale inspired by my years living in Cornwall when you do. You'll also be sent an invitation to join my Subscriber Family Birthday Club. Sign up today at www.annajensen.co.uk/news

Follow me across my various social media platforms. Or email me directly at hello@annajensen.co.za I'd love to connect with you.

Scan the QR code to access clickable links.

Printed in Great Britain
by Amazon